Where The Mind is Without Fear

Where the mind is without fear and the head is held high
Where knowledge is free
Where the world has not been broken up into fragments
By narrow domestic walls
Where words come out from the depth of truth
Where tireless striving stretches its arms towards perfection
Where the clear stream of reason has not lost its way
Into the dreary desert sand of dead habit
Where the mind is led forward by thee
Into ever-widening thought and action
Into that heaven of freedom, my Father, let my country awake.

Rabindranath Tagore
Bengali Poet, Philosopher, Mathematician,
Soul Mate of Albert Einstein

Taming Storm Surges

When Ecology, Engineering, and Faith Meet

Bob Onan

ISBN (13) 978-1-880654-33-0.
(10) 1-880654-33-4.

Library of Congress Control Number 2006901644.

Credits:
Interior design and typesetting by Percolator.
Cover design by Kelly Doudna, Mighty Media.
Matt Kania, Map Hero, Inc., for the maps at pages xii, 66, and 102.
Bill Stein, Artifex Studio, for the drawings at pages 213 and 230.

Acknowledgments

To Moira F. (Molly) Harris for her superb editing skills.

To Kelly Doudna of Mighty Media, Minneapolis, Minnesota, for the inspired cover design.

To Matt Kania of Map Hero, Inc., Duluth, Minnesota, for the maps.

To Bill Stein of Artifex Studio, Champlin, Minnesota, for the line-drawing caricatures of Bernice and Bertram.

To Dominic Baker for his graphic arts skills.

To Marilyn Parker of Write Away, Saint Paul, Minnesota, for her loyalty and word processing competency.

And, to my wife Gail, for her steadfast presence in my life.

And, to our five talented and resourceful children (their spouses/significant others) and our grandchildren who invigorate our lives in ways they may never know.

Table of Contents

Prologue

Dr. Rajiv Gaol, Chief Pediatric Resident at Evanston Hospital pauses. It is 1:00 a.m. His seventy-two-hour "on-call" has just finished. He stands outside on a balcony facing south just above the emerging foliage. It is May. The spring winds off Lake Michigan caress his skin. Central Street below him is quiet. Downtown Chicago is less than ten miles away. The Chicago skyline, day or night, is impressive. He'll always remember it.

It was his last "on call." He has come to the end of his eight-year trek here compliments of the Ministry of Health Care. He is basking in a newly reclaimed luxury: ruminating about lots of things.

In two short weeks he will be dispensing pediatric care in a most futile endeavor in the most impoverished country in Asia, Bangladesh, his native country.

His mind clock winds pleasantly ahead to eight p.m. this coming evening. After some much needed sleep and packing, he and several med school/residency comrades will gather at Dana Josephson's comfortable apartment in one of those old, three-story, red brick, wooden stair, Sherman Avenue buildings. The kind of place where people cook out on the back porches and purple finches congregate and nest in the joists for the floor above, swooping down for seeds or any tidbits.

It will be their last hurrah before each heads out into a lucrative career. Each of them that is, except Rajiv. His new position is way south of lucrative—the price of his eight-year free ride. He must now serve six years wherever and whenever in Bangladesh the Ministry wants him to go.

Debt free—on one kind of balance sheet. A ton of duty on another.

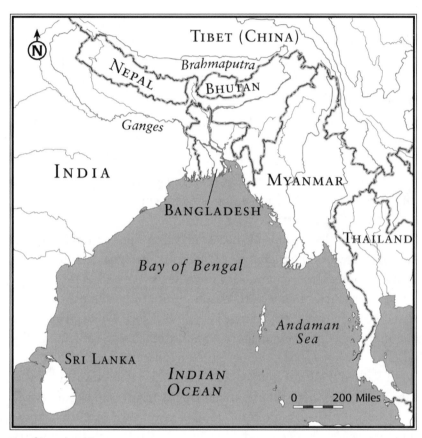

Bay of Bengal

CHAPTER 1

Abundance

The fire roared—literally roared—and flames rushed up the chimney. The room's occupants did not know this, but neighbors saw flames shoot from the flue on the apartment building roof. A yellow glow blazed in the room, radiating to the faces around it, the heat bringing cherries to their cheeks.

Dana rushed in from the kitchen.

"No more paper," she shouted. "Don't you guys know anything about fires? Paper can start a chimney fire."

Her four friends looked at her with sheepish grins.

Dana shook her head. "Obviously, no Boy Scouts here. And you..." She pointed a finger at a tall blond man with a U2 demeanor, fashionably disheveled.

"Aren't you from Minnesota, Wisconsin or some other woodsy place where people know about fires?"

Gus shrugged. "I'm just a city boy. Besides, it was cool."

"And dangerous," Dana said.

In moments, the flames subsided, returning to a more subdued crackling and popping. The room was littered with brightly colored wrapping paper—some of which had been fed into the flames, but the rest of which remained in a sea of splashy crumples on the floor. Wine glasses and beer bottles were scattered across coffee tables and end tables. A going away party, one that, like the fire, had roared earlier in the evening and was now ebbing. The hangers-on sat or lay near the fire, hypnotized by heat, wine and reflection. The former residents, now almost board-certified physicians, had spent the week congratulating one another with drinks, pats on the back, and extravagant meals they'd be able to regularly afford in their new stations in life. Tomorrow, they would scatter. While there was a possibility they would see each other again, for some it was remote.

Rochelle stretched her long limbs and let out a yawn, always a sign that the evening was almost over. "What time does your flight leave, Jiv?"

"Eight a.m."

His friends groaned. "It's not so bad," he said. "I'll have plenty of time to sleep."

"How long will it take you to get home?" Gus asked.

Rajiv ran his dark elegant fingers through his thick, jet black hair, cut in a slightly old-fashioned style with a side part. At almost six feet, he was tall for a Bengali, and his long legs were stretched out in front of him. He raised himself off of one arm and ticked off the legs of his journey on his fingers—from Chicago two days by air, including the usual layover in London, then Calcutta. From there, half-a-day by train to Dhaka, then boat or train to Sherpur up near the Bhutan-Tibet-India corridor regions. "Two, two and half days," he said.

His friends fell silent. Within a few weeks, they'd all be somewhere else beginning their post doc fellowships or jobs in Illinois, California, Florida and New York. By this time next week, Rajiv would be a world away from them. In far more than distance.

"You're treating this like a dirge," Rajiv laughed. "It's not like I'm leaving forever. I'll be back."

"When?" Rochelle asked.

Rajiv shrugged. He had not been home in two years. Travel to Bangladesh was not only time consuming, but expensive. His arrangements had not provided travel money except at the beginning and end of each school year. He would, of course, be better able to afford travel once established in Bangladesh, but only barely. Government physicians made little more than U.S. residents. But government support for professional travel could be had, with arm twisting and political know-how.

"Why *are* you going back?" Keith flushed almost immediately after asking the question. "I mean, I know it's home, but you've got some incredible offers here. You'll make tons more money here. Enough to support that entire clan of yours."

Rajiv stared into the fire. As it flickered he recalled reading, ten or so years ago, a somber phrase in a text on the 1947 partition of India. "The future of Eastern Bengal (Bangladesh) would present very difficult problems since it is clearly not a viable unit." At the time he thought, how dare those departing British colonials offer such a harsh assessment. The prophetic nature of that declaration was becoming increasingly prescient.

"I'm sorry," Keith said. "A little too close to home."

Reticent by nature, Rajiv said little of his struggle as the end of their residency at Evanston Hospital neared, but it was no secret either. In the United States, he could earn enough as a pediatrician to send his two younger siblings to college and markedly upgrade his parents' comfort at a time in their lives when they deserved it.

Further complicating the issue was how much he'd changed. He was comfortable with comfort, and the life he was going back to would offer little of that. It would be easy to be a pediatrician here in the central USA, where medicine, equipment, supplies and money were plentiful. Sanitation and dietary standards were among the world's highest. In eight years, in spite of what at age 22 was an ironclad commitment to a higher purpose, he was now more American than he'd ever counted on. He looked down at his T-shirt, jeans-clad legs and Skecher tennis shoes. Rajiv grimaced at his naiveté. What had he known about the world at 22? Was there any higher purpose in futility? His cynicism about the "calling" to which he was returning had grown. His idealism had faded, maybe became jaded. Yet he wouldn't renege on his contract with the Comilla Health Ministry, which had subsidized his education.

"You could pay back that contract in just a few years here," Keith said. "Other students from Bangladesh have done that."

Rajiv met his friend's gaze. "Too many."

The room fell silent. There was something about the fire that was hypnotic and contemplative, although the melancholy, settling in among the group, was inspired more by alcohol and fatigue, Rajiv suspected, than by the blaze.

The fact was that while the district health ministries were cash poor, they needed a pediatrician far worse than they needed money. They'd been waiting eight years for him. His obligation was no different than ROTC residents, and he didn't know many military med students who got out of their deals. The Ministry had even chosen his specialty for him—pediatric infectious diseases—which he accepted without question. He would operate a roaming clinic in a vast multi-river delta. He would move from village to village where medical care was either inadequate or nonexistent. Australia had its flying doctors, in Bangladesh he'd be a floating one.

"I will be back," Rajiv said. "but I need to fulfill my obligation."

"How long?" Dana asked.

"Six years."

That was also the bargain he'd made with his family. He'd promised them that he'd complete his service contract, then return to the United States to start his own life and help his brother and sister begin theirs. His meager salary in Bangladesh would largely go to his parents in Sherpur to supplement their support of his siblings. But that was only enough to help his parents' cash flow. It would not send anyone to college.

"A toast." Gus raised his glass and there was a pause as Dana fetched the last bottle of wine, already half gone, and parceled it out.

"To Jiv," Gus continued. "Our very own missionary. And with my admiration of your incredible skills with your pediatric patients."

Rajiv smiled and raised his glass, but he was unable to feel the celebration that should have gone with the toast. He felt like an

ROTC student who, on arriving at boot camp, asked himself, "What have I gotten myself into?"

"Put another log on the fire, Jiv. At this point, we may as well stay up until your plane leaves."

"Sure." Rajiv handled the wood. Oak, he guessed. Earlier in the evening, he'd listened as Gus and Keith discussed the merits of various woods, birch over hardwoods; hickory, ash and applewoods were nice, if you could get them. They made such aromatic fires.

He had tempered his awe over the extravagant use of wood in the United States. The average American threw out more fuel in a year from cereal cartons, product boxes and newspapers than an entire Bengali family could have used for all its cooking and heating needs. A day's mail wasn't complete without at least one catalog that he'd not asked for and never ordered from. But he loved catalogs and could not wait for the next one. These quarterly connectors to Western lifestyle during med school and residency in Evanston; a quick purple line "EL" ride north out of Chicago's downtown loop, were a visual treasure trek.

He threw more wood on the fire and watched the shower of sparks fly back at him.

Fire, he once read, was the most powerful of the four major elements. It meant life's sacrifice, sustenance, love, and the ashes of death. Fire was as necessary for life as water.

Goodbyes for these class-team mates were joyful yet sad. He'd long remember the delicate scent of Dana's perfume; Keith's rugged hands and attentive eyes; Gus' established competitive bent disguised by his always roaming eyes for womanly hips, thighs and calves; Rochelle's brown fluid hair and her professional chin. If he remained here, she would be his cardiologist. Dana's hands suggested her surgeon's skills; Keith, like Rajiv, was a pediatrician; and Gus, a neurologist with an electromyography emphasis. Would the day ever come when these already trusted and respected professionals would visit him on the medical Guadalcanal where he'd be stationed? Or would he be too uncomfortable to let them see him at work in the villages?

CHAPTER 2

On the Job in the
Village of Sagaria

On Hatiya, a Barrier Island on the Bay of Bengal

Eighteen months later. Hard months of drastically limited supplies and severely limited budget for staff, and constant travels.

It had been an exhausting day in the clinic. Rajiv had not kept track of how many patients he had seen. Fifty? Sixty-five? Rajiv had not realized just how soft he had become when his clinical duties began in earnest. As he had told his friends, it had taken him two days to reach Calcutta, just over the border, and then another day for his journey north to see his parents. It had been a short reunion. He'd been allowed a week in Sherpur, then reported to his first clinic in Hijla back south on the coast of the Bay of Bengal. Then, he'd been on the aquatic road every few days for the last seventeen months.

Manja beckoned him into their home. He removed his shoes at the door and took his seat on a jute mat. Manja Singh was a midwife. She stood 5'5", had glistening black skin, and feminine but seasoned hands. Her movements were easy. Her eyes were her trademark. Large, beautiful, penetrating eyes. On her smallish nose were half glasses which emphasized her penetrating observational skill. She

7

is a listener, a very attentive one. Her feet are petite—only the soles are calloused. Rajiv had met her during his first tour of the southern end of Hatiya island.

In the United States, many physicians scoffed at midwives. Here, Rajiv depended heavily on them. And they were revered in Bengali culture. In the absence of medical facilities, Manja not only delivered the area's children; she also tended the medical needs of most adults. When he entered a village, the first thing Rajiv did was to locate the midwives. They became his nurses, having the most health care experience of anyone in the area. The midwives provided medical histories and knew which children had the most pressing medical needs and how they'd been treated thus far. Midwives were also a vital bridge of trust. People knew them. The midwives had earned village respect.

In larger towns, Rajiv stayed in boarding houses and hotels arranged by the Comilla Health Ministry. But on Barrier Islands and the Sundarbans, he often stayed with the midwives and their families. They considered it an honor, and the system set up by a predecessor had become tradition. Logistically, it saved him making arrangements in advance where communication was often extremely difficult. Manja had perhaps three days' notice of Rajiv's arrival. Her home was scrupulously clean, but not because of his visit. Rajiv was sure that she kept the jute floor mats spotless, and the clay floor freshly swept. Rajiv stopped to admire Manja and Sabjada's basket and quilt work, hung from bamboo rafters in the hut.

Manja's husband, Shukendu, and their two sons were not yet home from the rice fields. The rains were fast approaching, and it was critical that the crop be planted at least three weeks before monsoon season. The root structures of the rice plants had to be developed and imbedded.

Sabjada's hands worked deftly, managing two pots at once as she prepared her family's evening meal of dal, a lentil soup, and fish curry. The enticing aroma of payes, a rice pudding, wafted through the air. It was clear the ten-year-old was no "Daktar's" apprentice when it came to cooking. She looked up when she saw Rajiv standing in the door with her mother, Manja. Sabjada smiled. She loved the gentle and funny way Daktar Rajiv related to the children of her village.

The young girl ladled Rajiv's dinner into a tin plate before serving her mother and herself. As she handed Rajiv his food, he noticed the burn. A blister ran the length of her left arm, deepening as it reached her wrist and spread into the palm. Rajiv watched her handling the plates. She favored the arm.

He turned to Manja. "When?" he asked, gesturing to the wound.

"Four days ago," she said.

"May I?" he asked. He knew that Manja had already been treating it, and he didn't want to suggest in any way that her treatment had been inadequate. Cooking accidents were common, particularly among young girls who'd reached an age where they began to assume family duties. Most rural Bengalis cooked over open fires, scrounging wherever they could for fuel. If a ten-year-old's attention wandered (he had never met a ten-year-old whose mind did not wander), it took only a second for a gauzy cotton sleeve of a sari or the tail of a dupatta to go up in flames, causing horrific scarring on the faces of thousands of girls. In over the past eighteen months, he'd seen many such burns, but he guessed Manja had seen far more. Such was a reality of open fire cooking.

Manja nodded and signaled Sabjada to submit to Rajiv's attention. The girl lowered her head and held out her arm. Rajiv stretched out the limb, Sabjada winced. The wound was clean, but deep. It was a second-degree burn, perhaps worse in places. As he examined her daughter, Manja described her treatment, which had consisted of cool compresses. Rajiv nodded in agreement. It was a matter of making do. It was what he would have done—without any medical supplies whatsoever. It was what his own mother had done to treat burns on her own children.

"Does the village well still work?"

Manja nodded.

There was that, at least, Rajiv thought. Most villages had a well for drinking water, but no one used that water for washing clothes or for bathing.

"Are you drawing from the well for her compresses? And do you boil the water you're using?"

The crook of Manja's eyebrows was his answer. Infection was always a risk when the main water source was an adjoining river ripe with urine and fecal material, sewage and industrial waste. The closer to the cities one went in Bangladesh, the more toxic the stew. It was another reason to make close contact with the village midwife. If he was careful and did not insult her, Rajiv might impress upon Manja a lesson in hygienics more important than teaching her to stitch wounds. It was often difficult to convince a midwife to break away from practices handed down over generations. As he treated patients throughout the day, he quietly and matter-of-factly dispensed tidbits of knowledge to Manja these past seventeen to eighteen months, knowing she was absorbing them like a sponge. He had praised one woman at a pond whom he saw filtering the water for her jug with a sari folded several times. The simple technique circulated by Comilla and Matlah Health Services had proven effective filtering out the plankton to which cholera attach. The Matlah Clinic was a world renowned health facility funded entirely by grants and donations from Europe and the U.S.A. While examining one robust pregnant woman, Rajiv praised Manja for her supervision. Heavier mothers were less likely to deliver the underweight infants endemic to Bangladesh.

Rajiv released Sabjada's arm, and the girl returned to the cook fire. The depth of the burn must have made it uncomfortable to be near heat, but she did not flinch from her duties. The damage on her hand was also deep enough that an ensuing scar would restrict the use of her fingers. As the wound healed, the scar would tighten, drawing some fingers into a claw.

He turned to Manja. "She has received superior care. As have all the children at Sagaria." Manja smiled.

"Of course, the timing of her burn is not good," Rajiv continued. "The rains are coming. It would be best if the wound was well on its way to closing before then." The constant moisture in the air would work to prevent the burn from sealing. The risk of infection would double. Fungal infections were common on the coastal plains and the islands. The humid conditions and constant rain made many otherwise simple ailments difficult to treat.

Manja nodded slowly.

"I would, with your permission, like to leave a burn salve for Sabjada. It will help the wound close before the rains come." The rains were already at their doorstep, but the antibacterial salve would help stave off infection. "I would also ask you to consider boiling the water you use for the compresses, allowing it to cool, of course, before using it," he said, knowing she would probably not do this. Gathering water for the entire family was a cumbersome enough chore. And, it was probably one of Sabjada's chores to fetch the water from the river. She no doubt eased some pain each day by dipping her arm in the water. But Manja nodded.

"I have some salve for you in my bag," and he got up to fetch it. He looked at Manja knowingly. "Use it for *Sabjada*." The temptation, he knew, would be to save it for another case if Manja thought Sabjada was healing to her liking. There would be barely enough in the tube for Sabjada, let alone to parcel out for other treatments with an ineffective dab here and there.

"And when she is healed, Sabjada will be the apprentice midwife of Hajiya! It won't be long and the two of you will replace me."

Mother and daughter looked at each other and smiled. They were both embarrassed and thrilled.

"Sabjada wants to be a nurse. A registered nurse."

"Then you must accompany your mother for tomorrow's clinic." He turned to Manja. "Can you spare her from home? It would be good for her to watch, and perhaps she could help with bandaging, things like that."

Manja agreed, and Rajiv could see that the invitation delighted the girl, whose face lit up like a firefly. He stole a final glance at the angry burn snaking up Sabjada's arm as she returned to the fire to prepare dinner for her father.

Later as he strolled outside, the evening was humid, the smell of coming rain heavy in the air. Rajiv heard Manja and Sabjada murmuring inside their hut, excitedly whispering about tomorrow. Sabjada would join them at the village plaza after she finished their short morning meal, and prepared a lunch for them at midday. Rajiv looked at the cluster of homes, most, like Manja's, made of bamboo, a little wood—very little—and jute mats lashed into walls and roofing material. Most homes had one room with bamboo curtains, forming the interior walls. Most families in Sagaria were preparing evening meals, and the village was relatively quiet. Soon, the men and boys would return from the rice fields. This moment, between shifts in village life, was Rajiv's breathing space, his time to reflect on the day's cases.

CHAPTER 3

Reflections

Since he'd been back, Rajiv had had little time to himself except for the days in Sherpur, a city on the Jumuna River (Brahmaputra in India) north of Dhaka. He remembered the country air of Sherpur, its clarity wafting down range from the massive mountains of Bhutan and Nepal. By the time this air left Dhaka on the way to the Bay of Bengal, it was laden with the putrid byproducts of bacteria and disease. Only recently had he reclaimed his tolerance for this sad filth. Chicago air was pure compared to this. And he remembered how excitedly he, his father and brothers piled into their home when his mother beckoned the troops for evening meal. Her Naan breads, ginger-mango chutneys and hot fire tandoori chicken with cumin and cayenne quickened his saliva. Even in the lean years, he had never felt hungry. After his father's injury, the portions were smaller. Mother's deftly applied cheerful psychology, family singing and spirited word games camouflaged the loss of abundance. How quickly their folk singing became instrumental as his brother acquired music skills. And he was good. In his week in Sherpur, he'd listened long hours into the night as his brother alternately practiced and entertained while preparing to do a "recital" before an entertainment agent in

Calcutta. His sister dreamt of being a vocalist. But, according to Rajiv's ears, it might be a few years before this might be realized.

His father, Dal, was extremely resourceful with mat weaving and bamboo construction. The floor of their house was solid and two feet off the ground. The mats gave like two-inch foam. This made standing, sitting or sleeping very pleasant. Father, who could not return to mill work because his left side movements were limited by traumatic arthritis, had become the local mat and floor master. He was also highly skilled at bartering his services for meat, vegetables, flour, fruit and cooking oil.

His entire family was full of pride, self-esteem, and appreciation for others. The children were beginning to understand and appreciate the gifts their parents provided daily in values, traditions, intellectual exercises, and abidingly deep Agape and Filial love.

Eros was another matter. Apparently, medical school suppressed this until Angela came along. Eros erupted like molten lava during their fourth (clinical) year. When the relationship ended, the emotional pain drove his sexual self way deep into the subconscious. While containing this pain, he spit out venomously at female interns and residents. What had appeared as arrogance was actually pain disguised as anger at her family's rejection of his deep brown skin. Her family of Bible-toting, Sunday church-goers routinely failed to live out—the other six days of each week—the inclusive teachings of Jesus. Rajiv had been well on the way to Christianity until this happened. And his pain became so great he could not even find his way back to Allah. His faith was dormant. But safe. The occasions for re-examining spirituality were yet to come. He was unaware that safety was a bad trade off for the development of a deep faith which abided all.

And the reunion with his parents and siblings had been joyous, but bittersweet. His mother had prepared him all his favorite dishes. Koftes (onions and spices flavored meat patties). Biryani (long grain rice, an meat and spices). Chapati (An Indian bread often brushed with ghee-clarified butter), and all her naan with chokputi. He'd eaten everything with relish and gusto, but within a day, he'd fallen ill. His system had lost all resistance to the parasites common in the water of Bangladesh. He spent the rest of his stay carefully hiding his diarrhea from her, and dosing himself with oral rehydration salts and loperamide. It seemed his systems were purging themselves of his American life, replacing it with a new-old reality. He'd moved far away from those early days and had forgotten how far he had gone. He touched familiar furniture to make sure it was the same. With each clinic, with the steady onslaught of patient after patient, his life in America became a distant star way out in space.

He was confronted daily by the disparities between life in Chicago and in Sherpur. His parent's home seemed more crowded than he remembered. Four rooms for five people. In Evanston, Rajiv had shared a similar sized unit with just Gus.

Rajiv's other brother Assam, now 21, was working as a rice trader in Ranpur. He should be at university, but his grades, while excellent, had not made the cut for government support, and his family could not afford to send him. And the health ministry rarely selected two sons from the same family for the physician program. His sister Gerga, 19, was working in a textile factory, where she supervised a crew of children as young as eight. There she dreamt of the day when she would win a vocal audition. Her hands were raw with small cuts that looked like a network of spider webs stained with dye. His parents seemed frail. Trishana, his mother, now 61, was a computer-qualified teacher of three languages and home economics at a well-known girl's school between Sherpur and Dhaka. She was intellectually agile, well-read, long before the internet, and thirsty for information and knowledge. She knew the difference between the two and this was her wisdom. She imparted a sense of this to Rajiv. Rajiv's own intellectual agility often made him intolerant of the slower processing rates of some of his colleagues—an all too prevalent attribute of yuppies in Asia, India, London and major U.S.A. cities. Once he'd come to understand Adlai Stevenson's appreciation for the things you cannot see, he began to perceive a darkness somewhere in his brain. This seeming gray-black void made him uneasy when he was ruminating. For now, he just dismissed it.

And as he'd begun his work, he understood the hardships to expect. But being aware of difficulties versus living them were two different things. These past months had been hard on body and spirit. He was a guest in someone's home almost every night. At the moment, he saw his apartment about twice a month. What he craved most was solitude. As an honored official in the villages he visited he encountered nonstop social interaction between clinical sessions.

He thought of his friends in the United States, and the life he'd enjoyed there. He did not much miss the fast-food trappings of burgers and French fries. But he did miss Carmen's deep dish pizza with pine nuts in Rogers Park just west of Sheridan. He often sought out Indian restaurants in Chicago, which, like most Indian restaurants in the West, were actually run by Bengalis.

He missed abundance. Food. Medical supplies. Firewood. Enough doctors and nurses. Middle class families with abundance. The air of want and the absence of dignity in Bangladesh was oppressive. It was everywhere.

The dearth of supplies had been discombobulating at first. Once he was treating a boy in Bandar for an abscessed ear and out of habit ordered up amoxicillin. The midwife just stared at him. There was none.

He had lost patients before during his internship in an emergency room in South Chicago. It was very traumatic watching patients die, no matter how it happened. But there he knew that all possibilities had been exhausted, that supplies and medical talent were virtually limitless. The resources in one emergency room in Chicago would serve several thousand children here. It was emotionally draining to examine child after child ill with a relatively minor disorder, such as dysentery, and know they might die, where in the United States they could be bouncing around a day later. IV solutions, antidiarrheals, better food. He had treated a girl of eight already crippled with polio who had never been vaccinated. There had been a global immunization effort by wealthier nations which provided vaccine, but getting it to the villages was another matter. So polio still existed. Once every few years, workers from around the world spread out into villages in Bangladesh and other developing countries, tracked down unvaccinated children, placing a couple of drops on their tongues. But some children were always missed. Rajiv and most country physicians couldn't stock the vaccine, which required refrigeration. And, of course, AIDS was rearing its ugly head.

He thought about wells and water. He had spoken to Manja about her village well, but had not asked if it has been recently tested. Back on the mainland, he was constantly on the lookout for arsenic poisoning. The big push in the 1980s had been to install pipe wells in villages throughout Bangladesh to ensure a healthy source of water, since the rivers and ponds were cesspools. But now scientists were discovering industrially-dumped arsenic in many pipe wells, sometimes fifty times more arsenic than is considered safe. When he noticed skin lesions on the hands and feet, he knew that a village well and its people were in trouble. In villages "lucky" to have been among the first to have a new well, more people were being diagnosed with cancers of the liver, bladder and kidneys. Clean water was so basic, and yet so elusive in Bangladesh. In the filthy black water rivers of China, industrial pollutants were daily piped into streams and rivers. In Bangladesh it was arsenic in the wells. The consequences were beginning to show up.

Perhaps it was best that he had so little time to think. Looking toward the edge of the village, Rajiv saw Manja's men returning from the fields.

Shukendu Singh was, like most men in Sagaria, a rice farmer. With rainy season fast approaching, he had but a few weeks to plant a crop upon which his family would depend for food for much of the year. Shukendu was smarter than most. He owned his plot. More than two-thirds of the farmers in Bangladesh rented their plots or worked as day laborers for others. His clan's entire holdings were only a few hectares, of which less than a hectare belonged to Shukendu. The traditional Muslim inheritance system decrees that a man's land should be divided equally among all sons upon his death. On his small plot,

Shukendu had neither the resources to grow multiple crops every year, which required irrigation to bring water from the rivers during the dry season, nor the capital required for rapid growing, short-season seed varieties and fertilizers. His one crop was everything.

Shukendu embraced Manja first before he welcomed Dr. Rajiv. It was clear their love was solid and reinforced daily. He was lean but handsome; his arms lanky and muscular. His hands were his most important feature. They were large, long and seasoned in the waters of the rice fields. There was something special about them. Was it the way he held them or was it that he spoke with them? And the emphasis it seemed resided in both index fingers. His affection toward Sabjada and her brothers was tender. The smiles of these children in return were telling. When Shukendu took Sabjada's burned arm, he was very careful. The way he examined the damaged tissue and the redness of the surrounding forearm showed his concern. Rajiv used this moment to apply the salve. With Manja and Sabjada's permission, he applied it to the worst areas with a tongue depressor (no cotton swabs here) while Shukendu held her lovingly in his arms. He shared her pain as he watched this painful ordeal. The invisible transmission of such empathic love could not be missed. Rajiv only hoped that, by morning, her arm would look better before Shukendu left for the fields.

Shukendu and Rajiv chatted briefly before Shukendu and his sons sat down to eat Sabjada's meal. He explained the improvements he and his brothers had made on their rice paddies, building up embankments that provided some protection against flooding. The dikes had taken most of two years to build, and this year, they hoped to see the fruits of their work. While the rice needed vast amounts of rain to thrive, their plots were close enough to the river that extreme flooding and currents could sweep away the tender shoots, leaving the farmers devastated for the year. This often forced landowners to sell.

Four years ago, some of his clan cousins who owned nearby plots had sold their land to a wealthy landowner in Dhaka, for extremely modest compensation. Such circumstances were all too common.

Land ownership in Bangladesh was concentrated. The percentage of the absolutely landless had grown beyond 65 percent. Once they lost their land, his cousins had joined the renters and day laborers in a system like sharecropping in the southern United States. Last year, his cousins had moved to Chittagong to work in jute factories. Shukendu had visited them once last year.

"They live in a bustee along the railroad," he said. "A house of paper and very crowded." He shook his head.

Rajiv nodded. Once they lost their land, farmers joined the "floating people," those with nowhere to call home. He had regularly observed the bustees as he rode trains out to his coastal village posts. The filth was overwhelming. There were no sewers, so human waste was everywhere. The only thing in abundance besides people were rats and flies. And disease. The shacks never withstood hard rains, let alone monsoon conditions. One statistic spoke to Rajiv: infant mortality rate in these ghettos was more than fifty percent. The same rate was 7 per 1,000 in U.S. ghettos, 3 per 1,000 in Europe and Scandinavia.

As if the conditions weren't enough, mustans (the collect and protect gangsters) terrorized the bustees. These mafia-like warlords exacted small but persistent fees for land rental in the slums, as well as for the right of rickshaws to travel on public streets in the larger cities. Rumor had it that many mustans in Dhaka were connected to political parties, and that much of the student violence at the universities was due to politicians who thrived on unrest and violence. But the mustans were particularly nefarious in the bustees, where the poorest of the poor had little money to spare on bribes.

Yet the bustees were growing at an alarming rate as failed farmers moved to the cities in faint hope of a better life. Shukendu was among the few who understood the emptiness of that hope. Holding onto his land was his best chance in life.

"Perhaps you would like to tour our work?" Shukendu asked.

"Of course." A glimpse at the quality of area's farming gave him a bird's eye view into the region's health. As everywhere, good health followed nutritious food and clean water.

As they walked to the fields a mile away, Shukendu explained the project, and Rajiv heard the pride in his voice. His clan had embarked upon the dike system two years ago. It had been back-breaking. All the dirt had to be moved by hand, one shovelful at a time. Even getting the soil for the embankment was troublesome. They'd scrounged rock from wherever they could, along with bamboo and trash. Then, they stole precious top soil from their own fields for the final layer.

Soil was less a problem in Sagaria than on the coast north of Hatiya island. The island was all silt, the result of annual flooding that redistributes soil from the upper river basin to the delta. Even Hatiya was shifting. The eastern end was washing further out into the Bay of Bengal, the western end was growing.

Rajiv, Shukendu and his sons stood atop one of the narrow dikes, now covered with a fine fur of rough grass. A swell of children and men had followed, flowing behind them like an incoming tide. Shukendu introduced Rajiv to his cousin Pradeep, who owned the plot next to his, and whose family helped build the dike. Like Shukendu, Pradeep had had a rudimentary education and was able to read and write. He had helped with the research on diking efforts in other areas of Bangladesh.

"You've done good work," Rajiv said.

The men accepted the compliment. "It has not yet been really tested," Pradeep said. "We've had two rainy seasons, and it has done well. But no severe flooding yet. This has been good. It becomes stronger each season. The root structures of the grasses help a great deal."

The weather provided opportunity for the grass to grow, which would stem some of the erosion flooding would bring. And each year the planters walked up and down on the dikes to compact them, giving them added compressed strength.

"The village council has begun planning an embankment around our homes," Shukendu said. "But it is slow."

Besides the problems of physical resources, a village-encircling dike system required a fair amount of labor and cooperation, and most families had their hands full with their own subsistence. The national government had begun investing in monsoon shelters in the larger cities. A monsoon shelter had concrete floors and walls whose roofs could resist 175 mph winds. The structure stood ten feet tall above deeply driven concrete stilts. Each monsoon shelter could protect 1000 people. Surviving a monsoon was a matter of luck, location and wealth.

"Everything worthwhile takes time," Rajiv said.

It was dark when they returned to Shukendu and Manja's home. Rajiv was exhausted, a state to which he was becoming accustomed. His morning would start early. As he drifted off to sleep, he heard the music of rain on the bamboo roof. These intense brief rains were the harbingers of monsoon.

And he had been right about the antibiotic salve. Manja had gently wrapped Sabjada's arm before bedtime and as she removed the wrappings in the morning, despite Sabjada's pain, the salve had wrought a small wonder. Dr. Rajiv was pleased. Manja was comforted. Shukendu's face lit up like a Halloween pumpkin as he looked at the arm and saw Sabjada's smile. He firmly grasped both Rajiv's hands in his, in an appreciative male-to-male demonstration of gratitude. The tremor in Shukendu's grasp was surprising to Rajiv. And it felt so good. He did not understand but he felt emotionally nourished.

CHAPTER 4

In Fulfillment of Duty

River Boat Clinic at Site #14 on
Rajiv's Coastal Itinerary for the Month

"Daktar Gaol?"

He met the woman's gaze steadily. She held her listless toddler, a boy of about three.

"Diarrhea? Vomiting?"

"Before, he held his stomach when he cried," she said. "Now, nothing."

"Has his skin been itching?"

The woman nodded.

Rajiv gently opened one of the boy's eyes. The whites were beginning to turn yellow.

"Has he had it before?"

Again, she nodded.

Hepatitis. Fairly advanced. The child's stomach was distended, but when Rajiv pinched his skin, the wrinkles stayed. He was dehydrated. He turned to Sabjada and directed her to the case of fluids behind them in the village school they were using as their clinic. He was careful in dispensing Pedialyte. It was heavy to carry the bottles with him, and there was little follow through to make sure the child healed. Hepatitis was growing in the island's southern areas. There the waters grew more toxic as they added factory outflow and sewage in their journey to the sea. Bangladesh was losing too many children to out-of-control diarrhea.

He began instructing her on water hygiene, then stopped.

"Sabjada, come here."

The girl scurried to his side. Sabjada had shadowed him since her arrival, watching intently as he bandaged and in a few cases stitched, administered shots and advised. She was not only the youngest nurse he'd had, but also the most attentive.

"Explain to her the importance of boiling the child's water."

As he used a disinfectant wipe to sterilize his hands for the next patient, he listened. Gloves were in very short supply. Pure water was an illusion. Sabjada enjoyed the status of her role, and she accurately reiterated the methods he'd been preaching to families over and over. Boiling. Filtering.

He turned to Manja and nodded his approval.

This clinic on Hatiya at the far western end of the island had been going since early morning and he'd seen three dozen patients already. They'd had malaria or the flu. Several had risky pregnancies, which entailed leaving detailed instructions with Manja. Two children, victims of amputation from wounds that had become infected, were eligible for leg prostheses. He measured them and put them on a list already too long. There were more burns like Sabjada's. He asked Sabjada or Manja to describe the treatment of boiled water, sterile dressings which he supplied, and antibacterial salve when available.

They broke briefly for the lunch which Sabjada prepared and brought them. The girl was bright and watched his every move with intense interest in the purpose and rationale of each procedure. He found himself explaining treatments as much for her as for her mother. And he found himself enjoying the instruction. Watching the girl follow his orders without deviation gave him hope. He wished there were a dozen girls like her in every village. That would be the way to create a health care knowledge delivery system, he thought to himself.

At mid-afternoon, he told Manja to advise the people that they would take no more patients after the last person currently in line. He needed to be on the mainland in Dhaka by tomorrow. Hatiya's one main road leading to an airport on the mainland was impassable once the rains progressed in earnest, and if conditions worsened, he could be stuck on the island for several weeks, which would throw his clinics way off schedule.

At four, they closed up shop. Shukendu came in from the fields, and he, Manja and Sabjada accompanied Rajiv on the quarter mile to the ferry. Their sons brought the trunks of supplies and equipment that traveled with Rajiv in his nomadic practice.

Rain began to fall, again gently at first, and then harder, and after loading his goods on the boat, everyone crowded for a few minutes beneath the station shelter, exchanging formalities. As he turned to board the ferry, Sabjada stepped forward.

"For you." She handed Rajiv a bundle, and when he opened it, he found a *nakshi kantha*, an elaborate quilt made of worn saris and other used cotton clothing. *Nakshi kanthas* were artistic expressions of Bangla culture born of necessity. *Kanthas* were also believed to be lucky and had at one time been popular as infant blankets. A prevailing belief was that Allah would ignore someone swaddled in rags but would cherish one wrapped in a *nakshi kantha*.

Rajiv turned the *kantha* over in his hands. The background was black, a traditional color, and stitched into it in yellow, blue, pink and red thread was an entire village of people; many were children. The villagers were clustered around a woman, who held a single child aloft as if offering it to the sky. It was the story of a midwife. Rajiv's first instinct was to say that he couldn't accept the gift. The piecework was elaborate. It must have taken Sabjada and Manja many evenings of spare time to quilt the *kantha*. Most women and girls saved such pieces for dowries or sold them to tourists for critical extra cash. But he knew she would be hurt and Manja insulted if he refused.

He smiled and said, "I needed this. Luck will follow the *kantha*." He put his hand on her shoulder. "Be a good student. Study hard. I will send you some biology books from my collection. When you are ready to apply to university, come to me. I will help. And I will see you next month."

Sabjada ducked her head, but Rajiv could see her smile. She was glowing.

"Salam-a-lekum."

"Salam," Shukendu said.

The ferry blew its horn, and Rajiv nodded in final parting before dashing through the downpour as much as anyone could while carrying three large bags of supplies before squeezing onto the lower deck. As the ferry moved away from shore, he saw Sabjada's smiling face and her brightly colored *dupatta* flapping in the growing fury of the storm. He watched her, until the sheets of rain became an impervious curtain. To have a daughter like Sabjada some day. How precious that would be.

CHAPTER 5

Effectiveness Introduced

Editorial Page

"Politicians like to arrange for dike projects being awarded to construction relatives of clothing magnates. Dikes for railroads from clothing factories to shipping ports gain funding over impoverished areas every time.

Senator Ram Mukherjee and his cronies seem to have forgotten they are elected to serve all Bangladesh. Safety for the masses has no priority.

And an Ananda Marga leader has called for Mass Protests and Picketing of the Senate."

—*Chittagong Daily Press*

Rajiv had to reach Chittagong to catch a flight to Dhaka. If he had had the luxury of time, he would have taken the train. As the small jet lifted from the Chittagong airport, sun sparkled on what appeared to be water rather than land. The rains had been falling sporadically for two weeks and rivers were rising with added melt water coming down to the Bay of Bengal from the mountains of Tibet and Bhutan. The coastal plains were flooding. As the plane rose to cruising altitude, a mist wafted over the lake that was now Chittagong. The morning's sun was a welcome respite as they reached flying altitude.

It is easy to romanticize flooding, as writers have through the ages. But Rajiv had not missed it when he was abroad. The rains were like the snow. Back in Chicago, his friends rhapsodized about the first storm or two, hosting sledding parties to break the academic stress they faced. By mid-December, they were already weary of slush, slick sidewalks, traffic pileups, and the bone-chilling, wet Chicago wind. By February, everyone longed for a week in Cancun or Florida. So it was with the rain in Bangladesh. First, relief that there was rain for the crops. Then, resignation. Finally, loathing.

Almost 70 percent of Bangladesh was submerged every year, and while the farmers depended on the rain, mostly everyone suffered through, or more accurately, waded through it. The Chittagong province where Rajiv spent much of his time bore the brunt. In June and July, Chittagong might get as much as 24 inches of rainfall each month.

Cyclones were the worst. Bangladesh was cursed with more cyclones than any other place on earth, due to a variety of factors. For one, the tides were large. The coastal configuration and Bay of Bengal topography increased wave height which, coupled with high tide surges, easily submerged the low flat terrain. The cyclones wrought their special havoc on Bangladesh about every two to three years. Chittagong province was among the most susceptible because there was so much deep water in this city on the sea. In 1970, between 300,000 and 500,000 people died. The exact count would never be known. In a disaster, the poor are the most undercounted in every nation.

The flight to Dhaka was short—less than 30 minutes—and much of it was spent getting to altitude, then descending, and watching the water. Located at the confluence of the Burhi Ganga, Dhaleswari and Lakhya rivers, Dhaka at only thirteen feet above sea level, would also be flooded, although its average rainfall was less than that of Chittagong. But Dhaka also had more hills and more natural protective resources. Rajiv would not have to spend so much time in

Dhaka with his feet wet. But he, too, found himself longing for a sunny someplace.

Instead, he was headed to a seminar for Comilla Health Ministry physicians in Dhaka. For two days, they would hear updates about the progress—often the lack thereof—on health issues in Bangladesh. It was Rajiv's fourth such seminar since returning home, and he had already learned about the real business of the seminars.

In the evenings, the health care folks would commiserate about the lack of supplies, the unending workload, and the Sisyphus-like nature of their work. They would socialize with politicians in hopes of gaining further funding. That was, by far, the most important part of seminars.

The plane descended. Rajiv leaned toward the window, but the glare of light off the water blinded him and he looked away. Already some of southern Dhaka was under water.

The humidity was oppressive. And by evening, the physicians and government officials were glad to shed their dress coats, unbuttoning their collars for whatever air movement came into the ballroom chosen for the evening reception. Large ceiling fans were in overdrive.

The first day had provided a fascinating, if demoralizing, look into public health throughout the nation. Rajiv heard evidence that the health struggles in the southern coastal provinces were indicative of the rest of the nation. He knew, too well, this harsh reality. And yet the mood of the conference was upbeat. It was noted several times that in the last decade the Ministry of Health had nearly doubled the number of physicians working in floating clinics, due largely to the recruitment of men like Rajiv in scholarship programs. A presentation by a deputy of the Health Ministry, Amit Das, noted the government's expectation that many of these men and women would choose to stay on in Bangladesh after their contracts were completed. Rajiv felt a twinge of guilt, and a downturn in his spirits. That's what they were depending on, re-enlistment of men like him. Rajiv had looked around the classroom and saw he was not the only government service doctor with doubts. Another doctor whispered to Rajiv, "I wouldn't stay if my salary quadrupled!"

Rajiv's national loyalty and patriotism kept him torn between duty and his vision of a pediatric practice in a Chicago suburb. He surely would not renew without a signing bonus and at least doubling of his salary.

The camaraderie of the conference was good for Rajiv. By the end of the day, he'd made contacts that would help him when it came time to work through red tape or for consultation. After dinner dishes were cleared, they moved into the hotel ballroom for after-dinner drinks or, for strictly practicing Muslims, tea and nonalcoholic refreshments. Rajiv drank brandy. In the ballroom, small clusters of doctors, health officials and government workers mingled, further cementing relationships.

"It was a most interesting case." Dr. Taj Doyal, a physician in the Comilla Dhaka division, paused to sip his cocktail. "The child worked in a clothing factory as a hemmer. A needle pierced his index finger and as he pulled away, he tore the digit. It was, of course, infected by the time I saw him."

The group of physicians surrounding him nodded. They were familiar with the lot of the clothing workers.

Most newer physicians kept their heads down and passed cryptic notes to each other.

Rajiv had not yet become accustomed to discussing his cases with such clinical detachment, which he knew was necessary if he were to survive. But he found himself thinking of Sabjada and her burn. Dr. Doyal had introduced himself to Rajiv during the meal and had offered to introduce him to the other doctors in his circle. Dr. Doyal would be leading a session the next day on injuries specific to the clothing and jute industries.

"The infection was the simple part," Doyal continued. "The problem was how to save the tip of the finger. Without it, the boy is useless in the clothing factories. He needed the index finger to push the material through the feeder beneath the needle."

But the fingertip was black by the time Dr. Doyal arrived on the scene. His course of treatment started with the removal of the fingertip from the second metatarsal, followed by a round of antibiotics administered by a village midwife.

"When the nub had properly scarred, we fitted him with a pros-
thetic glove." With his hands, he described the glove, which was really an elastic finger sleeve fitted with a poly tip. Wrist straps kept it
in place, giving the boy much of the use of his own index finger.

"How old was the boy?" Rajiv asked.

"I believe he was nine," Dr. Doyal said.

"Perhaps he shouldn't be working in the clothing factories," Rajiv said quietly. During the 1990s, Bangladesh had become a target
for international protests about child labor in garment factories. Most
garment factories were in the Dhaka and Chittagong divisions. Rajiv,
too, had seen more than his share of injuries. To be missing the tip of a
finger was lucky. He had treated a woman who had lost her hand when
her sleeve got caught in a weaving arm, pulling her in as she struggled
to free herself. "An industrial setting is no place for a child. I was there
for two years when I was 11 and 12. And our literacy rates will never
rise beyond current levels unless we can keep the children in school."

Doyal was a small, almost petite, dark-skinned man. His blazing
eyes darted from side to side as he spoke. It was clear he was also a
masterful politician.

"Ah! If only it were that simple," Dr. Doyal said. "Yes, it is unfortunate that the children must work so hard when they are so young.
Historically, factory workers rarely achieve even a rudimentary education. The work is dangerous. Yet there is the issue of money, and
food." He fingered the edge of his cocktail glass thoughtfully. "I've
seen such ideas put into practice, and well-intentioned as they are,
the results have often been tragic. Children barred from the factories
do not go to school. Instead, they go into less-savory professions like
begging, prostitution, or stealing firewood.

"You know, there is some suspicion that the anti-child labor
movement is being encouraged by the American labor unions, who
aren't worried so much about the children as they are about the competition. You'll remember how rapidly the focus on children in the
jute factories shifted when the industry faltered."

Attention to jute factory children had waned as manmade fibers
like Dacron and polyethylene took over much of the world market

previously held by jute as backing for carpeting and for shopping bags. In the last decade, hundreds of thousands of Bengalis lost their livelihoods as prices for jute plummeted, accelerating land concentration in the hands of the few and the movement of more poor to the bustees. The welfare of the children was not forgotten, but many were nostalgic for the days when the factories were full of children, and the jute market was healthy. In the factories, they were fed, some were actually educated. All received health care.

The group fell silent. Few had been accorded an American education, and Dr. Doyal's statement was a veiled indictment of Rajiv, a suggestion that maybe he had adopted the thinking of his medical school compatriots without question. Perhaps, Dr. Doyal seemed to be saying, Rajiv had become too Western.

It was not the first time he had faced such criticism. There was a fair amount of jealousy directed at the candidates educated abroad. And there was a nugget of truth in Dr. Doyal's argument. At the wages offered, most families needed three or four wage earners to survive, a fact that armchair activists, often trust beneficiaries with full stomachs, sometimes overlooked. Most labor class children came from families without fathers; they had no choice but to work. Older children often worked in the factories so younger siblings could receive an education.

"I know few Bengali children who do not work hard, whatever their labors," Rajiv said. "My own brothers and sisters have worked in the factories." He waited for that to sink in. "But the question is really about safety standards, which should be higher because of the presence of children."

"Such as?"

The circle of doctors turned deferentially to the voice. Rajiv saw a man, a big man, about 50, wearing the traditional dress of blue silk coat or sherwani and pajamas with a cream stole trimmed with gold tassels. His gray hair was thinning to a semicircle, but it was clipped short in a distinctive, executive cut. He was dashing and had commanding presence.

"Senator Mukherjee," Dr. Doyal said, stepping forward to take the man's hand. "It is so good to see you again, although it is no surprise to find you here." He turned to the doctors around him. "Senator Ram Mukherjee is the parliamentary representative for the Chittagong area. As most of you know, he has a keen interest in health issues, particularly those for children."

The group murmured their respects, and the senator returned his attention to Rajiv.

"What kind of advances would you recommend in the factories? I am interested."

Dr. Doyal shot Rajiv a look that urged caution and diplomacy. Rajiv chose his words carefully.

"I understand that there are plastic shields that can be attached to the machinery to prevent accidents like the one of which Dr. Doyal spoke, which would prevent a worker being able to insert their finger beneath the needle. There are also implements workers use to push the material beneath the needle so their fingers are never in harm's way."

Senator Mukherjee studied Rajiv closely. "You mean in American factories. Many of which are closing now, losing their market share to factories in China, and here."

Rajiv did not respond, and for a moment, no one spoke.

"We are in a delicate place in terms of Bengali development and we are on a global economic teeter-totter," Senator Mukherjee said. "For the first time, we are advancing in the global garment industry. Did you know that most of the T-shirts in the world are made here in Bangladesh? We are the seventh largest, soon to be sixth, clothing supplier to the United States, where clothing factories are practically a thing of the past. As the quality of our work grows, we are on the cusp of producing brand-name clothing. Soon, Levis will be made here. Our people hunger for those jobs."

"Our people hunger for any jobs," Rajiv said, "not just clothing labor."

Senator Mukherjee pursed his lips. "You have others?"

Rajiv smiled. "Touché."

"Child labor does not exist in a vacuum," the Senator said. "It is difficult turning a starving child away from work, real work. I would have trouble doing it. Wouldn't you? What they need, what all Bangladesh needs, are choices. You come to me with choices, and I will listen."

Rajiv heard hard notes of censure in the senator's voice, and didn't know what quagmire he had stumbled into. But he did know it was best to back out gracefully, and now.

"That is a formidable challenge, but a fair one," he said.

"He'll get back to you with solutions to all of the problems of Bangladesh," Dr. Doyal said to the group. "In a few years perhaps."

The laughter in the group broke the tension, and Senator Mukherjee smiled. "Good doctors, enjoy yourself in Dhaka. I will see you all tomorrow evening."

Rajiv watched as Senator Mukherjee moved to the next cluster, ever the stately politician cultivating potential voters.

Dr. Doyal's eyebrows crooked, and he breathed a heavy sigh of relief. "That was close. Mukherjee married into the Kapoor family."

For a moment Rajiv drew a blank. Then it came to him. "As in the Kapoor clothing factories?" Rajiv asked.

"The very one." Dr. Doyal pulled Rajiv away from the other physicians toward the bar with a firm grip on his elbow. "Dr. Gaol. You are new to the politics of public health. I would advise that you be careful in the future."

"Discussion of these matters is important if progress is to be made," smarted Rajiv back.

"You are impatient. I remember my first few years here." Dr. Doyal dropped his friendly tone and his voice became firm. "But you risk too much antagonizing the very hands that feed us. You have people to look after, and which would you rather be: a doctor with adequate supplies, or one who depends on just these?" He held out his empty hands. "Think about it. Think of your patients before you exercise your 'freedom of speech' next time."

He shot Rajiv a final warning look before striding away.

Suddenly, the humidity in the room, crowded with physicians, minor government officials, and politicians, was oppressive. Rajiv blinked at the drops of sweat stinging his eyes. He waded through the throng to the exterior doors, looking for an escape. He stepped out onto the veranda and wiped his brow with a large cotton handkerchief. The air was thick. More rain was surely on the way. A breeze kicked up, and Rajiv closed his eyes and thrust his face forward to receive it. He stripped off his suitcoat and was surprised at how quickly his damp body took a chill. The winds grew stronger. Rajiv frowned. A razor of lightning shot across the black sky, then another. A formidable storm was moving in. Bangladesh had not seen a full-fledged major cyclone season in several years. It was as if global warming and sea level rise were getting ready to topple his fragile country into the Bay of Bengal.

By morning, the storm had hit. Appropriately, Rajiv was attending a seminar on the storm shelter movement. This 1991 cyclone was stronger than those of the infamous season of 1970, destroying four times as many homes. But the death toll was less than half that of 1970, largely due to the growth in the number of storm shelters and better advance warning techniques. Storm shelters had been built in heavily populated areas of Chittagong, and often doubled as schools or government offices. The shelters were offered as proof the nation was moving to address its age-old problems from flooding and as evidence that the nation was becoming more modern. Of course, rural areas lacked such a shelter system completely.

Clean water availability remained a key factor in the control of an epidemic. In the countryside more tube wells had been sunk, and in the major cities of Dhaka and Chittagong, water authorities had taken steps to protect the water pumping stations themselves from being submerged under the flood waters. The seminar speakers made it clear that Bangladesh would not surrender to floods, but everything they discussed dealt only with the aftermath. Little progress had been made on flood prevention. It bore more than a passing resemblance to Katrina, New Orleans and Pass Christian.

A thunderous wind pounded the building. Rajiv looked up from his notes to see rain pelting the windows, whose glass shook with the force of the growing gales. The lights blinked. The speaker, a government engineer, paused first because of the flickering lights, then because a hotel worker had come to the front of the room.

"Gentlemen, we are going to ask you to move to better shelter. We have just received word of cyclones moving up toward the north end of the Bay of Bengal. We believe Dhaka is safe, for the time being, but officials are advising that we move to a higher ground facility, just in case."

The doctors rose and scurried to gather up their papers and brief cases.

"Has it hit the mainland yet?" Rajiv asked. "How about Chittagong?"

But the man had already left, moving on to the next room as the hotel prepared for evacuation.

Rajiv went to his room and jammed his belongings into his bag. By the time he reached the lobby, it was full of people crowded around television sets. Rajiv elbowed his way forward for a view of sideways rain in Cox's Bazaar and another of submerged bustees southeast of Dhaka awash in the flotsam of what were once beggars' homes.

"Any news of the islands?" Rajiv asked, breaking the somber quiet of the watchers. "Sandwip? Hatiya?"

One of the men shook his head. "There will be no pictures of the islands until this is over. And then...." He did not finish.

And then, what would there be to see? Water, debris, filth and the cloak of apprehension that tragedy was to follow.

It was more than a week before travel resumed to the southern divisions, and then only by boat, which meant another day of travel before Rajiv landed in Chittagong, where he'd been ordered to report to an emergency clinic at Battali Hill. He was able to hail a cab, which had a high-water mark on the side that seemed to suggest he would be tucking his feet up on the seat if he wanted them dry. The cab took a circuitous route as it plunged through small inland seas in which Rajiv could see rats swimming, slicks of various chemicals and oils, and the occasional body. Already, the threat of typhoid and dysentery was great.

The scene at the clinic, a converted elementary school, was

chaotic. For once however, there appeared to be enough medical staff and supplies. Beds, benches or even dry spaces for the injured and sick were at a premium. Medical staff and ambulatory patients threaded their way among the prone bodies of adults and children who awaited care. The airports had not yet re-opened, so supplies from the United Nations, UNICEF, donor nations, and personnel from Doctors Without Borders and Oxfam were stalled. The rooms were eerily quiet despite the suffering they held.

Although housed in a grade school with no books or blackboards, pupils or teachers, this makeshift clinic was a functional triage facility. This facility had equipment, supplies and, of all things, standby power. Nobody else in Bangladesh had the electric power so vital for instruments, lighting for diagnosis, blood and other tests, and treatment. This could not happen without connections and a well-oiled political process. Rajiv could sense the hidden hands of Senator Mukherjee and Dr. Doyal. The two generators, one Japanese, and one American, were on separate trucks. The standby generating engines were humming at a steady, reliably sounding, cadence.

If his normal clinic days were draining, days in the emergency clinic were off the exhaustion end of the chart. Working by the artificial light, Rajiv and the other staff members worked until they could no longer stand. They were told they would have the generators for two more days. Most of the region's generators had to be shared by hospitals, where full surgery was being performed, and government offices trying to coordinate relief and disaster centers. He treated people for rat bites, infected cuts and wounds, and dysentery. Many younger patients had swallowed flood waters filled with a host of bacterial maladies and poisoning from the surge in industrial pollution which now made its way into the rivers as the waters rose. Rajiv finished bandaging a nasty cut on the head of an elderly man whose eyes were stony.

"Do you have any family?" Rajiv asked.

The man just stared. Rajiv looked to his nurse, who stood behind this patient and dejectedly shook her head. The man was in shock, yet there was no room for him at the school, which was full of others in worse shape. The nurse gently took him by the elbow and escorted him to the door. He sloshed through an ankle-deep puddle like someone who had lost everything, from family to hope.

Rajiv rose from the stool that he'd been perched on since, it seemed, forever (actually eleven hours), and felt himself becoming dizzy. A hand on his shoulder steadied him. When his vision cleared, he turned and saw Dr. Doyal. The elder physician's gaze was grave. Doyal had been observing Rajiv every chance he had. He was very impressed with his diagnostic skills and how rapidly he processed patients without being harsh. Admirable skills under these conditions. In Dhaka at the seminar he worried that Rajiv was just another flash in the pan whose long-term contribution to Bangladesh would likely be marginal. This fellow had gumption. Doyal's opinion had clearly changed.

"Go rest."

Rajiv protested but Dr. Doyal was firm. "You must take care of yourself. There will be many more days of this. You are of no use to these people if you are sick yourself. Come. Let us take a break."

They made their way past the bodies of the sick and exhausted, on gurneys and floors, to the back door of the school, where there was a loading dock, a dry space because of its elevation. Dr. Doyal put a Camel cigarette into his lips and offered one to Rajiv. Rajiv didn't smoke regularly—but often wanted to—but he took the cigarette gratefully. They puffed in silence for a few moments, looking onto the playground. It was pitch black except for the glow off the tips of their cigarettes and the sliver of a moon, which had just risen over rooftops and bustees. Moonlight glistened on the slick mud coating everything, illuminating a vague rustle here and there, usually of rats. Somehow, the rats always, always survived. He thought of the moon that had watched over him in Chicago while he was a medical resident just nineteen months ago. The moon was the same but he was not. Rajiv felt exhausted, dazed, and shell-shocked, as if he'd been through a war or had walked across a mine field. His limbs trembled.

"When did you get in?" Rajiv asked.

"Yesterday. They're pulling doctors from other regions to serve

Chittagong. Is this your first cyclone, that is, as a physician?"

Rajiv nodded. "First time as anything. I'm from the north, and when the storms of 1991 hit, I was too young. My parents wouldn't allow me to join the relief efforts. I've never seen them firsthand." Outside the clinic, in the quiet, he felt bone-weary and he leaned heavily on the wall. His neck ached from the constant stooping over patients, and his eyes stung from the concentrated evening's work. His clothes and hair smelled of fuel, and he knew that potable water even for drinking was scarce. He would have to boil whatever he used to wash, and he was too exhausted tonight even to bathe. He'd been given a small cot in a janitor's closet in the school-turned-clinic, up off the floor so that at least he wouldn't have to compete for floor space with all of the insects scurrying in any dry space they could find.

"I won't say, 'You'll get used to it,' " Dr. Doyal said. "You don't."

"Do we even have an estimate yet?" Rajiv meant bodies. One judged the severity of calamities in Bangladesh in terms of body count.

"Nothing official. I've heard, however, people think perhaps fifty-sixty thousand. Injuries, maybe three times that. About 200,000 homes."

Rajiv was not shocked by the casual tone in Dr. Doyal's voice that discussed fifty thousand lives as if they were grains of rice.

"Have you heard anything of the islands. Hatiya?"

"Hatiya?" Dr. Doyal studied Rajiv before speaking. "There are now several Hatiyas." He exhaled a long cloud of smoke. "I saw a clip on the television this morning. You can see a few hills and trees, but mostly there is just the sea. Many survivors have come by boat to Chittagong until the water recedes."

Rajiv's head snapped up. "Where?"

Dr. Doyal shrugged. "They're spread out all over, but I know some are at the Medical College Hospital at Cox's Bazaar. You have people on Hatiya?"

Rajiv threw his cigarette into the pool beneath the loading dock where it landed with a hiss. "Friends. Maybe I can find word of them."

"You're not going tonight?" Dr. Doyal said incredulously.

"With all these untreated patients? There will be no time until late tomorrow," Rajiv said, moving as if to go.

Dr. Doyal put his hand on Rajiv's arm. "I meant it when I said you must take care of yourself. My first cyclone, everyone's first cyclone, you think you can save them all. I became seriously ill with hepatitis my first cyclone out of medical college. Then, of course, I saved no one. You will go tomorrow."

"But there are patients here…."

Dr. Doyal said. "The sick are like the poor. They are with us always, everywhere. I will arrange for you to go to the Medical College Hospital for the day. Tomorrow, in between patients, you can look for your friends. But tonight," his voice became stern, "you will eat, and sleep. Understand?"

Rajiv felt his chin bobbing like a doll, and any argument washed out of him. With effort, he shoved away from the wall and stumbled through the elementary school to his closet sleeping area. His dinner of bottled water and cold lentil soup sat on a shelf. He slurped both down without tasting either. When he fell onto his cot, he was asleep.

The mood at the Medical College Hospital was more somber than at the makeshift clinic. Patients here had lost more—more family, homes and livelihoods. In between cases, Rajiv interrogated patients in the hospital and on the outlying campus, where tents fashioned of blankets and tarps were already rising from the soggy patches of grass. "Are you from Hatiya? From Sagaria township? Have you seen anyone…? Do you know the Shukendu Singh family?" Singh, unfortunately, was like "Smith." Instead, he began asking for "midwife Manja." A few people recognized her name, but they had no news. Most people had their own sad stories to tell. It was so hard, so very hard to hear. It was slow going. New refugees arrived by the minute, many of them doing just as he was, searching for people they knew, for parents, for children. Out on the grassy commons in front of the main hospital building people were searching moving from one cluster of refugees to another, bowing their heads for a moment before moving on to the next.

By dusk, Rajiv was again exhausted, but today, he decided to take Dr. Doyal's advice on self-care seriously. He signaled his nurse to wind down his line of patients. When he rose from his stool, his back cracked in protest. He was stiff from head to toe. Outside, he scanned the commons, not that he would necessarily recognize any newcomers. His mind was crowded with new faces. Since he'd come home to Bangladesh from the United States, there had been constant new faces. Familiarity was a lost luxury.

He made his way to the street, where a steady stream of refugees continued to pour onto the grounds. He glanced back on the crowd one more time, and met the gaze of a man who was staring down at him from a low wall, a favorite perch for searchers. The man, like most of the other refugees, had a beaten-down look about him. His clothes were muddy, and his eyes were anxious and despondent. He looked like every other cyclone victim. But the man's expression changed as Rajiv returned his gaze, and he jumped from the wall and moved toward him with eagerness. Suddenly, Rajiv recognized him.

"Pradeep!"

"Dhaktar Gaol!"

They embraced. As physically and emotionally exhausted as he was, Rajiv could feel the quake of trauma and near starvation in Pradeep's body. Rajiv began moving back toward the medical college where he could better examine Shukendu's cousin. As they moved, they peppered each other with questions. They had both been searching for information for days.

"Your family?" Rajiv asked, gesturing toward the courtyard.

"I have two of my sons with me." Pradeep's voice dropped. "I cannot yet find my wife and daughters."

It was a common refrain among refugees. Too often, the women of a family had not developed swimming skills, which probably would not have saved them from a cyclone but increased their mortality rates in the flood surges that followed. Sadley, Rajiv knew that when space in storm shelters was scarce, families tried to save sons first.

Rajiv braced himself, and asked the question he'd been waiting days to ask, but to which he feared an answer. "Do you have any news of Shukendu's family?"

Pradeep shook his head sorrowfully. "I have no news of Shukendu and his wife, Manja. Their hut is gone. Before my sons and I were evacuated, we waded through where the village was...." His voice faltered. "We found Sabjada and her brother, Rohit... in the water, so lifeless...."

Rajiv was taken sharply back. His professional detachment mode vanished. He was stricken.

But, then he quickly turned back to his professional demeanor. "First, let me take a look at your sons and get you all something to eat. It will save waiting in line."

Pradeep fetched his two young sons, ages eleven and fourteen. Rajiv steered them back into the building in which he'd been working, taking them into a serving kitchen where they enjoyed a degree of privacy. He summoned a nurse and asked her to round up rations. She returned in a few moments with thin lentil soup, ruti and bottled water, along with a handful of oral electrolyte rehydration salts. Pradeep and his sons gulped down their meal. When they were finished, Rajiv offered to have them accompany him to the school. His sleeping accommodations were meager, but they were inside. Pradeep politely declined.

"We were told that many of the Hatiya refugees are coming here."

Rajiv nodded. The quest for Pradeep's wife and daughters would supersede all else in the coming days, and possibly weeks.

"I will be back tomorrow," he said. "You can find me in this building. Come, and I will see if I can find a tent and some other supplies for you. Tell them I am part of your family so they let you in."

"Thank you."

Rajiv put his hand on Pradeep's shoulder in a silent good-bye, and left.

In the darkness outside, Rajiv began to absorb the news about Sabjada. He cycles through his memories of this lovely child-woman, one he had thought would be part of his future floating clinics. Alone, he sobbed with a rapidly heaving chest as he remembered her gift, the *kantha* and his last view of her and her brothers at the ferry landing that rain-filled day. He composed himself as best he was able and headed back inside.

Now, because of his fatigue, he suddenly felt, in one of the most densely populated places on earth, isolated and alone. Sabjada was hope to Rajiv. Sabjada and her mother, Manja, were symbols of what Bangla health care could be. They were the closest thing to friends he'd made since returning to Bangladesh. Manja had been his first student. Sabjada his second. His back ached. He trembled and shook uncontrollably, his grief became an explosive, all consumptive infection. His mouth went dry and his eyes puffed up.

He longed to see the faces of his med school friends and residency colleagues. He needed to see his mother and father.

CHAPTER 6

An Altered Perspective

Dr. Doyal was almost right—35,000 dead, with another 15,000 missing, and perhaps 10,000 of those dead as well.

It was a month before relief efforts solidified, the waters subsided, and food supply lines were running more or less smoothly. By late July, Rajiv was preparing to return to duty out in the delta/Sundarbans. He then would move down the coastline of Chittagong province to other areas hit by the storm and flooding. He would still be in disaster relief mode, treating mostly the infections induced by dirty water and increasingly cholera and typhoid.

"So, you've gotten your feet wet, so to speak, in the monsoon cycles," Dr. Doyal said to him. They had just finished their work one evening at the school refugee camp and had stepped onto the loading dock for what had become this nightly ritual cigarette. The workload had eased, but there was still so much to do.

Rajiv had come to value Dr. Doyal's companionship and counsel. He was experienced in the bureaucratic snares that often brought their work to a halt, and he knew what strings to pull to make government clerks rush medicines and supplies to their clinic. Rajiv realized how well-connected Dr. Doyal was. He could reach mid-level officials, and members of parliament, especially Senator Mukherjee. He knew his way around and was very effective. Little did Rajiv realize that the Senator and Dr. Doyal had had several conversations about him. He had already been marked as one to consider for future positions.

"Yes," Rajiv said. "How long before the next one?"

His tone was mildly sarcastic, but the question, unfortunately, was real. Both knew that cyclones with their sad toll, would recur.

"It is the price for being Bangladesh," Dr. Doyal said.

Rajiv exhaled a stream of smoke. "Does it have to be this way?"

Dr. Doyal smiled. "Young doctors. You all want to save the world."

"No. Just my corner. And there must be better ways."

"*My*, what an interesting choice of words." During their weeks together, Rajiv had shared with Dr. Doyal some of his conflicts, both monetary and personal, about his return to Bangladesh. The elder physician had not preached, just listened.

"It is, and will always be, my home." Rajiv wasn't sure when it started to happen, but sometime after the cyclones hit, in the absolute worst of times, he thought of Bangladesh as home. This was a reclaimed feeling. It was as if he had been handed a real estate deed, "in fee simple absolute." Somehow, his country had called more to him in this tragedy than in ordinary times. He felt commitment and a resurrected pride. The sort of pride he'd felt when, as a nine-year-old school child, he had scored off the top on a country wide English test. His mother had gently said, one evening, "You would thrill your father's and my heart were you to become a national health care physician. This country needs strong, intelligent, devoted people to care for our nation's poor." Obviously, he had been listening.

"What do you have in mind, Dr. Moses? Will you part the waters of the Bay of Bengal?"

"I'm serious. Other nations have devised ways to manage the consequences of these cyclones. Why," Rajiv found himself asking, "is it that some nations seem so capable of handling such water problems or at least fighting them intelligently? Bangladesh appeases just like Neville Chamberlain did with Hitler. "The Dutch, for example.

I've read on the Internet about how their coastal protection systems are so effective. How much have we studied their system?"

"That's pretty heady subject matter for a government service doctor, Dr. Gaol."

Rajiv laughed, but became serious again. "Why not?"

Dr. Doyal seemed contemplative. "That is the question to ask." He was silent for a moment. "Are you serious about exploring this?"

"I wouldn't know where to start."

"With a study. You're a man of scientific technique, first and foremost. Never forget. Everything starts with an idea—it matures to a concept, then proceeds to a hypothesis. Then, investigation." He turned to go back into the clinic, signaling an end to their evening session. "I have a friend in the Minister of Internal Affairs office. I'll call him and see if he can help. Maybe he will put you in touch with a few people, if you are still interested."

Rajiv looked out over the night sky. He could hear bulldozers digging graves for Muslims. He could also smell smoke from funeral pyres for Hindus everywhere, as the nation made efforts to deal with the cholera dead. Curls of black smoke rose from cities and the countryside, as if the nation were at war.

In fact, Bangladesh had always been at war—with her very best friend, the water. But everything was done after the storm and the flood. There had to be a better way.

"Yes, I am."

Dr. Doyal nodded, turned and left.

Politics was so frustrating. Rajiv really wanted no part of it. By the middle of September, Rajiv was uneasy over the futility of trying to advance some new ideas. He'd written letter after letter, stealing time from his clinic work to do so. Nothing but empty words came in reply. "Thank you for your concern, Dr. Gaol." That type of thing. He'd returned to the country, working up and down the Chittagong coast, where he saw first-hand the devastation in the rural areas. Mud was still a foot thick in most fields. The rice crops were mostly ruined. Once again, many would be hungry.

But a month after he left Chittagong, he was summoned to Dhaka for a meeting with Doyal's contact, the first assistant to the Minister of Internal Affairs. Sanjay Rao was courteous, politically smooth and noncommittal. They spent the first hour reviewing—showing off, actually— Bangladesh's cyclone recovery efforts. Sanjay seemed overly anxious, Rajiv thought, to prove that despite 45,000 dead the government was doing all it could and that it had been prepared. They spent the rest of the day touring storm shelters around Dhaka. Since the casualties of 1991 and 1998, the government had invested more in storm shelters high enough to avoid flooding and strong enough to withstand the high winds of a typhoon. Many structures doubled as schools or government offices. But building storm shelters was just a beginning.

"Our progress on storm shelters has been instrumental in limiting casualties," Sanjay said as he hailed a cab for their return to his office. "The casualties in Chittagong and Cox's Bazaar, two areas that usually experience the highest tides, were greatly reduced in the most recent storms."

From the back seat window, Rajiv looked out onto the streets of the capital, dusty with the drying mud from the floods. The storm surges had traveled directly up the rivers, and Dhaka, barely twelve to thirteen feet above sea level, had experienced serious flooding. But the city was far enough inland that it rarely felt the full brunt of the typhoons, and he wondered if the relative comfort of dry homes and offices dulled the commitment of the officials who lived there.

"And the people in the country?" Rajiv asked.

"We have to focus our efforts where they help the most people," Sanjay said. "We have been the target of some very bad press from militant, revolutionary organizations. Eventually, we will have adequate storm shelters throughout the country. We are moving as fast as we can."

"Storm shelters will never totally protect the country people," Rajiv said. For its density, Bangladesh had a high rural population. Almost 20 percent (28 million) of the nation's 150 million citizens lived in the most vulnerable rural coastal areas.

Sanjay's eyes widened. "We're talking about typhoon-like storm surges, and people with homes of mud and straw. It's the three little pigs and the wolf all over again."

"What I'm saying is that storm shelters, while admirable, are approaching the problem from the post-storm standpoint, after it's already begun its devastation on crops and homes. What if we could stop the tidal surges from hitting land?"

"Ah. You're talking about barriers." The tone in Sanjay's voice was flat, bored, as if he'd heard this argument too many times before. The cab pulled up in front of a nondescript office building which housed domestic/interior agencies. Sanjay paid the driver and began walking into the building.

"You don't sound enthusiastic," Rajiv said as he followed him.

"It is hard to become enthusiastic about the impossible," Sanjay said.

"They're not impossible," Rajiv said. "It's been done."

The hallways of the building were cool in the mid-day heat. Sanjay nodded to several people as they walked through the corridors to his office, a sunshine-filled room that faced onto a central courtyard where other government workers were lunching and meeting. It was clear he was a person to be respected. His desk was covered with neat stacks of files and correspondence waiting his attention.

"One place." Sanjay sat behind his desk and invited Rajiv to take one of the chairs in front of it. "One place in the world has built such a thing, and even that is largely untested. They have yet to experience a full-force storm—10 to 12 on the Beaufort scale—since it was finished." Rajiv was impressed. This fellow knew his business.

Rajiv did not sit in the offered chair, but instead walked to the courtyard window. It never ceased to amaze him how just two months after their nation was torn apart, people were laughing again. His people were resilient. He knew, as a physician, that in the face of great tragedy, the human mind worked overtime to block its pain. But why was amnesia such a strong component of recovery? Bangladesh had come to believe that the death toll from cyclones was inevitable. It happened every year and always would. As a nation, this was part of their character and fate. This was, perhaps, a huge piece of the problem.

"It is interesting, however," Rajiv said finally, "that the Dutch built their barrier when 1,800 lives were lost. How many times that have we lost? Thirty-five thousand this year alone." He turned to face Sanjay. "How can we not at least try in the face of thirty-five thousand people every other year?"

Sanjay looked at him for a long time before speaking. Then, he nodded. "There is someone you can speak to who might be able to help. I believe you already know him. Doctor Doyal says you've met."

Rajiv closed his eyes and rolled his head. Not *him!*

Sanjay laughed. "I see you've met, but don't yet *know* Senator Mukherjee. Believe it or not, he's more flexible than most members of Parliament. Did you know that he was educated in the United States?"

"No, I didn't know that."

"Yale man, I believe. He's a lot like you."

Rajiv winced. That seemed sarcastic.

"No, really. He straddles two worlds, and understands how to get things done." Sanjay leveled a serious look at Rajiv. "He could be your chief ally here. He's a member of the Awami League, which just came to majority power. That's not a small thing. The party is reformist at its core. They advocate change. But he can become your adversary with one misstep. Like everyone else, he has his own agenda."

Sanjay closed with a promise to arrange a meeting. He led Rajiv to the door.

"People don't mind examining the idea of a surge barrier. But when the idea comes close...." He shook his head. "Something like this could change the face of Bangladesh. Not everyone is interested in that. You must be very careful. Presentation and packaging can be art forms as much as content."

As he walked back out onto the busy street and hailed a rickshaw, Rajiv thought about Sanjay's parting words. He had the ominous sensation that he was beginning to cross a field of claymore land mines. What was he doing here with his idealism pinned to his chest?

With surprising speed, the meeting with Senator Mukherjee was arranged the next day, before Rajiv left Dhaka. The Senator's office was a startling contrast to Sanjay's bland government-issue, engineered curtain wall, building and furnishings. The Senator's room was spacious, and full of rich, dark woods—rosewood, mahogany, teak. When he was ushered inside to wait for the senator, Rajiv's sandals sank into a thick rug of hand-tied wool knots, an import, no doubt from nearby India. The office faced a plaza of fountains and manicured gardens. As he took in the gently flowing opulence, Rajiv's attention was drawn to a colorful wall hanging. He walked up to it and recognized a *nakshi kantha*. He shivered as he remembered Sabjada so proudly handing him her package. This piece was large and museum quality, on a red background bordered with gold thread. As in Sabjada's quilt, the figures told a story, which took place along a flowing blue river running from the lower left corner across the piece to the upper right. At the river's origin were men and women making cloth. At the center were women and girls sewing clothes, saris, but also western-style shirts and skirts. At the end of the river and the journey were figures embroidering on cloth as if making the *kantha* itself. The story was the life of cloth in Bangladesh, spanning traditional methods and new manufacturing processes.

"It's a striking piece, isn't it?"

Rajiv turned to see Senator Mukherjee breezing into the room. He was elegantly dressed in a traditional black silk sherwani coat and pajama pants, a cream silk stole was draped around his neck. His shoes were embroidered jootis. As a member of Parliament, Mukherjee was expected to wear indigenous clothing. He seemed right at home in them, as if born into them. For a Bengali, he was tall, almost six feet, and stocky, but not obese. In America, he might have been a running back in his younger days. Once again, he made a commanding figure.

"A gift from my wife's family," Mukherjee said, coming beside Rajiv. "She and her mother worked on it, along with other members of their family. Of course, it speaks to the Bengali textile industry and its place within our society and history."

"It's beautiful," Rajiv said. "I was also recently given a *kantha*."

Mukherjee's expression was one of interest. Around the room

were baskets, wall weavings, and pounded copper scenes, a small museum of Bangladesh art.

"From a patient, a girl on Hatiya. We lost her in the recent flooding." He turned his glance away as the emotions erupted barely behind his eyes and in his throat.

Mukherjee's face clouded and his look became guarded. "Tragic. Very tragic." He gestured Rajiv over to his desk. "Of course, that is what you're here to speak about, the flooding."

"Specifically, the cyclones. I've been doing an Internet study of the Dutch system, and am interested in furthering my research."

Senator Mukherjee pursed his lips. "An interesting hobby for a physician. But of course, you've spent the last months treating cyclone victims. I do get reports, but seldom do I have the opportunity to speak directly to a clinic worker. How is that work going?"

Rajiv appraised the senator. His interest appeared to be genuine. What Rajiv did not realize was how badly the senator was smarting from the recent accusatory press.

"Our biggest enemy right now is cholera, along with diarrhea. People are dying of simple dehydration because we never have enough IV fluids." He gave a soft snort. "Because of too much water, people are dying of dehydration." He looked up and saw the senator studying him closely, and forced a clinical tone back into his voice. "Furthermore, people are quite dejected by their losses. Low mental state impairs the body's ability to recover. We're beginning to treat for trauma-induced shock and depression."

"Yes, yes." Senator Mukherjee looked to the door where a woman bearing a silver tea service had entered. She placed it on the Senator's desk. Mukherjee did the serving, pouring first for Rajiv and then for himself.

"Lemon or cream?"

"Lemon," Rajiv said slowly. He realized what made Mukherjee a politician of such renown. He was a man of protocol, etiquette, and context. And if his concern wasn't authentic, he certainly made it seem so.

"I am familiar with the Dutch system," Mukherjee said as he

poured milk into his tea. I had an opportunity to see parts of it a few years ago, when I was part of a delegation from Bangladesh to the Netherlands. Fascinating."

Finally, they were getting to the meat of the matter, Rajiv thought. "After the dignitaries' tour, did Bangladesh ever complete a cost analysis study?"

Senator Mukherjee sipped his tea. "It has surely not escaped your attention that Bangladesh is a poor country."

Rajiv bristled at the patronizing tone. "That has not escaped my attention, Senator."

"Do you know how much the Dutch system cost, how many years it took?"

Rajiv looked down in answer.

"Eight billion Euros, or twelve billion in 2005 U.S. dollars. They started in 1958. The Project part was finished in 1986. Almost thirty years." Senator Mukherjee spread his hands. "We did not need a 'cost analysis study,'" his tone gently mocked the term, "to understand that Bangladesh was without the capacity to summon such funds. And no international finance seems to ever come our way."

Rajiv was silent for a moment. He looked at the tea platter in front of him, sterling, no doubt antique, worth enough to supply an entire village with IV fluids and antibiotics for a year. As a symbol, it suggested he'd come to the wrong person. And yet it was clear that Dr. Doyal had been steering him toward Mukherjee from the start. Rajiv was missing something, some key to the puzzle. He and Doyal had begun some sort of dance culminating here, but Rajiv was missing some information. What was it?

"Senator Mukherjee, I understand you attended university in the United States."

Mukherjee's eyes lit up at the reference. He turned to the wall behind him, where his diplomas hung. One was from Yale in philosophy and political science, as Sanjay had suggested. Another, an MBA came from M.I.T. This was totally unexpected. Rajiv studied the rich pieces of parchment, reflecting for a moment on his own diplomas, stuck in a box in a cabinet back in Sherpur.

"What was your undergraduate field of study, if I may ask?"

Mukherjee hesitated for a moment. "Political science."

Rajiv thought for a moment, and then the seed of an idea came to him.

"Our new Prime Minister has declared high hopes of reducing the corruption that plagues the bustees and suppresses the economic abilities of individual family units."

Mukherjee nodded, and waited.

Rajiv explained how former Prime Minister, Mrs. Zia, campaigned on a platform of economic emancipation for a larger slice of the population, the daunting nature of his medical work and how, looking farther ahead, technical mechanisms had been developed which might diminish flooding along parts of the coast, suggesting land values could then rise, as would crop production. Rajiv then proposed that Mukherjee could announce a study showing the public and the newspapers that the Awami party was serious about economic reform. He concluded, "As you suggested in Dhaka, we cannot solve the nation's poverty by attacking its few healthy industries. We must create additional options."

"Perhaps." Mukherjee was studying Rajiv again, his fingertips together, tapping as he thought. "Do you have an estimate for the study, then?"

Rajiv shook his head. "I have no idea."

Mukherjee smiled. "We will require an estimate. At the very least, I think you should go to the Netherlands to see this 'Eighth Wonder of the World'. We have money for travel and for a small initial look-see study. I'll have my assistant make the arrangements, for two-three months from now—for say, one week? You can meet with Dutch engineers—they are beyond ingenious—and talk through your ideas." Rajiv had the distinct idea Sanjay Rao and the senator had been discussing him and the Dutch on more than one occasion.

Rajiv began to protest. "I have six clinics every week. I'm sure the health ministry will not be willing to grant me so long a leave...."

"Ahh," Senator Mukherjee said. "My dear Dr. Gaol. Let me tell you a little bit about the nature of such undertakings. Half the battle is building the fire. You hold an intriguing candle. Allow me to speak with Dr. Doyal about a brief leave of absence and coverage for your clinics."

"I don't understand."

"The will. The desire. If we assign this to some bureaucratic government worker, what do you think the chances are that the study will ever come to any useful conclusion?"

He did not wait for Rajiv to answer. "Zero." He rose, signaling their meeting was over, and began escorting Rajiv toward the door. "Do you know how many studies of flood control have been completed in Bangladesh? Perhaps 300. If you truly want something to be done, do it yourself. You must ultimately develop a hard proposal for a first phase comprehensive study and recommendation. We may be able get you part of the funds for this. The Dutch engineers are as expensive as their Delft-ware. We are probably talking about many, many millions. You will have to develop significant non-government forces."

Out on the street, Rajiv wanted to walk before hailing a taxi. Now he was frightened and way off his turf. How would he ever find money for a study? Next to Mukherjee's diplomas were a series of vibrant pastoral pictures, featuring modern agricultural methods in Bengali fields. Mukherjee stood next to a shiny Japanese Kubota tractor, smiling broadly. He was vested in the clothing industry and he was also a landowner. Adversary or ally? This felt so mysterious. As he rode the taxi to the airport, he felt safer as he returned to the clinic life he knew. This political, construction and economic world was very foreign and intimidating. And he wondered how Dr. Doyal fit in. Was he somehow in conspiracy with this master politician?

CHAPTER 7

Amazed? A Maze?

Rajiv had really improved his Internet research skills at Northwestern. One night, armed with a case of Boddingtons Ale, he and a classmate had gone through contemporary search strategies and keystrokes until 3:00 a.m.

Now, he had to reclaim those techniques. He had the skills but was going nowhere. Actually, he was going everywhere. He had so much information, so many titles of articles, names, topics, it felt as though he were in a Windy City blizzard. He lacked the precise keys to open the myriad of Dutch water agency resources he was compiling. He had 50 names and 300 topics. He was struggling to establish connections.

He remembered a Dutch resident he'd met during rotation in his second year of residency. Van den Issel was his name. Egad, what was his first name and where had Rajiv parked his e-mail address? It took him several days of back and forth e-mails with some fellow residents before one responded with David's name and address. Yes. David Van den Issel. That was it.

"Dr. David," wrote Rajiv.

"You may remember we served together at Oak Park Community

Hospital in Residency Part 2. Well, now I am a pediatric physician in coastal Bangladesh, serving my six year 'sentence' in return for the education my government provided me. Actually, I do river boat clinics at villages on the Barrier Islands and in the massive India boundary wetlands (really wet) known as the Sundarbans. I hope this finds you well and prospering.

"I have a non-medical request. One of our national senators has encouraged me to contact the Netherland's coastal erosion people to explore their helping my truly lowland, low country survive our cyclonic surges. The effects of these storms are compounded by global warming and sea level rise. Who can I talk to? Do you know anyone who could help me reach the right people? This is not urgent but is pressing. If you could get back to me within a week with a name and an e-mail address, I would be ever so grateful. If you send your mailing address, I will send you some photos of my river boat children's clinics. Let me know how your practice is going.

Regards,

Jiv."

The next day he received a response. David would provide some details in a few days. Rajiv was delighted. He plunged into a full week of clinics, actually two week's worth in one. At noon Saturday when he browsed his e-mail manager, his dark face lit up when he saw a lengthy response from "D. Van den Issel, M.D." It was laden with information on a group known as the Royal Water Service (RWS), based in Delft, Den Haag (The Hague) and Amsterdam. There were names, addresses, books, reference texts. There was an attachment of considerable interest from a lady in The Hague named Annecke Van Leerdam, who worked for the RWS as a Public Relations media writer.

One paragraph was electrifying to Rajiv. It read:

"… The RWS is quite a large institution. For your colleague, cutting through these layers could be a very frustrating exercise. I took the liberty of calling a resource I have interviewed for several articles on Netherlands coastal protection, Krystian Kpoczek. He enjoys a fine reputation, nationally and internationally. And he had major roles in the Delta Project—our largest and, by far, most complete project. It took 30 years (I have only been on board the past three years.) Krystian is the ultimate no-nonsense fellow. Only because I did a respectable job expressing what he told me—and begged him to edit my writing—did he come to trust me. His opening remark to me was telling; 'Bangladesh is a severely economically depressed country with major challenging coastal issues. It is a salt-water desert like the central Sahara. I will respond to the doctor, but I cannot be optimistic that we could ever help.'"

The closing sentence on her note to Dr. Van den Issel read:

"Please ask Dr. Rajiv Gaol to copy me on any note to Krystian.
Tot Ziens.
Annecke Van Leerdam."

Rajiv is thrilled. He prints the message, holds it as though it were a 10-carat Burmese ruby and fires off an appreciative note to Dr. David. Then he heads for a long deserved nap, one which lasts seven hours. Over dinner at an open air tandoori café, he composes an introductory note to Krystian, cc: A. Van Leerdam. It is too ragged to send off. He realizes he needs help—help from someone he can trust.

One of his friends, Pog Marenjar, writes articles by day for a rice growers' coop and runs a graphic arts business after hours. He calls Pog on his cell phone.

"Pog here."

"Hey, Pog. It's Jiv. Got a minute?"

"Sure, Jiv. How goes it?" They rap for a few minutes. Then Rajiv explains what he is doing and that he needs some help in writing a respectable communication to Mr. Kpoczek in the Netherlands.

"Jiv, what in hell are you getting into?"

"Pog, things are only getting worse in coastal Bangladesh. We can't help Sundarbans villagers or Barrier Island peoples unless and until we make a real stab at tidal surge protection on a very broad scale. Survival of the entire area is the issue."

Marenjar asks him to e-mail the draft, which he does. Two days later came the response from his friend:

Mr. Krystian Kpoczek
Senior Project Manager and Communications Leader
Royal Water Service -- Delft

RE:Bangladesh
Mr. Kpoczek:

A medical residency colleague of mine, David Van den Issel, inquired of RWS Public Relations (Annecke Van Leerdam). She provided your name and asked to be copied on this inquiry—which I happily do.

I am a riverboat pediatrician in coastal Bangladesh. I was trained at Northwestern University in Evanston, Illinois, USA. We do clinics at villages along both our barrier islands and in the Sundarbans. I work for the Comilla Health Ministry, our government health service. We work very productively to serve these village children. However, limited resources impair our ability to be more effective.

Of greater concern, however, are the significant consequences of global warming, manifesting themselves here as higher than usual tidal surges from cyclones. Dutch responses to tidal surges keep surfacing as effective and thoughtfully executed.

I have done considerable research and taken my concerns and the results of this research first to our Ministry of the Interior and, upon their nod, to an influential senior senator of our ruling party. He has authorized me to connect with and visit an appropriate Dutch resource to explain our situation. If a positive Netherlands response is forthcoming, I would explore a first phase study paid for by my government.

Our government has agreed to cover my travel expenses for eight days. I would like to visit you or a colleague in the Netherlands. I would bring such information as you might require. I must have this trip completed within 75 days of this date. Once our monsoon season begins, we are all fully involved in responding to the overwhelming health care demands.

I will also bring a letter of introduction from Senator R. Mukherjee (the Senator referred to earlier). He will have it signed by the Minister of the Interior so my visit will be government-sanctioned.

Please advise the possibilities for a three to four-day visit specifying dates. I will promptly book flights. Would you kindly recommend a hotel for me? I will guarantee any debt you incur there to book reservations.

I suggest we might proceed to prepare an agenda once these matters are firmed up.

I look forward to the opportunity to meet you and learn what might be a reasonable approach to these matters.

Rajiv T. Gaol, M.D. – AIPP/BNMC

P – cell

P – Comilla Health Care

E-mail – Rgaolmd@comilla.Bengl.gov

E-mail alternate – Rgaolmd@yahoo.com

Pog had done a masterful job rewriting Rajiv's draft. Rajiv finished it up, added address and phone information and a CV (as an attachment). He sent copies to Senator Mukherjee, Annecke Van Leerdam, blind copies to Dr. Doyal and Pog.

Several days later, Mr. Kpoczek responds. Rajiv is certainly welcome, but there are only three consecutive days possible in the next six weeks. This thrills him, but places him in panic. He forwards the response to Senator Mukherjee, Dr. Doyal and Pog. It will take five days to receive authorization from the Senator's office to cover the travel charges. Kpoczek has promised to send a possible discussion agenda as well as information on several proposed site visits. A copy of Kpoczek's response is posted to "M. deBouter RWS." Rajiv wonders who this fellow is. All in good time, he muses.

Pog calls. He is happy for his friend and says, "My fee, Jiv, will be lifetime medical care from you. We'll start with a visit next week. By the way, Jiv, where will the money come from for such a study?" This question jolts Rajiv into reality. He wonders where and who and how much. This could get sticky. His anxiety drives him to a café for some Sri Lankan high hill tea to soothe his nerves.

"How much money would be needed?" he wonders. Would it cost a million dollars? Ten million dollars? He has no idea so he arranges tea with Pog to brainstorm some ideas. Realizing he has to get started now, he and Pog, over the next two weeks, have several "tea" sessions.

At one of their tea meetings, Pog lays out his perception of those who benefit versus those whose economic ox might be gored by such efforts. On the benefit side, Pog and Rajiv list shippers as #1, the construction industry as #2 and agriculture as #3. Over on the "Will oppose at all costs" column is the clothing industry. Fear of that competition for their work force which would surely force wages up. Also party-in-power politicians are likely to be very frightened about such activities as would any move away from their jealously guarded status quo. Pog's common sense wonders if after some early successes politicians might just want to claim that this was their idea all along so they could claim credit for helping the population and thus nail down votes. Clearly Pog has studied the earlier press attacks on legislators who trumpet window dressing fixes while pocketing referral commissions inside the family. Rajiv does not agree but is willing to remain open minded.

At another session, a new thought surfaces. The entire Sundarbans and coastal lowlands flood plain are becoming devoid of trees. Trees. Timber-log lumber, planks, panels. How might timber interests benefit from this? This riddle may be worth cracking. Neither has an answer.

Rajiv figures any young trees planted would just be snatched up for kindling and firewood by the masses. He knows that the better organized timber companies would hire security forces to guard tree plantations. "But how could this become a planning asset?" Pog reflects out loud. "We may have to reorient our perspective to list planning assets and beneficiaries." Pog's eclectic mind ponders timber interests in other parts of the world. How do they operate? He knew that the rapid growth of timber was one reason paper companies shifted paper manufacturing operations from cold climates to warmer climates, where annual growth rate was double, often triple. Made sense. There might be something there, the two agreed. But they decided to think about other resources who might want to become involved.

One day about a week later, Pog called to say, "Jiv, our country has no trees in spite of rainfall and a growing season close to that of a rain forest."

Jiv says, "Pog, you may be onto something. What if we put together a little outline to stimulate some interest by our timber people? What if we could show them a way to double their harvestable timber in say ten or twelve years?"

"That would be great," said Pog. "But how?"

"Haven't the foggiest," responded Rajiv.

Pog answered, "Well, let's ponder this for a couple of weeks and exchange e-mails."

"Do you think we might broach this with the Netherlands coastal protection people?"

"You couldn't lose," said Pog.

The month flew by as Rajiv prepared for his trip. Mr. Kpoczek had a list of twenty items that the RWS wanted to see before Rajiv arrived. In a panic, Rajiv requested an appointment with Senator Mukherjee to seek help responding to these requests.

"A very, very comprehensive list," mused the Senator as he studied the requests. "Sedimentation data for our rivers, the Sundarbans, sound waters inside the barrier islands, aerial photos of our entire coastal area, elevation contours, tidal data. My goodness, with only three weeks before you leave, this requires immediate attention. I will ask my chief of staff, Khalil Ghazowi, to help and have him contact you. In fact, I will get him on the phone now," and he buzzed a secretary to execute this task. While the Senator talked to Khalil, Rajiv, once again, glanced at the comfortable but elegant office suite décor, while he sipped a succulent tea served up by yet another attractive, female aide.

He wondered again how was he could feel so comfortable in such an opulent space. This made him wonder about the Senator's life. What were his parents like? How had he been raised? What then, was the difference between this master politician and himself? For a moment, he felt immensely proud of his own accomplishments; how he had been a top student in this entire country; how he had been selected to go to one of the finest medical schools in the USA; how he'd been recognized as an achiever both in medical school and residency. Perhaps the Senator treated him as someone special because he was special. He had not acknowledged this since he left Bangladesh for medical school. It felt good.

The Senator ended his conversation with Khalil. He provided Rajiv's e-mail, cell phone and mail address, and made it clear this was now top priority. This support was well beyond what Rajiv had found in his medical practice here but it was overwhelming, energizing, and frightening all at the same time.

Khalil performed yeoman service preparing Rajiv with responses to the Kpoczek-RWS list. And Dr. Doyal took him to lunch one day about three weeks before Rajiv was to leave. He had arranged for Rajiv to be fitted with two business suits, a sport coat, slacks, dress white shirts, ties, and a lined top coat (for the Netherlands wind and rain). In response to Rajiv's gratitude and wondering about the source of the funds, Dr. Doyal said, "Well, I have a rainy day fund and it made sense to do this for our newest ambassador. We don't have too much to be proud of in this country. But we are proud of you. Very, very proud."

CHAPTER 8

Will The Sun Ever Shine?

Three weeks later, Rajiv flew into the Schiphol Airport in Amsterdam, landing in the early morning amid a foggy, gray drizzle. He had slept during most of the flight since leaving Kolkata (Calcutta). He had just collected his luggage when he heard his name.

"Dr. Gaol?"

As he turned, Dr. Krystian Kpoczek introduced himself to Rajiv, as the senior special projects hydrologist at the Royal Water Service, the national coastal management office.

"We arranged the rain to help you feel at home," he joked. Kpoczek did not look like the Dutch man Rajiv imagined. He was slender, blue eyed and blond, with a neatly trimmed mustache. He wore pressed khakis and a cotton shirt, which Rajiv would learn was the daily uniform for coastal water staff. "I believe the rainy season is coming upon you back home?"

Rajiv nodded. "And we haven't finished drying out from spring."

Kpoczek shook his head. "Yes. You had a very bad time of it this year. I saw much of it on BBC television news, and wanted to see it for myself but wasn't able to get away." He led Rajiv toward the train station, which would take them near his hotel. "Cyclones elsewhere are of great interest here. Whenever the public resolve about our investment in the storm surge systems wane, pictures remind everyone what's at stake."

They boarded the train to Delft. Kpoczek continued, giving Rajiv a brief history of the storm which stimulated the monumental response in Netherlands. Because much of the Netherlands lies below sea level, normal tides would daily inundate half the country every day if previous generations had not raised dikes and dams. Severe storms often caused surging tidal waters to crash into dikes and push upstream into rivers and estuaries. The most vulnerable areas are the large tidal inlet formerly known as the Zuider Zee and the Delta cre-

"In March, 1953 . . . the storm of the century howled across the North Sea and into the Netherlands, testing the strength of the Zuider Zee enclosure."

ated by the rivers in the southwestern corner of the country, next to Belgium. It had Eastern (Ooste) and Western (Wester) sections.

Dutch water engineers had long proposed that the Zuider Zee be dammed and drained, but the government was reluctant to tackle such an immense project until 1916, when a furious storm hit the northern provinces. The agricultural production demands in wartime coupled with the need to eliminate the constant floods paved the way to dam the Zuider Zee. This created a new vast tract of rich, cultivable farmland. People settled and built homes and livelihoods there. To this day, it is considered a huge success and a model for other low countries.

But the sea was not done with the Netherlands. In March 1953, what the Dutch referred to as Watersnoopdramp, the "storm of the century," howled across the North Sea and into the Netherlands, testing the strength of the Zuider Zee enclosure. But the enclosure held, with only some damage to a causeway on top of a dike. However, the country's unprotected southwest region took the full brunt of the storm, with water surging through dike ruptures, over seawalls and up the wide waterways of the delta (Scheldt). More than 1,800 people lost their lives, and livestock numbering hundreds of thousands perished. 200,000 homes were destroyed. It was a national disaster of the highest order.

"Those lives inspired the nation," Kpoczek said. He asked the next question almost hesitantly, aware of the disparities in numbers. "What was the final death toll from your typhoons this summer?"

"Thirty-five thousand," Rajiv said, staring out the window into the rain. "And yet, it is an endless battle convincing people that something really significant needs to be done."

"Of course," Kpoczek said matter of factly. "Projects of this size always have opponents. The key is to find the "price tags." And by this I don't mean the cost of the project. It's best at this stage not to even consider that. It's too daunting and you will simply give up. What I mean by "price tags" are opportunities needed to convert opponents. As you have wisely noted, Dr. Gaol, vast health care improvements in Bangladesh will result from coastal surge protection."

Their train pulled up near a small hotel and Kpoczek helped gather Rajiv's luggage. "Everyone," he said as they stepped onto the street, "wants certain tickets." Rajiv was intrigued by this concept.

"Take an hour to rest up, have some tea, or Dutch chocolate. Your tour guide to the Delta project, deBouter, will be here in about 90 minutes. The two of you will see the Delta Project and I will join you both for dinner about 2000 hours. Tot Zeins!" And he was gone.

Rajiv took it all in. The clean streets, polished 3-star hotel façade, red sharply sloped roofs, woodwork and all. The lace curtains in each first floor window made the place warm and inviting. Check-in was easy. He was an RWS guest. This was all that mattered. His room was up one floor. The clerk offered to have his bag taken up while he went to the small Dutch blue and white coffee shop. The lace curtains, actually half curtains with a delicate valance above, were intriguing. He decided he would look for some for his mother and for his modest apartment. While he sipped the luscious hot chocolate, tempered by steamed milk, the waitress wrote down the name of a lace shop. This strong cocoa recharged his sagging energy level.

His room was well lit by windows facing west. There was a soft feather comforter folded at the base of the bed, and a flat screen Phillips (was there any other in the Netherlands?) TV. He had time to freshen up and change for the field trip. He took a sport coat and, on Krystian's advice, wore the long sturdy rain coat.

Just as he was unpacking, his room phone rang.

"Dr. Gaol. This is Maartje deBouter of the RWS. I am your taxi driver and guide for this afternoon's trip to the Delta Project."

He was very surprised. He managed to politely respond, "I'll be right down."

It was a woman. Did Kpoczek send a secretary? Oh, well. He belted his rain coat and headed down. In the lobby was a tall lanky, 5'10" lady about 31 with dark-framed designer half lens glasses, large warm lips, intelligent eyes, a three-quarter length wool coat, and a scarf that must have been seven feet long, wrapped around her neck and draped over each shoulder. The scarf framed her smile.

"Hi, Dr. Gaol. I am Maartje," and held out her hand boldly. "And where is your hat? It will be very windy where we are going."

"Ah, yes," said Rajiv. "I planned to buy it tomorrow."

"Dr. Gaol, you'll have pneumonia by morning if we don't get one right now. I know a decent hat and cap shop on the way out of Delft. We'll make a quick stop. May I take your suit coat?"

"Yes, yes," mumbled Rajiv, still amazed that M. deBouter was a woman.

"Do you work for Mr. Kpoczek, Miss deBouter?" asked Rajiv.

"I work for Beatrix, Queen of The Netherlands. However, Krystian is my direct boss. He shovels whatever engineering projects he wants at me. Since I am only three years out of school, I take whatever he gives me. And please call me Maartje, Dr. Gaol."

"Only if you'll call me Rajiv, Miss deBouter," he bantered, smiling warmly. He was already feeling better about this.

"Certainly, Rajiv," twinkled Maartje's eyes, nose, and mouth, as they climbed into a midsize Opel diesel, comfortable and narrow, suited to European streets.

Delft streets are ancient but extremely well constructed stone roads beefed up by solid curbs for drainage. At low speed, cars rumbled. Maartje was a very much in control driver. The hat shop was on a narrower side street. The car jumped the curbing, they climbed out, and went in. "You'll want a woolen cap, probably British or Welsh and tight enough so North Sea breezes cannot blow it into the sea, especially when we are 100 feet above the water. It is a little difficult to retrieve from there."

Rajiv remembered how he'd dressed for Chicago–Evanston winters. Warm hat with ear protection, a goose down REI jacket, and wool lined boots were for the bad days. He had carefully ordered some fleece-lined hiking shoes for this trip but figured the hat could wait. (He enjoyed browsing through glassy catalog photos.) But, it was early November now. The Northwest winds coming across the North Sea were sharp and wet.

He chose a Harris tweed hat with ear flaps, imagining himself wearing such a hat while at the wheel of an MG like one of his med school professors. Maartje gave her approval with a nod and flickering eyes. If the lady was really an engineer, she had communication skills.

The one-hour drive to the north end of the delta was pleasant. Maartje asked many questions about America, Bangladesh and his medical schooling. She compared her M.I.T. years with his time at Northwestern. No wonder she could communicate. Now he found himself off balance and did not understand why. He tried to show his best "professionally detached" residency discipline. The lady was an enigma. She was intriguing as well.

Their conversation never halted. After asking him to share his educational and family background, she inquired how a riverboat physician became a point person for major national water issues. In return he asked about her family and technical responsibilities. She beamed as she spoke of parents, grandparents and siblings. It was clear she had a quite decent upbringing. Might be fun to eat a Dutch country meal at her parents' some day. With his dark skin and fine lips, he might feel odd man out. However, he didn't dwell on this reality, just tucked it in and pressed on.

Rajiv could hear seabirds and feel the cool North Sea wind, but could not see the water. Not until he climbed a long manmade terrace about 45 feet high could he see it. Before him stretched a large bay, its yellow-green-gray colors suggesting rich nutrients. The rain had briefly given way to a sunny day, which sparkled all the more because a good cloud bath had washed the concrete and stone and made the late autumn gray slopes and fields green once more. Behind him lay a rich delta, its composition not unlike those in Bangladesh, only the fields appeared rich and productive with lots of trees. Solid farmhouses, villages and acres of Holland's famous flowers dotted the landscapes. None had a direct view of the sea. In the middle of the bay stretched what looked, from where Rajiv stood, like a bracelet with many large links in the middle.

"The crown jewels in our system," Maartje said.

Rajiv turned to his tour guide. Wisps of her brown hair had escaped from her braid, blew at her cheeks and eyes. As she spoke, she kept reaching for strands and trying futilely to tuck them behind her ears. In this wind, his new cap was just right.

She described the "bracelet," the Oosteschelde surge barrier, also known as The Delta Project which, in the impact it provided on the lives of people living in the Delta, was truly a precious jewel. The links were actually made of 66 concrete piers, each 148-feet high and weighing 18,000 tons. The piers supported sixty 300- to 500-ton steel gates rising about 120 feet out of the water at high tide. The "charms" dividing the barriers were two large man-made work islands. The entire work extended about three kilometers across three channels formed by the two islands and a 128-foot-high dike.

"The goal is not always to hold all water out," Maartje shouted over the wind. "When storm surges thrive, we raise the gates a little, and if wave pressures increase beyond a design limit, the gates are opened more, which allows moderate flooding, but on a far lesser scale. Yet even then, surges, the worst part of the storm, are essentially prevented. Remember, tides rise and fall in roughly eight-hour cycles. So we rarely deal with more than four or five hours of disastrous water.

"Also, the gate system preserves ecology in the waters inside the gates. Most of the time the gates are down, allowing the flow of water into and out of the bay.

Ecologically, we share much in common with Bangladesh," Maartje said. "There is a reason we are called the "low country." Large sections are below sea level. Both countries have river delta ecosystems. And like Bangladesh, we live below sea level. If our surge protection systems fail, the bathtub fills with water and overflows. And we live on the bottom of the tub. If the Rhine and Waal dikes were to give way, cities, villages, houses, and farms would be covered by water. We depend much on engineering—our own.

"We thought having you see this first would make our discussions easier over the next few days."

"Maartje. I'm no engineer," Rajiv said. "But I don't understand how the sea floor can support these massive structures."

"The footings are an engineering story all by themselves." The wind picked up, making it harder to speak. Maartje pointed Rajiv back to her car. "I'll take you to the museum. It's a good place to start, and easier to talk there. Krystian was a major force in the design and placement of these footings."

Inside the museum, she led him to a huge scale model of the entire delta, which showed currents, water depth, storm surge barriers, islands, and the New North Waterway surge barrier currently being built to protect Rotterdam.

She pointed to the various dike systems snaking around the country. "Of course, the dike system is the historic fairy tale for which the Dutch are known. It is our earliest form of protection, hundreds of years old, and if I may make the comparison, in terms of flood protection development, we think Bangladesh must be now where we were in 1953.

"Our greatest advancements are storm surge barriers, which is what you've come to see." She began walking through the museum, showing him photos of the dry dock where each of the ten-story piers was made before being floated and towed to location. Maartje was particularly interested in flotation. In the last month, she'd been on the Hibernia drilling and production platform off Prince Edward Island in Nova Scotia, studying a water ballast and balancing system used to stabilize platforms while in tow and at final position.

Maartje continued, "Using laser telemetry, and GPS, each pier was eased down during slack tide. Not one is more than 1½ inches off its design location."

She moved down through the walls of photographs. "You asked how we stabilized the ocean floor. This explains it." Like a school teacher, she explained each photo. She pointed out, "The piers were embedded 35 feet into the sea bottom. To prepare the site, the pier base areas were dredged to remove silt. Then we compacted the bedding materials to depths of 50 feet using massive vibrators, and then we deposited three feet of coarse sand. To keep the sand from washing away, we constructed 'mattresses' beneath each pier."

And she explained how her present Director, Jan Greilingen, was Project Design Leader for these mattresses. The mattresses, she told Rajiv, were a high-tech sandwich of sand and gravel between the bread slices of a space-age fabric, Kevlar-reinforced plastic material. "The lower mat was 15 inches thick. The top mat was the same as the bottom. These mats prevent erosion and provide footings at the base of each pier. Around the base of each pier are graded layers of stone, the outermost made up of hard basalt rock. Maintenance of the footings is an ongoing process. We're working with an American engineering firm using underwater drones with acoustics to track scour holes sometimes made by ship anchors and deepened by sea currents. Once detected, these holes are immediately filled with rip-rap. The equipment was developed from that used to locate the "Se-ñora Nuestra Atocha," the Spanish gold bearing galleon, which sank in the Florida Straits between Key West and Cuba in the 1600s.

"And now, a close-up of what we've been talking about." They walked to her Opel. She drove down the coast on top of the structures until they were at the south end of the barrier. Along the two-mile road were inspection and maintenance entrances to the works below. At a parking area designated for RWS employees, she pulled over and reached into the back seat for two hard hats and safety glasses.

"Let's go."

An interior elevator took them down twelve stories. There, Rajiv saw the immense gears used to lift each gate. They appeared to be 15 to 20 feet in diameter.

"No template existed for the machinery for these barriers," Maartje said. "We designed all of this from scratch."

As Maartje enthusiastically described the technological aspects of the barrier, Rajiv's doubts about such a project for Bangladesh grew. The Dutch were clearly a race of engineers, inspired by their imagination for such a project. Could the people of Bangladesh ever envision such ideas? Most important, could its politicians? How would he ever put this across?

Back in the car, as they left the barrier behind, they rose above fields of cows, greenhouses growing flowers, canals, and a presently benign sea on the other. Next, Maartje took him on a brief road tour along the Scheldt River.

"The shellfish and much of the marine life of the Eastern Scheldt depend upon tidal movement for nourishment and oxygen. Sea movement means food for these little creatures." Maartje pointed out the dense grasses, shrubs and trees along the sea coast and the river banks. That was part of the solution as well. The grasses and shrubs help prevent erosion. Stopping this erosion helps maintain the gates. Otherwise, silt would overwhelm the footings and weaken the structure.

Inside the quiet of the car, it was hard to imagine such a scene back home in Bangladesh. The sea, the orderly fields, neatly painted houses and barns in the midst of a cyclone—it seemed impossibly different.

Rajiv turned to Maartje. "It works? The sea barrier. It really works?"

"We have not had a storm the magnitude of the Watersnoop-dramp since the barrier was finished in 1986, but it has clearly contained the damage from quite serious storms and paid for itself. Actually, our cost analysis studies show the storm barriers are more cost effective than dikes, when maintenance and enhanced sea food harvest effectiveness are factored in." She looked at Rajiv, and he sensed that she understood his real question: Had it been worth it? Could the money and the political struggles justify the results? Maartje returned her gaze to the highway. "But yes."

After their field trip, Maartje dropped Rajiv off at his hotel to rest while she returned phone calls and checked e-mail. She left some materials for Rajiv to read, and it was his full intention to spend his afternoon studying them, but very quickly, he fell sound asleep. When he awoke, he'd had to rush to shower and change out of his wrinkled clothes into fresh ones. He was unsure of the night's attire, but it was a business trip and for once he was out of the swelter of Bangladesh, so he'd worn a new charcoal gray wool suit. As he studied himself in the mirror, the tie seemed a touch too formal, and he left it behind choosing instead a creamy silk Bayonet shirt. His hair was still damp as he scanned the bar for Krystian and Maartje and tried to awake from the fog of sleep.

The hotel restaurant was comfortably full, with a mix of tourists, locals, and business people capping off their day with evening drinks. Piano music washed over the murmurs of conversations in French, Dutch, Flemish, English, some German and a variety of other languages.

Krystian hailed him from a table, where Rajiv saw the two of them seated and waiting.

He saw that Maartje had also changed out of her engineer's uniform, trading it in for a gray linen skirt, jacket and silver colored silk blouse open femininely at the front. Her hair was sleekly rebraided, fastened with a gold clip at the nape of her neck.

They took a moment to order drinks and some appetizers before reviewing their day.

"I'm very impressed," Rajiv said, "and, I must confess, intimidated. It's hard to imagine such structures in the Bay of Bengal."

"Yes," Krystian said. "But first *you must* try to imagine. A child without dreams does not become a productive adult."

"As a doctor, I am always addressing cyclones at the other end, after they've wrought their havoc." Earlier, he had described to Maartje his clinic duties, and he presumed this information had been relayed to Mr. Kpoczek. "Even in normal times, I am discouraged by the futility of my work. But I just went through my first cyclone as a physician and watched thousands of people, many of whom I'd come to know and treated, get swept away. And for what?" He shook his head. "The other physicians saw this as an initiation rite to be experienced again and again. I cannot accept that to be the case."

"You must always keep those scenes of devastation before you," Krystian said, "To remember why you pursue this."

"You know, many people here still honor relatives who died in the Watersnoopdramp," Maartje said. "I lost an uncle, my father's brother, a man I had never met. He was gone before I was born. His picture keeps today's efforts alive. Every year on March 23, we gather to toast his memory at the place where the storm surge ruptured the dike."

"I would think Bangladesh would have even greater motivation to act now," she continued. "It's not just the cyclones of today you have to worry about. According to the better predictions, sea level is expected to rise three to seven feet over the next 100 years. Global warming," she explained. "In Bangladesh, that will submerge 22,000 square kilometers of land, which translates to the homes of 17 million people. I can show you the computer models back at the office."

"I would like to see them," Rajiv said. "So if we do nothing, our grandchildren will be at this very table 100 years from now, struggling with an even greater problem."

"Yes," Krystian said. "But the fixes will be astronomically more difficult."

"But what little I understand about politics in Bangladesh has not been encouraging," Rajiv said. "How our politicians would ever support something like this...." His voice trailed away.

"I would like to suggest you consider another perspective," Maartje said. "You will never get agreement. So try to let go of such a fantasy." Rajiv felt a sting from this straight up talk and clearly, he was not used to such assertive statements from a woman. Of course, he remembered several brassy women residents. But that was in a world 5,000 miles away.

"Then how.... "

"Before 1953, the Dutch had never achieved agreement on a Delta Plan," she said. "And yet after the Watersnoopdramp, our hydrologists knew something very, very major had to be done. So, they sought out their opponents' goals and worked them into the design." She smiled at Rajiv's puzzled expression.

"People look at the Oosteschelde barrier and think it is a superior and colossal engineering achievement, and of course, it is. But it's more than that. The Delta Project is a marriage of the goals of its opponents." She linked her hands together, twining her fingers as illustration. "Most people think of lives lost and the destruction prevented as its social value. But," she said, raising one finger at a time, "our commercial mussel industry considers the barrier a valuable tool for maintaining an optimum environment for their fisheries. Our environmentalists, who were at first among the most ardent and violent opponents of the barrier, now cite it for the way it preserves the tidal-based ecosystem—and not coincidentally the economic well being of large segments of our country.

"Finally, this engineering marvel has actually come to be prized even by traditionalists. It's become a point of nostalgia and pride in the seaside culture of the Zeeland. In the design of the visitors center we saw this afternoon, Krystian and his team made it possible to capture and the preserve some ways of life that were vanishing. The motto of the Zeeland province is 'Luctor et emergo.'"

Rajiv strained but only for a moment recalling medical school Latin. "I struggle, and survive."

"Yes," Maartje said. "They now claim ownership of the barrier as evidence of their historic struggle. It is emotionally very powerful."

She sipped port from her glass.

"I once heard someone describe this in terms of the story from India, of the blind men and the elephant, the one in which each feels a different part and decides it's a completely different being or thing."

Rajiv nodded.

"Your project will probably be like that. Everyone will see the project as something different. And yet, it will come to exist as one entity. And perhaps you must start with the so-called squeaky-wheel."

"What do you mean?"

"Realistically, any plan for large construction in Bangladesh should probably start with Dhaka, its largest population center," Maartje said. "You've seen the North Sea wall. Tomorrow, we'll brief you on the New Waterway Storm Barriers that will protect Rotterdam. It's the future of surge protection in the Netherlands that will allow us to close off rivers and waterways from the surges that push large high tide storms far upriver. Such gates would be easier to sell in Bangladesh. It's a more self-contained project, and the results would be more immediately visible."

"Even so, it is impossible to ignore the disparities in national wealth," Rajiv said. "The Oosteschelde barrier cost the equivalent of 8 billion U.S. dollars. That's close to the gross national product of my country, which is hugely dependent upon the aid of three dozen international aid agencies just to hold down starvation."

"Small steps," Krystian said. "You're getting ahead of yourself. Our plans for strengthening our existing water defenses and pumping stations are estimated to cost $19 to $25 billion. These are enormous figures if you had to spend them all at once, but we're able to spread this over 60 to 100 years. And if we had to start from scratch and build the infrastructure you've seen so far, you'd probably just want to surrender the land to the sea. We build on what we have. Begin where you are.

"Maartje and I have worked up some figures of what it might cost to study the issue. We think the preliminary study would involve two hydrologists, two engineers and two ecologists-biologists. We're recommending a British firm, HKV. Maartje has worked with them before, and the Royal Water Service may be willing to assign Maartje to the project. We're probably talking about 4-6 million Euros for the preliminary study."

Rajiv grimaced. "I assumed it would be in this range."

"First we must address erosion in the regions that feed silt into the Bay of Bengal," Maartje said. "As I showed you, for the storm surge barrier in the Eastern Scheldt, we had to establish firm foundations for any large structures. As here, I suspect any structures eventually built in the Bay of Bengal would involve high-tech stabilization techniques. But in the meantime, the silt rate must be slowed. The amount of materials coming into the water now would overwhelm any footings in a matter of years. Silt is an ongoing problem for us. I told you today that the Oosteschelde barrier works, and it does, but water is never done with us. Now we're looking more seriously at how we contribute to flooding." She paused again to sip her wine.

"In 1995, here in the Netherlands, we were threatened with flooding from within, from the rivers. Heavy rains and unusually high snow accumulation in the Alps combined with Western Europe's increased urbanization and deforestation along rivers contributed to record winter floods. Both the Rhine and the Meuse overflowed their banks upstream, long before they reached the Netherlands. The swollen rivers go through Switzerland, Germany, Belgium and the Netherlands before reaching the North Sea. We pay major attention to river embankments and deforestation along the rivers throughout Europe. Because these areas and adjoining wetlands act like sponges in times of flooding, we are trying to get our farmers and those in other nations to give wetlands back to the rivers." She went on to explain that land in the Netherlands was so precious people gobble up every bit. "The current plan called for 222,000 acres to be surrendered by 2050 so river flood plains could be increased and turned into forests and marshlands. Another 62,000 acres of pasture are to be earmarked as temporary storage pools for floodwaters. Land use practices on another 185,000 acres are to be changed so the fields and crops can tolerate soggy conditions during winter and spring. We may grow cranberries, for example."

"Yet there are places where people should not be living, and places where vegetation must grow abundantly. There," she paused for emphasis, "is your starting point. And that alone may take years. Because of the tragic consequences of Hurricane Katrina in 2005 in Alabama, Mississippi and Louisiana, we are predicting a re-creation and re-dedication of wetlands in the Mississippi Delta which were sacrificed for direct canals to service the offshore oil industry."

Rajiv was silent for a moment. He tried to imagine getting just one farmer on Hatiya to give up his plot of land in the name of flood control. Or how he'd persuade Senator Mukherjee to give up one hectare of his land. This project was unfolding to a magnitude he had never imagined. He was no longer sure what he imagined when he began asking questions. He knew only that cyclones did more than flood his country. Floods took away people's dignity and destroyed government motivation as well. There was a nagging sense that he should step back from this Quixotic mission and return to the medicine he knew. And yet, he knew that one cyclone had a far greater negative impact on public health than any positive health care effect he might have in his entire lifetime.

"Dr. Kpoczek, Miss deBouter. You've given me much to think about, and the only hope I've felt so far about this undertaking."

Maartje answered, "Please. If all goes well and you are able to raise these funds, our team will be spending considerable time over the next several months in Bangladesh. It would be nice to have a friend like you there." This sharing of feelings was pleasant.

Rajiv thought of his friends in the states and how their support had borne him through seven years away from family.

"This calls for a toast." Krystian summoned the waiter and ordered a round of old *genever*. "Our national liqueur," he explained.

Krystian explained the difference between old and young genever and told the two he would order the milder old *genever*.

The waiter brought them a tray with three crystal cordial glasses filled with this Dutch version of gin. The glass in Rajiv's hand was icy cold.

Krystian led them, lifting his glass, "To the water."

Rajiv and Maartje followed, and for a moment, the overhead light from the chandelier shown on their glasses, sending long flickers of light around the table.

"To the water," Rajiv said. "Luctor et emergo."

"By the way," Rajiv asked, "does the sun ever shine for a full day on the Netherlands?" Everyone laughed.

CHAPTER 9

A Pleasant End to the Beginning

The rest of Rajiv's time was spent on field trips and in informal class-room sessions dealing with a myriad of coastal erosion protection issues. He saw new gating concepts, rapid deployment of large transports filled with aggregate for weakened dike areas and the rapid movement of equipment. These methods were a far cry from the standard "fill the sand bags" activities he had seen and read about on TV and in the newspapers in the U.S. The morning of his last day was spent listening to and questioning economic, public relations and political staff members who were either part of the RWS staff or under contract to them.

Dinner the last evening was arranged by Krystian. In the after-noon, an RWS contracting officer spent the better part of three hours going over the likely contractual arrangements. He gave Rajiv a de-tailed outline of contractual articles the RWS would require. Rajiv took copious notes, asked for and received a duplicate set for Senator Mukherjee. Neither Krystian nor Maartje were with him during this session. They were very busy on current projects.

They picked him up at his hotel at 7:00 p.m. Rajiv wore his very best white silk shirt, tie, sport coat and slacks. The cashmere coat and an elegant dark brown wool slacks suited his coloring. He liked the fellow he saw in the mirror. It had been years since he had tended himself like this. And he insisted on hosting the dinner.

The restaurant was in Scheveningen, a North Sea fishing and oil rig service community. It was located just behind a massive Dune-Dike. Its harbor entrance to the North Sea was guarded by 60 foot-high hydraulically-operated gates, again to fend off storm. North Sea commercial fishing and rig service boats had high, broad, wave spreading bows because of the 30 foot and 40 foot waves they frequently encountered. The bow height in turn made higher pilot house structures necessary so skipper and helmsman could see over the bow. In heavy weather, the helmsman's vision was terrific as his vessel crashed down into the valley between large waves. Pounding up-wave, these monsters obscured everything. North Sea helmsman by definition, have to be very, very capable sailors who command respectable wages.

As the three walked from parking at the back side of the harbor, the air was full of salt mist so common to sea coasts. Maartje, in yet a different color coat, now cashmere, scarf, and Krystian in black leather coat with a wool cap, Rajiv in his raincoat and Harris tweed cap were a handsome trio. As they strolled along, Rajiv offered his arm to Maartje who grasped it snugly. Krystian seemed to be looking at the boats. They walked without speaking a word. Rajiv was hesitant to talk—not certain what to say. He pulled his bent arm and elbow in close to his body to make certain Maartje could depend on this support as they walked against the stiff, brisk, 25 mph wind and sea spray. The lady was technically capable yet very feminine—she was in fact a stretched out version of his own mother. His respect for her was growing and he nestled his feelings into a tight, little cerebral cubicle that said, "It's just the good, intellectual stuff which flows among and between people working together on a common project." They were the sellers and he was clearly an interested buyer.

The restaurant was rustic and nautical; the lighting subdued and welcoming. Krystian introduced the red-cheeked hostess to Dr. Rajiv Gaol, host for the table and a visitor from Bangladesh. Having transferred "table authority," Krystian politely stepped back and asked for everyone's coat. He piled them on the fourth chair of the fairly small table. He left to go to the restroom. Maartje smiled and asked Rajiv if he wanted any help on wines and appetizers. "Thank you, Maartje. I had no idea what to do."

The waitress arrived as Krystian returned. She provided appropriate deference to the designated host. Rajiv smiled at her saying, "Miss Maartje will make the selection for both drinks and appetizers. We will enjoy these for half an hour or so. Then would you kindly explain the dinner options to us?"

"Certainly," she replied. Maartje ordered two liters of wine; red from Italy, white from France. For appetizers, she ordered cod cheek skewers with butter and also a cheese dip, wine flavored herring and Swedish eels, baked in a buttery mousse of wine, cheese, garlic and butter.

Before appetizers arrived, Maartje explained the baked eel, in answer to a grimace from Rajiv as she ordered them. "My brother, who farms, is, in season, an inspector for Dutch imports of foreign eels. He goes to the Swedish coastal islands to inspect them as they are taken from the sea. These eels are not pretty but they are excellent for dining. The recipe here is like one used by my sister-in-law. The preparation is excellent and whatever you do not care for, Krystian and I will finish, fear not."

"With this explanation, I will try them," and Rajiv smiled, hesitantly.

Krystian turned to Rajiv who was busy chatting with Maartje about project stages. "Here are some names of Finnish timber companies and contacts who might be interested in an incentive plan to acquire timber properties in Bangladesh for pulp wood. I've added a Swedish company. They manufacture timber harvesting and pulp wood defribators which pulverize logs into a fiber size for pulp stew cooking in paper making processes. This might be a stretch for them but perhaps not. I know they are into building and selling turnkey paper mills in a global joint venture with some other Swedish manufacturers. This is really not far afield from timber land for paper stock. You may use my name as a referral source. As a courtesy, I would not use my RWS title, just my name. The RWS is a little jumpy about such informal connections. I am sure you understand."

"Of course," nodded Rajiv. "Your logic on connections is sound," he added. "I am embarrassed to be so naïve about these business realities. I think I am pretty good at medicine. But anywhere else, I seem connection-challenged."

"Rajiv," spoke up Maartje. "Do you have any idea how difficult it is for a practicing physician to jump into the complex world of water, tides, coastal and riverway erosion? Both Krystian and I marvel at your ability not only to take in data and information but how well you abstract it to knowledge. Please, do not change your approach or style. You give yourself a formidable credibility by never losing the focus of why you are doing this. Allow Krystian and me to support you. We'll be your technical resources/references when someone challenges your technical background."

The appetizers are enjoyed by all. Even Rajiv manages the bite size morsels of eel. He ate four and clearly enjoyed them as much as Maartje or Krystian. Krystian explained the cod cheek delicacy. They were succulent. Rajiv was adapting to and enjoying both European mealtime intimacy and the company. More and more all three were sharing family intimacies as they talked. Krystian spoke less guardedly of communist rule in Czechoslovakia. It was clear by the facial tension that he harbored an intense dislike of Marx-Trotsky-Stalinite communism. Maartje told what it was like being the technology expert in her family now that her father, the engineer, had retired. Rajiv found himself sharing the times of sacrifice when his father was injured. But he was not yet able to share the unfortunate toll this hardship period imposed upon his sister. This pain lay too deep. Would the time and place ever come, he wondered, when he could get his heavy stuff up and out—as his psychiatry professors taught—"expressed feelings change?" He bore this pain as part of his baggage, knowing it affected him a great deal at certain times. But Maartje was wont to share more of herself. She willingly talked about her parents.

Once again, they finished their repast with a glass of sharp, icy, freezer cold, *oude genever*. But it was Rajiv who sought to render a final toast to close out this first phase (maybe last) of a newfound relationship. It was awkwardly delivered but eloquent:

"To thank you, Krystian, and you, Maartje, for being so welcoming and tolerant of my limitations;

- For helping me see coastal protection and erosion matters from new perspectives;

- For helping me understand how I might proceed to have this matter bear fruit for the mutual benefit of Bangladesh and the Royal Water Service;

- And for an absolutely thorough and charming introduction to your country and its impressive resourcefulness.

- You have changed me, inspired me, and have created a beacon for the national darkness we regularly dwell in. I hope we are able to work together and meet again many times and I thank you for the memories."

Maartje and Krystian beam. Each smiled at the other two warmly as they absorbed the genever to prepare to go back out in the biting North Sea wind.

Krystian understood that either Bangladesh would drop its idea as un-economic or that Rajiv and whoever this senator was would take a few months to get back to the RWS. And he chose for himself the one he thought most likely.

CHAPTER 10

A Fund Raiser

In the morning before he left for the train station to the airport, Rajiv made contact with the Finnish resource Krystian had given him and also one from Sweden. Rajiv made clear that reforestation of Bangladesh was a vital part of any coastal erosion project. Both were polite, listened carefully and, in true Scandinavian style, were utterly non-committal.

They exchanged e-mail addresses and Rajiv told them they would either hear from him or from Senator Mukherjee's reliable staff chief, Khalil. However, in the conversation with the Finn, there was a distinct shift of interest when Rajiv alluded to the necessity for Bangladesh to incent foreign investors to gain their participation.

As he rode the train from Delft to Schiphol, he was pleased over the visit and how the wheels were already turning towards the next phase. As he pushed his luggage cart toward check-in, he looked at the six pounds of RWS material he'd been given over the previous four days. He'd have plenty of reading matter for the flights.

As his Airbus lifted off, all was foggy, rainy and cloudy until the plane reached cruising altitude. The sun popped out at 8,500 feet. He had some tea, then promptly fell asleep for the next two hours.

Eleven more hours remained on this leg to Johannesburg, South Africa, where his flight would be refueled, cleaned and re-stocked with food and beverages. He thoroughly enjoyed the luncheon cheeses he was served along with juice, black Dutch coffee, croissants, cookies and British jams and jellies. Then he read for almost four hours, fell asleep for one and one-half, and dazed fitfully for two more. When he awoke, he was famished and it was at the end of daylight even though they had gone essentially south.

His dinner was a 10-ounce steak with mushrooms, onions and new potatoes, wine, a miniature French baguette, Dutch butter, a German blau kraut, tomato and cucumber salad with a delicate champagne dressing. He had three desserts with Darjeeling tea and promptly fell asleep again until the customs slips came around. He had only read about 150 pages of the 600 when the wheels hit the Johannesburg runway.

During his ninety-minute stopover before the flight to Calcutta, he shopped for his family. Mother loved perfumes, Dad enjoyed foreign photo calendars, his brother (unbeknownst to their parents) loved single malt scotch, his sister, fashion books. In Delft, he had purchased a four cup and saucer Delft-ware tea set for his Mother, some Dutch lace material for mother and sister, and a bottle of oude *genever* for himself. He wanted to buy three but they were more expensive than expected.

The flight to Calcutta was seven hours, then on to Dhaka. He read and slept, caught the news of the day on CNN and read the *Financial Times*.

He was travel tired when he got to his apartment but took time to outline the report he would prepare tomorrow for the Senator and Khalil. His outline was more philosophic than technical:

A. Goal of this trip.

B. Parties engaged.

C. The Netherlands approach to the Sea.

D. Feasibility study for Bangladesh (by the RWS).

E. Probable cost with recommendations toward
first phases.

F. Silt.

G. Reforestation.

H. Possible Finnish and Swedish connections.

I. Necessary incentives to obtain foreign interest.

J. Resources to develop.

K. Making allies out of adversaries; an approach
Bangladesh might consider.

L. Public relations.

Sleep came quickly as he knew his report-writing day would be very long.

"The goal of this trip to the Netherlands," Rajiv read off his laptop screen, "was to explore hiring the RWS (or, Royal Water Service) to perform a study and report on the feasibility, methodology, sequences of the various phases and the cost of a major, national project to address, in realistic stages, coastal and barrier island erosion from storm surges, flooding, the consequences of sea level rise from global warming, and other climate change."

A secondary goal was to attract foreign investment for the first phases of any construction. Knowing this report would be seen by many legislators and ministers, Rajiv understood that it had to recognize "local content" and "value added" contributions by citizens and businesses of Bangladesh, a heavily populated and, except for the clothing industries, under-producing economy. Rajiv also knew that Pog needed to wordsmith this report. So he kept going. It took four and one-half hours before he cleaned it up and fired it off to Pog.

Then he dashed off a moderately formal note to Krystian, cc: Maartje and Annecke, his first RWS contact. He understood from Krystian that she was to be kept in the loop.

Pog quickly transformed Rajiv's articulate, but stilted and formal, draft into a user-friendly communication. His key edit was one sentence which read, "Until Bangladesh successfully attracts major foreign loan guarantees and investment similar to Taiwan, Malaysia, China and Poland, it will be vital to incent foreign investors with both short-term and longer (20-40 years) returns which are all but guaranteed by our government. A respectable beginning might be to build a formidable timber (lumber and paper pulpwood) industry using joint ventures where the foreign investor is the dominant partner."

This line caught the eyes of both the Senator and Khalil over tea the next morning. The timber industry was falling on its ear because the population scavenges every scrap of wood to build, cook with and heat their homes. The Senator pressed Khalil to develop a list of wealthy Bangla citizens who might be willing to meet with the Senator. Before polling, however, Khalil was to develop two separate, incentive-based systems including legislation to implement a concept that emerged from this meeting. As the Senator and Khalil parted, the Senator said, "I believe we can generate, legislatively, one million of the five million Euros the RWS wants, maybe two million. But without a four million Euros infusion, from abroad, we will go nowhere. Four should be the price of being entitled to the incentives."

"If we do not limit the number of hectares, the country could be swallowed up by foreigners," said Khalil.

"Ah, fine point, my boy," said the Senator, very proud that he had picked Khalil to be his top staff aide. Senator Mukherjee knew that if he were not careful from this point on, his career could be over. As Khalil rose to leave, the Senator was already thinking who among his many contacts would be willing to "contribute" now and thus be incented to recover this up front in a reasonably short time.

Thinking further, the Senator wondered just how fast he should move this thing along. Because he had been continually stung by harsh press, he was inclined to move rapidly. The current legislative majority and political climate suggested an outcome the press might look favorably upon. If we do this successfully, he wondered, will our low, wet little country at the base of the massive 'rooftop of the world' mountain ranges, the Himalayas, and the Karakorums be viewed, finally, as a player—however small—in the big boys' world? Status was very important to those who didn't have it.

CHAPTER 11

End With a Finnish

Khalil's proposal required work but had promise, thought the Senator as he read through it:

- Exclusive occupancy to substantial acreage in Bangladesh,

- Foreign investors may own up to 70 percent of the production off the land,

- Access to water, transportation and railroads,

- Fifty-year rights to timber, mineral, oil, natural gas and any other natural resources found on or under this land—no rights to the produce of the sea nor ownership of any waterways, and no right to control the waterways,

- For each 1,000 hectares (2400 acres) a foreign investor must pay 250,000 Euros up front,

- Limit of 10,000 hectares per foreign investing unit/s having a common partner,

- Thirty percent of all rights and privileges must be owned absolutely by citizens of Bangladesh who reside in Bangladesh,

  – At the end of 50 years, the land interests end and the 70
    percent reverts to the government of Bangladesh,

- Bangla investors are entitled to a depletion allowance
  each year based on their proportionate (value) (# of trees)
  (board feet) of timber harvested—only for trees older than
  12 years,

- Bangla tax rate on income of foreign majority-held firms
  not to exceed 17.5 percent.

After the Senator and Khalil met, they invited the Ministers of Revenue and Interior to a discussion of the draft. This time Khalil folded in margin paragraphs of rationale and persuasion. His Powerpoint presentation was well done.

When Khalil returned to his desk, there was a copy of an e-mail to Rajiv from someone named Lakki Tuomi of FinnForest, a paper maker about 300 miles north of Helsinki. The company and Mr. Tuomi had clearly made contact with Krystian. They expressed interest in any forestry developments in Bangladesh with respect to incenting foreign investment. Mr. Tuomi asked ten questions about acreage, mean height above sea level, feasibility of building and owning a paper processing plant in a seaport complex, duration of timber rights and government security to protect foreign investment incentives were.

Also, would there be "local" value-added content requirements for timber and paper employees, and tax abatement until the first harvest year. Lastly, he advised Dr. Gaol that representatives of FinnForest would come to Bangladesh to discuss opportunities after they received responses to the questions and an invitation either from the government or Senator Ram Mukherjee.

Khalil took this e-mail immediately to the Senator's executive secretary (Senator Mukherjee was at a Kapoor family baptism) telling her this was very important. Then he called Rajiv who was very pleased at these developments. At no time did Khalil leave any hint that the Senator had already selected the patriarchs of three Bangla families—two in clothing and one in agriculture—as thirty percent investors. Nor did he mention that the Senator was a participating partner with several others in a syndicate which sought the first opportunity of owning any major government construction and transportation projects which would surely include something like site preparation for a paper mill.

Rajiv was awed by the effect of one man's (Krystian's) influence with a major Finnish company.

"My, my, what an education in business I am receiving," he said to himself.

He called Khalil to see whether he should confirm receipt of Mr. Tuomi's inquiry. "Yes, yes," barked Khalil. "Tell him the Senator will tend to this immediately. You and the Senator will report back to him within one week. And tell him the invitation is in process."

Over the next weeks, answers were prepared for the FinnForest inquiries. The formal invitation and responses were e-mailed with hard copy to Mr. Tuomi at FF. About three weeks later, the Finns proposed a five-day visit by a team of four executives. They were particularly interested in a first day helicopter tour of the land areas available for the grant of timber rights. The Senator directed Khalil to arrange with the Bangladesh Air Force for such a tour—two helicopters for sure, better three. The dates were fixed. Rajiv was to go along on days two and three. The Senator wanted him front and center as a national symbol of intellectual strength and developing business acumen.

A late afternoon reception followed by an evening dinner was set for the second day to be attended by the "potential" Bengali 30 percent holders, their spouses and an appropriate retinue of ministers and legislators. The negotiating team was selected: the Interior Minister whose family was slated to be one of the 30 percent stake holders, the deputy Revenue Minister and Khalil who was to be the big picture fellow to protect the Senator's interests and make sure Bangladesh did not give up too much. Khalil was to be sure that any receipt of wire transfer monies was done simultaneously with the execution of any timber rights documents. The Attorney General was the legal draftsman and these documents were to be e-transmitted at least two weeks before the Finns left Helsinki. Two sticky issues had been identified: the tree planting period and security to protect the fledgling timber. This last concern forced the Senator's team to markedly consolidate the timber area into two large tracts. Khalil and the Senator knew just how difficult it would be to prevent piracy. Scavenging in this impoverished land had become a national ethic. Everyone on the Bengali team was troubled by this issue. The word went out that some new ideas were desperately needed. When Rajiv received the e-mail on this, he immediately patched it to Pog Marenjar saying, "Pog, this piece is vital. Please put your head to it."

The Bengali team remained at wit's end to devise an effective, affordable "forest"security system. The Army, Air Force, and Special Forces were unwilling to commit beyond four years. The Bangladesh team was now forced to adopt a potentially deal-breaking position: that four years was it.

It was Pog who suggested that in year four, using random selection techniques, special forces teams could injection-drill a certain percent of trees to have radio micro-transmitter strain gauges installed which operated like an EPIRB (Emergency May Day Beacons). These could trip a land based alarm with GPS coordinates rapidly sent to nearby Special Forces bases. Special forces loved the idea because they viewed it as a funded training activity. Budget conscious legislators winced at the cost but understood they would have almost two years to get ready. Khalil was very uneasy about the four years. However, he thought the Senator could sell the 30 percent group on having their employees take training from the military so they could help from years four to eight. Beyond this would be up to the Finns—another possible deal breaker.

The Senator was gloomy and losing optimism. Khalil was strung tight as a violin string. Pog was uneasy but his humor kept him professionally detached. Rajiv was more curious than anything else because he was learning political, economic and global ways of transacting business. And he was trying to figure out how this means of raising money could be linked to storm surge protection and coastal erosion reduction. He could not yet visualize the connection. But there had to be one.

During the month before the Finns' visit, everyone was busy. The draft documents from Bangladesh were transmitted on time to the

Finns. Characteristic of the Scandinavian culture, there was a polite acknowledgment of document receipt. No commentary on the merits. Khalil was certain these would not come on to the table until day two of the visit. He scheduled an extra set of meetings with the negotiating team to make certain the Bengali negotiating strategy was in place. It was clear the genetic mathematical genius of this culture would play a major part in the negotiations. The Finns knew trees and paper-making. The Bengalis knew math, economics and analytical technique. They welcomed the opportunity to create an economically-sound deal.

Meanwhile, Senator Mukherjee was operating on two wave lengths. One involved the possibility of major land ownership at a new seaport and construction bids for his investment group. There was another more elusive goal. But this goal remained well-hidden, subterranean.

The Finns were extremely curious and attentive. The helicopter pilots later reported they had never been put through such intense flying for such long periods. They had maps (NATO), and with their laptops and GPS instruments, they plotted every leg of their look-see day. Two rode in each helicopter, one overflying a proposed forestry site, the other two at a second site and the barrier islands. The pilots both reported hearing Krystian's name spoken several times. Other than this and the frowns on the faces as they studied the sandalwood beige-brown ribbon of erosion and silt moving into the Bay of Bengal, there was little the pilots could report to Khalil who debriefed them while the guests were transported back to their hotel. The Bangla team was kicking itself for not having pilots with Finnish language skills. They had blown a great opportunity. But they would recover for the negotiating sessions. Khalil concluded the likelihood of the Dutch RWS coming to be part of a very significant project (or several) was exerting a positive influence on the Finn's intentions.

Day Two

The Finns were allowed to rest and dine on their own this first evening. Early on day two Rajiv made his way to Senator Mukherjee's palatial office to be part of the welcoming team. Khalil filled him in on his day one observations. He had previously asked Rajiv to prepare a broad brush treatment of the likely approaches Maartje and Krystian had thrown out in their discussions. But Khalil, seeing this as a marketing piece, encouraged Rajiv to speak in terms of 10-15 years rather than 15-50 to implement major construction phases. Meanwhile, the Senator was wondering how any paper the Finns made would be transported to the markets.

After formal welcomes by the Senator and the Ministers, the group settled in to a large, comfortable, conference room. It took almost three hours to elicit the Finnish response to the Bengali proposal. Translators for both teams labored mightily to present and clarify communications. It became clear the Finns wanted 65 years and a more advanced timber security system than the Bengalis were offering. These would be tough issues, especially because they seemed wedded to 12 years of security supplied wholly at Bengali cost.

During a two-hour lunch break—the Senator and Khalil ventured to the Bangladesh team that some trade-offs would be required; to cut a deal; raise the €250,000 per 2400 hectares to 400,000 Euros, shorten 12 security years to 6 years, 3 years government, 3 years Bengali business partner but decided not to present this until day three in the afternoon. The Bengali math-genes matched up well against the Finnish business-deal-savvy-genes. Rajiv was absorbing this and politely threw in a suggestion that the tax rate after year 25 could be adjusted to 24.5 percent from 17.5 percent. By then the amortization of plant construction and start-up would be nearing the end. This way, Bangladesh, over the next 30 years, could recover early security outlays for the years one through six or beyond, if negotiating outcomes required this. The team was grateful for the suggestion and modified it to a negotiating strategy. Whether he knew it or not, Rajiv was beginning to get the "it" of business negotiations.

Toward the end of the day, Rajiv gave his presentation. He used visuals from the RWS sessions to illustrate the RWS interest in Bangladesh. This clearly stimulated the ever stoic Finns to a higher level of interest. As the group adjourned, Khalil sidled up to Mr. Lahki Tuomi whom he correctly identified as the lead member of the team.

They chatted quietly and briefly. It was clear, as Rajiv watched, Khalil was preparing Mr. Tuomi for some negotiating possibilities the next day which might move the parties toward compromise.

The outdoor reception took place at the Textile Club, across the plaza from the meeting room, as the sun set on a cool, low humidity, evening. Each member of the visiting entourage, translators and all, was given by the Interior Minister and Senator Mukherjee, a cream colored evening silk jacket tailored in the last 24 hours to each visitor's specific size. Graciously, all guests followed Mr. Tuomi's lead and doffed their suit coats in favor of these gifts. Group photos were taken. The taller Finns looked quite tropical and appropriate in their jackets and relished the comfortable feeling of wearing them. They presented each Bengali host a set of four Finnish crystal glasses in addition to toasting glasses they had brought for everyone, some three dozen in all. In the candlelight, these looked like hollowed out melting ice cubes as the refracted light shimmered inside and out.

Dinner was served indoors. The peppery aroma of spices was pleasant and the appetites of hosts and guests alike had been whetted by a hard working day. The seafood courses and the naan breads were relished by the guests. The chicken and beef courses were East Indian flavored with hot peppers and onions, but tempered by a prudent chef and his maitre d'hotel. The remarks by the hosts were inclusive and generous. All the Finns could do was to smile, stand, toast all their hosts and say "thank you." They were very businesslike. They understood day three was likely to be a tense working day.

Rajiv was thrilled to be part of this gathering. He had attended several medical society gatherings in Evanston and downtown near Chicago's loop, but never one where the setting was so tropical, warm and the food so succulent. To close the evening, the Finns provided Finnish vodka to their hosts who struggled, smiling mightily to swallow, in one breath completely, the two-ounce freezer cold portions served for the toasts. The entire group was mellowing. As the group broke for the night, the Senator quietly, but urgently, implored Khalil to remain right at his side to make certain he did not fall down, so potent was this potato liquor. Rajiv knew he was in trouble so he drank three quick cups of strong coffee and two bottles of Evian before he left the table. After his taxi dropped him off at his hotel, he drank two more bottles of water, read the Finn responses for an hour, then blurry eyed, faded into a deep sleep, a very deep sleep.

Day Three

Day three began with a Bengali-team-breakfast in a private room off the lobby restaurant. Khalil and the Interior Minister were finalizing strategy and discussing "time out" gestures to use, if warranted. It reminded Rajiv of the hand signals Big Ten coaches sent in to offensive and defensive units during football games at Ryan Stadium. He never could understand the gestures but he would watch the team captain react and the players adjust quickly and sometimes very effectively. Thus Rajiv backed into business negotiation strategy.

Khalil opened the session by softly responding to the 65-year (or 5-6 timber harvests) proposition by suggesting that it could be done, on two conditions: first, the tax rate could be adjusted in year 25 to a 25.5 percent rate; second, the downstroke (the "usage royalty" as it was deemed) would be €500,000 Euros. Rajiv gulped. He thought the Bangladeshi team had agreed on €400,000. Then, he saw Khalil was creating negotiating room, €100,000 worth per plot. On timber security, there was no way the government of Bangladesh could provide 12 years worth. They would do three and then, at their own expense, train the Bengali 30 percent partners to do the next three. The Finns grunted and on some invisible pre-arranged signal Tuomi suggested a short recess. The recess lasted one hour and fifteen minutes. When the Bengali team was called back into the conference room, one of the Finnish delegation was on his cell phone—Nokia, of course—talking Finnish, no doubt back home. It was clear authority was being sought from corporate headquarters. This time the Bangladeshi team had the linguistic ally they lacked in the helicopters. One of the translators was fluent in several Finnish dialects.

What the Bengalis did not know however—and would not learn for several years—was that the Finns had been doing some genetic engineering on a tropical variety of tree indigenous to India, Burma and Thailand. On the basis of this research they concluded they could plant a newly engineered strain and harvest it in 9-10 years. Thus they would have seven harvests rather than five leaving a two-year margin to effect a timber planting start-up. They also sought an 18-year tax abatement on a new paper mill which they would install in year 7 or 8. Because this was non-negotiable, they would pay a €450,000 Euro royalty per 2400 acres. The tax rate adjustment was agreeable "only if agreement were to be reached on all other terms." Among sophisticated contract negotiators, this last condition foreclosed the, "But you've already agreed to" trap.

The Senator signaled Khalil that a recess was now in order for the Bangladeshi team. It was near lunch and a two-hour break would occur.

Over lunch the Bengali team chatted like sparrows in a tree. The negotiations were down to security and the new facility tax abatement. The Senator said, "Everywhere in the Western world these abatements are negotiated. We need to do this." The revenue minister rejoined, "But we have never done one for more than 12 years." To do otherwise would establish a very bad precedent. After discussion they instructed Khalil to hold firm at 12 years. Rajiv was awed by this process of negotiations and time outs because he was still trying to find a connection between money for plots of land, reforestation and shrubbery which the Dutch insisted upon. He struggled the rest of the day, perhaps still slowed by last evening's vodka.

When the discussion resumed, Khalil set forth the "final and best offer" but without saying so. The entire Finnish delegation frowned throughout his soliloquy. Tuomi's response eased the tension, "We will undertake security beginning in year seven if, at the expense of Bangladesh, your Special Forces will train our corporate personnel for six months at the end of year six. This is the only way our security employees will be able to understand what they are dealing with and how to put a lid on major thievery breaches. We are also willing to enlist some NATO capabilities at our own expense to begin our preparation. If the abatement is limited to 12 years, we do not like this, but it is a major commitment by Bangladesh and, in fairness, you have only had two days to comprehend our response to your position which you so timely submitted to us. This unfairness to you has historically been part of our "stoic" if you will, culture. Many people who have negotiated with Finlanders complain about this. For years, we laughed among ourselves and said, 'It works, why change?' Now we realize how important it is to create a cross-cultural sense of fairness. So we try—very imperfectly, we are sure."

The Bengalis simultaneously applauded Mr. Tuomi. He blushed.

The Senator seized the moment to say, "If we had been more rapid at perfecting our tolerance for your vodka, we would toast you with your vodka. But we don't dare risk it yet and perhaps won't for several years. (Everyone laughed heartily.)

"However, let us have some early afternoon Indian Hill Station tea, clearly milder."

The Senator rang the service bell and two attractive waitresses appeared. "In the meantime, I wish to raise the question of how many 1000 hectare plots you intend to commit to? And which years?"

Tuomi turned to one of his team. The gentleman spoke up, "Six this year. Six next year and six two years from now."

Rajiv quickly totaled 18 times 450,000. That equaled almost €8.2 million. He could not believe it. Now he understood the term, "fund raiser." The Revenue Minister piped up, "Payments should be made in January each year."

Clearly, the Finns wanted fast growing pulp wood. Equally clearly, Bangladesh wanted, up front, the funds that came from helping them get there.

Tuomi responded, "February first each year will be acceptable."

An elegant tea service arrived to be served by the one man and three lovely Bengali women, Khalil said, "If we were to recess now for tea and for the day, might it make sense to turn the preparation of our memorandum to our legal department so we might anticipate signing about 2:00 p.m. tomorrow afternoon?"

"Agreed," spoke Tuomi.

And a fine tea it was.

CHAPTER 12

Study Time

From the air, the land looked like a slice of gray-green, Roquefort cheese. Rich veins of water cut through the fabric of fields, villages and cities, simultaneously separating and joining them. Bangladesh is defined by several major rivers, the Brahmaputra (known to Bangladeshis as the Jumuna), the Meghna, the Ganges, and the Padma. But from the helicopter, what stood out were the hundreds of tributaries that fanned out for miles, liquid highways to many destinations. Again and again, the helicopter pilot followed a stream which seemed to go nowhere, yet it connected five villages in the course of a few miles. The waterways were like threads in a shirt. It was the water which held everything together.

Maartje took copious notes and snapped photographs as they flew. She had arrived a week ago and quickly started with an aerial survey of the major waterways and tributaries. The subcontracted British HKV team had preceded her by two weeks to begin silt testings just seaward of the coast. Rajiv had been in contact but had been working in his clinics until this morning when a helicopter landed at a village heliport and whisked him away. Two hours later, he joined Maartje 90 miles away.

It was an interesting scene. Two attractive adults very much looking forward to seeing the other; each very hesitant to show excitement. But emotion took control and they embraced excitedly. It was a happy first reunion.

Conversation was difficult over the engine noise, but every now and then she would point to a denuded stream bank and raise her eyebrows. From the right altitude, he could see the demarcation between normal stream current and the muddy cloud of water billowing out from a village's banks, a clear example of topsoil washing away every day. The expression on Maartje's face was one of intense interest, and Rajiv could see she was in her element.

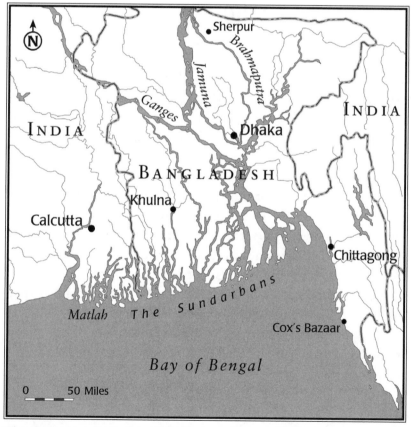

"The waterways were like the threads in a shirt. It was the water which held everything together."

The pilot waved at them from the cockpit as he was preparing to land in a small village near Lohagara, a city in the Khulna division. This area was selected because of the vast denuded acreage and silt loss. As part of recent flood preparation work, the federal government created heliports in each of Bangladesh's 460 counties. The heliports were built to speed delivery of emergency medicines and food following floods and cyclones. A man and a woman waited just off the landing pad, and as the whir of the blades slowed to a whine, Maartje headed their way. Already the heat and humidity of the day were affecting Maartje.

Rajiv smiled and spoke, "Maartje, I'd like you to meet Mr. Junaid Caterlee and Miss Smeeta Pal, a grass, foliage and shrubs specialist and animal biologist respectively from the Federal Water Development Board (WDB) and Interior Department."

Except for darker complexions, they resembled Maartje in appearance: khakis and cotton shirts. Smeeta carried a laptop briefcase, and Junaid clutched a leather case bursting with papers and folders.

"There is no point duplicating work already completed and paid for," Maartje said. "My preliminary study helped us understand how much useful work the WDB has already done."

Together, they began walking toward the village, where Junaid and Smeeta had arranged working space in a village commons building where they spread out papers. Junaid had ready some soil sample studies and hydrological data.

Rajiv turned to Junaid and Smeeta. "If so much quality study has been undertaken, why has more not been done?"

"The flood protection already accomplished is actually quite remarkable," Junaid said, "given the resources available and complexities of land formation. There is far more water to deal with here than in the Netherlands, or, almost any other inhabited flood plain in the world."

As these discussions proceeded, they entered the shady meeting building and settled in a small bright room. Junaid and Smeeta had arranged for a lunch of *catni* and curry. While they ate, Junaid,

Smeeta and Maartje briefed Rajiv on their work, which had begun earlier in the week with a review of two earlier flood plans.

Moved by the aftermath of the floods of 1987 and 1988, the French government developed a flood action plan for Bangladesh. The French proposed a traditional levee system to contain the major rivers. They did not, however, offer funding for the implementation of the plan, estimated then to cost $10.2 billion.

"The idea," Maartje said, "was to seek funding from countries such as Japan and the United States. However, neither nation was interested. The Japanese, whom it should be noted also face cyclones—and, worse, Tsunamis—favored a system of better flood response and disaster relief."

"And the U.S.?" Rajiv asked.

"The U.S.," she said, "was re-examining its own levee systems along the Missouri and Mississippi, particularly following flooding in 1993, when those systems utterly failed. Then along came Hurricane Katrina in August 2005. They have finally come to see levee systems as a diminishing part of the costly, and endlessly expensive, battle with nature. And, many believe the cost estimate for the French plan was hyper-optimistic. Annual maintenance alone was a horrendous $1 to $1.5 billion."

"The plan also faced opposition from inside Bangladesh," Smeeta injected. "Besides the money, the other issue is land. The plan required taking 21,000 hectares, that's about 50,000 acres, of land out of production, affecting 680,000 people. The study implied that greater development in Bangladesh would ultimately offset the costs, but many of us doubted this. On top of everything else, because of the setback from the river of the proposed embankments, the plan left almost five million people unprotected. If they stayed where they were, immediately next to the rivers they could only await the next colossal disaster. If we moved them ..."

The group was silent for a moment, but the impact was clear. This plan involved hundreds of thousands of people losing their homes and land.

Nor did this plan address the reality of rice growing methods,

Maartje explained. "Rice requires flooding. So once embankments were built, farmers had to turn around and irrigate, and irrigation does not work as well as inundating fields. A Bengali farmer clearly could not afford irrigation."

"Interestingly, one study has shown that personal nutrition is highest in areas that routinely flood," Junaid said. "It's lowest in routinely dry areas, probably because fish and rice are, of course, more abundant in flood-prone areas."

"Here's another interesting fact," Maartje said. "In a World Bank study done about 10 years ago, the majority of Bengalis most likely to be affected by the French plan said they wanted protection from large-scale flooding. They were willing to deal with ordinary floods. The people understand, often better than scientists do, how vital water is to their well being."

"So the French plan fix actually created many significant problems," Rajiv said.

Smeeta nodded. "The problem was largely due to the fact that it was created by non-Bengalis. We do recognize our need for outside guidance," she nodded toward Maartje, "but the failure of past plans is that they were often designed by people who looked at flooding here and saw it as too different from their own experience. They thought water could only be contained or excluded, ignoring its many attributes and possibilities."

"What this suggests," Smeeta said, "is that you Dutch are on to something with the idea of movable sea walls and river gates, as planned outside Rotterdam. Those systems regularly allow water to flow tidally and are closed only under extreme surges. Otherwise, normal sea and river currents continue. The European Greens presented these issues against earlier designs of the Delta Project. The "close ranks and defend plan" attitude of the Dutch planning groups almost derailed the entire project. Although these protests were nearly violent, the Greens had a prescient approach."

Junaid smiled ruefully. "Of course, discussion of any flood control plans among Bengalis has not been without problems."

The three Bengalis in the room knew the political infighting to which he referred. Large projects are subject to politics in any nation, but the young government of Bangladesh posed a unique set of difficulties. It was risky for the agencies to even to talk about politics. They did not know each other very well. Much of the problem lay in the nation's distinct and autonomous ministries, like the Water Development Board. Inter-agency cooperation was rare. The government of the 1980s and early 1990s had been too weak to unite agencies for meaningful flood control. Corruption and partisanship were the norm in awarding lucrative water control contracts. District government and sub-district bodies had little power over staff representatives of various ministries. Rajiv suddenly realized Maartje had already gone to considerable effort to smooth ruffled feathers by working with these folks and their supervisors in the water ministry, those who had turf, jobs and contract work at stake.

"We understand Senator Mukherjee is supporting this newest endeavor," Junaid said cautiously in his deep voice.

"'Support' is perhaps too strong a term," Rajiv said. "I would say he seems interested."

Smeeta and Junaid exchanged a glance. "His backing would be significant," Smeeta said. "He has the power to force..." she stopped and corrected herself, "to unite various agencies."

"He also has the ability to kill such efforts," Junaid said, adding diplomatically, "if in his best judgment it is ill-thought out, unwise or contrary to the interests of his constituencies and, of course, his in-laws."

Rajiv looked at the two and realized they weren't necessarily supporters of the Senator's efforts. Perhaps they thought of him as a meddler, or naïve amateur in what was essentially their life work. But they clearly wanted Rajiv to cultivate his ties to Senator Mukherjee. "I do not know him well," Rajiv cautioned them. "And," he laughed, "our introduction was more abrasive than smooth."

"But you've spoken with him, and obtained funding for this first work," Junaid said. "That's more than you think. It may signal that he's ready to move forward on something larger. He could be the catalyst we have long needed for effective change."

"I'm not sure I'm the best go-between," Rajiv said.

Junaid leaned back from the table and spread his hands in the air. "You've already been chosen. Mukherjee has chosen you. For some reason, he has anointed you."

Rajiv returned Junaid's smile uneasily.

"Shall we break for a few minutes?" Maartje rose from the table and waited for Rajiv to join her. "Let's walk for a moment," she said, steering him toward the door. "I want to show Rajiv an example of erosion control down by the stream," she said to Junaid and Smeeta, which made it clear that she wanted some privacy. They agreed to meet later to continue their helicopter tour.

They walked silently for a moment, moving through the center of the village toward the stream bank on a path barren of foliage.

"Look, they've been dealing with such efforts here for years. It's their life work and they have been frustrated time after time," Maartje said. "They're going to be suspicious."

"Yes, and I am impatient and intolerant."

Rajiv was surprised at how freely he was able to express to Maartje some honesty about his critical nature.

Maartje stopped. "Prepare yourself. There will be many floods, and casualties long, long, long before you see the results of your labor."

Rajiv grimaced. "I understand."

"May I ask you, as a doctor, do you expect to save every life?"

"No."

"And every day, people die of cancer, AIDS, and other diseases for which a cure doesn't exist?"

"Yes."

"Does the inevitability of their deaths mean you stop trying to help them, or that research should stop?"

"Of course not. I get your point," he said. He looked into her warm eyes. For the first time, he was comforted. But he was also aware of other feelings.

As they moved toward the water, they saw several dozen children swarming around a man carrying a knapsack. With him were a half dozen American college students, some of them carrying small insulated bags slung around their necks. The man with the knapsack was older, perhaps 63-65, wore brown slacks and a clerical collar on his short-sleeved shirt. He handed out candy to adoring children, while the students pulled children aside and placed a few drops from vials upon their tongues.

"Polio vaccines," Rajiv explained to Maartje, who was clearly curious.

"And the man in the center?"

"A religious 'tourist' from the United States. They came around several times a year." He could not keep disdain out of his voice. "I've met the type so often. They come once or twice a year, hand out used clothing or, candy. They go home satisfied they've done their charity for the year. They give speeches before their congregations about everything they've seen, say a prayer, pass a collection plate, and go home to Sunday dinner where they eat more food than many Bengali families see in a week."

"But what do they hurt?" Maartje asked. She was struggling to understand his sarcasm and bitterness.

"They dispense false hope with their candy," Rajiv said. "These bleeding hearts promise things they cannot deliver. I hate to hear children talk about salvation that comes from other countries; salvation, when they should be saving themselves.

"We are a sick, flooded, poor, hopeless country. A thousand of me will not change this, nor a thousand of him. Futility is the endless chaos we have all the time." The pain in his eyes and voice was unmistakable.

Rajiv was clearly irritated and angered by such do-gooder volunteers. Actually, he had not realized how much they bothered him, until he saw the man standing there.

"It's an industry," he said sarcastically. "They book vacations in New York or London that promise the fulfillment of philanthropic desires. It's a feel better vacation."

"I am sorry for your pain." Very sorry, her body language said. "You and I are two—Krystian three, the Senator four, Jagdish, Khalil, Smeeta and Junaid make seven." Rajiv felt to a flicker of hope from her gentle support. "But they don't have to come," she said. "They could go sun themselves on a beach in Tahiti."

Having vented his emotions, Rajiv shrugged. He watched the man pause, dispense his treats and at times, put his hands on a child's head in a way that, to Rajiv, seemed patronizing. Bengali charities asked tourists to avoid just this activity, in part to help preserve a shred of national dignity, but also to curb the growth of an age old profession: begging. There were even parents who intentionally maimed a child, chopped off an arm or gouged out their eyes, so they would be more suitable beggars in Dhaka.

"Some people consider it adventurous to travel to a developing nation to rub elbows with the poor rather than hiking in the mountains. I just don't like seeing children as entertainment."

Maartje shook her head. "I understand why you may be angry. But look at it another way. That man," she said, pointing to the cleric, "cares on some level. He is here. He is probably well-intentioned. I concede that maybe some others are not. And yes, he'll probably return home and tell people what he saw here. Maybe, if we're lucky, they will care on some remote level as well. Bangladesh needs more individuals who care. If there are enough such people and their efforts are supervised by appropriately skilled people, why get in their way?"

"I become embarrassed at my country having its hands out to the world." Rajiv almost spat the words. He was, he knew, tired of the effort it took even to get his rounds as a physician completed, always having to ask for more just to deliver basic care. And the magnitude of assistance needed for long-term flood relief overwhelmed him. He was weighed down with the sense that after much effort, anything he tried to do in his country would fail.

"You know, as a physician, you could make 100 times what you make here if you were in the Netherlands," she said. "Yet you are here."

"I have to be here," he said flatly.

"You would stay even if you didn't have to be," she said. A look of surprise crept across her face. "You don't know that about yourself yet, do you? Well, it's true. And that being the case, I'm not sure I see much difference between you," she pointed across the clearing, "and him."

She started to walk away, toward the candy man.

"Where are you going?" Rajiv asked.

"I have a sweet tooth," she said.

As she approached the throng of children, the man looked up, and looked not toward her, but toward Rajiv. His gaze was intense and somehow targeted something unexpected in Rajiv: grief. Until this moment, Rajiv had hidden his pain and anger from that night at the emergency clinic when he first learned of Sabjada. Now, suddenly, tears welled in his eyes. This had not happened since he'd lost his first patient as a Cook County intern.

From across the path, Rajiv watched the man's expression soften as Maartje approached him. He smiled at her, as she accepted a piece of candy and popped it into her mouth. Then, the pair turned to Rajiv and after a word or two from Maartje, they began walking toward him.

The man was older than Rajiv had thought, yet he walked with alacrity. He was nearly bald, except for a thin circle of snow white hair that rimmed his head. His eyes were bright, piercing blue, a shade that reminded Rajiv of ice.

"Rajiv," Maartje said. "This is Theophane."

Rajiv took his hand, which was intensely warm. When Theophane released his grasp, Rajiv's hand felt like it glowed.

Theophane was an American cleric, a monk from an order based in Wyoming whose ministry served children in the world's poorest nations. He had been coming to Bangladesh for 20 years, usually to rural schools. Because he was fluent in local dialects, he often was asked to accompany medical workers who came to dispense vaccines to the children.

"And the purpose of the candy?" Only after he asked the question did Rajiv realize how mocking it sounded. But he could not quell the sensation that this man, like others he had seen, reveled in seeing a knot of children trailing after him. They fulfilled so many quaint images of the poor.

Theophane smiled. "It's sweet."

Maartje laughed. "That it is."

Rajiv was unable to share their amusement, and frankly, he didn't understand what was so funny. "You'd be better off giving out tooth-brushes. The candy isn't any better for them than it is for American children."

Theophane's eyebrows crooked in amusement. "Or worse. Children are much the same the world over, aren't they? They love the same things."

Maartje nodded at his sagacity. Rajiv did not realize he was frowning until he saw the quizzical look on her face. He thought Maartje naïve, even childish, about this complete stranger. When she turned toward Rajiv, a veil fell over her eyes. They became hard. She was irritated at him.

"What brings you to Bangladesh?" Rajiv asked.

"Our monastery contributes any way it can to your government's health care efforts."

"Education is good for education's sake." Theophane gave a small chuckle. "God comes to us in many forms and in many types of work, and for that matter, through many religions. Also, for all of its politi-cal infighting and intrigue, the social climate in Bangladesh is more stable than in India and in Pakistan. One of the reasons is because the government here makes a stronger investment in schools. In Pakistan, of which Bangladesh was once a part, extremism is always a threat, largely because of the private Muslim schools. These Madrasas, run by the mullahs, are the only place many poor children can learn to read. In spite of that nation's cooperation with the United States on terrorism, American agencies are reluctant to pay much more for ed-ucational reform because of the billions already squandered. Much of it has gone to land barons rather than the children.

"And in India, the deadly fighting between Hindus and Muslims rears its ugly head again and again, in part because the government has tolerated divisions on smaller scales everywhere. I'm not saying that corruption does not exist here in Bangladesh. It exists every-where. But in my missionary experiences, I've found it far worse in countries with education systems that exclude, rather than include."

Theophane stopped and looked at Rajiv for a moment before speaking again. "You are lucky. You live in a country where there is hope."

"Theophane..." Rajiv stumbled over the name.

"My name in the order," the monk answered. "When we enter, we choose a name that signifies leaving one life behind, the secular life, and taking on a new identity for God. The name means 'the presence of God.'"

"Do you believe God is everywhere?"

Theophane nodded.

"Even when floods claim thousands? Where is God then?"

Theophane hunched low to the ground and began tracing in the sand, and for a moment it reminded Rajiv of the women folk artists who worked in colored sand, creating intricate works. Theophane's strokes were purposeful, yet Rajiv could not make sense of the image emerging.

"You have lost someone very special to you in the flooding," Theophane said. Maartje was struck by the insight.

Rajiv snapped. "Everyone here has lost a precious someone to the water! If not this time, then next time!"

Theophane ignored his tone, kept his composure even becoming more calm. "I had been working with the children in Chittagong province when the storms hit."

Rajiv shot a glance at Maartje, and wondered if she had told the monk of his ties to Chittagong, but from the interest on her face, he could see the detail was fresh news to her.

"You know, even though I work with them only a short time, the children are precious to me," Theophane said. "I write to many from the States when I return, to encourage them to continue their studies. They love—as I do—receiving mail from somewhere far away. There were more than 120 children there, before ..." His voice trailed off. "I will not be writing as many letters when I return home."

He rose from his squatting position and leveled an intense look at Rajiv. "And, yes, God was there then. He was with me when I toured the village after the flood, and when I helped bury many of those children. God is with us perhaps even more in death and destruction than when life is going smoothly. In death, the curtain between worlds parts, just for a moment."

Rajiv looked down at Theophane's scribblings which looked like a child's face, but just then, the wind came up, and the image disappeared. The breeze was cool, and piercing.

Rajiv did not consider himself spiritual. He had been raised, like the majority of Bengalis, as a Muslim. But as a scientist, struggling to appreciate things he could not see, he had stopped praying. Like many who stop praying, he had shelved his belief in God. But now, a snippet of prayer popped into his head, one he had heard the children in Sabjada's village sing. "Oh Allah please hear my prayer... may I serve none but thee."

Then he realized Theophane and Maartje were bidding each other farewell. She put her arms around the monk.

Theophane extended his hand to Rajiv. He grasped Theophane's hand tentatively.

"Are you in Bangladesh for much longer?"

Theophane shook his head. "I return to Wyoming at the end of this week. I hope to return to Chittagong before the end of this year to help rebuild a school there."

"Perhaps we will meet again? Would you please provide me with your mail, and perhaps, e-mail address and phone?"

Theophane smiled. "I would like that very much."

Theophane took his leave, and followed the immunization volunteers who were ready to move on to the next village. Theophane reached in his knapsack for more candy, handing it to the tenacious few who remained. Each time he laid his hand gently on the child's head in a silent blessing. As they made their way out of the square, he turned one last time toward Rajiv, ducked his head in benediction, and was gone.

Maartje and Rajiv watched the empty square in silence for several moments. "I suppose we should head back to Junaid and Smeeta," Maartje said at last.

Rajiv nodded, and they began walking.

"Interesting fellow," Rajiv allowed.

Maartje murmured, "He really cares about them."

The sounds of evening prayers were rising over the village, and he turned his head. He could hear a muezzin rhythmically calling the men to prayer. When the sun had completely set, they would begin their prayers.

CHAPTER 13

Swarovski Action Plan

In the morning, Smeeta suggested that they tour wildlife areas which were losing their trees as firewood-seeking Bengalis invaded what should have been protected areas. Smeeta described it as an ecological tour to broaden the team's understanding of the root problems causing silting in the Bay of Bengal. Now they were joined by Krystian who had arrived yesterday, and had flown out by helicopter from Dhaka.

The copter banked east to head up the Jumuna River. Rajiv listened on and off as the engineers talked of rates of diffusion and water absorption. What he saw from the air disheartened him. He had last visited this region as a schoolboy of sixteen, on a camping trip. He remembered forested area full of lovely foliage. Now, along the river banks, he saw mud-packed earth devoid of trees. Bangladesh had once had vast, dense tracts of jungle and hardwood forest. But as population grew, forests gave way to villages. Silt was a very unfortunate consequence.

Forty miles north of Dhaka, the helicopter swept west, heading for the Madhupur Forest Reserve, a tract about 35 kilometers square; the last remnant of what was once a moist, deciduous, old-growth forest which, at one time, extended hundreds of miles over the Dhaka division. Around the forest on all sides were rice fields. The sharp delineation between the tree line and rice fields created an image of green paddies of Pac Men chomping at the forest, inch by inch.

The voices in the helicopter quieted as they approached the southern edge of the forest. They could now see black scars of land recently cleared by slash and burn methods.

"Tragic, isn't it?" Maartje said.

"It happens everywhere," Smeeta said, "and always with ecological consequences. In America, the Dust Bowl resulted from poor farming practices as prairies were stripped of hardy grasses for crops." She turned slightly to Maartje. "In the Netherlands, if you turn wetlands into farms, rivers flood. Wetlands are vital natural sponges for flooding. They are able to hold vast amounts of water for long periods."

Maartje nodded. "Our government finally instituted a program to return parts of the polders to wetlands, but it's increasingly difficult getting farmers to surrender such productive land."

Rajiv found himself thinking back to the farm photos on Senator Mukherjee's wall. He wondered whether the good senator would surrender a single hectare in the name of flood control.

"As in the Netherlands," Maartje continued, "flood-control must address silting, short and long term. Sufficient wetland systems stem the wash of sediment into lower deltas stopping silt movement pre-stages, tidal surge barriers, and flood gating."

"How long would that process take?" Rajiv asked.

"Not as long as you think," Krystian said. "In the Netherlands, by planting grasses and shrubs on the sea dunes and river embankments that feed the scheldt, the sedimentation rate slowed markedly. Actually, these efforts keep soil from becoming the suspended particles which are silt waiting to happen. For the Delta Project, the sea floor was carefully dressed and built up for the five years before the barriers were placed."

"Those trees there," Maartje pointed at neatly planted rows of forest, "what are they?"

Junaid looked where she pointed and frowned. "Sometimes, well-intentioned economic development meets with tragic results, because ecological impact has not been carefully considered," he said.

"In the early 1990s, our forestry department received a grant to help farmers supplement income by planting rubber trees. The idea was to have farmers plant trees on land that was already cleared. The extra money would actually curb the need to clear other land for crops. But in practice, the incentive only encouraged farmers to clear more land. They began opening new patches, which they claimed as old clearings to qualify for assistance. Initially, forest officials turned a blind eye to the practice, but when the practice was discovered by the international media, it became a scandal. The assistance was terminated. Now, you see rows of unproductive rubber trees where once healthy and diverse forest existed.

"Other parts of the forest have been destroyed for the usual reason: the value of the wood," Junaid said. "The sal tree is as valuable to woodworkers as teak. Gewa is made into pulp for newsprint." I'll bet the Finns know this, Rajiv thought to himself. "And, during monsoon season, people need warmth and drying out. So, much of the forest is burned for cooking fuel."

As they passed over the forest, Rajiv saw areas of open land within the preserve. He pointed down and looked at Smeeta and Junaid for explanation.

Some interior forest lands were privately owned, Smeeta advised. This was of little concern when the primary owners were Mandi, a tribal group believed to have emigrated from Burma. They were not farmers, and their traditional life depended on a spacious forest. But as Bengali farmers encroached upon the forest from the outside, many tribal members sold off their lands and headed to more remote areas farther north, creating a vicious cycle. The farmers who bought the land made speedy work of felling the trees, which they sold for their lumber, creating more farmland. In response, more Mandis sold out.

The helicopter set them down in Muktagacha, a small village on the Tangail-Dhaka road where a government utility vehicle—an ancient Land Rover—waited for their forest tour. They were welcomed warmly by Jagdish Rao, a forester assigned to the preserve.

Jagdish had buck teeth, large warm eyes and often tilted his head inquisitively to the left. He wore tropical weight khaki shorts, a matching short-sleeve shirt and ankle-high boots. Judging by his long beard and traditional turban, he was Muslim. His eyes danced as he spoke. His words turned up with the deliberate cadence of old-school British spoken with a heavy Bengali accent.

"You have chosen a fine day to visit Madhupur Forest. The sun is shining. The weekend is over. When the weekend weather is too good, we are often overrun with campers."

He directed a porter to take their luggage to a forestry guesthouse where they would stay overnight. Then he ushered them into the Land Rover. Something about this place triggered an old memory for Rajiv. When he realized where they were, he turned to Jagdish and whispered a few words. Jagdish smiled and he nodded. Rajiv then turned to the group to explain.

"We will visit the Gopal Pali Prosida Monda," he said bowing happily. "They make the best monda in the country."

Krystian and Maartje exchanged curious glances.

"Smeeta has a sweet tooth," Jagdish said, smiling, "and this village is home to the most famous candy shop in our country."

As Jagdish drove, he told the story of the shop. "About a century or so ago, a local family cooked a specialty, a type of sweetmeat, for the zamindar, a large landowner. The zamindar was so delighted that he hired this family to cook exclusively for him. During the partitioning of India and the two Pakistans, East and West, the landowner's heirs left for West Pakistan and the cooks opened their own monda shop."

He finished the story just as the Land Rover pulled in front of a simple one story building with a tapered roof and a lion over the door. There was no display area or counter, just an area in the shade with tables and benches. Rajiv ushered them to a table and a young man soon came out for their order for tea and monda, a spicy sweet macaroon of boiled milk with a dry, grainy texture.

The man delivered the monda on small trays, which they balanced on their knees along with the tea. Maartje and Krystian nibbled at theirs. The Bengalis ate politely, but with obvious relish.

"It is an acquired taste," Smeeta said, smiling.

Rajiv made short work of his. An outing to this place, lush with boyhood memories, lifted his spirits. He ordered another. Smeeta and Junaid looked up at him in surprise. Monda was a treat eaten in small quantities, like chocolate. Most Bengalis loved it. Cost was the only constraint.

"When will I find myself back in Muktagacha?" he said in defense. "And we work hard. What is a little indulgence in monda?" He signaled the clerk and ordered more for Junaid, Jagdish and Smeeta, who protested, but barely so, before graciously accepting.

"And you," he said to Maartje while the clerk waited. "Another?"

Maartje sipped her tea and nodded. "Indeed," she said pensively, "when will we be back in Muktagacha?"

The group laughed, and in the fading sunlight, Rajiv felt more at ease, a feeling he had known among his medical school friends. It felt good. He had not realized, until just now, how stressful the recent formal dealings with so many new persons, one after another, had been. Everyone had been so guarded with one another.

Full of monda and tea, they piled into the Land Rover and headed for the forest. They drove forty-five minutes before turning onto a forest service road. Gewa, sal and banyan trees towered over them as they drove down the main road. Some were 100 feet high; most were two feet or more in diameter. The driver slowed, and as the passengers looked out the windows, a civet darted in front of them. Krystian opened his briefcase and fished out a set of binoculars. They were Swarovskis.

"Are you a bird watcher?" Jagdish asked.

Krystian grinned. "The most amateur kind. But I read up before coming here, and I thought if I were lucky I might see one of the owls the forest is known for, maybe a dusky owl, or if I'm lucky, a brown woody."

The Land Rover rattled from every door, window and body joint as Jagdish drove deeper into the forest. Conversation was difficult with the road noise. The road, however, was well maintained, packed gravel and they made good time. An hour later, they pulled into a camp site. Limited camping was allowed in the forest, although be-cause they had come during the week, it felt as though they had the place to themselves.

They got out. Jagdish became the tour guide, walking them down a short path.

Rajiv smiled as a movement overhead caused Maartje to start and Krystian to swing his binoculars up to his eyes. He glanced upward and saw a langur—a bushy-tailed monkey. The animal peered down on them as if he were the tourist and they, the oddity. Interesting perspective.

"The forest is home to a variety of wildlife," Jagdish said. "As you've already noted," he nodded to Krystian, "there are several owls here. We will probably also see rhesus monkeys. That fellow up there," he pointed at their gawker, "is a golden-capped langur."

"Are there tigers here?" Maartje asked.

Jagdish shook his head. "Once there were thousands, but they've been hunted out of central Bangladesh. I understand you're headed to the Sundarbans next. If luck is with you, you will see one of the remaining 300 down there."

Suddenly, a chattering filled the air, and the trees exploded with movement.

"The welcoming committee," Jagdish said. "A colony of rhesus monkeys."

They continued walking and came to a swamp that was now dry, since the monsoon had come and gone. The overgrown meadow was bathed in early afternoon sunlight. Compared to the relative quiet of the forest, it was abuzz with butterflies, insects and songbirds. Maartje's face lit up. Krystian's binoculars were glued to the bridge of his nose.

"Their songs are beautiful," Maartje said. Rajiv smiled as he watched her smiling face light up over his country's birds.

"A black vested swiftlet," Jagdish said, pointing out for Krystian. "Over there, we have a Swinhoe's minivet. And a petrel, I believe," he said, squinting.

"These wetlands are the ecological sponges we spoke of," Junaid said. "While Bangladesh has probably been prone to flooding since the beginning of time, the severity of the floods is increasing." He went on to explain this was due to diminishment of wetlands. "Wetlands, properly respected, serve as major flood control functions and storm surge buffers. If politicians would only listen, wetlands are nature's original zoning. Wetlands are places where development should not take place, since vegetation, soil composition and water levels declare that, by nature, they are prone to high water overflow. Second, wetlands are containment systems for seasonal heavy rains. Much wetland vegetation shares attributes of desert succulents; plants go dormant during dry seasons, but green up rapidly as water arrives. These 'floating meadows' possess a capacity to absorb and hold millions of gallons of water, which they then release gradually over the dry months. In the Florida Everglades, after the Corps of Engineers helped kill it with levees, the water could only flow into the rivers."

"In the Netherlands, we've also discovered the folly of emptying wetlands," Krystian said reluctantly, surrendering his binoculars for a few moments. "First we built dikes to keep water out, but as we claimed more and more land from the sea, the water continued to creep up from below. We installed pumps to carry the water over the dikes. But when aquifer water is used for consumption, caverns open up far beneath the surface. As the land dried, construction began. People built homes, farms and whole towns on top of the former wetlands. It was such a crushing weight that over the last two hundred years, the land gradually sank. Much of the Netherlands was once *at* sea level. Now, a growing portion is *below* sea level as the polders continue to sink. Some hydrologists believe the Pudong area on the Huang Po river in Shanghai, China, is experiencing the same effect. We've actually increased the potential for disaster. Now, if one of our sea containment systems fails—a dike, a sea wall—the floodwater will rush in even faster and create immense inland lakes."

"With all those homes and towns at the bottom of the lake," Junaid said.

"Yes," Krystian said. "Wetlands maintain a balance between aquifers below and land above."

"They serve yet another function," Maartje interjected mischievously. She twirled in her fingers a small flower she picked from a bush. "They draw tourists, and money and folks with birding binoculars like Krystian's. This broadens the base of an economy beyond farming."

The group turned to listen. "This should be part of the strategy if a flood containment plan is to succeed in Bangladesh," she said. "You need economic reasoning to keep land out of production, and certainly to remove any from production. You have to convince officials that tourists will come here to see this." She gestured to the clearing and back to the forest. "And they will."

The problem, Smeeta explained, was that it took decades to convert even a small part of a national economy from agriculture to tourism. Asking for flood control monies before tourism could take root seemed a stretch. It was difficult to argue to a poor nation that it must be patient to see the results of investment. Bangla people had so many compelling "now" needs because nobody believed they would survive long enough to benefit from any long term rewards. Smeeta's insights were fairly astute, thought Krystian.

Krystian interjected. "What you're saying is true for traditional tourism, the easy, armchair sightseeing. But in the west, we're seeing a recent travel industry movement called eco-tourism, service tourism, where people come not only to see a unique landscape, but also to participate in rebuilding it. It is considered a form of "servant leadership." This is already happening in Costa Rica and Guatemala. Bangladesh has an advantage over neighboring countries in that it is relatively safe for foreign visitors to travel here. Yet it feels adventurous. Off the beaten path, so to speak."

"It's a little bit like Theophane, 'the religious tourist,'" Maartje said to Rajiv. "People come to sightsee, yes, but they also come to help. The model spreading across South America right now has drawn many people in their twenties, many of them fresh out of college, but now it is bringing retirees who bring interest. And something else, donatable funds. This broadens the support, and funding base."

Rajiv was beginning to see where this was going. Once again, he was being educated. More importantly, Maartje was exuding a charm which eased his learning.

"Eco-tourists often support places they've visited long after they return home and so do their children," Maartje said. "Not always, but many become continuous fundraisers for these fragile systems. At the very least, they spread awareness. Such caring is powerful. It is spiritual."

Jagdish steered them back to the wooded path and in twenty minutes they were back at the Land Rover. He had brought a light camper's lunch—stir fry vegetables, naan breads, fruit and a dried sweet-sour pork soup—and he expertly prepared the dishes over a gas fired cook stove at the camp site. They ate with gusto. Each held an elegant square rosewood plate with steamed, fluted rims. Everyone chattered like the monkeys they had met. Smeeta and Maartje's cheeks were flushed, and they tucked back wisps of hair into their braids. Krystian scanned the trees. A birder is always a birder.

"It's a small part of the overall puzzle, but it was the support we spoke of in the Netherlands," Krystian said. "You must gather support from every possible corner to optimize your chances for success. As with all things, it's better to see for yourself. Smeeta observed that there was an organization already working in Bangladesh. It was on the edge of the Madhupur Preserve."

Jagdish nodded, his eyes dancing. "Yes. A European-based group, and I must say, I was skeptical at first. But I've been very impressed with their progress. You'll see. But we must hurry. We are nearing the end of their work day."

He cleaned up the lunch materials with Maartje's help. They loaded back into the Land Rover and drove out to the main road where he took yet another service road, but this time one that was pitted with washboards and potholes. "Hang on," Jagdish stuttered. Rajiv suddenly understood the need for the 4 x 4 vehicle. Thirty teeth-jarring minutes later, they came over a rise and saw the bank of a small stream in the midst of a slash and burn clearing. Several dozen children and what looked like college students were working with forestry workers along the stream bank. They were broken into pods, a cluster of children in colorful clothing assigned to each student, backs bent over the soil. From a distance, they made a moving, changing collage.

"They look like a Seurat painting," Maartje commented. "Dabs of color against the gray-brown mud of the bank."

"Their work is even more beautiful," Jagdish said. He put the Land Rover into gear and drove closer to the work site. They got out and stretched their legs before approaching the workers. Close up, Rajiv saw that each pod was furiously planting shrubs and grasses along the stream banks. Their hands and arms were muddy all the way up to their elbows. Sludge encased their feet like boots.

"This is the way this particular enterprise works," Jagdish explained, "Students—from American and European schools—are required to pay their own way, and, they also have to find funding for the plants they intend to reintroduce to the recovery area. Some earn college credit for their work. They work with a forester to devise a plan in keeping with the natural vegetation of the area. This area had been legally cleared and burned by a neighboring farmer, sadly one of many, but these philanthropic service groups helped the Forestry Ministry return it to a natural state."

"How long would it take them to do this area?" Maartje asked.

Against the treeline were rows of tents where the students and children apparently bunked overnight. Rajiv could see local women wearing bright-colored saris hovering near the tents, minding various fires. A veritable construction "company town" traveled with them as they worked from sunup to sundown.

"We've found that with the aid of the children, they can replant about 25-30 hectares in a month," Jagdish said. "For that reason, many students gather additional funding to hire area children and also some mothers, who prepare meals and mind the children. The students make their work a cross-disciplinary project drawing on economics, plant biology, and forestry, all related to the idea of servant leadership."

"Twenty-five hectares a month," Krystian said. He was thinking.

Jagdish offered the more upbeat assessment that progress at any pace was only good. In Bangladesh, high precipitation and temperature allow replanted vegetation to root quickly, and in fact, the banyan tree had been a reliable resource except in urban areas. There its strong roots spread so rapidly it could destroy modest buildings in a few years. Bad news for building caretakers, but good news for forest caretakers. He looked toward the sky. "We must be heading back now."

It was 6:00 p.m. The light was beginning to fade, the temperature was dropping. It would be dark in another hour. Rajiv took a final glance back at the clearing. The students, forestry workers and children were finishing for the day and walking toward their tent city. Their banter echoed against the forest walls. He tried to picture the clearing overgrown with lush grasses and bushes. He closed his eyes. It was not so difficult to imagine. An idea was taking shape. Actually, the very barest bones of one. These students and the local children were painting a picture before his eyes.

After a decent night's sleep and a good western breakfast, the helicopter wash buffeted the canopy of trees and the water as they came into the Dhangmari Forestry Station in the center of the Sundarbans. Here the buildings were on stilts, and the helicopter pad was on a portion of ground built up somewhat like a dike, but supported with gravel and hard-packed mud.

There were no permanent villages in the park. But from the air, they spotted occasional (there used to be many more) government timber camps. They were also on stilts or platforms built in the trees. The forestry camps were particularly interesting. From the air, they could see cutters (*bawalis*) cutting with axe-like hand tools and, a few chain saws. The ground was too spongy for bulldozers and heavy machinery. This made forestry manpower-dependent. The Sundari trees for which the park was named were prized for lumber. The trees grew to about 80-100 feet, were fairly straight and had few branches. When submerged, the lumber was immune to air-borne vermin and became rock hard, valuable in a water-logged country. Sundari trees made excellent lumber for building ships, electric poles, and materials for house foundations. Like the Madhupur preserve, the park was home to *gewa*, which produced useful planking.

There were also *pasurs* and *groans*. From the air, they could see one sad consequence of the harvesting. There were many large patches of mud, naked except for stumps.

When they landed at the station, they met another forestry official, Nafis Ahmad, who, like Jagdish, wore the usual forestry uniform of khaki shorts, shirt and boots, but he was clean shaven. Instead of a turban, he wore a baseball cap. Where Jagdish was reserved except for his eyes and spoke in moderate tones, Nafis was animated. Rajiv guessed that he received part of his education outside Bangladesh. His English was far too good for any other conclusion.

As they stepped from the helicopter pad, they discovered the ground was treacherous. Maartje slipped. Rajiv caught her elbow just in time to save her falling into the muck. The gray earth was shiny and the muck was everywhere. My goodness, he thought, her skin feels really tender to the touch. He wasn't expecting this.

"Ah, please. Watch your step," Nafis warned. "The entire floor of the camp is barely above water. We live in and just above the mud."

They climbed the stairs to a forestry office dominated by wall maps. It was a wood frame building painted a serviceable yellow brown, about 600 feet square with three ceiling fans. On the maps, the amount of blue told much of the preserve's story. About half of the region was covered with water, river channels, canals and tidal creeks varying in width from a few meters to almost a mile, significantly more than the Netherlands canals (grachten), thought Krystian.

"These are dry season maps," Nafis said. "In spring, even more land is submerged by tides, perhaps 50 percent more." He put his finger on the map marking the station and traced the Sibsa River south. "You can see the best way through the Sundarbans is by water. This will be our highway today. We should see a great deal before sundown." His finger stopped at what appeared to be a fork in the river, but was really an unnamed tributary snaking through the Sundarbans. "Here I'll take you inland. If we get off the main channel, we are likely to see more wildlife."

He ushered them to a dock where two aluminum motorboats awaited, along with several dozen wood rowboats and attendants awaiting passengers. "The shoreline is difficult to navigate on foot because the mud is very slippery, as you've already discovered. This station marks the farthest point into the park for roads, so tourists make it here by bus, then hire a tour guide."

Maartje and Krystian, complete with his binoculars, looked every inch the ecotourists. And, in a sense, they were. Like Nafis, they wore khaki sports clothing. Maartje's brown cotton fedora was rimmed with ultra fine green nylon netting fastened to the brim with Velcro—mosquito netting she could lower when needed. Junaid and Rajiv had opted for T-shirts and light-weight long pants. Smeeta's traditional sari was the most practical. The light fabric skirt was cool, yet afforded protection from mosquitoes. The scarf around her shoulders also doubled as insect wear, if needed.

"Is tourism significant in the Sundarbans?" Maartje asked.

Interest in the Sundarbans was high, Nafis explained. Traffic was more pronounced here than in other Bengali parks, perhaps because wildlife was more abundant here. Tourists came to see Bengal tigers and also the birds Krystian has been sighting.

"And some tour guides are not reputable," Nafis said. "We have reports of some conducting hunting excursions. Many do not bag trash and human waste created in a day tour, and even more so in an overnight stay. They simply dump it into the water."

Accommodations were typically unclean, mosquito-ridden and poorly maintained. Most tour operators kept guests on pontoon boats for overnight stays. The few land facilities available were government-owned and in poor repair. Poorly paid employees expected bribes. Political turmoil in Bangladesh had not led to quality in guesthouses, Nafis said. There were also other hazards. Pirates were a real factor in the Sundarbans.

"Pirates?" Maartje said with surprise.

Nafis waved his hands. "Where there is poverty and isolation, we have pirates. Dacoits. They avoid boats where they see uniforms and armed personnel." He reached down and patted his Austrian-made Mannlicher. "We will be safe."

As they stepped into the boat, Rajiv asked about the lumber camps.

"Controlled logging is part of forestry management everywhere," Nafis said. "But even more crucial, native lumber is in extremely short supply. Lumber is very expensive to import. Imagine the cost of building if every beam came from abroad. Our economy desperately needs revenue from lumber. We carefully select the areas where logging is allowed, and the camps are run by the government. The logging areas are spaced to lessen impact on wildlife. It is an imperfect system but we live with it."

"Other countries offer inducements to forest preservation," he said. "The United States recently canceled a portion of Bangladesh's debt and allowed future interest payments to be shunted to a fund that supports only forest conservation efforts, so there is hope," he said. Rajiv was already feeling better about the Finnish Deal not because growing and slash cutting pulpwood was inspiring. He realized that he was part of a bigger concept and the Finns were leading him to it. Must be the vodka, he smiled to himself.

Nafis chattered happily as he steered the motorboat into the main channel. True to reputation, the Sundarbans were rich in scenery and wildlife, much of which seemed undisturbed. Within minutes of leaving the station they saw spotted deer drinking at the water's edge. The park was home to 30,000 of the delicate animals, Nafis said. Their antlers were felted. As the deer stepped gingerly back into the trees, a group of monkeys appeared, dropping keora leaves.

Maartje laughed. "What are they? Another welcoming committee?"

"Yes," Nafis joked back. "We don't know what inspires the behavior, but the monkeys follow the deer. They throw the leaves on the ground around the deer. My theory is that the monkeys hope to preen the deer—gather insects and parasites from them—and the leaves are an incentive to have the deer stop."

Krystian was in bird watcher heaven. The binoculars became his eyes, the Czech lenses the ultimate in clarity. The park was home to 300 species, and Krystian spent the better part of the tour calling out specimens.

"That is a snipe. There, a crane of some sort."

Nafis directed their attention overhead. "An eagle."

They passed by a white and gold heron, but a smaller bird with bright yellow and red plumage caught Maartje's attention. "He looks so sad."

Nafis squinted to where she pointed. "Ah yes, a madan-tak. They always look dejected."

By day's end, Krystian would be more than delighted. He'd added almost forty different species to his birder's list.

After an hour, Nafis pulled the boat through the silt laden water onto a mucky spit of sand point broken up by small clumps of Saccharum grass. "I think we have a story here," he said.

They got out, taking care not to slip on the greasy sludge from silt. The shore glistened, as if covered in slime.

Nafis instructed them to stand back while he studied the scene. He threaded his way through mud containing hoofprints. Then he smiled. "Yes, a good story, better than I thought." He waved them closer.

"First, there was a casual gathering. Perhaps the chital were coming to feed," he gestured toward the grass. "All was going well, until an intruder appeared." He walked toward a place where the grass met with the treeline. Rajiv saw giant paw prints, and a depression in the mud where something big had waited, hidden partly by grass.

"He was a very patient intruder," Nafis said. "He watched and waited for some time. Then his trap snapped shut." Nafis took five steps further into the grass where there was a smattering of blood and signs of a struggle. Around the crime scene, other hoof prints were dug in deeper. All but the victim had scattered. Nafis followed a few light drag marks, then went back to the treeline and fingered a bloody leaf on a shrub. "Then, the intruder decided to dine in private."

He looked at Rajiv and grinned. "We see evidence of tigers far more often than we see tigers. They take their kill into the brush, where they can't be seen by any river traffic, and the tides won't float it away."

Maartje and Krystian were mesmerized.

"When do you think he was here?" Krystian asked.

"Not long ago," Nafis answered. "The tide comes in every six to eight hours and wipes the slate clean."

Junaid and Smeeta were not as captivated as the Netherlands team. Junaid seemed to sweat more profusely. Smeeta pulled her sari tightly around her, as if it would ward off a tiger.

"We should go," Nafis said.

They continued downriver, where they encountered tour boats and fishing trawlers—large boats with thatched roofs and cabins. "Sea gypsies," Nafis said. The group had arrived just before the beginning of the larger fishing season, during which thousands of fishermen from Chittagong converged on Dublar island at the southern edge of the Sundarbans to net schools of shrimp moving through. Fishing in the preserve was legal, and the bounty supported hundreds of thousands, perhaps millions of people. A pair of otters sat on the deck of one trawler. Some families used trained otters to chase fish downstream from small creeks and tributaries into waiting nets, Nafis explained.

Hunting, however, was illegal in the preserve, although the well-connected and wealthy routinely circumvented the law. Despite his upbeat nature, Nafis could not hide his contempt. "It is one thing to poach for food, another to poach for sport. The privileged should protect our treasures, not plunder them."

As promised when they started out, ninety minutes into the trip, he turned up a small tributary. Compared to traffic on the main branch of the Sibsa, the backwater stream was secluded and enchanted. Out of the current, Nafis killed the engine and turned to his oars to maneuver the boat. The sounds of the jungle enveloped them. Birds and monkeys chattered away at them. No one said a word.

As they rounded a bend in the waterway, they could see something swimming in the water about 200 yards away.

"Ah, it is a lucky day," Nafis whispered.

They quietly drifted closer to the animal, who noted their appearance, but he did not seem overly troubled. His head was a light golden color with white accent. He moved against the current with force, leaving a small V-shaped wake behind him. He was a powerful swimmer, crossing the wide channel quickly. They watched him climb onto shore, and realized with a shock that he was an almost entirely white tiger.

"A triple lucky day—a white," Nafis interjected. "They used to be found in Siberia and Thailand, but hunting and poaching by the aphrodisiac trade took a huge toll." He reached into the breast pocket of his shirt, took out a small notebook and began scribbling notes. "A male. Three or four years old. Healthy. Yes. We've seen this fellow before."

The tiger shook himself vigorously, and turned, almost as if he were strutting before an audience. He stretched almost ten feet long from his massive head to the tip of his tail. He perhaps weighed 500 pounds. He turned toward the boat and leveled a yellow glare at its passengers. His tail twitched. Krystian and Maartje were captivated; Krystian was glued to his binoculars. Rajiv saw goose bumps on Maartje's arms, reminding him of the Indian and Bengali legends of the animal's hypnotic powers. Junaid and Smeeta looked stricken. The color drained from Smeeta's face. Her hands gripped the side of the boat, and her knuckles were white.

"My trip is complete," Krystian said. "I knew they were here. But I never thought we'd get to see one."

"My God," Maartje whispered. "What a magnificent animal!"

The tiger's ears perked at the sound of their voices, and his tail twitched. Then, implausibly, he waded back into the water and swam toward them.

"Time to go," Nafis said. With a quick pull of the start cord, the engine sputtered, and they were again moving. This did not deter the pursuer. The small boat moved down the creek, and the tiger followed, about 75 yards back at first, but gaining. Rajiv was suddenly aware how overloaded the boat was for its small engine. Their pace was agonizingly slow. He stole a glance at the Dutch team, and realized they were oblivious to what was happening. Krystian had pulled out his camera and was zooming in for a shot. Maartje had taken his binoculars and was watching the animal advance—and she was smiling. Nafis was concerned. His expression turned grim. Circles of sweat beneath his arms had grown, and it was clear he no longer considered the day lucky.

"Does anyone else know how to operate a boat?" Nafis asked.

"I do," Maartje said, not putting down the binoculars.

"Come take over," Nafis said. "Now."

Maartje looked at him, puzzled at his tone, but she carefully stepped to the rear of the boat, keeping toward the center. It was clear she understood the tippiness of smaller boats. Nafis turned over the tiller handle, telling her to keep it at full throttle and to watch for floating debris in the water. "It would be bad to hit a log just now," he said.

He reached down for his rifle and brought the butt up to rest on his hip, all the while watching the tiger, who was now barely 50 yards from the stern of the boat.

"You're not going to shoot him," Maartje protested.

Nafis did not answer, as he raised the rifle to his shoulder, aimed well over the tiger, and fired. The effect was not immediate, but the tiger paused, as if he were weighing his options. Nafis fired again. The tiger swerved off course, cut a wide turn in the water, and swam toward the muddy bank. Maartje eased off the throttle.

"Do not cut the engine!" Nafis barked.

When the animal's feet touched bottom, he took one violent leap, and the grassy shrubs swallowed him up. Except for the motor, the boat was deathly quiet.

"The tide is coming in," Nafis said. "That's better for us."

"I felt almost as if we were his prey," Maartje said.

Nafis had not stopped scanning the shoreline. "We were," he said.

They went back to the station without delay. No one spoke. Each was lost in thought. All eyes were riveted on the overhanging trees, now aware the very thing they were looking for could see their every move and knew exactly where they were. The coolness of the coming evening descended on the water, and they wrapped their arms around themselves for warmth. Occasionally long shadows fell over the water, and the fading light created such reflections that it was difficult to tell where water stopped and shore started. Rajiv looked at Maartje and Krystian, whose eyes were on the shoreline. Like most Bengalis, Rajiv had been raised to respect tigers, and to fear them. He watched the muddy jungle. He saw no tigers, but knew they were there.

Once at the station, Nafis directed them over suspended walkways to the guesthouse so they could clean up and change clothes before dinner. As Rajiv had observed, the guesthouse was marginal. The beds were military cots topped with sleeping bags of government-issue green. They were clean, but worn. Heavy mosquito netting hung over each cot. The windows were screened, and protected by heavy bars. The men were assigned to one room, Smeeta and Maartje to another.

Junaid and Krystian went to freshen up while Rajiv strolled out onto the deck where Maartje was already waiting. The night was growing cooler. The tide was rising. It already reached the bottom steps of some buildings, and the floating docks had all risen a good two feet. The tides rose one meter every seven to eight hours, giving the forest an ever-changing face. As the water kept coming, the forest appeared to float. Tree trunks disappeared into the river, which overflowed its banks and claimed the jungle.

"Smeeta is quite shaken," Maartje said. "She can't wait to leave the Sundarbans. I wonder how real our danger was."

Rajiv was more taken by Maartje's delicate feminine scent.

Across the way, they saw Nafis on the upper deck of the main building, speaking with another forestry official. From their serious expressions, Rajiv saw they were discussing the tiger. When he saw them, Nafis' expression lightened. He waved and began making his way toward them across a suspended walkway.

"Dinner is just about ready. Shall we?" He ushered them back the way he had come.

"What happened today…?" Maartje opened.

"Yes, I'm sure you have many questions," Nafis answered. They reached the dining hall, where some forestry workers were finishing their meal. "We can talk, at dinner, about the subject of being dinner." He grinned and directed them to a table laid out with serving dishes, more beautiful rosewood plates and platters. Junaid and Smeeta soon joined them, and dug into their meal. Rajiv had not realized how hungry he was until the first spoonful of an excellent fish soup crossed his lips. He looked up and saw he was not the only one who was ravenous.

"So," Nafis said after a few minutes. "You've only been in the Sundarbans for a day, but what do you think?"

"I think I discovered how sheltered my life has been," Maartje said. The group laughed.

"I was watching the expressions of our little group as the tiger came in and out of view," Rajiv said. He turned to Maartje. "You were not afraid. Why?"

Maartje shook her head. "Because we were in the boat, which gave us some protection."

"They can tip small vessels like ours," Smeeta said quietly. "They are powerful swimmers."

Maartje turned to Nafis for confirmation.

He nodded. "They will even board launches with housing."

"I read that tigers in the wild rarely attack humans, unless they are old or sick," Krystian said.

"Except in the Sundarbans," Nafis said, pausing between spoonfuls of dahl. "Here, because of habitat and prey depletion, man has become a food source."

"An attack was actually possible?" a stiffer, worried Maartje asked. Rajiv could see and hear her concern.

"An attack was imminent. That tiger had chosen someone on our boat as his next meal," said Nafis carefully. "If you think about it, pound for pound, humans are easier food for a tiger than deer or boar. People don't have sharp tusks or hard antlers with points that slash and penetrate."

"But you had a rifle," Krystian said. "Surely…"

"A deterrent, yes. Some people believe tigers recognize a rifle, and choose unarmed victims, which most workers in the Sundarbans are. But my one rifle was of little protection. It's just a high powered BB gun. If he wanted one of us, he would have succeeded."

"Why here?" Krystian asked. "Why are the tigers man-eaters?"

Nafis shrugged. He explained. Sundarbans tigers had proven adaptable. Some believed the tigers developed a taste for human flesh during the cyclones and heavy flooding, when bodies floated down the rivers and into the Sundarbans. Or perhaps tigers associated humans with food by waiting near the nets of fishermen. According to another theory, brackish saltwater that the tigers drank damaged their livers over a lifetime, making them irritable and changing their normal habit of avoidance.

"How many people do they kill every year then?" Krystian asked.

Nafis hesitated. "Hard to say. Government officials believe that citizen villagers exaggerate the number. On the India part of the Sundarbans, people who lost families members to tigers were compensated for their loss. But deaths were underreported among the transient poor who worked in the Sundarbans. Those people did not report when family members were killed out of fear that they, too, could be punished for being in the wrong place at the wrong time. Officially, between 40 and 60 people are killed by tigers on both Indian and Bangladesh sides each year. Unofficially, we don't know. Some put the number as high as 300 a year." Nafis told of one researcher who calculated that given their population in the Sundarbans, if man constituted a staple of the tiger's diet, the human death toll would top 20,000 a year. Even park officials had trouble separating reputation and myth from reality.

"Villagers mistrust all tigers, so they report every single tiger, whether threatening or not. This makes it difficult for the rangers. The rangers simply ignore such routinely overstated reports.

"More often and even worse, villagers simply take matters into their own hands. Last week, a group of villagers attacked a young male, trapping it with fishnets and clubbing it to death. Upon investigation, we discovered he had not attacked anyone. His 'crime' was venturing too close to where they were cutting wood. Illegally, I might add. It's an endless and serious problem."

"What does the government do when this happens?" Maartje asked. "When people kill the tigers illegally?"

"If poaching, they are prosecuted. But you can't arrest an entire village because they are afraid. Fear is the tiger's real enemy in Bangladesh," Nafis said. "That is why when I see one, I pronounce it a harbinger of luck. If enough people believe it is luck when they see one, we change the perception of fear. This is not to understate the danger. Tigers are predators."

In particular jeopardy were *maualis* (Mow-Lees), the honey gatherers who pile into western regions of the forest in April and May to gather maua, a spicy honey known for its healing powers. Bees in the Sundarbans produce a half million pounds of honey a year. The maualis were mostly poor day laborers. They worked in small groups from dawn to dusk, finding hives by following bees.

"In their hurry to find honey, some are careless about watching for tigers, or remembering to make enough noise to scare them off. Instead, they run through the brush, which mimics the noise of a deer or boar running. And, they carry no protection. Tigers always attack from the rear, and they crush a man's head in a microsecond." Clearly, Nafis knew the reality.

"They kill by severing the spinal cord," Rajiv interjected. "Death is instantaneous. But they eat the belly first, since it is the largest nutrient source. They will return to the kill later for the rest of...." He looked up from his plate and noticed that Smeeta and Junaid had stopped eating. Perhaps the clinical side of the tiger's diet was not a proper dinner topic. He masked a smile, but let his sentence go unfinished.

"When we are working on land, we sometimes wear iron masks that protect our head and necks, and in India the maualis do use them. The masks have proven quite effective," Nafis said matter-of-factly, making tigers sound about as dangerous as mosquitoes. "But honey farmers in Bangladesh historically do not use such gear, and the masks are heavy and hot. Mostly, they pray to Bonobibi, the forest goddess. Sometimes they place sweets on the ground as soon as they step ashore from their boats."

"Does that work?" Maartje said.

Rajiv tried to gauge her expression, and saw she was serious. He was impressed that she might believe in such a spirit. Angela had belonged to a dogmatic, bible-thumping church. This lady was quite different.

"Not always," Nafis said. "Honey farmers claim that five to ten people are eaten by tigers every year. But we have trouble tracking down either victims or survivors. 'Man-eater' remains a case of reputation exceeding fact," Nafis said. "In this case, reputation is not good for endangered tigers."

The tiger god was Daksin Ray. Some prayed to Daksin Ray as often as they did to Bonobibi. Villagers assigned all sorts of mythical attributes to tigers. Some believed tigers could fly, which Nafis believed came from a tiger's capability to leap 20 feet, even while carrying prey. But much of what people believed about the animals gave them an evil persona, and whenever an animal was deemed wicked, historically, its existence was threatened. People create justification for killing animals.

"We know this," Nafis said. "Tigers are smart. So far, tigers thwart every effort to minimalize problems."

He described measures, some of which drew smiles from his audience. In addition to the iron masks, there were plastic masks worn on the back of the head. Because they refused to attack from the front, one researcher had a village of more than 2,000 try wearing cheap plastic masks on the backs of their heads when they worked in the jungle. He went on to explain that the masks had worked, that is until the tigers figured them out. About five months after the experiment began, tigers had already learned to distinguish between "real" faces and fake ones. Attacks resumed. The forestry department even tried building freshwater ponds deeper inside the park, thinking that with a better water supply, they'd stay farther inland, where people weren't supposed to go. The tigers used the ponds, but they still drank brackish water from the rivers and canals.

Rangers also tried releasing more pigs into the park, trying to boost a natural food source. This really helped. Blazing ballpark lights stood in some villages at night around the park to keep the tigers out. Electric fencing surrounded much of the park.

"Fencing did not solve the problem. It kept tigers in the park. It didn't keep men out. People continued to put themselves in the tiger's path."

"What are the tiger numbers in Bangladesh?" Krystian asked.

"Other places," Nafis said, "tiger populations are actually growing. As recently as 1990, researchers predicted their extinction from the wild by now, but in many parts of Asia, they are coming back. We have about 3,000 tigers between all of India and Bangladesh—and about 275 to 300 in the Sundarbans on both sides—but these numbers are shrinking, not growing. Between here and India, there were as many as 80,000 just one hundred years ago."

Once upon a time, he said, a popular Indian saying held that two maharajahs could shoot 2,000 tigers in their lifetime. That was just for fun and to prove to their farm workers that they would be safe. Tigers were under pressure from a variety of factors. For one, there was simply the pressure of population on habitat. What was happening to the tiger paralleled the near extinction of wolves in Europe and North America. When the human population grows, other forms of life are squeezed out. Land and water can support only so much.

The problem, Nafis explained, lay in the tiger's prey. As population increased, the deer, wild boar and other small mammals the tigers had gobbled up "like hamburger" began to disappear. Deer and wild boar in particular became a popular supplement to diets of villagers. Deer were still plentiful in the Sundarbans, despite poaching, because there were few permanent settlements. Assuring a food supply allowed tigers to thrive.

Also in recent years, Nafis explained, population gains had been enhanced by species preservationists who took the ingenious step of pouring over ancient Chinese texts to find substitutes for tiger bone. One was bone meal from a rodent common in China. For the last decade, researchers and preservationists had publicized the substitute and its cost benefits among practitioners. To a degree, the strategy had worked.

They finished dinner. Nafis and Krystian pulled out cigarettes and began smoking. The windows were open and a breeze swept through the room. Rajiv found himself relaxing and he accepted a cigarette from Nafis. The day had been adventurous, but somehow, he felt as though he were on vacation. He could see why tourists flocked to the Sundarbans. This was a world apart from daily living. Away from his normal rounds, he was rediscovering part of his old student self, and feeling the excitement of discovery. His work was rewarding, but also draining. He wondered if he'd become interested in flood control out of a public health concern or because he was running from the futility of his work.

Relatively speaking, the Sundarbans appeared to be in better shape than most other Bangladesh parks, Maartje observed. With the exception of permitted logging, the deforestation was far less than Madhupur.

"Make no mistake, the Sundarbans are shrinking, just more slowly than anywhere else in Bangladesh," Nafis said. "That's due in part to the seasonal flooding. The land cannot be cultivated. And the tiger actually protects the Sundarbans. He is the guardian of its soul. People fear and worship him. This helps the tiger population."

"You know, the Sundarbans play a more fundamental role in our mission," Junaid said as they rose from the table. "May we go back to the map room?"

They walked along the boardwalk to the main office, a stroll Rajiv found invigorating. A partial moon shone brightly on the water, interrupted by overhanging gewa, created a dappled brilliance that played hide and seek with them as they walked. The forest quiet was broken by the hum of generators lighting the camp and nighttime insects waking up. The lights from the maintenance buildings drew moths, mosquitoes and gnats, which batted against the screens. The women covered their hair with their scarves. Rajiv thought Maartje looked terrific in such a scarf. Maartje, on the other hand, was thinking Rajiv was pretty neat in shorts and a jungle shirt.

Junaid and Smeeta were not very relaxed as they watched the treeline.

"Interestingly, tigers avoid villages, and of course, our camp," Nafis said. "Hunting is a matter of knowing the odds, and tigers know the odds are better on their own turf."

Junaid did not relax until they reached the main office, lit by the glow of a single light bulb hanging from the ceiling. Once inside, he immediately focused on the map.

"The Sundarbans provide important protection from cyclones for the more populated inland areas," he said.

Junaid explained. The Sundarbans were critical storm buffers in Bangladesh, and India because the mangroves absorb and dampen much of a storm's power. Also, important was the climatic effect created by the mass of vegetation and water. A blanket of cool air suspended over the water, surrounded by warmer air over land bordering the forest, channeled a cyclone's force into the park, where estuaries and trees dampened the wind. Junaid traced the east and west edges of the park on the map with his hands, showing a V open at the Bay of Bengal and closing inland.

"You mean the Sundarbans influence cyclones?" Krystian queried.

"Yes. Studies suggest that as the Sundarbans shrink, cyclones increase in intensity," Junaid said.

"A cycle exists here," Junaid said, "which is being ignored. From the beginning, we've talked in terms of flood walls and gates as you have in the Netherlands. These would be welcome. But the Sundarbans offer a natural flood wall capable of buffering half of Bangladesh and much of India during monsoon. As we chip away at it, we deconstruct the very protection we require."

A new thought came to Rajiv. "This plays into the integration of missions you spoke of in the Netherlands." He turned toward Maartje and Krystian. "If I recall correctly, your storm surge barrier project required a marriage of interests. Perhaps preservation of the tiger, preservation of the Sundarbans, and flood control might be related."

"Well put. Do not forget economics," Maartje smiled. "Any plan must improve economics for the villagers. There must be incentives. Without other means to sustain themselves, villagers will continue extracting firewood and eroding the entire area. That's a given. But the edges of the Sundarbans might be a good fit for fish farming. We're trying to encourage it in the Netherlands. It uses an existing water environment, and does not require using precious land. Some actually create fish 'beds' in existing bays or inlets. Why not create more formal fish farms and re-train traditional farmers to raise fish this way?"

Junaid and Smeeta looked doubtful. Cooperation between agencies to such a degree was rare in Bangladesh. But Rajiv was in a hopeful mood. He was tired of abandoning idea after idea because of bureaucratic turf issues. Let someone else be the nay sayer for once. Maartje looked to him to see what he thought.

"And perhaps our man-eaters could become, as they say in the West, man's best friend," Rajiv said.

Maartje looked at him with puzzled interest.

"I don't have a firm idea yet, but I think I can put together something we can take to Dhaka to show our politicians there." He laughed. "Maybe Daksin Ray is speaking to us." And he glanced over his shoulder toward the forest, as if for affirmation.

CHAPTER 14

The First Light
of a New Dawn

Rajiv's sleeping bag was damp when he awoke just before dawn. He dressed quietly, not wanting to wake Junaid or Krystian, and slipped out of the room.

A morning mist hovered over the water. So thick that it obscured the few shrubs on the banks, and most of the camp. The camp was eerily quiet. From the deck, Rajiv could see a faint light from the dining room. He stood there for several long moments enjoying the silence. He'd slept soundly, exhausted by the previous day's excitement and activity, and they'd talked late into the night.

After the group went to bed last evening, Rajiv mulled over the tiger encounter. In the West, animals sparked more compassion than people. That world could ignore, had ignored, the tragic reality of scores of Bengalis dying in floods every year. But when tiger habitat was threatened, an international symphony of outcry ensued. When he was in the United States, he'd marveled at the outrage ignited over abuse of pets. He'd even read of a group in Hawaii which raised $50,000 to rescue a dog by helicopter from an oil tanker abandoned and on fire. A single dog. The tiger could become an ally here, particularly given the role the Sundarbans play in cyclone control.

Could they be made into project mascots? He wanted to talk to Pog about this.

Thoughts like this were ephemeral. Maybe one strong wind could blow it all away. It could be the next monsoon. More likely, it would come from Dhaka. He looked out at the fog. The Dutch system of integrated flood control made very sound sense—in developed parts of the world. But in Bangladesh, politicians still favored capital-intense micro—not macro—projects. Such was the irony in a poor nation. But projects vested in heavy construction had many political advantages. If they got off the ground at all, they were often funded from international sources, bringing in cash. And they provided, for the press, images of a government doing something for its people. Preserving wetlands was perceived as doing nothing. Preservation of wildlife was a luxury in poor nations. Conservation efforts were far more popular in wealthy nations. When survival for the largest segments of its population was no longer an issue, a country then could turn its attention to the land or wildlife.

Until then, it was a tough sales job convincing impoverished people and their elected representatives of a vital link between economic security, protecting ecology and the environment. Advanced nations polluted at will long after they industrialized. He imagined presenting to Senator Mukherjee an idea involving ecology and using tigers as poster children to gather support. The Senator might enjoy nothing more than a good laugh. Rajiv was uneasy and he pondered how this could be presented.

Soon, Maartje and Krystian would be going back to the Netherlands. Krystian had to leave a day earlier than Maartje because of commitments back in Delft. Back home they would assess the material from their trip, look at previous studies, the soil and water samples, the geological surveys they collected, then try to connect the sciences of economics and water. And politics. The latter perhaps more important than any other.

He needed tea. He walked toward the dining hall light and nearly stumbled over Maartje.

"You startled me."

"I'm sorry," Rajiv said.

She looked a little frightened, and Rajiv smiled. Maybe she was beginning to respect Daksin Ray after all. She had not expected to find anyone up yet. Her brown hair fell in waves on her shoulders, not yet braided for travel or work, and her face was bare of make up. She was dressed in Western-style camping clothes, jeans, pastel plaid cotton blouse, minus hiking boots. She wore instead woven sandals like those sold at street stands throughout Bangladesh. She had beautiful feet.

"An early riser too?" he asked.

"Sunrise is the best part of the day," she said. "It's a daily affirmation of our hopes. A visible manifestation of promise. Don't you think?"

Rajiv nodded in agreement. "It's also the time of day when your thoughts are clear and the world hasn't bombarded you yet."

"I like that," he said. "I was heading over to the hall to see if anyone made tea. Join me?"

She nodded, and they began walking across one of the boardwalks. They strolled together, comfortably and closely.

"You head back in two days," he said. "Would you have time to meet with Mukherjee, if I can arrange it?"

"I think that would be good. We need to acquire a better sense of where he stands before we proceed much further. What do you think our prospects are?"

"Frankly, not good." And he began to pour out the obstacles they faced in such a nontraditional project for Bangladesh. "People here believe in bricks, piles of dirt and mortar, not heady, strategically planned, macro concepts."

"Even if bricks, mortar and dirt don't work?"

He shrugged. "Could you persuade your people back home they'd be better off without those flood gates on the New Waterway?"

"Touché."

They walked in silence for a moment. The mist around them created feelings of privacy and attachment. The others were sleeping, but these two could have been on another continent. It was a moment of easy, unscheduled intimacy. Each was privately feeling comfortable from this closeness.

"How is it you became an engineer?" he asked.

"My father was a civil engineer," she said. "From the time I could walk, he took me on construction sites all over Europe. My mother, my brothers and I would visit him when he was working away from home, and he always showed me bridges, tunnels and roads he was building and explained how the project was engineered. Once he took me through the fantastic construction displays at a German museum near the Isar Tor in Munich. As I became older, he explained, in more detail, the science of his profession. He never assumed I wouldn't understand. So I grew up with the language and the milieu of engineers. Now he has retired back to our family farm. And guess what, I am the family engineer."

"And of course, in the Netherlands, the Royal Water Service is a major employer. I chose hydrological engineering because I love water," she said, "and this lets me work with rivers, oceans and even the rain. As you learned from your first visit, we hold the patent on rain in the Netherlands except for your world during monsoon. Of course, then I spend time at a computer or at my desk poring over technical details, maps. But I get to spend part of my year on the water. Water is magic. I love to sailboard and swim."

"Interesting choice of words," Rajiv mused. "We're spending so much time fighting the same water that enchants you."

"Our work is really about recognizing and accepting the power of the water," she said, "including its mysteries, and, yes, its spiritual qualities."

Rajiv's eyebrows shot up. "Spiritual?"

She laughed. "I don't get much support from other hydrologists on this. But yes. Every religion reserves a sacred place in its theology for water. Baptism, Creation, all of that."

"So a quest for the divine drew you to hydrology."

"I prefer the word 'magic.'"

"And what about a family?" he asked. "Where does that fit in your plans?"

She smiled softly and warmly. "I would like very much to be married and have children some day. As advanced as the Netherlands is socially, some things are the same the world around. When I have children, I will miss assignments like this one. For now, this is what I live for. And this includes meeting people like you." They looked at each other, quite comfortably for a long time. And in these moments, it seemed an emotional blacksmith was at work gently hammering out a product from their separate metals. Each knew something was going on but did not realize the affect on the other.

They could hear the sounds of the river and wildlife, the slapping of water against the sides of the boats, the quieter sounds of trickling and lapping as the water made its way to the Bay of Bengal.

"And if I'm not mistaken, your mother is plotting a wife for you," she said. "Isn't that the usual—after the education, the Indian or Bengali son is expected to take a wife? I assume parents still arrange marriages here?"

He heard the gentle teasing in her voice and smiled a huge smile. "My mother despairs of ever having grandchildren, at least from me. Yes, some families still pick spouses for their children. My mother regularly suggests I turn the matter over to her. Then I would be married with all due dispatch—and no fuss."

"You're not in the same hurry, I take it."

"What do I have to offer? My life is not conducive to being a marriage partner. At present, I have only a modest apartment, too modest for a wife and children." He looked at Maartje. "It's like your work. In a month, I may visit seven different villages or towns. I stay with whomever the village leaders choose for me." He thought of his obligations to his brothers and sister. Even when his tour of duty as health ministry physician was up, he had to help them through college. He explained the role of health ministry physicians and the funding for his education. In U.S. dollars, his pay averaged a little more than $200 a month—high by Bengali standards, but hardly comparable to even the tollway fees his med school associates were shelling out monthly.

"Of course, there's no comparing my work to that of my friends in the United States. Do you know how many patients I've lost during my first year here? My colleagues would be appalled."

Softly and carefully, she ventured, "I can see the brochure: 'Dr. Rajiv's clinics for volunteer physicians. Come for two weeks. Return for a lifetime.'"

He smiled.

"It is probably hard for Western doctors to comprehend living conditions in Bangladesh until they see for themselves. Do you keep in touch with your med school friends?"

"A few e-mails, but I'm often out in rural areas without access."

"You should invite them over. I bet they would jump at the chance."

"Do you think so?" He looked at her curiously. The thought had never occurred to him.

"Of course. It may take a little packaging. There is something enchanting about Bangladesh. It seems untamed, even in the heart of its most developed cities. People crave such places. Bangladesh is beautiful. I love it here."

He was struck by this.

"Funny. But people here want more of what developed countries have — clean water, good roads, good factory jobs, better health care — and they struggle to appreciate what we have, which is nothing. You seem to appreciate the beauty of nothing."

Maartje shook her head and smiled, "You mustn't be impatient. Perhaps medicine involves more immediate gratification than the projects we work on. You have to move quickly to be of any use, and a human life, after all, is relatively brief in the scheme of things."

"And how is this not so for engineers?"

"Practically everything we do involves studying the long-term impact of our 'science' on the world," she said. "Short term is ten years. We design for two hundred years."

He stopped walking and turned to stare at her. Such sanguinity about progress at a snail's pace was difficult to absorb. For him, a hundred years only translated into thousands of lives lost. And who knew what would become of the Sundarbans in one hundred years? How much would be left?

"I take it people in the Netherlands were impatient for change after the floods of 1953," he said.

"Of course. That's what people in the know said after a mere 1,800 people died. Progress will take time. We must be patient. But of course, people were impatient. Actually, they were frightened." Her eyes were bright, and she was annoyed. "But impatient or not, it took more than 30 years to complete the storm surge barriers, and we're still building as we arrive back at the conclusion we should have come to in the beginning: Societies should not create farms and cities in vital buffering wetlands."

She put her hand on his arm. He felt her soft touch and saw warmth in her large lips. "Your impatience serves a vital function. It gets people moving. It is one of your greatest strengths. Use it, yes." She lowered her voice, but her tone was pressing. "Approach this not only as a Bengali and human being, but as the scientist you are. If you don't, you'll burn out and give up. The cyclones are hardly new, but what's stalling progress here is the paradigm that these losses are inevitable. They are not." And her fingers dug into his forearm. In this moment their connection was more a touch of fusion.

They stood there a moment, and Rajiv felt his confusion easing. She was right. He smiled and placed his hand on top of hers, which still held onto his arm. "Tea. I'm ready for tea."

Rajiv's hand felt good, very good.

She smiled back. "Tea it is." The tea was good. The moment was precious.

They were in luck. A meeting with Mukherjee was possible in the mid-afternoon of the day before she left. Krystian had just departed for Calcutta and home. As with Rajiv, Mukherjee was a model of decorum, lavishing attention on Maartje. His questions were pointed, intelligent, informed and inferred genuine interest in their work. Once again, Rajiv found himself cautiously feeling hope. Maartje and he explained the direction of the plan, blending immediate conservation of vital wetlands, the Sundarbans and other fragile ecosystems on the Bay of Bengal, followed by flood control systems such as a series of sea walls along the Chittagong coast and flood gates on rivers leading from the bay to Dhaka and other inland cities. At Rajiv's suggestion, no mention of tigers was made. Rajiv wanted more time to develop this piece.

Senator Mukherjee sipped his tea and nodded appreciatively. "This is good news. All good news, for the long-term. And we have other good news." He did not mention that yesterday he'd been lambasted again in the press. "Parliament has decided to fund the extension of the dike system along the Chittagong coast, effective immediately."

"A dike system?" Maartje said.

"Yes, you have many such systems in the Netherlands, I believe."

"Yes, although dike systems are crude by today's standards, and they've proven utterly ineffective at stemming larger storms. And long-term, they're very costly to maintain."

Senator Mukherjee's expression froze, but only momentarily. He would have been a good poker player, Rajiv thought. "Yet, they're a start. Much as they were for the Netherlands."

Maartje pressed on. "Senator Mukherjee, the French plan Bangladesh rejected 15 years ago was based on dikes. From my research, I understood the consensus was that dikes were too unwieldy, expensive and prevented water flows necessary for rice farming. And they do nothing to prevent storm surges from rushing up the rivers. In fact, operating as funnels, they facilitate this."

"In Bangladesh, we take victories wherever we get them," the Senator replied. "We already have limited funding in place for this, and construction begins immediately. We are, of course, interested in other ideas you may have. The funding for your preliminary study exists. But significant funding for other flood-control projects would be difficult to gather support for at this time."

Their meeting went nowhere from there. It was all very polite. Senator Mukherjee again verbally encouraged them. Perhaps there would be sufficient funding for the next activities in two years?

Outside in the plaza, Maartje shook her head. "Long-term, it won't work," she said. "He is playing with us. He rates our odds about 1 in 20,000. I don't like it."

Rajiv looked up at the impressive stone edifice of the Parliament, thinking of what he'd said earlier about bricks and mortar.

"But why would he support something he believes will fail? Yesterday's paper prodded Parliament for its yesterday fixes for tomorrow's country. Press relations, appeasement of someone or something, I am sure.

"Dikes are not good for farming. But the dikes offer immediate, albeit limited, visible protection for the country. Mukherjee is vested in the clothing industry. It's a hunch, but I'm guessing he has interests that lie behind those dikes," said Rajiv.

"The dikes and levees won't protect his factories from cyclones," Maartje snapped.

"My guess is they're far enough inland to survive. But several times a year the flooding reaches quite far inland. Dikes sometimes help remedy that."

Maartje shook her head. "All that money wasted, and levees create a very artificial sense of security. It's a disaster waiting to happen. Look at New Orleans in August 2005."

Rajiv nodded. "Maybe this is why. Disaster is one thing we're never short of in Bangladesh. It's part of our daily diet."

He was watching Maartje chew her braid—actually something she had not done since middle school.

"We will complete our recommendations," she said. "And I'll be back in three months."

"Remember, I have an idea regarding tigers," he said. "I'll e-mail it when I have something ready. It's about grants for tiger habitat and other species enhancement efforts."

Maartje looked at her watch. "I should be getting to the airport."

Rajiv waited in the lobby while she and a porter fetched her bags. The bellman hailed one of the colorful and ornate rickshaw carriages that Bangladeshis are so proud of. As she climbed in, he reached inside his satchel and brought out a fairly large but soft package wrapped in brown shipping paper. "A gift, for you."

Maartje's expression showed he'd caught her off guard, and for a moment, he feared she might refuse it.

"Please don't open it here," he said. "Wait until you are on the plane. It's something to break up the long flight."

He nodded to the driver, and watched from the curb as Maartje's rickshaw blended right into the colorful, undulating sea of Dhaka traffic.

Several Hours Later on the Calcutta to Amsterdam Plane

At 36,000 feet, two hours after take off, she unwrapped the package slowly, the waxy brown paper giving way to a vibrant blue and buffy brown. She held up a sweater unlike any she'd seen before. It was clearly handmade. On the front was a singing bird perched on a tree under a setting moon. There was a Bengali inscription knitted into the sleeves, with characters running up one sleeve and down the other.

It was beautiful.

Beneath the sweater was a note from Rajiv. His script was very neat and tidy, unlike his usual scribbles. He seemed to have taken great care with this letter.

> After I returned from Delft, I called my mother and asked her to make this for you. I made a few suggestions, but the design is her own. When I saw the way you and Krystian watched the birds at Madhupur, I knew my instincts were right. The inscription is from Tagore. 'Faith is the bird—who feels the light and sings while the dawn is still dark.'
>
> "The sweater is a thank you. I did not want to be involved in this endeavor. I just wanted to convince others to make it happen. Frankly, being a doctor in Bangladesh is daunting enough. But with your help and visit, I feel my spirits lifting. I cannot put my finger on it, but like many other human conditions, I am beginning to believe hope is contagious. I have not always felt this way.

Maartje's eyes grew large and were glistening. She unbuckled her safety belt and slipped the sweater over her head. How unexpected to receive such a gift when it seemed all their efforts could be for naught. She gazed out the plane window and saw the stars.

She felt a tingling sense from fingertip to toe as she thought about this gift. It came from a country whose people, land, water and culture were almost bereft of hope but abundant with spirit. And the donor was a medical man who was stimulating some very special feelings.

CHAPTER 15

Root Canal Therapy

Three weeks later at the labs in Delft, Maartje and Krystian are huddling with several engineers, scientists and some construction managers. Maartje began.

"Silt is a major impediment, a project killer unless it can be essentially halted. What I learned from a capable forestry—agronomy team there is that the Bengali equivalent of mangroves and certain river grasses will, if left intact, create a soil retention system. You need a minimum of one to two years to see the first successes. "

"Why not do that project first?" asked Krystian. "It should be relatively easy and low budget, especially if local conservation groups and their industrious children are involved. And I do mean industrious."

"There is a far deeper problem," explained Maartje. "The effort would work only if local village people leave the plantings undisturbed. Right now, they have not, they will not and they cannot. They scavenge all over the country and especially in the Sundarbans for kindling and other fire wood. For most of them it is their only source of cooking heat and warmth during the windy phases of monsoon. We must suggest a firewood alternative for at least three years.

Because it has far longer growing seasons, then major parts of the country could be reforested and selective harvesting principles could be taught to the populations. And this would only work if the new shrubs, grasses and trees were kept intact. Until the people are free of worry, a three-year supply of foreign firewood must be provided to all coastal peoples. The village people must be convinced they don't have to pirate, hoard and sneak daily supplies of firewood. Actually, a by-product of such an effort could be more time, for the local people have to be taught why they should not take shrubs and small trees. We need one to two hours a week for educational efforts. And enough time to prove this to villagers."

The problem was that there was no idea—save an undeveloped concept by Dr. Rajiv—about how to import and pay for a three-year supply of firewood. Then distribution had to be done equitably, to avoid destructive, disruptive riots and other social upheavals, any of which could derail the best of efforts.

An engineer in the room asked, "What is the concept this Dr. Rajiv proposes?"

Maartje replied, "It needs some cerebral embellishment but simply stated, it boils down to this: tiger populations throughout India, Bangladesh and Burma are under severe pressures. We believe there is major grant money available for programs which help increase tiger population. All require amplification of tiger habitat as a major component. Simply put, this means trees, grasses, shrubs along all canals, bayous and rivers. Thus there can be a synergy between saving tigers and stopping silt by such 'root-canal therapy.'"

"It's either goof ball or genius," commented one introspective soul.

And he added, "Preliminary research indicated a $10-15 million grant is a possibility. The RWS could be partly paid with some of these funds for our Phase 2 efforts."

"However," commented another financial expert in the room, "all those funds may not be enough for this 'replant and secure' effort. So, how and where does the firewood concept become funded? I doubt that the timber owners and woodworkers unions in the U.S., Canada, and South America are just waiting to donate three-years worth of wood. That is a massive amount." Everybody laughs.

Maartje speaks up, "My rough computation (just made) says a family of five needs 500 sticks of kindling and 250 to 350 three–five inch in diameter logs 16" long to prepare two cooked meals daily and provide three months of heat during monsoon. The coastal population of Bangladesh is 40-60 million. This will require an armada of supply ships, deep water ports for unloading and distribution facilities. It's D-Day all over but by a multiple of 50."

Krystian responds, "You are absolutely correct. Obviously, we do not yet have a workable solution. Please brainstorm this over the next week or so. To secure any major funding, we must solve this."

As this meeting proceeds, halfway across the world, weather in the Bay of Bengal is taking an ominous turn. A storm is coming. A 1200-mile wide cyclone is forming in the south of the Bay about 2000 miles south of Chittagong. Weather and meteorology experts in India, Bangladesh, Australia, Europe and America (at Colorado Springs) are busy analyzing—in real time—satellite and weather data. There is major e-chatter. A grim forecast goes out worldwide: a Beaufort Scale Force 9-12 cyclone has formed and is moving north toward East India and the coastal areas of Bangladesh and Myanmar. Landfall is projected in five to seven days. Dissemination of this information begins immediately.

Along the Bangla coast, the people who fish and farm daily, already worry. They watch local birds and monkeys who immediately sense significant barometric pressure changes. Like the birds and animals, these people feel it coming and prepare as well as they are able. But, even an advance warning of two to three days leaves millions extremely vulnerable, especially those who live within 30 miles of the coast. Small fishing boats reef their sails and head up river, mothers gather children and possessions and head to the highest ground—about as elevated as the Netherlands or Florida. They know that if the storm makes landfall on an incoming high tide and severe winds ramp up the tidal waters, perhaps 50,000 people could perish through drowning, disease, or accidents. High winds throw projectiles, walls collapse, ordinary flotsam can become deadly weapons.

Krystian suggests, "Let's stop until a week from today. Same time but I want to ask someone from Smit Transport to help us. I will brief them and Maartje, will you call them as soon as I have firmed up a contact? I know you are going skiing later this week. Please make sure you are back here by 1:00 p.m. next Monday."

Maartje shakes her head, "This Bengali project is too complex to skip out on and I have already shortened my skiing trip. If we do not solve this wood problem, there will be no work for us in Bangladesh now or for a very long time. I'm off to e-mail Dr. Rajiv, Senator Mukherjee and the forestry people to elicit their help on the firewood situation."

She walks back to her lab desk and her computer. She types the following note addressed only to the Senator with (protocol) copies to all others:

"Senator Mukherjee...

"Have just left our team meeting. We are intensively at work on silt and have reached a hurdle we must surmount. Might you help us? There are so many questions. No matter how successful we are at replanting (restocking) soil, retaining shrubs and embankment grasses in the Sundarbans and other low-lying areas in Bangladesh, the endless foraging by the population for firewood will defeat us before we get off the ground. How might we protect these plantings for two to three years? How would we set up a system for importing a two- to three-year coastal supply of firewood? Where will the human resources come from? How might the wood be distributed? How would the government prepare people for this so they do not panic when the first wood arrives? What will be the shipping costs? Who will pay them? How should we treat woods not indigenous to your country so we do not import predatory vermin? Would Bangladesh supply the 'value added' by its people so your country has politically acceptable local content? In areas like the Sundarbans what vessels (lighters) are available to move wood, cut and split, to the villages and peoples up all the tributaries? What available systems might be used to prepare people as a way to head off chaos?

"Frankly, I think we are searching for a new perspective. Until we escape the one we operate under, success may not be forthcoming.

"On blind distribution copies, 'A copy of this goes to our entire RWS team for your consideration. We meet a week from today.

"Thank you all in advance."

Rajiv sees this e-mail a few hours later and he immediately calls Pog Marenjar, his artist friend. "Hey Pog. Jiv Gaol here."

"Good to hear from you, Jiv. What's up?"

"I need three sketches or caricatures of two medium size tiger cubs and a very little one. Their names will be Bernice, Bertram and Banjo."

"Egad, Jiv, what odd names!"

"Pog, as you know, we are working on a coastal management plan to make life in the Sundarbans and other coastal areas a little more secure and less crisis driven. We want to use these caricatures to market our ideas with tigers. I want Bernice to be a darling adoptable tiger cub that kids would love. Bertram should be a boy maybe a little scruffy. Bernice could have ribbons (pink, of course) on her ears and tail."

"Can you give me a week? I am backed up for the next three to four days. But I'll have something in this time frame. I assume you want these in color? Do you want some background like foliage and water?"

"Yes, but separate the backgrounds from the tigers. In some cases, maybe one tiger without a background. That could be the logo for a presentation.

"The trick, Pog, will be to make all the tigers appeal to all ages. They should be not too humorous, not too serious and very engaging. Banjo can be more funny than serious. Our PowerPoint presentation will have from 25 to 50 digital segments in a two-hour presentation. And Pog, I have a budget for this so give me an idea of the cost range."

"Jiv, from 300-500 Euros should be the range. If this is a work-for-hire, add 200 €."

"What is work-for-hire?"

"You own the caricatures totally. I cannot receive any future royalties, however often these characters are used. So, I charge a flat rate for giving up those rights."

"Thank you. I get it. I think we should do work-for-hire. Do you want some up-front money?"

"Sure. How about 400 Euros whenever you can get it? I'll start work without it."

"Hey, Pog, can you do them on a CD-Rom so we can get others to do the logo layouts for a computer-generated PowerPoint presentation?"

"Sure, would have done this anyway. In this day it has become automatic. And I will have a file copy for back up. Do you want an extra?"

"Yes, that would be perfect. Actually, two back ups. I'll send it to my counterpart in the Netherlands. Maartje deBouter.

"And Pog, here is my cell phone number. Call anytime. If I am out of range and you cannot reach me when I am doing clinics in the Sundarbans, leave the message regardless.

"Pog, what do you think of posters and stuffed animals as a way to market the project? They might appeal to species preservation groups, zoos, grade schools, and environmental-ecology programs in communities and at universities."

"May have merit. Let me think about it."

"Where would I go to get stuffed animal samples?"

"Sit tight. I will Google that and get back to you. Do not overlook copyright protection, design patenting, and other legal stuff. I have to think about this all the time. My own literary solicitor is very capable and reasonable. And she returns phone calls and e-mails very promptly."

"Wow, I never thought of this. Would you get her to do what is necessary to protect our caricatures and any stuffed animal design? Again, let me know the cost."

"Good move. Assume I am on it and she will be. I'll have her give you a call. Her name is Asmat Robja. Her office is in Cox's Bazaar."

"Pog, I really appreciate all of this. Tell her these designs may go to Western Europe and America, too. Right now, I am working on gaining access to a group in Boulder, Colorado. There's a species preservation society there with Bengal tigers on its top 10 list. They could be players for several reasons. I'll explain later. I'll keep you posted on a drop dead date for the final caricatures. This could happen fast, like maybe a month. Do what you can. Once I receive your final efforts, I'll need two weeks to roll them onto the PowerPoint visuals for this appearance and Pog, stay buttoned up on this, please. There are some status quo clothing manufacturers who may not be happy at all about the social changes produced by these concepts. Until we gain funding and other momentum we are very much at risk."

"Got you, Jiv. You know my wife is from a clothing family with political connections, so I will confide only in you and Asmat. Do not call me at home except on my cell phone. By the way, Asmat is from a coastal village in the southeast. She may be very sympathic. She lost family in the cyclone two years ago."

"Pog, you know these crises come rolling at us so often we do not think of them as major anymore. The rest of the world must be horrified at our nonchalance. If my medical school classmates saw what I was working with for supplies and our completely open air clinics and hospitals, they would quarantine me. I do the absolute best I can but until we can protect villages from storms, tidal surges, and disease, I doubt we will do any more than put band aids on human pain and loss. So, if you wonder why I spend time and energy up in this ether, it is because I need this to cope with some hard daily stuff and not go crazy. Of course, I could drink after work. That might be cheaper than flying to the Netherlands."

"Jiv, call me for tea whenever you are bogged down. I'm no therapist but I come from a family of healers and some of this has worn off. And do give me a chance to meet the Dutch lady, Marcia is it?"

"No. Maartje. Like Mart-cha."

After talking with Pog, Jiv thinks back to his residency farewell party in front of the roaring fireplace. How abundant firewood and paper were and how incredibly available were what came from trees: paper, rolls of Viva, newspapers, catalogs like Land's End and Eddie

Bauer, tissue paper, wrapping paper. What could it be like here 5 or 10 years from now, then 15 or 20 after several phases of a really good program? Ah, such a luxury to think so hopefully.

How long had it been since he heard the bird singing as mother taught him? He remembered it had been the night of his father's mill injury. How frightened his whole family was until they learned Father would live. He remembered. Yes, he remembered. The bird sang. And they kept faith. Rajiv began thinking of how healthy his Father was and how proud he was of his doctor son. And yes, Father, Rajiv softly, privately, promised himself again, I will keep you proud.

One evening Rajiv was finishing his weekly report to the Matlah Community Health Project. One of Rajiv's duties during his six years was to copiously compile and report his health care data to Matlah. This world renowned Bengali facility was a gathering and dissemination point of a health care database. With 150 million people in a country barely larger than Illinois, the data from studies of health care is on a par with major USA and European clinics. The national willingness of the population and health care providers to report, detailed, useful data on illness, diagnosis and treatment is skillfully converted to useful knowledge by researchers all over the world. Matlah's scientific paper production exceeded 2000 and was growing rapidly. The now widely used and inexpensive technique of filtering water through old sari material for a major cholera reduction program is an outgrowth of Matlah data. Rajiv does his reports religiously.

As Rajiv works on the creative fix for the firewood—roots-soil—silt—tiger puzzle, he wonders how he can connect the children of Bangladesh to children around the world.

Meanwhile, Maartje has just settled down on the train for her six-hour trip to ski heaven. As she relaxes, she thinks of aromas she detects whenever she is around Rajiv; delicate musky male somehow mixed with those of an Indian spice vendor's stall.

"I've never been close to such a combination. I rather like it," she muses. One of her high school boyfriends who came from a family of fishermen always smelled of fish and diesel fuel. She thought Rajiv was a definite upgrade.

CHAPTER 16

Seilbahn (Cable Car Transport System)

It is Thursday. Maartje has arrived in Lech, Austria. Snow and skiers everywhere. She is alone and glad for this. She also is deep in thought.

The Kinderdorfer is a classic county Gasthaus with thirteen rooms, a large dining room opening to a U-shaped bar with a distinctively Tyrolian flavor; dark trim against creamy plaster. The outside has floral (call it Austrian Rosemaling) accents. The interior walls are laden with hunting and mountain gear. The spirit of the place, the *Gemütlichkeit*, manifests itself through multilingual conversations at the long tables over the excellent food, beer, especially Pilsners, and beer with liquor shots. A table may have Asian, Czech, New Zealand, Danish and American folks. Not many Japanese anymore.

She checks into the Gasthaus and goes down to the Kleine Stube for a Pils nightcap. Then back upstairs to her low European bed with goose down pillows and comforter. Windows are partly open, the heat is off.

Early the next morning, she dresses, eats a European hard roll with plum jelly, cheese, sliced meat, and one soft (sort of) boiled egg breakfast, grabs her skis and poles and tromps off the quarter mile to the Lift Station. The queue is moderate compared to tomorrow's expected weekend hordes. While waiting in the rapidly shortening line, she studies the bull wheel, a giant horizontal 12' diameter sheave about 10 feet above her head. It moves the cable through the gondola platform, and transmits power from the 750 horsepower electrical motor and worm gear reducer to drive the cable up, actually pulling it down on the return side. Then she studies the four person gondolas. A frown, then a smile, indicates she is shaping an idea. Her gondola arrives and off she goes for the first of eight runs, maybe eleven if she is really lucky. The snow is powder—the best—fresh and has a deep base. Couldn't be better except in Alta, Steamboat Springs, or Mammoth Mountain, California, where the powder in March and April is the "other worldly" snow skiers talk about over Evian and coffee. At day's end, (she managed ten runs) she takes off her skis and clumps over to the wheel house to talk to the operator.

"Can you tell me who manufacturers this lift and where they are located?"

The Operator, a twenty-eight-year-old with careful eyes and agile mannerisms, replied, "This is a Kloppleser. Here's the name and headquarters. It's in Bildstein, Austria. That's only about 75 km from here, not far from the Bodensee. Here's their phone. But I think our manual has a more current number. Let me check. They are very good, exceptionally good, especially about safety and wanting us to call them if we have operating questions or concerns. Not like that other ox on Jenner Berg over there. It's poorly made, poorly maintained, and 30 years old. I think the company was bought by a Japanese firm. I believe we are replacing it in two years with a new Kloppleser Seilbahn—if that one doesn't kill a bunch of skiers before then. God, I hate it."

Maartje studies the wheel house, the control board, and the process flow monitors. She is very impressed with what she sees. She writes down the relevant information, thanks the operator and heads off to her little Gasthaus. Instead of going down to socialize with other skiers at the end of the day, she is on the phone for an hour connecting to the Kloppleser sales department. Finally, she works her way through to the vice president of sales, Kleinhold Dalmer.

"Mr. Dalmer, I am Maartje deBouter from Lisse in the Nether-lands, near Keukenhof Gardens."

"How do you do, Maartje. What can I do for you?"

"I work for the Royal Water Service—Delft as a civil engineer in hydrology. We are engaged in flood management systems in the Netherlands and abroad. Currently, we are working on a preliminary study of the Sundarbans river delta-flood plain and other coastal areas in Bangladesh, if you will, beginning just east of Calcutta and on the coast. One project parameter requires the movement of large num-bers of people inland and to higher ground before flood stages and tidal surges. Another parameter will likely require the movement of significant amounts of firewood along those same routes. I am skiing here at Lech and, if I reduce your lift bahn and gondolas to a blur, I can see a system like yours (or several) becoming a significant part of such a dual cargo system in Bangladesh."

"Ms. deBouter, clearly such is possible but I do not want to be an information source for someone to take to our Italian, Swiss and Japanese competitors."

"Mr. Dalmer, this is not my intent. I am just trying to take a very embryonic concept and grow it. I would gladly give you a non-use, non-disclosure covenant of the type we require our prospective cus-tomers to sign before we share any data with them.

"This may suffice. Why don't you send me a request by e-mail when you get back to Delft-Lisse? Include a draft non-use, non-disclosure commitment. I'll have our risk manager look it over. I will tell you we have been hired to propose a system for moving military personnel and fighting equipment across and among rugged moun-tains, plateaus, over rivers, steep valleys and glaciers. I'm not sure there are insurmountable differences between your concept and this one. I do know we would require you to agree that if we issue a pro-posal, you agree to deal exclusively with us for five years on any sys-tem comprehended by the proposal."

"You drive a hard bargain as do we. I would expect a similar com-mitment from you on using or disclosing any of our information for any reason other than our project. That agreement should last for the same five years so we have a head start at perfecting our concept. I will send all this material as a ZIP or JPEG file. Is this okay?"

"Yes, either is fine."

"You'll have it by next Wednesday. How soon might you be able to respond?"

"In seven to ten days. What we really sell, Maartje, is solid footings to large, tall, wide base towers and tons of lift cable. All the rest is decorative—not quite—but you get the point. Our gondola clamps are as good or better than any in the world. They are titanium and fatigue-free. And I'm sure you've already noted, our bull wheels are seamless single bloom forgings, not weldments, such as most other seilbahn, excuse me, cable system manufacturers use—for the obvious cost reasons. We can talk about the Keystone, Colorado and Mammoth Mountain, California lift disasters—neither were our systems. Both were poorly welded bull wheel fatigue failures."

"Mr. Dalmer, I was aware your bull wheels were not welded but that's about all. My metallurgy is kindergarten."

"Maartje, when you come here, as I hope will be part of the process, I'll give you a short course on castings, weldments, and forgings. And we'll also talk risk and cost."

CHAPTER 17

The Two-Way Highway

Senator Mukherjee has taken Maartje's e-mail regarding wood to two of his business partners. He says, "We may, just may, have a solution to our perennial freight problem. The Dutch are proposing that we import a three-year supply of firewood. Mind you, that is enough to supply the coastal population requirements of Bangladesh for three years. While this by itself, may seem ridiculous, when combined with some other ideas namely the Finnish pulpwood deal recently agreed upon by our government, modern storm surge protection, tiger habitat and species enhancement, the firewood idea becomes less ludicrous and more appealing. Presently unsolved is a wood distribution system and security to protect the firewood after off-loading. Can you imagine how some timely booked shipping charters could help if we did so before shippers knew what was happening?"

One partner says, "Maybe we should charter a tandem of super tankers for this period. Think how many (cords) of wood one would carry. Allah be praised. Because there has been a huge world-wide inventory of unused oil tankers for almost 20 years, we should be able to negotiate some fine, fine rates. I realize this is changing given current oil prices. I assume these can be converted to carry items like wood, rice, and clothing. The ships may have to be scrubbed and disinfected after the wood is off-loaded. The Interior Minister proposes treating all imported wood so we don't import any vermin harmful to indigenous trees and shrubs. I am sure it will be so. And where will the vessels dock?"

Another partner responded, "If the firewood is treated on the ship before off loading, this will surely be a cost item we must address. What do you think about this? Is this beyond our interest? We will probably require the services of a shipping accountant. Do you know one, Ram?"

Mukherjee responds, "I have contacts in Hong Kong. Should I ask them? How should we handle cost? Can we treat it as an advance for a limited liability company we could set up? Do we want to capitalize these items so we might amortize them? Let's ask the accountant we used for the mill construction a few years ago. She was very capable on these issues."

"OK. Yes. Let's do this—at least for a look-see."

Delft, Netherlands

Maartje is at her desk e-mailing the RWS confidentiality agreement to Dalmer at Kloppleser. It is very comprehensive. He responds within five days, saying, "The matter has attracted interest here and some ideas have been put forth about conversion of lift gondolas to wood containers. We should have something for you within 30 days. Please make certain you execute our attached (JPEG) confidentiality document and return it at least two weeks before we transmit our thoughts. It is a blend of your ideas and ours. I leave for Patagonia for a week beginning Saturday. You can reach me only by e-mail until Sunday week late. As part of this trip, I will visit Iguaçu Falls. This has been on my dream list for 20 years and now the development of the South American ski industry is helping this dream come true."

Maartje receives an e-mail from Khalil. It explains that the Senator seeks the name of a wood pest/vermin expert. The Senator is concerned that importing pests which might overrun Bangla forests—such as they are—would generate a political barrier to any silt reduction programs. She answers, "Khalil, (cc: Senator M and bcc: Dr. Jiv). I have a tentative resource but will not have a name or CV until later this week. After we evaluate this resource, I will report back to you forthwith."

Maartje doesn't tell Khalil who she is seeking help from. He probably would not understand the connection. Maartje contacts Martin Morgan, Technical Representative—Sales Support, for Ivory Tower Chapel Bell Company in Queens Park, London. "Martin, I remember when I toured your facility in 2000 as part of the International Hand Bell Symposium, a tour I will never forget, you explained your 425 year-old company's search—across the world—for hand bell woods that were vermin-free. And if I remember correctly, your wood consultant evaluated several hundred from everywhere, then eliminated almost of them on the basis of rot, insect or fungus vulnerability and I filed that away for future use. Little did I realize then how useful this might be.

"This request has nothing to do with hand bells. It is for a project we are researching for a flood control client on the Indian Ocean. Many details have yet to be developed. However, we are under pressure for a partial report shortly."

Maartje meets in Krystian's office with Krystian and the Executive Director of the RWS, Jan Greilingen. Jan is a seasoned, deft executive who maneuvered himself onto the short list for the post during the years of glory after the Delta Project was completed and dedicated by Her Majesty Queen Beatrix in October 1986. He was project manager for the woven fiber "cloth" laid on the North Sea floor before the giant piers were placed. His credentials are significant but his willingness to risk the good name of the RWS has not been tested. Jan turns to Krystian and asks, "Tell me the status of your review of the foundational data for silt elimination and resulting compression strength worthiness of the areas where we would be recommending gating piers for a surge barrier."

Krystian replies, "Because the data is only partial, I cannot say whether coastal floors are suitable for the pillars. However, the borings reveal that below the silt, the compression strength data are excellent. As you know, Jan, our efforts will initially focus on reduction of silt, renourishment of shrub, tree and grass with retention techniques for canals and river embankments."

The director is not convinced and asks, "Well, how then—either of you, please—can I sign a report and recommendation which put us in a spotlight way across the world where we must live up to what we recommend? All this assumes Bay of Bengal tides will sweep most of this silt out to sea way beyond a zone where this could be problematic."

First Maartje answers, "Director Jan, our report and recommendation will be based on the assumption that Bangladesh succeeds in its soil retention efforts."

"But, Maartje, doesn't this depend on a hope, no more than a hope, that a massive supply of firewood—from outside Bangladesh—will be magically delivered to a new, and as yet unbuilt, deep water port. Then, that it will be successfully distributed by a means which insures, and I mean insures, delivery to all those millions of scavenging people? For us to depend on success of a program we cannot control triggers all sorts of alarms in my fear center. Simply stated, without a higher quantum of evidence or proof that significant silt reduction is going to occur, I am very uncomfortable having us guarantee performance of heavy construction mandated by your critical path outline. I cannot sign off on this report until we have better evidence the silt management has a reasonable likelihood of succeeding."

"Director Jan, two items. First item, we will need to have our first report delivered and signed before we can apply for a Grant for $10 million USD.

"Second, the Bangladesh Senate will not approve its matching grant funds without our report and recommendation."

Jan says, "Yes, yes, I understand these things. I know a World Bank consulting engineer. His efforts caused a decisive veto by the World Bank for participation in the Three Gorges Dam on the Yangtze River. This fellow concluded the dam would likely experience extremely costly ongoing maintenance due to silt and pollution. The

World Bank voted down a 25 billion Euro loan. That is a lot of money. And it meant the risk of diminished World Bank participation in other Chinese projects such as proposed pipelines from Kazakhstan to Shanghai.

"Krystian and Maartje, I'd like to see a higher likelihood of silt success. And I think you should find this engineer from the World Bank. Find him, hire him—even at a consultant's fee—so we can have the benefit of his expertise. I would like to give you more than 30 days to do all of this, but you know how busy the agency is. We have to consider other projects that may advance to the slot we are holding for Bangladesh. Let's set our next review for 30 days. Now I must leave. I'm giving a lecture at the Koophandel den Haag in one hour. I'm going to tell them about the types of projects the RWS is working on around the world and how we compete against top drawer engineering firms from the USA, Germany, France and Japan. Thank you both for your usual candor. Tot Zeins."

Heading toward Maartje's work station, Maartje and Krystian walk down the hall together, feeling overwhelmed. Maartje says, "My God, how can we ever do this in 30 days?"

"Well, Maartje, will you find that World Bank engineer? I want to contact the Senator, Dr. Jiv, and the Agronomy and Forestry people in Dhaka. Maybe, just maybe, we can put together a more convincing case for the Director. He is concerned about the reputation of the RWS. He's focused on silt. We have to be doubly thorough because of this. This is not all bad. We should have thought about this long before this meeting. Clearly, the ball is in our court. Find this engineer. I have the feeling if he respects our upstream silt management, Director Jan will believe in our efforts and, Maartje, perhaps, just perhaps, we will have opened a door to World Bank financing of phases two and three of this project."

"Krystian, that would be major. I've been wondering about this since our trip there. What I am unable to visualize is how we will differentiate our selves from the Three Gorges. Maybe the answer lies in our own files. We have a long history of preventing silt movement toward the North Sea from the Maas and Rhine rivers.

"Krystian, I think we need one of our more seasoned project historians to crack those older files to provide some ammunition."

As they talk, Maartje's computer beeps the presence of a new e-mail. It is a communication from Martin Morgan. After Krystian and she part, she taps into the message.

"Maartje, of course, I remember you and your Lisse Bell Choir.

"And yes, I have a name for you. She awaits your contact. Her name is Anna Marie Godsen. Her phone is (dialing from the Netherlands) 011-33-87-406-224. Her e-mail is AMGBUG@Eunet.com. Her painstaking efforts for us have been well affirmed by our field experience with bells in Sri Lanka, Indonesia, China, Malaysia, Brazil, Peru and British Columbia. She has, as you will see, degrees in Forestry Studies and Entomology. Two degrees from Cambridge and a Masters from Guelph University in Montreal, Quebec. We placed a great deal of trust in her and the results were worth it. Now she is collaborating with a genetics fellow at the University of Wisconsin stem cell research labs in Madison. Briefly, we wanted new strains of our favorite wood with an enhanced density. We thought this combination would preclude vibrations which interfere with particular bell sounds. It's an interesting lab. Their scientists are also working on a new bamboo variant for pandas. All the best and before I forget, we are developing a line of J Stroke hand bells so we can compete head on with several U.S. hand bell foundries. This is a big step for us and we are very excited. It helps to be a 425-year-old company from the west end of London. We are planning to fly 250 English hand bell choir directors from the U.S. to our facilities for a two-day tour. We have chartered a 747-400 for this purpose. The visiting musicians will have four additional free days for their own leisure before they return. It will cost them four days of meals and lodging—not too expensive if they stay at the hotel we have negotiated with. Best, Martin."

Maartje replies, "Martin, you are a grand soul. Thank you. I will call Anna forthwith. Best of luck on the J Stroke bells. Your promotion sounds ingenious. Keep me posted on the genetic project."

Her call to Anna is brief and focused. "Anna, I am Maartje de-

Bouter. I believe Martin Morgan has spoken to you of our concerns. Briefly, I work for the Royal Water Service in Delft, Netherlands. We are doing a study of flood management projects in Bangladesh. Coastal Bangladesh is losing its trees and shrubs to a huge firewood scavenging population. One of our recommendations is that in order for Bangladesh to restore its trees, shrubs and grasses, it must import a supply of firewood for up to three years from around the world. The Bengali political and forestry people are concerned that foreign vermin like the Dutch Elm beetle and gypsy moth will come along and destroy such remaining indigenous foliage as they have."

Anna replies, "Maartje, I believe their concern is justified. Just now, I am working on a situation here in Great Britain where a voracious little ant from South China has arrived and is wreaking havoc on a local stand of basswood. If we do not create a fumigant promptly, all English basswood will be at risk. Here, that's like an assault on the crown jewels. I think we are close but we haven't completed the studies of the proposed fumigant. We do not want another DDT mess."

"Specifically, Anna," Maartje continues, "we need to know whether we can do treating on board ships the size of oil tankers. What insecticides or fungicides must be used? How should they be applied? The Bengali government is likely to require certificates of treatment before the ships enter Bengali waters."

Anna sounds amazed. "Wow, not a small issue. Would you give me a week to think out the parameters of such a project so I might estimate the costs for you? When is your report due?"

"Anna, I wish I could give you more than 60 days but these issues arose yesterday for the first time and this aspect of our report is due in 90 days."

"Maartje, you may have to pay for some overtime support personnel but if you can cover this, I will make sure you have my recommendations in... let's say 55 days from next Monday. I will start my assistant listing vermin and fungus by region. It would help if you were to prioritize the source of wood by geographic regions."

"Anna, the USA and Canada come first. Northern and Western Europe are second. Recent developments suggest Finland may be a player. And we will cover all your efforts from today through next Monday regardless. I will confirm this immediately in an e-mail. Will 2,000 € cover it?"

"Yes, it will. Maartje, I will set this project in motion immediately. Thank you for the call."

Maartje promptly e-mails the Senator, Dr. Jiv and her Royal Water Service team about Anna Godsen and her willingness to undertake the project. She details some of Anna's credentials, which are impressive. She does not, however, elaborate on an idea she has been nurturing, which is the genetic enhancement of grass roots. This she quietly and privately pursues on her own.

She leaves work early but is on her cell phone in the parking lot to an engineering school classmate from Mongolia who works at the Philips Research Labs in Nijmegen near the German border. "Solongo, this is Maartje deBouter calling."

"Why Maartje, how is life at the Royal Water Service? I still remember how excited we all were for you when you got that great job working with their senior hydrology engineer."

"Oh, Solongo, it has almost been too much. He is so capable. He shares all the credit and shoulders more than his share of responsibility, a remarkable and gifted person. He comes from the Czech Republic. He has given me lead engineer status on a project in Asia. And the support he provides is formidable. The project is huge. It may last 20 years. Tell me, how is Philips treating you?"

"Maartje, this is a fine company. I am part of the high density television project. We have an excellent, well tested product line, now into its third phase of production. All the European airlines and train stations are converting to our flat screen TV's. Our team received a ten-day all expenses paid trip at a five star Dutch resort in Curaçao off the coast of Venezuela. The weather and snorkeling were fantastic. Spouses were included. My husband and I had an excellent room with a balcony and view of the water from the fourth floor. Tell me now what prompts your call?"

"Do you have a phone number or e-mail for the plant genetics fellow you introduced me to at school?"

"Henri LaVie, you mean. Yes, I have both. He is at a plant institute in Antwerp. Does plant genetics for a consortium of seed companies. Here is his e-mail. BetterPlantsHLV@ Euronet.com. His phone is country code Belgium + 46 32 22 47. He really knows plant engineering. He won an award last year and shares a patent for a strain of celery with a ginger flavor which already has a huge market in Asia. I purchased the celery at the farm market in Breda. It is wonderful. Especially in stir fry cooking. Tell him I said so."

"Solongo, do you have any idea how lovely it is to be chatting with you again? After I finish this preliminary report in a couple of months I will call you and we will meet say halfway—maybe Utrecht for dinner. You will be my guest. Your information is worth more than the price of a good dinner."

"It's a deal. Whenever you are available."

Maartje fires off an e-mail to Henri.

Meanwhile, Krystian has learned the name of the World Bank expert and made e-mail contact. He is Royce Brenden, a civil engineer with an MBA from Indiana University. He works with an engineering consulting consortium in Denver, Colorado. His firm is on retainer to the World Bank. His work on the Three Gorges Dam is the stuff of legend. His analysis on the effect of silt and garbage on generators in the dam is viewed as a model for all future such evaluations. The Chinese government was so troubled by his unwillingness to support the project that it sought to bar the World Bank's publishing of his appendix report to the rejection. A full meeting of the World Bank Board of Directors concluded that the Chinese government's efforts were ill-founded and detrimental to the best interests of the World Bank. Brenden said nothing, did not get into the bickering and came out on top.

Krystian sends the following e-mail to Brenden:

"I am a senior hydrology project manager at the Royal Water Service here in Delft. We study, design and supervise public and private contractor construction of flood management systems. We deal primarily with fending off high tide storm surges for low countries like, of course, the Netherlands.

"We are engaged on a preliminary study and recommendations which will likely become a series of major projects in Bangladesh. One situational parameter is excessive silt coming down the numerous rivers, tributaries and canals which empty into the Bay of Bengal from the central and western Himalayas and Karakorams. We are proposing, well before any construction, rather significant grass, shrub and tree restocking to reduce the erosion which produces the silt. We have consensus on this throughout our team and the Bengali Project people. However, some of our concepts are not yet proven. Your name was raised because of the Three Gorges Yangtze project. We were told that you understood silt and how harmful it can be for any construction or embedded structures under water. Our Director (my direct boss) asked me to contact you for your views. I believe that if you feel our methods are sound and hold more than just a chance of success, he will embrace our recommendations and we can thus proceed to perfect these concepts. And we can fund your efforts, regardless."

Brenden responds a few hours later. "Sounds interesting. How compressed is your schedule?"

"29 days from today," Krystian answers.

"If you or an informed associate can be in Denver early next week with your sedimentation data, we will commit to complete our evaluation 28 days from today."

"I'll arrange it. Please provide a cost estimate ±15% within 48 hours. VTY, K.K. RWS."

Krystian then rings up Maartje and says, "Can you be in Denver Tuesday next week? I've contacted Royce Brenden, the World Bank Engineer. He will undertake to evaluate—a day before our drop-dead date—our silt management proposal. He wants our data, at least 48 hours before you show up. Also, e-mail him a descriptive outline of our silt solutions. Do not get Brenden tangled up in the firewood importing issue unless he raises it. For him, that is collateral. Be ready if he does address it. Any questions, Maartje? I have to tend to a project discussion on our Northwest Australian coast study tomorrow. I will send him our silt data tomorrow for sure."

"Krystian, I will leave Tuesday and return next Friday. I will do the best I can. Tot Zeins."

Then, Maartje fires off a brief e-mail to Dr. Jiv explaining her trip to Denver. He replies, "While you are in Denver, please talk to somebody at the International headquarters of the Global Wildlife Federation (Boulder) about their priorities on species protection. I am working on a concept (but do not discuss this with them) to present to them. Just confirm that the Bengal Tiger is still on their top 10 species preservation list."

Maartje makes her travel arrangements. Then, just as a thought, fires off a short e-mail to Nafis, saying, "Can you tell me what your number one and two recommendations for grasses and bank shrubs to retain soil throughout the Sundarbans and why? Please let me hear from you by this Sunday a.m. (our time). We have some concepts we are considering and I believe your recommendations will carry great weight. And if there were to be some genetic engineering of the best features of any two or three grasses and shrubs, which features of which plants would you seek to combine and why?"

By noon the next day, Nafis has sent a responsive e-mail with some very interesting commentary on a root structure Jagdish found in a Sundarbans embankment. Maartje is ecstatic. He has provided her with some pieces of the puzzle for Dr. LaVie. And she passes this directly on to LaVie. Dr. LaVie's response is quite technical but the essence is laid out in a summary paragraph at the beginning of nine single spaced pages. Genetically they cannot marry the features of the two species she proposed. However, her "rooty grass" has a distant cousin found in South China about 100 miles north and west of the Kowloon peninsula. It is used on the banks of irrigation trenches for terraced rice paddies. There the flows are very erratic.

LaVie said, "The roots of one plant are sheltered from the flow turbulence by grass which is from 12-18" long lying right upstream of the roots for the next grass plant downstream. Maybe we can genetically graft the sheltering grass onto the plant whose roots have a high soil retention index. How do you feel about this approach? Fee wise our standard genetic enhancement charge is $45,000 USD plus a royalty of 5% of any seed your client might purchase. The royalty is non-negotiable. Time wise, we quote 45-60 days to the first plants and then 100 days to generate the first 50,000 seeds. After this, it is a cakewalk because reproduction is exponential. Just like you Netherlanders do with tulips and hyacinth. We might also discuss cloning.

"However, I need the PH and soil alkalinity where these seeds would be placed. I prefer having samples—sealed—so we can do our own quantitative analysis. From soils both above and below the water and six of each from proximate but not adjacent sites. This provides a higher statistical base for germination and let me assure you we do not use first generation 'terminator' genes like certain companies. What we deliver will be very fertile for reproduction and replanting. Those who will benefit the most will be your contacts in Bangladesh. The word will spread and we will do okay. Our pricing policies express this confidence. If our front end load is problematic for you, we could reduce it and raise the royalty percentage."

Maartje asks, "May I see those figures within a day or two? This may ease some constraints."

"You will have it tomorrow," says LaVie.

Maartje proceeds to outline the description Royce Brenden requested as she prepares for the fast trip to Denver. The foreboding tone of the Director's admonition concerns her. Because she does not know whether he is a zero risk person or an assertive—assess-risk take-risk—leader, she worries. She reports to Krystian on the grass possibility found by Jagdish and Henri LaVie's initial genetic analysis. They also discuss royalties vs. front end load and tentatively conclude that a lesser up front charge is the better option since sale royalties will be ultimately borne by the Bangladesh government. Then RWS will have less project cost to absorb. And perhaps the up front lump sum might be recovered in project add-ons.

Krystian thinks the Director may actually be more interested in genetic root structures and long grass. This may be more important to obtaining the Director's initial report sign off. He decides, after

Maartje returns from Denver, to have a team dinner at Zierikzee, a little estuary village between the Delta Project and Rotterdam.

Krystian will distribute a list of some currently baffling issues to everyone several days before the dinner. That will start them processing. Then they can have a two-hour hard hitting discussion before any drinks. Dinner will cost Krystian maybe 800 Euros out of his budget. Time and again, this casual dinner meeting approach helped the RWS end up on its feet, especially during the horrendous cost escalation period on the Delta Project when legislators were very serious about scrapping the entire Delta Project. Twenty-eight years ago, Krystian, with his Director's blessing, took an idea from a similar dinner meeting directly to the Prince, who said he would do anything to help the project succeed. The Prince personally met with the most reluctant legislators and convinced them with poignant pictures from his helicopter flight the morning after the 1953 flooding—barely 12 hours after the outer-dike rupture was discovered. The royal family manifests an acute sense of responsibility to the Dutch people and has translated the perception into a duty to facilitate a meaningful response to a major and recurring, natural hazard.

It took the Prince weeks to recover from the sad sight of drowned people, their livestock, and the total destruction of farmland—from salt poisoning—and damage to fields, homes, barns, roads, and fences. Singlehandedly, "silver spooned" royal had come forth in a dark hour to inspire even the most recalcitrant legislators to take a new perspective. That, thought Krystian, was leadership. The right amount of courage so necessary for a monumental moment in Dutch history.

CHAPTER 18

In a Theatre of Competence

Maartje's flight to Colorado is uneventful. The Amsterdam-Chicago leg through O'Hare is almost on time. She sleeps hard. She has felt for the past several weeks as though she were staving off a major sinus and respiratory infection. The stress on this project is intense and she is very apprehensive that a failure of any early piece will embarrass the RWS to the point where the French dike proposal could easily regain the inside track. She cannot escape these apprehensions especially because she is so uneasy about trusting Senator Mukherjee. He seems too smooth and elegant.

As she rides the van to her hotel in downtown Denver from DIA, she marvels at the engineering risks taken on this new airport. She remembered reading that one group of consulting engineers was very concerned that a chalky layer of Bentonite 10–12" thick would produce severe settlement, side slippage, and 3–5" vertical concrete cracks within six to ten years. Even with this dissent, the project was green lighted. There was an article in a business school journal about two years ago with a very analytical discussion about these risks and the projected "fix" costs from years 5 to 25. Dutch political figures would never take such a high level of risk on a major project like this. But so far, the attention was all about the start-up failures which plagued the luggage handling systems. Shifting and settling has been within tolerance.

Denver is right at the western edge of the prairie and the beginning of the Rocky Mountains. Approaching the mountains seemed to her like breaking out into the North Sea from the sanctuary of a breakwater. Very energizing.

When Maartje arrives at her hotel, a message from "Royce B" is waiting. "Ms. deBouter, call me when you are settled in. Give yourself a few hours rest to acclimate (I'm serious) to our air at 5,000 feet above sea level. I'll pick you up about 6:45 p.m. for dinner (if this works for you) about 10-15 minutes south. My wife, Laura, will be with me. My cell is 303-321-5936. 2:00 p.m. Royce.

"P.S. Take two Tylenol and drink a liter of bottled water or two before dinner!"

Maartje calls Brenden and confirms that she will be outside under the entrance canopy at 6:40 p.m. She asks for a wake up call at 5:30 p.m. and is asleep almost before the phone is in its cradle. A hard, good sleep ends with the wake up call—which comes way, way too soon. She showers and before she dresses, she reviews all her materials for her dinner meeting—just in case a social meal turns to business.

By 6:30 p.m., she is in the lobby, dressed in casual black slacks with a magenta blouse. She heads outside at 6:40, just as Royce pulls up in an A8 Audi. He hops out, introduces himself and Laura, and holds Maartje's door while she seats herself and fastens her seat belt. After a short ride, they arrive at the front of a small, quiet seafood restaurant called Pompano. It has the essential feel of her favorite restaurant at Kijkduin, a coast town near The Hague. Mrs. Brenden is graceful and friendly. The conversation is easy. It is clear the Brendens have traveled to many spots around the world, including several times to China. Royce suggests ending the evening before it is too late and says, "For tomorrow when we start at 9:00 a.m., I will be particularly interested in learning what measures your team proposes for reducing the erosion of silt that gets into these three rivers and ends up in the Bay of Bengal and how you will measure and quantify any such success. Also, what do you know about the dissipation of silt in the Bay of Bengal?" Maartje blinks. She is thrilled. They are on the same page.

"Maartje," says Royce, "I like what we have seen so far of your influencing parameters approach. On the Three Gorges project, the Chinese project managers were instructed to say anything they thought we wanted to hear. It was pitiful. Their empirical data was fabricated, incomplete and unsophisticated. The project people were intimidated by party higher-ups. The silent message was to have the project approved regardless of any worry about safety or functional concerns." The evening ends pleasantly and early.

From her room, Maartje looks up at the shadows of the Front Range mountains. They are 30 miles away but, in mountain country, seem at one's feet. For a low country native, the quiet presence of mountains contrasts to the endlessly noisy presence of the North Sea, the wind—the endless wind—and, of course, the pounding waves, the fog, clouds, and rain.

Maartje settles in for a cool, dry night of sleep with windows left open. Her sleep is deep. Again, the alarm goes off way too early but it is show time with Royce Brenden.

She dresses in a brown suit for the day and takes a taxi to the International Engineering Company offices and research labs. The firm has about 50 engineering and research scientists and 100 support personnel. A male receptionist greets her and takes her coat. The reception waiting area has mountain views northwest toward Boulder and Fort Collins. She notices the scale of the chair and sofas. Everything is three inches higher—an ergonomic recognition by Brenden's firm that people are taller in 2004 than they were in 1940-1960. Maartje, being tall, enjoys the comfort. Brenden is dressed in a plaid Colorado viyella shirt pressed, creased jeans and two-tone brown Kangaroo boots.

"Maartje, you look very rested. I assume you slept well and our desert air has not dried your nose and throat too badly." He stops near a refrigerator and pulls out two 20-ounce bottles of spring water. "Here, drink four of these a day while you are here. Six at Vail. It's 3,200 feet higher. If you get headaches, it is likely due to altitude adjustment. Water is best. For some reason, soda pop is not good.

"We are going to a small conference room where I will introduce you to two team members on your project—Erika Swenson from the Swedish Institute of Technology and Bill Allaman from Purdue. Bill is a silt researcher and Erika is apprenticing here for three years to study Colorado Creek beds and banks to help us better understand the behavior of water, rock, stone, foliage, and roots—a study perhaps of use in your project. It was very helpful of you to transmit your satellite images of the 10-mile strip proximate to the Bay of Bengal. Very helpful imagery but how alarming to see such diminished foliage. Now we understand how this contributes to the significant loss of soil."

He proceeds to explain that they are currently under contract to a Midwest timber growing, logging and marketing concern which is becoming image-conscious after a century of strip logging in the Pacific Northwest. Now they are doing damage control on what appears in the public mirror. Major destruction of mountain trout habitat in their forests in western Washington, Oregon, and Northern California has produced a board redirection. Seven of the sixteen board members are trout fisherman. Environmental and fly fishing groups have been publicly deriding them, but they stand up and take it and explain they are changing and working to redress these wrongs. And they are slowly turning the tide. Other timber concerns were taking notice, not wanting to be next into the environmental frying pan.

"Maartje deBouter, I would like you to meet Erika Swenson and William Allaman. As I informed you two last week, Maartje is Assistant Project Manager for the Bangladesh Project of the Royal Water Service in the Netherlands."

"Maartje," says Erika, "I have been sail boarding with friends several times inside and outside the Delta Storm Surge Barrier. The piers and gates are awesome. What a thrill it is to sail between the piers. My, what a project! What an underlying commitment! And such a beneficial outcome."

Maartje replies, "Erika, I wish I could claim credit. I began work 15 years after the Project was dedicated by Queen Beatrix."

"But Maartje, just to work in the presence of such large scale, processes must be inspiring."

"It is, Erika, but some days it is intimidating. My boss was the chief hydrology engineer of the project for the last 10 years. He is an analytical giant."

Brenden calls them to attention. "Well, let's get started. Maartje, I understand the scope of our assignment is to render a written opinion on the probability that your phase one proposal, respecting upstream silt management and downstream reduction, has sufficient promise so that your director will bless this initial study report and its preview of further phases—what I would call the design and build phases of a major coastal storm surge system. If these first phases are successful, by a definition I do not fully appreciate, additional phases will be implemented for other parts of the coast and river-ways."

Maartje says, "Yes, this is well stated."

Royce then asks, "Maartje, please take a few minutes to trace out your plan for Erika and Bill."

She proceeds with her presentation. "Bangladesh, like the Netherlands, is a low country with large amounts of water flowing out of the mountains of India, Bhutan, Nepal and Bangladesh in many rivers, including the Brahmaputra (in Bangladesh, it's called the Jumuna), the Ganges and the Meghna. At certain times of the year, collisions occur between the outflowing waters and surges coming inland off the Bay of Bengal driven by massive storm systems—cyclones. When these two forces converge, massive flooding occurs. Thousands—as many as 250,000 people die; farms are flooded and fields are salt poisoned; the coastal rail system is severely disrupted; and disease, especially cholera and dysentery, run rampant. The people living in these coastal areas are fishing and rice-farming families. Often they can't afford to buy coal and other fuels for cooking and warmth. So, millions of them forage every day for kindling and firewood. The result is that many areas are devoid of foliage. Thus, when the rivers back up and the storm surges force their way inland, massive soil erosion occurs. This suspended silt flows out into the Bay of Bengal. In coastal engineering, there are enemies; the worst is silt. Piers or dam structures cannot be placed on silt.

"Now let me compare the Bangla situation to what we did in the Netherlands. On the Delta Project, the RWS contractor had first to remove millions of cubic meters of silt and clay. Then they compressed the bed using a massive, specially designed ship which lowered tall hydraulic vibrators into the bed, often 30 feet or more below the sea floor. Then smaller, revetment grade rock known as fill rubble was barged in. A cleverly designed plastic mattress 24 inches thick was placed and anchored. On top of this mattress was an 18-inch thick structural mattress, which took sand fill and was so designed that it trapped sand despite strong tidal currents working to dislodge it. This technology predated the nanotechnology now being used for micro-biological applications. Then the piers were placed. Then granite was placed in three layers. First, small, then medium size rock, then massive boulders into which were drilled lifting and lowering hooks. These all prevented scouring away of footing material. Divers regularly check to make sure all is well down at the base.

"In the Netherlands, tulip-dahlia and other flowering plant technology was used to develop canal grasses which had two root characteristics; long, tough runner roots and periodic embedding roots. We learned that the runners, which were thought insignificant, possessed a formidable ability to mesh or create webs with runners of other grass plants. The runners became, quite unexpectedly, a support system to fend off canal tidal flows until the embedding roots were securely locked into the banks. The Dutch conditions were at least as severe as tidal currents in the Sundarbans and river deltas of Bangladesh."

She continued and now took a huge risk. Krystian had told her not to mention the firewood idea but she felt these people could understand and grasp the concept. They seemed so competent. "To do this, we envision a massive inflow to Bangladesh of firewood by ship for two to three years. And yes, I realize this seems novel. Two to three years appears sufficient to refoliate trees, shrubs, and grasses in most major defoliated areas. And by using what was formerly wood scavenging time to educate people (and there are millions) about careful and selective harvesting techniques will probably require an almost military regimentation. Then after we assure that methods for distribution of imported wood are effective, we will proceed to do plantings of grass, shrubs and trees. This is a bare bones outline of our concept."

"Maartje, is this relatively short external supply period due to the tropical rapid growth rate for grass, foliage, shrubs and trees?" Erika asks.

"Yes, Erika, everything grows at almost triple the rate of the Netherlands and most of Northern Europe. Now, how will a 2 to 3-year supply of firewood happen? Tall order; perhaps taller than any other construction issue. However, an important Bengali Senator is working with a group of wealthy businessmen to create a deep water seaport. They seek massive cargoes to be brought into Bangladesh so their chartered ships productively carry cargoes each way. Option contracts are being negotiated, as we speak, for minimum and maximum periods. Now, I am sure you will ask where will the wood come from. Here several diverse interests converge."

"Maartje, how will Bangladesh distribute the firewood?" Bill queries, while Brenden asks, "And avoid an invasion of bad bugs or tree diseases that could devour such grass, shrubs and trees Bangladesh has?"

Maartje answers, "You are both squarely on point. We have retained a noted British authority on diseases and destructive insects. Her task is to help perfect a shipboard system of fungus and vermin elimination. For political reasons, i.e., value added local services, all the ship off loading and distribution of the firewood will be done by Bengalis. As you may already know, boats in Bangladesh are like bicycles in China. The Bangla are people of the water."

Then Maartje poses what seems an off-base remark, "This may seem ridiculous but do all three of you ski?"

Everyone laughs as Erika replies, "Maartje, deliveries of Colorado babies are often complicated because the babies are born with skis attached."

"This is delightful," smiles Maartje. "Can you imagine a large number of ski lift units at the coast moving inland?"

Erika shakes her head. She can't grasp where Maartje is heading. "But Bangladesh is so flat. It doesn't begin to rise until the India corridor on the north—the sliver between Bhutan and Bangladesh."

"Yes, Erika, true. However, my idea involves horizontal cable systems, not vertical. As we speak, the ski lift gondolas are being redesigned to carry firewood. We expect this to be a significant method to deliver firewood to those who live in isolated areas, especially the coastal zone. It will supplement delivery by boats."

Royce says, "Oh, this is clever, very, very clever."

Maartje continues, "We are expecting very shortly a proposal from a European ski lift manufacturer to sell Bangladesh these cable systems. In fact, they are so intrigued with the concept, we at the RWS were required to agree to deal exclusively with them for five years. Otherwise, they would not even propose to us. And the government of Bangladesh must (this is also in process as we talk) guarantee the exclusive dealing covenant. A drawing of the wood gondolas should arrive within the next 10 days. Already they are pleased with their design. They must perceive a new market."

Royce asks, "Maartje, speak to us about soil retention as a means to control silt. I ask this because the designers of the Three Gorges Project were totally unwilling to consider soil retention measures to reduce silt movement. They laughed behind my back at my suggestion that given the money they were spending, earmarking funds to reduce or eliminate silt was important. My concern was that silt would build up and plug power generators causing devastating burn out loads on turbine shafts and bearings. From experiences on several major dams around the world, I have seen what happens when soil retention systems such as rip-rap, anchors and rock are implemented miles and miles upstream especially at the bends where rivers generate excessive turbulence. There will be an ongoing inspection and maintenance cost, of course."

Maartje's answer is, of necessity, lengthy. "Mr. Brenden. I promised this earlier in my remarks. On the Delta Project, we spent 20 years gathering interpreting and re-evaluating data. We were most concerned with sea bed preparation.

"It required three years to build the first massive piers to hold the gates. We were, of course, finalizing the design as we went. Our design was completed one year after the entire project was dedicated. For obvious reasons, I would appreciate your not broadcasting this last item.

"One of our team and several Bengali counterparts are working to enhance soil retention against turbulence by using a synthetic fabric to keep soil from being extracted from the banks. We used to think only of roots. Now we think about non-decomposing materials anchored to canal banks. If this approach works, then grasses and shrubs have time to develop and inter-weave with other plants and roots as they normally do in lesser velocity water.

"Nanotechnology offers some exceedingly advanced techniques. We try to stay close to the research."

Maartje does not put on the table her genetic engineering concept. She rather wants this to develop quietly and privately. Her intuition tells her that it is better to get the concept nailed down first. She understands the "bird in hand" philosophy. She can wait. Bangladesh can wait. The silt can wait. Getting the money cannot.

For the next several hours, Maartje, Royce, Erika and Bill discuss helicopter surveys, satellite imagery, tidal data and the supplemental data e-mailed by Nafis and Jagdish after Maartje left the Netherlands. They work whole eating their box lunches and well into the afternoon. At 4:00 p.m., Royce, sensing the benefit of a timeout says, "I suggest we break for the day to allow Erika, Bill and me to discuss the matter in light of your presentation. We would offer to take you out to dinner, but fairness suggests you be left alone. Is this satisfactory?" Maartje says, "Yes, I would love to go back to the hotel and freshen up. Would you recommend a restaurant for dinner?"

Bill says, "There are two in Cherry Creek near where we were last evening about a 5-minute taxi ride from your hotel. And there is

Lola, a fine Mexican restaurant. It's over in Lodo right near the Platte line. I'll get the addresses and phone numbers for you. "

Erika says, "I'll call you a taxi, say in 10 minutes?" Maartje thanks her and asks what time the morning meeting will be. Nine o'clock, Royce tells her so they will be able to finish by noon. Her flight leaves at 4:00 p.m. so she will need to be at the airport by 2:00 p.m. or even thirty minutes earlier.

After Maartje departs, Royce says, "Well, what do you two scientists think?"

Bill is impressed, "They are far more cautious than the Three Gorges teams. I would like to learn more about the fiber mats they are developing and their thoughts about nanotechnology. That is currently hot stuff. For many applications, they are slated to be far better than Kevlar."

Erika is more concerned with the local population, "I am concerned about policing any projects. Any engineering successes could be overridden by pilfering and thievery. It will take an army of security to sustain a two-three year growing period. Maybe two armies."

Royce, "I agree. However, we can sidestep any non-engineering issues—as not within our purview—by reciting certain assumptions and conditions for which others are accountable. But I'm looking for consensus among and between us on whether we can support their analysis and phase one recommendations."

Erika says, "These people are thoughtful, parameter sensitive, and cautious. I'm inclined to support them. However, I think the funding and firewood concept is a stretch. Maybe however, this is an assumption condition."

Bill concurs.

Then Royce wonders about the staffing needs. "I wonder how many more armies it will take to pull this off. What would you estimate, Bill?"

"I envision forestry, agronomy, shipping, distribution. I like the concept of horizontal ski lifts to move firewood and people. What's the difference between moving people over water rather than land—except light years of perspective? Then imported firewood may be more palatable. An army of communication and public relations, an army of donations (money or wood)."

Erika adds, "Don't forget policing and health care, Royce. How about an anti-terrorist army?"

"Medical care?" says Bill. "Isn't medicine far beyond our project scope?"

"Well," answers Royce, "sure, but without it and without a group like the World Food Program and UNICEF, our—or their—most brilliant engineering becomes futile. Long before any wood arrives, lest there be panic by millions, these lowlands people must be prepared and instructed about what they will receive, where to go—and when—to collect firewood allotments."

Erika salutes and agrees, "Quartermaster corps thinking."

Bill, "Precisely, Erika."

"Now," says Royce. "I have another question. Philosophically, are we to be done when our report is delivered or do we seek add-on work?"

Bill nods, "Very good thought. I vote for add-ons, like Maartje's RWS team. I would like to be attached to this kind of project for ten years."

"I'd be in favor of that," says Erika, "I don't think I will be here in two years but I agree. There is a large, do you say, reduction of human suffering component here. I feel a need to attach—in some way—to it. Perhaps that would be best through the Dutch RWS."

"True," says Royce. "Certainly it's safer from a funding-payment standpoint. The Dutch are incredible business people. They know how to perform, deliver and charge and get paid. We might learn from them."

Royce thanks his team, adding, "I feel a consensus of support with caveats, assumptions and limitations. Erika, I want you to flesh out the content of our report by Friday. Get Bill's input and let's meet Friday at 8:00 a.m. to finalize. I realize this is tight, but their backs are against the wall and we have agreed to the 29-day deadline (now only 20 days). And this means we have *our* backs to the wall."

Already Erika is beginning to rethink her return to Sweden. Some new hues of career choices are flickering in her mind. But there are concerns. Her parents are aging and expect her to be home in two years as their care-taking safety valve. Her relationship with Johann Akalund, a Swedish government inspector for shipyard construction may not survive a multi-year absence. Yet, something her carpenter grandpapa taught her is flashing in her head like a neon sign, "When you involve yourself in something bigger than yourself and it has the promise of helping others less fortunately situated, pay attention, participate, and make the commitment." Until the last two weeks, the routine in her life was leading comfortably toward a secure future in Sweden.

Back at the hotel, Maartje is clad only in her cotton underwear and is scrolling through her 156 e-mails. Then she sees one from Doctor LaVie, copied to Rajiv and Nafis. LaVie says, "We have reviewed your request for a genetically enhanced blend of water environment grass with a lengthy deep root. We will do the project but with two pricing variables; to save money we could include terminator genes. The price will be only 10,000 Euros. If we drop the terminator component, the price becomes 75,000 Euros. Obviously, if we are unable to make annual sales because the plants bear offspring, our consortium members cannot create future cash flow and profit. This forfeiture has a price as I am certain you can appreciate. We will require frequent and regular acknowledgment that this grass was developed by and came from us. We expect 60-90 days to complete the design and beta prototypes and another 90-150 days to produce two million fertilized seeds. Best, Henri. P.S. We can also do the royalty thing we discussed earlier."

Rajiv's e-mail is ecstatic. He reports on Pog Marenjar's caricatures and attaches them as a JPEG. As Maartje studies them, she thinks to herself, "God, how will we ever convert these to firewood and money?"

Jiv asks, "If you approve these, I will superimpose them on a series of presentation transparencies. Senator Mukherjee has approved them and has already paid Pog's first bill, so I am whole again. I am wondering about a comic book rendition of any presentation so kids here and everywhere can begin 'selling' the idea to parents—or maybe grandparents. I think this will take two to three years to bear fruit. I know you are in the USA but please give me ASAP your opinion of Pog's work."

Then he adds, "It feels very good every time I hear from you. Have a safe and successful trip."

Maartje replies to Jiv, "The caricatures are excellent. Proceed. The comic book is a great way to disseminate our project. I think we can expect to harvest the first small wood in two years assuming a six-month build-up of inventory before distribution and an intense resupply schedule." She closes her note by saying, "I feel so good when I read your e-mails and reply."

Rajiv replies, "What do you know about the ski lift proposal? I believe it is due next week. And what does your bug and fungus resource think?"

Maartje replies, "Won't know about either until late next week. And I realize the Senator is anxious to obtain this information but I am certain this is because his cronies are into ship charter negotiations."

Maartje heads off in a taxi. Her head is spinning from the intense day at Brenden's office. She feels congested and tired. The e-mails please her but remind her just how much has to be pulled together to obtain Jan's initial okay. And she must report to Krystian before she falls asleep. He will be coming to work about that time. He has a high need to know. It is clear that Director Jan's ambivalence troubles him. Maartje thinks Jan's expertise is misplaced. He is an expert at fabric design and technology, not decision making and personnel.

Perhaps, she thinks, Krystian could ask Jan to design a specific embankment fabric to assist in this project. She knows he would love to, but until his decision is made on the report, he would not respond to any such interest.

Her dinner at Lola is superb. Table-made guacamole, corn flour tortillas and margaritas are such a treat.

Maartje becomes very tired in the taxi on the return trip to the hotel. And she is not feeling good. But she does fire off a guardedly optimistic report to Krystian saying, "tomorrow is the day." She believes International Engineering will support the report and recommendations, but the conditions attached may be onerous, too onerous. She doesn't tell Krystian she mentioned the firewood.

Sleep comes rapidly. She is out until the 7:00 a.m. wake up call. Her head, especially sinuses, are plugged but she jumps out of bed, runs to the shower, and starts the coffee to reinforce her marginal "sort of awake" state. She wears a beige suit with a cream color blouse. Bags packed, she heads down to the desk, pays and checks out. She takes a quick cab to IEC and is there at 8:55 a.m. RMT. Royce pops in and asks her to sit tight for 15 to 20 minutes since he, Bill and Erika, are not quite finished. So she cranks up her laptop with its wireless modem. As expected, Krystian has replied, "I like the idea of a fabric designed by Jan. Once you tell me that Brenden and Company will support us, I will broach the fabric project with him. Actually, he is a natural for this. And he will do an outstanding job, one we can literally go to the bank with. I am lunching today with Joop Groot-emat, a Dosbouw (construction firm) Project Manager. He is capable and was very close to the mattress laying phase of the piers. He will help me think out embankment issues in the Sundarbans. I wonder how we will anchor this fabric so it stays where we want? This piece troubles me because the satellite pictures show the banks to be so unstable without tree, shrub and grass root structures. I wonder if the anchors might contain a bioengineered underwater grass which takes root after the anchor is in place. The generally fresh water supply could nourish the plants until they anchor their roots. Also, I wonder whether that fellow, LaVie, could build in a snorkel stalk which gets the plant up to the surface of the ground right above the business end of the embedded anchor?"

Maartje is taken back. This is a really stellar idea. He has such wide knowledge yet focuses so sharply on specific engineering concerns.

Erika comes through the door. "Good morning, Maartje. Sorry for the wait. We are ready—come." They meet in the same room as yesterday. Royce is on the phone rattling off some concrete strength numbers. His tone is frustrated. He ends the call, saying, "God damn.

I wonder when safety margins will become acceptable to the Asians—these folks from K.L. They want to cut corners everywhere. They do not care what happens five years after a project is completed. Shit. Just like the Chinese. Well, Maartje, let's get down to brass tacks."

Maartje looks puzzled.

Bill explains, "He means work. Idioms again. The bane of English as a Second Language."

Royce, "Maartje, we will support your report and recommendations. We believe the fundamental concepts are good, very good. The caveats we insert will deal more, as we discussed yesterday, with the success of the several extrinsic factors. To be candid, we think it will take several armies of resources to pull this off. I'll come back to this—actually Erika will. We commend your creativity and resourcefulness on the silt containment plan. It far exceeds anything we have seen before in China, here, Australia or South America. It should work. We are certain more R&D is necessary. But we believe you are on a sound footing, figuratively and literally. Frankly, if you pull it off, this may become an upstream working standard anywhere silt is problematic."

Erika hands her a single sheet of paper, "Maartje, here is an outline of assumptions we will attach. It is as tough as we hope it is fair."

Maartje thinks to herself, "These people appreciate the worth of their opinions and are very careful." The conditions do not comment on the processes used to cut back severely on silt movement. Instead, the outline reads,

- **Condition 1.** Silt containment in all waters flowing out toward the sea in the designated project blocks must be 30% effective within 2 years and 50% effective within 5 years.

- **Condition 2**, a supply of combustible wood, including kindling, must be sufficient to meet the requirements of coastal peoples in project block areas 1 through 14, 16, 17 and 21, within 32 months after written acceptance of the RWS report by the government of Bangladesh.

This, thinks Maartje to herself, is the keel of the ship the report is constructing.

- **Condition 3**, appropriate local wood distribution systems whether boat, cable systems or other must be in place and operative, in all material respects, 30 days before the first firewood shipments arrive in Bangladesh cleared by customs, unloaded and ready for distribution. These system(s) must be secured by troops or other firmly empowered forces, to resist panic by masses who fear they will not receive their first and second allotments of wood and also from terrorist attacks. We at IEC reserve the right to amend this condition to specify a flow volume of wood that renders the local population secure in its belief that free access to wood will essentially eliminate the need to forage for wood to burn.

- **Condition 4**. IEC is not a human services firm. It seems clear that a culturally acceptable public relations program will be required in advance. The timing and clarity—perhaps with illustrative pictures—would be very important. Unbelief or lack of support from local leaders (who must receive extra wood allotments to incent them); if it is too late could cause rioting and panic. The other conditions deal with the underlying accuracy of the data provided by the RWS and Bangladesh Interior Ministry.

They spend an hour going over all the conditions. Maartje is guardedly pleased. But Krystian will have to sell it to the director. A master politician must put this across.

She says, "Mr. Brenden, Bill and Erika. This is a careful and thoughtful opinion letter. You have honored your commitment to have it done on time. While I return to the Netherlands, would you e-mail it to Krystian Kpoczek at the RWS—you have his address. May I take this with me?"

Royce assents, but adds, "Certainly, but distribute only the one we send to Krystian." Then he takes her copy and writes, "Ms. deBouter's eyes only. Not for any distribution. RLB, IEC, Denver."

Maartje agrees, saying, "Of course, and please be assured that we may need your services further if our Director approves the report. You have touched on the concept of supporting armies for this project to succeed. This is beyond our current thinking. As you realize, we must clarify and amplify our thinking considerably."

As their meeting begins to break up, Maartje volunteers the bank grass development she is coordinating between Dr. LaVie, Jagdish, Nafis and Smeeta. Bill is very pleased with this. So is Erika. It is clear Royce is a steel and concrete fellow but as he ages, he demonstrates more interest in the soft, fuzzy stuff which facilitates and catalyzes project success. The value-added stages of big projects, the support stuff, is very important, and a first for him, because Erika and Bill are so committed, he is signing on emotionally. And he says so, taking a type of risk he is not known for taking, "Maartje, please keep us apprised about grass, fabric and anchor development. We have used an injection plastic designer who is very capable at mold and pattern design for the manufacture of both injection and blow molded parts. And routinely at realistic price/performance figures."

Maartje takes note saying, "We're not there yet, but send me an e-mail with his name and address and would you be kind enough to send him a note of introduction with a copy to me? I will pick up on it as soon as I return to Lisse. We must start."

"Gladly," says Royce, "his company is in Fort Collins about an hour north of here. I'll do it while you are flying."

They all say their goodbyes. Royce walks Maartje out to her taxi, insisting on carrying her two bags. Maartje says, "Please give my very best 'Tot Zeins' to Laura. She is charming and so easy to engage. No wonder the two of you travel so often together."

Royce thanks her. "She is a peach, a lovely wife and a wonderful grandmother. I will relay your greeting. And have a safe flight back. Our report should be on your computer in 12 to 18 hours."

"Thank you for your commitment and send your statement as a separate attachment so we can process it forthwith. Wire transfer seems the easiest. Include those bank routing numbers. But give us 20 to 30 days for our bureaucracy."

"Oh," says Royce. "I understand bureaucracy. Godspeed, Maartje. I am pleased we could be of assistance. I am very impressed with the multi-variate approach the Royal Water Service takes. No wonder your projects last 200 years."

While Maartje flies home, research is proceeding in the Sundarbans.

CHAPTER 19

The River Bank Dilemma

Nafis and Jagdish are hovering over a wooden examining table, each with a magnifying glass. Under their gaze are three specimens of river grass: one with 3-5" long whitish roots, a longer one measuring 12-16" and still a third, eight inches long but with many tributary fibers on the ends. Nafis says, "Look, the short root has more grass than root; the longest one has dense, not lengthy, grass. It was found right at the low tide level in a canal way up west in the Sundarbans. I've recorded the spot and logged the GPS coordinates. The roots are intriguing, but the vital point is that this plant survives on light entering the water and refracting. For three hours on each low tide it emerges from the water. If this strain could be reproduced in volume, it could markedly reduce silting. We must go back there to gather more. And we must air-ship this to Maartje deBouter or Dr. LaVie, better LaVie. He will find out about reproduction and genetic engineering. But we must pack it in water from the Sundarbans and try to assure some light so we do not lose it while in transit." They decide to use clear plexiglass containers.

Jagdish and Nafis decide they cannot, dare not, ship their single specimen until they secure another lest it be lost or destroyed in transit. They decide to return to the spot at the next low tide. They check tides, arrange for a departmental boat and load retrieving tools and pails. They also take shovels and boots. And they check on the weather for the next six to twelve hours. It will take two to three hours to get there, search for the plant and return. With the tide coming low going in and coming high on their return, they will require more travel time in each direction. They worry, too, over how to store their incredible sample until they obtain a second, maybe even a third.

They decide to keep it in the original container and under north light which is the least harmful to a partial-sun-only-plant. They mark it "Do not touch or move" and sign their names and date it as well.

An hour later, they pull away from a small dock and head northwest into a wide canal—against the tide which is now out flowing. The water is the murky sandy brown of suspended silt. They are careful boatmen and watch very carefully for tigers. They are also armed with the old 9 mm Mannlicher. Nafis is apprehensive about going in at low tide. That's an easier time for a tiger attack. Jagdish senses this and watches carefully as they travel. But they hear only birds and spot a hungry fish hawk carrying a still moving fish. They reach their search area just as slack tide occurs. It is quiet.

Jagdish says, "Here, Nafis. You be the body guard. Let me jump out and begin hunting. He puts on the tall muck boots which protect his feet from sharp items. His first six digs produce nothing, but the seventh is perfect. It is a specimen with 22-inch long roots." Nafis excitedly says, "Great job. Try for one or two more. Want me to take over?"

"No, you are a better shot than I. Allah called me to be a digger type."

They dig eight more plants from the bank as the tide begins flowing in at higher velocity. Jagdish yells, "Here's another, one not quite as long, but the tributary roots are better."

They admire it briefly, then pack up and head out into the middle of the canal. Once they gather speed, Nafis relaxes and says to Jagdish, "I'm glad we are out of there. I had a most uneasy feeling we were being watched. Low tide is very high risk. Incoming tide is a safety factor. Say, let's take a little extra water from this area before we get too far downstream. We'll need to aerate these samples and maybe refresh the water every few days." Next they test a sample of the water for PH and alkalinity. Another necessary test is gas chromatography on water and plants in case the Netherlands samples are harmed in shipment. Small samples for DNA analysis and reconstruction are preserved just in case.

Jagdish does the two analyses with chemically prepared strips and additives and logs the data. They return to the dock just as dusk settles in. With considerable relief, Nafis unloads the Mannlicher, thinking how good it would be to have a really powerful tiger gun. If he, Smeeta and Jagdish are to gather plants and grass samples and monitor tiger population, why shouldn't they have a hand held cannon?

Nafis thinks to himself that if the Dutch proceed with the project, he will ask for a gun as part of the project's cost. In fact, he has learned that another manufacturer, Steyr, has rhino guns. He has browsed on the Internet for images of these weapons.

He decides to call Dr. Rajiv early that evening on a Ministry cell phone. He knows Rajiv is working on the firewood project. How many large super-tankers will bring enough wood for two to three million families for 60 to 90 days? If they return every 55 to 60 days, maybe it can be done. They may need three or four such vessels. He has another idea. Perhaps some villages would consider, as an efficiency move, communal kitchens even if they need fires to warm their homes.

After they secure the boat and package the grass samples for preservation, Jagdish calls Dr. Rajiv on the doctor's cell phone. "Dr. Rajiv, Jagdish here from Forestry Section, Interior Ministry."

(Pause)

"Yes, I am fine. And how are you? We have been gathering samples of long rooted embankment grasses for Miss deBouter in the Netherlands. I assume she has spoken to you about this as a part of the silt program."

"Yes, Jagdish. This piece makes quite good sense. Are you having any luck?"

"Oh, yes, as of this afternoon, I am very pleased. Nafis and I found one beauty last week and sent it by DHL 2nd day delivery to Dr. La-Vie in Belgium. And today we found several more useful specimens. We will send him two and keep the others. Nafis will retain some plant material for DNA purposes. And how is the firewood project proceeding?"

"Believe it or not, we have only a few more things to work on. If we just find a few million dollars here or there, it's a go."

Jagdish says, "In Bangladesh, if you need people for a project, the project goes. If you seek money, the project dies. We are so poor." Banglas are culturally bound by this reality. It is so undeniably true they laugh about it.

"Yes, and only if we seek the funding offshore will we do any good. But you know the Senator has upped his promise to a 4:1 match. His bad press is actually helping us. Would you ever have believed this? Maybe he just feels so confident that we will never succeed at raising our share."

Jagdish reflects on what a pleasant person Dr. Rajiv is and how easily he crosses disciplines from medicine to flood construction to grass roots. It's the Monda that does this, not a doubt.

While these calls are taking place, Maartje is about to board her plane for Chicago. She calls the Global Wildlife Federation (GWF) in Boulder to discuss the top ten animals on their endangered species list and learn about grant application possibilities with Carolyn Mack, a staff member. "Miss deBouter, we are delighted with your inquiry, but the prospects for the Bengal tiger, which is number eight on our list, have been stalemated for lack of any realistic habitat proposal. It may drop next year to number 28 or 29 because we are close to a point of no hope. You say you are consulting on a storm surge protection system for coastal Bangladesh. What in the world could this have to do with tiger population and habitat? I am sorry to say I am not seeing the connection."

Maartje answers, "I have been called to board my plane. Dr. Rajiv Gaol will be contacting you within the next week with a grant feasibility request. He is a physician in coastal Bangladesh. But he is far more than this. His information and approach are interesting and, we believe, have scientifically sustainable validity. Please have your people give him attentive ears. He attended medical school in Chicago and has a fine world view. In short, I think you may be intrigued by his perspective. We at the RWS are supporting him and he has preliminary funding from the government of Bangladesh which is an almost impossible feat. Here is my e-mail address and I should observe that Royce Brenden, an engineer from IEC in Denver is working with us which is why I have been here for two days. Thank you and goodbye for now."

The GWF worker is befuddled. How could such a poor country have found money for tiger habitat and survival? What is the connection? The more she looks at it, the more out in orbit it seems. But Maartje seems to know what she is talking about. Carolyn phones a GWF director in Denver to ask if she knows Royce Brenden. Candace Carlton, the director, says, "Yes, he is extremely capable. If he is on the project, it is well worth your attention. One of his juniors belongs to our church and is also very impressive. They enjoy a reputation as being very ethical. I am only a psychologist, so I really don't know much about engineering. Do you want me to sniff around a little?"

Carolyn responds affirmatively.

"So moved," says Candace. "Give me a week or two."

"Not a problem."

Carolyn is now intrigued. Before she leaves for the day she wanders in to executive director Josephson's office. "Conrad, do you have a few minutes?"

"Yes, Carolyn. Sit down, please."

As she plops into one of his comfortable overstuffed chairs, she sighs deeply and begins explaining that she received a call from a "Maartje, M-a-a-r-t-j-e d-e B-o-u-t-e-r" who was in Denver for some meetings with a professional consulting engineer at IEC. DeBouter works for a Dutch coastal protection department. Her organization seems to be working with the government of Bangladesh on Bay of Bengal coastal protection proposals. This Miss deBouter inquired about the status of the Bengal tiger on the GWF endangered species list. And then she told me to expect a call next week from a Bengali physician who delivers health care to villagers in Bangladesh and along the northeastern border regions with India. The doctor wishes to make a grant application to us to enhance ecology, foliage and cover for Bengal tigers living in this area. Conrad, I do not see the connection, but perhaps you do."

"Carolyn, damned if I do either, but remember, first we listen."

Carolyn says, "I think maybe you should take his call."

"Wouldn't think of it, Carolyn. You are our point person and switching gate. Take the call, listen carefully—I'll work up a short list of questions. Then refer him to me or Jeanine. If we are not here, find out when we might call back. Be sure to get a time, date, and e-mail address. Then do a memo to us reflecting what he told you. And what you heard. They may be different. Do this immediately. It will be valuable."

"Also, Conrad, I just called Candace Carlton to inquire about Mr. Brenden. She will sniff around and get back to us in a week or two."

"Good move, Carolyn. She is a very committed, excellent director who gets it. Keep me in the loop. Let me think about this."

Before she leaves, he takes out a sheet of paper and the two of them sketch out a circular diagram which looks like this:

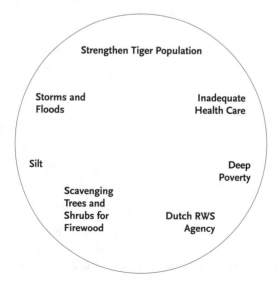

This helps Carolyn. She copies it and gets up to leave.

"Say hi to Jeff for me, Carolyn. How is his thesis coming?"

"He is on the home stretch. We are very excited. The oral defense went quite well. Only one chemistry professor worked him over roughly, on the error analysis section—the P. Chem computations. With luck, a year from now he will be a food nutritionist—one with a decent paying job. I do hope it is in Denver or here. He would love a faculty position. We love this area. You know how much I love this job."

"Carolyn, for what we are able to pay you, you have to love it. I wish our budget allowed more. But your review is coming up shortly. I appreciate having you around. We'll talk more in the next few days. I need to think this thing over. It's lucky we have the huge timber family endowment to generate grant income. Where would we be if you had not taken that phone call and blind drop-in visit three years ago? Do you remember how well you handled her?"

Carolyn Mack blushes.

"That's why you will take the call from the doctor. What is his name again?"

"Dr. Rajiv Gaol."

Conrad adds it to his card. As Carolyn leaves, he thinks to himself, if the Dutch are nibbling around the edges of this, maybe we should pay attention. They are the acknowledged masters of lowland protection.

Already the items in his concept circle are migrating. He knows he is days away from clarifying the connections, as he calls them. His basic process is to look for 'incented connections.'

He needs to know who will benefit by making these things happen. When he understands these, then he will be able to evaluate GWF participation. On the spur of the moment, he calls a colleague at the Colorado-based Atmospheric Research Center to acquire some updated knowledge about habitat loss and climate change. Dr. Jerry Beale is still there. Conrad asks his friend, "Say, Jerry, we are expecting a grant application regarding tiger population protection in coastal Bangladesh. What can you tell me about the impact of sea level rise, assuming our global warming rate stays essentially level?"

"Conrad, the Netherlands, the southeastern U.S. and Bangladesh are extremely vulnerable to sea level rise. Without coastal surge protection like the Dutch have and are continually enhancing, there is absolutely no hope for the survival of villages or foliage for animals."

Conrad ventures, "But Jerry, I understand Bangladesh has begun to work with the Dutch coastal protection agencies."

"This is interesting news, Conrad. That may be their only hope and I cannot overestimate this. Please keep me posted. Such efforts over the next 20 to 30 years could have a lot to say about the survival of both human and animal species there. I must dash. Doreene is waiting for me at that new French bistro. If I do not hustle, I will have my own climate change to reckon with. Let's talk after you receive the grant application. All the best, Conrad."

"Same to you, Jerry, and thanks. Blame me with Doreene. And give her my best."

Bangladesh

At the Matlah Clinic, Dr. Jiv is, as usual, hard at work summing up his weekly health care data for the organization. He sits in the Matlah processing center, which is twelve feet off the ground, on thirty-two 6" x 6" timbers which have been water-jetted eight feet into the ground. The one-story building begins ten feet above flood stage— an acceptable cyclone safety measure. It has standby power on the roof, air conditioning and data storage when hard wire power goes down—which it does at least weekly. Inside, it looks like an internet café but non-smoking and scrubbed clean.

He is tired but fulfilled. It has been a good week. No deaths other than a few elderly grandparents, no disease outbreaks and almost enough medicine and supplies to get by. He is looking forward to working with Pog tomorrow to roll the Bernice, Bertram and Banjo caricatures into his PowerPoint presentation. He will be speaking to the selected members of the National Congress for Bangladesh. And he wants Senator Mukherjee, Khalil, Maartje and Krystian to be critical as they edit more than sixty transparencies Maartje and he have located. The data must be perfect if they are to hope of obtaining government funding. He is troubled by the seeming delay (or is he just impatient?) in the vermin-fungus recommendations. However, the long rooted grass Jagdish and Nafis have located, retrieved and shipped to Dr. LaVie is a great discovery. Because the villagers already possess rice planting, tending and harvesting skills, they could be a first "army" of embankment planters and maintainers. And he thinks the RWS idea of an embankment fabric, a mattress, with seed embedded in fabric and anchors could be significant. Actually, on balance, he is feeling pretty good even after a long week. He does not remember how long it has been since he was doing so well on an early Friday evening. It is quiet on the water and in the lovely cover surrounding the data center. Even the birds, usually agitated about something, seem content. And the monkeys are quiet.

The gentleness of the evening causes him to muse about how loving and gentle his parents and siblings are, especially after the four tough years following his father's injuries. Maybe his family has come further than he thinks. Maybe he has, too. Yet he knows his country has not come very far. And he thinks about Sabjada, with her beautiful bright face and desire to learn. How he misses her. Maybe someday, if he receives a new clinic boat, he will call it the "Sabjada."

He finishes the data reporting and heads for his apartment. It is about a 30 minute taxi-ride. Fortunately, he has government vouchers for those, a real perk. Dinner comes first. He is very hungry and decides to head for some spicy, pork stir-fry with ginger and garlic at a tiny Laotian restaurant near his building.

Delft, Netherlands

Director Jan reads an early morning e-mail from Krystian: "Maartje is due in shortly. I will pick her up at Schiphol. She e-mailed me from Chicago while in transit to inform me that Royce Brenden and his staff will, with some conditions, support our report and recommendations. Their opinion will arrive shortly. It will come to my attention and I will e-post it to you. While we await this, I have a suggestion, assuming your response to the Brenden/IEC opinion letter is favorable. Is it possible that your North Sea seabed floor mattress design could be adapted to tropical embankment fabric anchored, somehow, to the banks of the coastal streams and tributaries? We think this approach could advance our timeline a great deal. The anchors must be special—maybe like porcupine quills. Once the anchor has been driven or injected into the soil, say 12-18" into the embankment, a slight retraction could force anchor prongs to open—like a parachute—to secure the anchors, which, if properly designed, will secure the fabric. Now, could the tips of these anchors be embedded with a plant seed and fertilizer that had genetically engineered 'snorkel like' growth to force a shoot to the surface from a depth of as much as 24 inches? I envision these anchors would be hydraulically injected. Because so much water in the Sundarbans is fresh, or marginally brackish during storm surge flooding, my thinking suggests we use, besides the soil, this water to facilitate germination. And the water, conceptually, could act either by pressure drop or hydraulically to move the fertilizer to the plant roots as they grew outside the tip of the anchors? This is my rough analysis and I offer it to the grist of your creative mind. I realize the anchors must have considerable impact strength. They should not degrade or decompose for a minimum of two to three years. We have PH and alkalinity data from several hundred water samples taken by the Bangla forestry staff. Maartje and I supervised the process. It is remarkably uniform. Our sample sites covered 50 canal/bayou/river miles. I am satisfied our sampling is statistically valid."

Jan leans back, scratches his head and looks up and out at the sky. My God, he thinks, when Krystian gets warmed up, there is no end to the horsepower he applies. This one idea is incredible. It might also work upstream of power generating dams. Think of the revenue we'd have if we applied for patents and protection to provide a royalty stream to the RWS. Clearly, Jan is motivated. Damn, he says to himself, Krystian knows exactly how to stir the kettle to solve a problem. He was brilliant when the Prince and his entourage came for that all day tour. And then they all went to dinner in that little town right there in the Delta. It was a charming end to a confrontational, all or nothing, day. What was the name of that charming 12th century town? He must ask Krystian. And did it still exist? That was 1981—25 years ago.

Little did Jan know, that at that very moment, Krystian was re-serving the same private dining room for a team dinner for the next week, Thursday, at the Eastern Scheldt Inn at Zierikzee. And yes, the same family (son and daughter-in-law) ran the place better, food wise, than had the parents. But the hospitable air of the papa and mama had not yet translated to the next generation. They were more busi-ness-like. The food was nutritious with Indonesian dishes sprinkled all over the menu. One cook was from Sumatra. And, the coconut milk cooking was to die for even if it presented cardiac concerns.

Dhaka, Bangladesh

"Snorkel shoots." My God. What next?! Senator Mukherjee's assis-tant, Khalil, is busy putting an analysis together and digesting a re-port from Anna Godsen, the bug doctor in Great Britain. This report says in order to secure 99+% freedom from vermin or fungus, the firewood must be autoclaved to force the combined fungicide-insec-ticide to the center of each piece. It would probably be a two-hour process and the chamber must, of course, be pressure welded. Khalil reports to the Senator and asks whether autoclaving should be done on board ship. The Senator responds that the risks would be too great to allow any untreated wood to leave ship. It must be done on board and during the voyage before any ship entered territorial waters. Just maybe, the Senator muses, a Bangla company could be created to manufacture these shipboard systems. How would they be shipped to the place where the unused freighters and super tankers have been put out to pasture?"

"Senator, why could we not have fabricating and welding shops, owned by us in those countries?" asked Khalil.

"Of course we could," replies the Senator. "My brother married into that Dhaka steel processing firm and has good connections. Perhaps our shipping partnership could own the fixtures, dies, and

CAD-CAM software. A license could require them to only use our technology and equipment."

"Ah," says Khalil, "clever, clever. But Senator, how will the flow of insecticide/fungicide be metered, monitored and reused? Dr. Godsen's report indicates the cost of this material."

"Good thought, Khalil. I will ask my brother whether we might develop a reclamation system for the excess sucked back out by vacuum pumps as the treatment is being finished." Khalil is wondering how in the world any odor can be dissipated.

The Senator is meeting later this day with his investment partners. Today the topic is public relations and education of the coastal masses. They need to select someone to sell this program. It must be a Bangla; must be Muslim-owned and staffed; must not be allied with any "reactive" political parties. There must be both women and men. Actually, a majority of women. Since so much of the cooking is done by women, the P.R. must speak in terms readily understood and accepted. Visual materials would be vital. The program will not be initiated until enough wood had been stockpiled and the distribution system tested and ready. Now, he wonders what had been learned from Dr. Rajiv or Miss Maartje about the cable system?

Khalil had heard nothing since their discussion a month ago. He suggested e-mailing Maartje to request an update. He also promised to think about the public relations possibilities.

Late in the day in the coastal waterways. Dr. Jiv, who had just finished for the day, was studying Dr. Godsen's report. He was concerned. One of the more important courses he took at med school was Environmental Medicine. This course—a two-semester seminar—was merged into an old toxicology course to prepare fledgling physicians to deal with toxic fumes and other residues from complex hydrocarbon structures. Generally, insecticides were ultra-complex. If the villagers burned firewood treated with such products, they would have to know in advance the consequences of combustion-borne residues.

He composes a brief memo to Maartje and Krystian and e-mails it to both. For now, he does not copy Khalil or the Senator until more is known—no need to create apprehension. Once again he appreciates the benefit of his medical education and Professor E. J. Kim who taught the seminar. She was regularly consulted by toxicology physicians and medical directors of companies who manufacture and distribute fungicides and insecticides. Is Dr. Godsen aware of these? He wonders. Perhaps he can visit her on his next (if there is funding) trip to Delft. He can fly to London as easily as Amsterdam. Then he'd take the ferry or chunnel train to Belgium and a short train north to Delft.

He is beginning to sense, without articulating it that any successful flood management will require highly sophisticated project management skills and software, sort of like a moving spreadsheet and critical path chart, all in one. Maybe with hyper-texting. The macro view ranges from firewood to genetic engineering to concrete, steel, shipping, PR, politics and, worst of all, terrorism. Suddenly he remembers Maartje's interest in the monk, Theophane. He wonders why.

Maartje reads Dr. Jiv's e-letter regarding toxic fumes and sees that Krystian is copied in. She forwards it to Anna Godsen with a request for help. "Is this a problem or perhaps an over-reaction?"

Krystian drops by her office with a short response to Dr. Jiv's e-mail regarding toxic fumes, "We must determine this. In any culture, these issues can blow up. As a trusted healer, Dr. Rajiv is very sensitive to his responsibility. Nothing we do can be allowed to betray this trust."

They decide to ask Dr. Godsen to select a toxicology lab to evaluate the effect of various concentrations of residue in cooking or heating smoke. A solution must be buttoned down before the first wood laden vessels sail. That will be the drop dead date.

"Maartje, I will e-mail Dr. Rajiv on this. Will you take responsibility for the Godsen effort and keep us posted? As a matter of protocol, suggest—or rather I will—that Dr. Rajiv communicate this concern to Senator Mukherjee—when he feels it is appropriate to do so. It is not our role to get between the Senator and Dr. Rajiv on this."

"Okay, Krystian."

The next day the IEC-Brenden report arrives. It is concise, comprehensive and careful. Krystian reads it three times and sends it on to Director, Jan, and the entire team.

Krystian's cover e-mail says, "Thursday next at 1500 hours we convene at the Oostescheldte Inn at Zierikzee. In the private meeting room. We will work until 1800, then drinks and dinner on the RWS, adjourn not later than 2100. Discussions, agenda to follow. Please stay focused. We will have, for certain, a 45-minute open comment discussion for comments, questions and concern. Maartje will be our recording secretary. If we are on track by 1700, we will have some appetizers."

Right now however, an impediment has cropped up. Maartje is sick. Her cheeks are very red and her large lips are hot and wan. She is run down, needs to see a physician and then go to bed. She has worked and traveled herself into infection. Krystian sees this immediately and says, "Maartje, get your coat, cap and scarf. I am taking you to the clinic right now. We have way too much on our plate in the next 90 days to risk not having you at full speed by Zierikzee next week. And I do not want to see you here for three days at least. Use these days and the weekend to recover. And no e-mails in or out for 72 hours. Do you understand?"

The doctor concurs and says, "Madam, you appear very worn down. If you will not stay in bed, take four of these pills daily, drink four liters of fluids (no diet sodas) daily, I will place you in the hospital right now. And, if you are walking next week, you may thank Mr. Krystian for this. Do you have a private care provider? No? Well, you have two choices: we have a public health nurse on staff. She will come twice daily for 60 Euros a day. I believe 60 percent of this is government health care reimbursed. Pay her directly. I want to order blood and urine work on you. My nurse will be in shortly. I will call you tomorrow between 1100 and 1300 to report. And I will tell Mr. Krystian directly that you are not to report to work until our visiting nurse clears you. And one more item: you are to work no more than 4 hours a day during your first week back. This I will report to Mr. Krystian also."

Maartje is fully aware she is in bad shape. She has been fighting this. As the nurse comes, the doctor leaves to speak with Krystian in the lobby. Maartje comes out and is barely able to walk even when she takes Krystian's arm. He wraps her neck carefully in her beige wool-cashmere scarf covering her mouth and nose from the biting North Sea winds. It is winter in the Netherlands. All is gray, cold, wet and very windy. It will be another 60 days before walking on top of the dunes will seem refreshing. Maartje takes her first doses of antibiotics, sinus and chest congestion medication, drinks two cups of tea and collapses into bed. She cannot even answer the phone for ten hours and when she goes to the door of her apartment, she finds a gift. Krystian has left a case of mineral water in plastic liter bottles and eight tetra-paks of chicken soup. Krystian, the veiled and camouflaged, bird-watching romantic, had already sent Rajiv an e-mail describing Maartje's sinus-chest infection and state of exhaustion. Tears swell up in her eyes. She feels very cared about. This former refugee, engineer has far more on his plate than Maartje. Yet, he and his wife Arrianne visit every day. For the first time in her life, Maartje pauses to wonder who cares for the caregiver and whether someday she might be a caregiver. Since Rajiv gave her the lovely sweater, she has not felt this cared about. It's a good feeling, especially for one who never thought about needing it.

As she rests and the medicine begins to attack the congestion, her thoughts go to Rajiv. Desires, too. She has only been physically intimate with one man, when she was a junior in college. It was a good relationship and lasted until he graduated that summer and went to England. She had been too focused on her career to invest, emotionally, in the continuation of a long-distance romance. Anyway, he married that next year.

Her feelings about Rajiv are both unsettling and enticing. A caring e-mail from Rajiv is heartwarming and makes her feel better certainly emotionally. She responds warmly.

She is about as tall as Jiv and 20 pounds heavier than the lean, deep brown, tough skinned Bengali. Even the fact she is thinking about "stuff" is bewildering. For now, she attributes this dreaminess to the medicine and her condition. Medicines do this, you know.

Her mind wanders from Jiv to her family. Her parents and married brothers live up north near the Frisian Islands. Her brothers are dairy-pork farmers and cheese co-op members. Her parents retired so they could help the sons and spouses farm and care for their grandchildren—three nieces and one nephew. She misses her family and has allowed her job to keep her too busy. So she calls each household just to chat about being incarcerated by physician and boss.

Fortunately, all is well at home. The boys report that there have been losses due to the recent hoof and mouth epidemic and mad cow mess, both monumentally poorly managed by the government and EU. Twenty of their 108 Holsteins were tested and taken because they were distantly related to a sick bull in Belgium. Many farmers lost complete herds and the government had to burn barns using napalm if hoof and mouth infiltrated the herd.

One brother is a part-time eel inspector for North Sea eels, a delicacy sought Europe-wide, especially by those from Swedish islands in the Baltic. There twelve families own one particular island. The island is divided in 30 degree sectors for economically strategic reasons. Each sector owner owns the rights to all marine harvesting for a distance of three miles into the Baltic. Within those three miles lie the richest eel breeding and harvesting grounds in the Baltic waters. These rights earn between two and three million Euros a year. Not bad, even divided by twelve. Her brother, Hanno, travels there several weeks a year for inspection. The quality and taste of Swedish eels is exceptional.

But one year the harvest was markedly diminished and the eel's taste was harsh. A biologist using infra-red photography determined that unusual currents had sucked phosphorus-based fertilizer and effluent from farms on Sweden's south coast onto the eel breeding grounds. It was an economic disaster that year for the islanders as well as a public relations issue of major magnitude. In the end, the eel farmers prevailed. Since then, phosphate fertilizers have not been permitted on coastal perimeter Swedish farms anymore. This incident tilted the government toward the greens as it became politically unacceptable to advocate for the deeply entrenched phosphate fertilizer interests. Efforts are well underway to successfully dilute the effluent runoff by an e-coli munching bacteria added every ten acres to the tiled fields and swales. Water quality during this period is making a compelling environmental case. Except for the phosphate and nitrate fertilizer companies, there seem to be no losers and many winners.

Maartje marvels over how water quality can so affect livelihoods, here just as in Bangladesh.

At the GWF in Boulder, Conrad is working on his circular analysis. It has been bothering him a lot. This time, he starts with three points on a triangle:

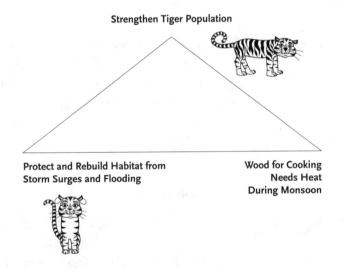

Strengthen Tiger Population

Protect and Rebuild Habitat from Storm Surges and Flooding

Wood for Cooking Needs Heat During Monsoon

This is vexing. After half an hour, he walks away from his chalk board. I'm making progress, he mutters to himself, but I'm not there yet. How in hell can tiger population improvement converge with human quality of life enhancement? He cannot see his way through this conundrum. Maybe the staff can help solve the riddle.

He calls Carolyn, "Say, would you come look at the charts I started last week? Also, would you find 15 minutes in the next day or two to gather the staff to brainstorm on this? I think I am on the right track, but I cannot visualize the connections."

"Sure, probably tomorrow about 3:00 p.m. Will this work?"

"We'll make it work," says Conrad.

So she puts out the word via e-mail. As she does this, an e-mail pops up on her screen from Dr. Rajiv Gaol. It reads just like Maartje deBouter advised over the phone. She jumps on it. "Dr. Gaol," she responds, "Maartje deBouter called us two weeks ago and informed us we should expect a communication from you concerning a grant application. As you request, enclosed as an attachment are our guidelines and the application itself. Do not hesitate to e-mail if you have questions. Miss deBouter seems quite capable and she speaks very highly of you. We have been waiting to hear from you. Per your instruction, Miss deBouter and a Senator R.M. Mukherjee and a K. Kpoczek will be copied on this and all further communications. If this list changes, just let me know. The guidelines are ten pages long. The application is eight. By the way, I understand you attended medical school at Northwestern University in Evanston. I was raised in Oak Park. Many of my classmates went to NU. All the best. GWF by Carolyn Mack, Coordinator. cc: Conrad, Senator Ram M. Mukherjee, Ms. Maartje deBouter, RWS, Krystian Kpoczek, RWS."

Bangladesh

In a certain graphic arts studio in Dhaka, Pog Marenjar and Jiv are engrossed in caricatures. Pog, always tongue in cheek, is seriously addressing Dr. Rajiv. "You know, Jiv, a long time ago Americans used to drive long distances to see the sights like the Badlands and Mt. Rushmore in South Dakota, the Tetons in Wyoming, and the Grand Canyon. One of the all-time successful advertising schemes ever on those long, Great Plains and prairie roads were Burma Shave ads."

"What is Burma Shave?"

"Jiv, it is shaving cream."

"Ah," says Jiv.

"There would be four or five wooden signs in a row about every

1/8 of a mile with rhyming and entertaining jingles. Kids loved them and so did parents. In my marketing classes in Calcutta, these were used as an example of superb marketing. They really made that shaving cream famous. Now you can't have a roadside campaign like that because you're not allowed to have the signs close to the road. But there are some enterprising Internet Web page designers who use this same concept."

"What's the point, Pog?"

"Well, Jiv, I think you might consider something like this to educate Bangla masses along the coastal areas and in the Sundarbans."

"Just don't make the signs out of wood or combustible cardboard, Pog," says Jiv.

"Yes, yes, they could be in plastic and they could be along the various canals and tributaries. I suggest using Bertram and Bernice on flyers that we will distribute, by the millions, by air, boat, and train to introduce the firewood programs. Tweaking the people to get them ready is what I am proposing. Here's an example:

Floods and cyclones won't destroy us. We will replant our forests.	**Bernice**
Free firewood will be supplied. And plenty. 2008.	**Bert**
We're Bangladesh, In this we trust.	**Both**
Watch for more information.	**Bernice**
	Marenjar.Pog@Bangl.net

"My God, Pog. It makes very good sense to do this during the year before distribution of the wood. Do you mind if I run this by Maartje, Krystian and Khalil, Senator Mukherjee's staff communications fellow? He's quite bright and does a good job getting the Senator's ear. We need material like this. And maybe I will try my hand at a set of these "Burma Shave" jingles. We could have some kids' cartoon books using caricatures to inspire connections between kids here and kids all over the world. Maybe we could lend tigers, perhaps to zoos in San Diego, Chicago, Helsinki, London, Munich. We could grow the species on foreign turf and (Pog jumps in), "Have the original cats returned to the Sundarbans after several successful breeding seasons overseas. That might placate some Mullahs who believe tigers have significant spiritual value."

Pog continues, "Very powerful. The fear of tigers here, in India, and China, is deeply embedded in the culture. Let's trade up on this to keep Mullahs from organizing people against this. The question is how do we begin a movement? At an appropriate time maybe the Senator could meet with several Mullahs to begin the process of enlisting their help—or at least keep them from working against it."

"Good, Pog," says Jiv.

"Pog, why didn't we think of this before now? Of course, we need to factor in spiritual dominion over the masses. We have to respect this and inspire it properly to build momentum."

"You know, Jiv, if we enlist their support, they may help us contain Bangla Bhai terrorist activities against the program."

"How so, Pog?" asked Rajiv.

And for the next hour, they debated the politics of including Muslim priests in the planning including a tiger Holy Day to bless the recovery of the species. Yes, and having Mullahs ride the cable rigs when they first distribute wood. All sorts of ideas like this.

"Some great thinking, Jiv. And they could bless the deep water container port, too. Just make damn sure everything is working right."

Delft

In Delft, discussions are centered on treating the wood.

"Krystian," said Henrik Van Stoors, a Smit Transport specialist, "I doubt there could be any successful fumigation of a whole ship cargo hold. Too many hazards for ship and crew. But we might think about specially designed containers for wood being moved into and out of a chamber on train tracks. A completed load could be pulled out while an untreated container was entering the chamber. Such a system could be engineered. I envision a series of rails or tracks underfoot and cranes or rails overhead."

Krystian says, "Henrik, if the containers are stacked 4 or 5 high in the hold, could the chamber be tall enough to accommodate this many? Maybe double wide as with mobile homes?"

"By God, Krystian. I haven't the slightest idea. But we have a very bright mechanical engineering lady in our Naval Architecture Department. Let me run it by her."

"Sure, Henrik, perhaps you and she would come to our RWS team meeting and dinner in Zierikzee next Thursday? It is a brain storming session. I think we need some fresh input to keep creative juices flowing."

He checks his schedule. "Sure, I am able to be there. Let me call Julianne."

Maartje is just beginning to feel better. It is Sunday, four days before the work session and dinner meeting. Krystian and Arrianne visit her Sunday afternoon. She is ordered to stay home Monday. She fights this until Krystian makes clear that, if she shows up before Tuesday, she will be uninvited Thursday. She knows she is in a box. She must be at least 80 percent for Zierikzee and needs to dialog with the Smit people. She has seen Henrik's e-mails to K.K. This is too important. Once again, Krystian added more skill sets to the loop. But fatigue beckons her into a long late morning nap. She has no sustained energy.

In Denver at the IEC, Royce Brenden is talking with David Beauchamp, a member of the World Bank's board. "Do you remember the fuss over the Three Gorges Dam?"

"How could we not? Egad, China wanted to assassinate you and cut the Bank off from our own long standing lines of credit throughout Asia and Japan. They were nasty. Luckily, we beat them off. They are not very confrontational and when you dug in your heels on the silt-garbage matter, they did not know how to deal with this."

"Well," says Royce, "we may have a new one coming over the horizon and I can smell a World Bank role 5-6 years from now."

"Royce, we are always looking for quality loan packages in politically stable countries. What is up?"

"Well, David, the Dutch Royal Water Service is doing a first phase consult for Bangladesh."

"Christ, Royce, that country is so poor it is not even on our list."

"Hold on, David. I smell some big local money and political power coupled with Dutch ingenuity and Bengal tigers—300 of them—in the coastal regions. These are some very sophisticated heads at work—here and there. They came to us for an opinion on silt management techniques. And I must say they are very advanced. We are conditionally blessing their approach."

"You know the joke about Bangladesh, Royce?"

"No, I do not."

"Bangladesh has two seasons—six months of soccer followed by six months of water polo. Same players, same ball!"

"Really bad, David. My point is this—if the preliminary phases are funded, I would think about putting yourself in line for some major loans. I will tell you that my skeptical wife, Laura, thought the Dutch engineer, a lady, was one of the more competent, committed people she has met. My team found her exceptionally mature for 32. She was prepared, innovative and cautious. A professional bundle."

"Must go, Royce. Only because I trust your judgment will I do some monitoring."

"Don't sweat it. You are several years away. I think you get the idea. Thank you for the ear."

Brenden heads off to meet with Erika and Bill who are completing their analysis of a South American project.

In Delft, Krystian is uneasy about autoclaving but it seems the only way to protect indigenous species and comply with Dr. Godsen's ideas on protective measures. Having an autoclaving facility in each seaport where wood is loaded would be way over the top, cost wise. Better one per ship. In fact, muses Krystian, it is sort of like a modern ship board total container inspection system on container vessels at sea.

Krystian e-mails Dr. Godsen:

"While Maartje recovers from a very bad sinus and respiratory infection, I would like to pick your brain on the firewood shipping concept. Logic says it would be prudent to have treatment done in transit. This way there might be only three to six autoclave treatment facilities depending on the number of vessels chartered. My thought is that by treating as many vertically stacked containers as the height of the pressure vessel can handle in one batch and using overhead cranes, rails, and specially designed firewood containers with holes top, bottom, sides and ends, or rigid wire cloth construction, we might be able to pressure treat in the chamber, then evacuate the excess chemicals by applying a negative pressure so the ship is relatively clean for a returning journey with clothing and other goods on its route to pick up another load of wood.

"Counsel us, please, whether this is 'far out' thinking. Maartje may be back tomorrow for half a day. Our entire team meets this Thursday at 3:00 p.m. for a work session. Any response before then would help.

Krystian Kpoczek, Bangladesh Project Director for the Royal Water Service—Delft."

It's now March in Bangladesh. Dr. Jiv is hard at work doing his Monday clinics. As usual, the limited supply of medicines and supplies is frustrating but, for the first time, he senses hope—a change from his prior frustration over those situations which in most other countries would be ordinary. But these patients hover so precariously in no man's land. So many are lost. But, something has been happening since his relationship with Dr. Doyal and the Senator has evolved.

It is clear there is an increased flow of medicines, anti-dehydration fluids, electrolytes, topical antibiotics and bandages. He must talk with and thank Dr. Doyal. A note of appreciation is certainly in order. Perhaps more. He will call this evening. May keep the pipeline open. But why does he have doubts about the Senator?

In the GWF offices in Boulder, Conrad and a couple of ecological types and Carolyn are in vigorous discussion. Carolyn says, "Conrad, I think firewood is the connector that catalyzes the tiger recovery and coastal protection. Let me show you."

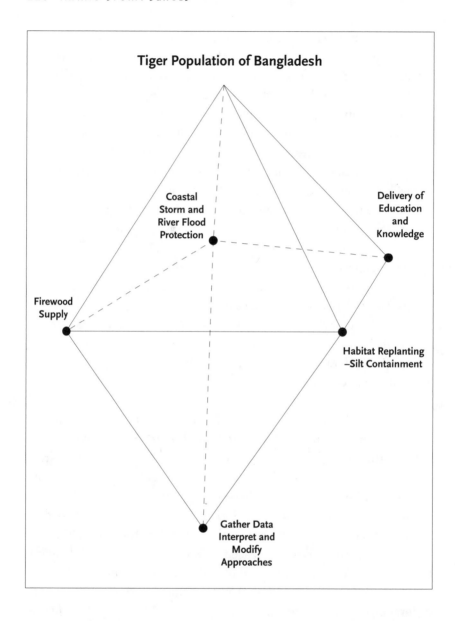

Conrad agrees, "You are right. Firewood has a lot to do with tiger population enhancement.

"Carolyn, clean this up and, when the Bangladesh application arrives add it to the GWF distribution package. Label it 'GWF Vital Connections.'"

In Lisse, Netherlands, Maartje is petting her sweater, the Dr. Jiv Sweater, as if it were sacred. She does not understand why she feels this way, but she is intrigued by this overworked, underpaid civil servant and his intense commitment to caring for village children. His vision for a better tomorrow is overpowering. She also thinks about Theophane. The pictures in her mind of the two men seem to merge into one blurred person—a pillar of commitment and yes, one of faith. She feels connected to both. Just as she puts on the sweater, Krystian calls and asks whether now is a good time to stop by. She says, of course, and hurriedly combs her hair for his visit in fifteen minutes. Her apartment is messy. It is in one of those old 2½ story buildings with the characteristic pyramidal orange tile roof, probably built around 1900-1910 and rebuilt after the Nazi bombings during the war. It is a dark red brick structure with much newer crank-out windows clad in white PVC . All her drapes are lace with a valance at the top and a half window below.

The rooms are well lit and orderly but clearly need a thorough cleaning. The entrance is warm and welcoming. All 31 family member pictures are on the walls or bookcases. The book cases are full of books on engineering, construction materials and handbooks and an array of MBA course books and seminar materials. Her kitchen-dining area is small but well laid out. Its centerpiece is a birch country-style table with sturdy chairs. It has a bouquet of flowers, begonias, caspia, tulips, and daffodils, nicely arranged. The flowers came from Krystian's wife. Maartje's bedroom is a shambles. Her queen size bed needs a change. Her health is improving but her place does not show this and it bothers her. She is half a homemaker, unlike her accomplished mother and sisters-in-law. She realizes this, perhaps for the first time. Maybe a cleaner, more comfortable nest would be a good thing. She does fairly well before Krystian arrives. Her Miele electric broom is her real cleaning maid. Sort of a hand-held Mercedes. And it runs so quietly. She loves it.

Krystian knocks. Maartje goes to the door, opens it and bids him enter. "My, my," he says, "you look quite a bit better and what a lovely sweater. You did not buy that here in Lisse, I am sure."

"Oh, no," she says. "Dr. Rajiv gave it to me. His mother knitted it. The words translate to 'Faith is the bird who feels the light and sings while the dawn is still dark.'"

"I like that. It suits you. Now, how are you and how do you feel about returning half days tomorrow and Wednesday and a late starting but full day Thursday?"

"I think I can do it, Krystian."

"Do not show up until 10 tomorrow and please leave at 2:00 p.m. sharp or I will send you home in a taxi. Do you understand?"

"Aye, aye, fleet admiral, sir!"

Krystian explains that Dr. Rajiv has begun work on the GWF grant application and is baffled by several inquiries. He asked for their help and Khalil's. They will discuss this on Thursday but he wants her to review these e-mails and attachments. It is a very pointed application. "Probably you and I should be with Jiv if he is invited to make an in-person presentation. Perhaps the Senator and Khalil should be there, also."

Maartje tells Krystian she thinks politically it would be bad judgment not to include them.

Maartje explains to Krystian that, in her assessment, the Senator has formidable skills as a statesman and perhaps he could begin, before Dr. Rajiv's PowerPoint presentation or better yet, he could summarize the presentation. He epitomizes the power layer of Bangladesh.

"The Senator could put across the person and personality of the country and he can close with his new quadruple commitment. Dr. Rajiv, you, Royce Brenden, maybe a minor role by me just to change tempo and provide a woman's perspective, could be useful. Depends how much time is allotted. My goodness, we are way ahead of things. They may sit on our grant for three years. Or worse yet, turn us down by return mail."

Dhaka, Bangladesh

Dr. Rajiv is working on the grant application when two new e-mails pop up on his lap top. One is from the RWS—Maartje or Krystian.

The second is from a medical school classmate he hasn't heard from since their last night party together in Evanston. "Jiv, how the hell are you? Wow. It has been five years since we squeezed drops from those bottles of red wine! I am in a fairly large radiology group in DuPage County near Wheaton-Naperville. We have a good practice, but guess what? Surgery has evolved from a sedentary 50-hour, weekends off, routine to a regular 65-75-hour per week grind. The development of minimally invasive techniques like heart stents, laparoscopes, vertebraplasty, and the like puts us on-call 24/7. It's do it or sink. I am barely attacking my debt. It was $212,000 when I started practice, now it's down to $140,000. My husband has been a real soldier. Enough about me. How is your practice going and how are you? All I read about Bangladesh is storms, floods and trauma. Hope this is not true for you. Give me an update when you can. Any chance of your coming for the 7-year medical school class reunion in Chicago? All the best, Dana (James) Josephson."

Jiv is warmed by this electronic probe to a long ago life. He has good memories of these comrades. Chicago seems a long way away, but wouldn't it be grand to be there? Maybe a pediatric conference for general practitioners would be in the cards. He makes a mental note to diary this reunion in nine months and twelve months. By then, the seminar announcements should be available from the American Society of Pediatric Medicine. This leaves him more than a little nostalgic and for the first time grateful he has zero medical school debt and only 36 months to go on his debt forgiveness from his government. My, where has the time gone? He pecks out a pleasant reply to Dr. Dana.

Maartje's e-mail thanks him for his message, asks about the GWF application, and suggests that he connect the Senator via Khalil. He does so promptly and also contacts Nafis and Jagdish. Their bank grass efforts hold promise and they are local. He notes that Royce Brenden, the World Bank consultant, is supportive of this approach. He tells Nafis and Jagdish about the grant application and notes that one of the RWS senior people is working on an embankment mattress and anchors which may hold seed and fertilizer. Jiv wants the grant application complete and clear for all. A medical school prof taught him this typically midwestern "open communication" methodology. Rajiv has never forgotten it. The method was so beneficial for resolution of complex patient care issues. Gathering and talking with the whole team, patients included, was so effective. Here, Rajiv has two patients: children and tigers. Maybe three, politicians.

Boulder, Colorado, GWF

Carolyn takes a call. It is Candace Carlton, the woman she spoke to about ten days ago seeking some quality information on Royce Brenden and IEC.

"Carolyn, I have some tidbits. Brenden is widely respected. He was a consultant on I-70 east of Glenwood Springs. His work was helpful. He is reputed to be an excellent communicator and is fearless in the face of skeptics. He can be brutally honest. This often threatens career political types, I mean those who operate like chameleons."

"This is very helpful, Mrs. Carlton."

"Carolyn, I will try to get more information."

"Thank you for the effort."

And Carolyn does a quick e-mail to Conrad summarizing this report.

At Matlah

In the midst of work, Rajiv's thoughts go to Maartje. When will they see each other? Perhaps in Boulder, if they receive a nod from GWF or Calcutta if she returns before any response on the application. Especially if Senator Mukherjee needs a technical gathering as he positions the Senate and National Assembly for the action he will direct on both seaport and quadruple grant match funding. All of a sudden Rajiv remembers Smeeta, the sharp lady they met when Maartje and Krystian were here. He has been remiss about keeping her in the loop. He jots off an e-note suggesting they meet soon so they might bring each other up to date:

"Smeeta:

"Sorry for not ringing you up sooner. We are progressing on all fronts. Perhaps Nafis or Jagdish has filled you in. We have a shot at a $10m (USD) grant from a USA based animal endangered species foundation. Bengal tigers are #8 on their list of the top 10 endangered species and they were about to give up as hopeless when we came along. Senator Mukherjee says he has preliminary commitments from our national assembly to quadruple any species preservation grant. A huge part of our proposal is habitat recovery and reforestation.

"Let's meet ASAP to review this and get your input on the 'firewood' piece of our concept. And I want to discuss Dr. Anna Godsen with you, too.

"Gaol, Rajiv, M.D.

"P.S. Best to meet late Wednesday next or Thursday say, 1800. I do not mind coming to you. Just tell me where."

Once again, Nafis is on the Internet surfing rifles to defend against tigers. There are Austrian (Steyr), Belgian (Browning), British (Weatherby) and American (Remington and Ruger) models and styles; .370 and higher. Only two short barreled models present themselves. He really likes the Steyr .370 magnum. At 100 yards, it will stop a 1500 pound rhino in its tracks. That should cover it, he thinks. But if he wants to include this in a budget for a project to save tigers it will take more than marketing. How about self defense materials for foresters and ecologists doing research in the Sundarbans? Not bad for a start. Safety tools for researchers in the Sundarbans. Of course, a 22-foot Boston whaler with two 225 HP Yamaha engines would also be another self preservation vehicle. But these would cost $50,000.

Long ago, he remembers his grandfather regaling him with tales of tiger hunts when countrymen beat the grasses while Maharajahs and British civil servants rode atop elephants with side-by-side short stock rifles. These were made in Germany—their mechanisms were flawless—and finished in Great Britain (value added to avoid import duties). These rifles were high caliber, short range. The range was calibrated right where the hollow point heads crossed, at about 78 yards. On top of the elephant mount right behind the mahout was also a double barrel—also side by side—long barrel pistol with large bore heavy black powder loads. While catalogued as a pistol, it was two small cannon barrels masquerading as a handgun. Grandpapa laughed when he described the kick. If, after a hit from a rifle the tiger kept coming, this was added safety. Grandpapa was a beater first, then an apprentice mahout. And he remembered Grandpapa had given him a book, *Big Game Hunting on Ceylon* by a gentleman named Baker. Where was the book, now? He thought his Mum had it. This book he wanted to reread. Talk about danger. Nafis thought, no wonder I am so interested in tigers or concerned about being stalked by one.

At Delft—Director Jan and Krystian are deep in conversation. It is becoming clear the director will approve the report with the conditions and assumptions plus a couple of his own. It is equally clear the embankment mattress interests him. He has been processing this ever since Krystian tendered it. He loves this stuff, but being part Brit, would never reveal pleasure at being asked to tear into this. The mattress is probably easier than the anchors. He is intrigued by Royce Brenden's reference to an injection molding firm in Colorado. This component is a bit foreign and the offer of technical help is appealing. Especially the idea of a seed carrying tip with exit holes for roots and a miniature pipeline to facilitate germination moisture. Clearly, the seed chamber must be located an inch or so short of the anchor tip and the "Root" hole tilted obliquely back so the anchor insertion process does not damage or seal the opening. All this is well beyond Jan's ken, but he trusts Krystian's assessment. And there may be some real incentive for Brenden to ride herd on this local company. Jan, however, wants the RWS to achieve proprietary protection for the mattress and manufacture process, if possible. These arrangements could create royalty streams for the RWS to help sustain future staffing and facilities. Sometimes it is a very, long, dry season between major projects, longer and drier yet for payment from some. Such an "endowment" as provides incremental payment streams may help a great deal. Jan decides to e-mail Brenden to open dialogue with the injection mold designer. Krystian helps him compose the communication. And bingo, it is done, except it is night in Colorado. So it might be a day or so before the three are in sync. Jan smiles. Scientists are so impatient when their minds need to slow down while technology catches up. But this is fun. Jan is back in his element.

He says to himself, "And damn you, Krystian. You just knew I was a patsy for this project. You are a real Zorro. You ride in, rescue the fair damsel (Maartje), start massive fires and vanish—until the next perceived injustice. What a gem the Czech Republic lost! Yet, another tragedy for communism. But his Netherlands culture is well known for being so inclusive and welcoming." This renders him proud. Recently, many talented Javanese and Indonesian scientists, physicians, and teachers have emigrated to escape extremist terror. God, he thinks, when will our own 9-11 terror happen? He shudders to think about what these foul creatures could do to the massive storm surge systems of the North Sea coast. Enough of this anxiety for now. Time to call it a day to join his wife, son and daughter-in-law for dinner in Haarlem. The seafood there is lovely. His stomach is ready. A glass of oude genever will taste grand. Maybe two or three. It's already been a long week. An exciting one, however. And he cannot wait to hear from Brenden. (And day after tomorrow, after Krystian's team meeting at Zierikzee.) I think this can be a very productive gathering if handled properly. He wishes he could be a little mouse in the corner. The focus for this one is three fold: first, are the primary construction stages feasible if silt is drastically reduced? Second, can the team support this 'firewood' thing? Third, will the Netherlands' experience with embankment grass effectively transfer to Bangladesh assuming some genetically engineered enhancements to root structures of grasses? This begs a larger question: How might Bangla forestry resources be empowered to take the point on this and what political support, funding, and security would be required to maintain presence for at least three years of firewood supply and distribution? The team's response to the Kloppleser design memo (just in this a.m.) will be important.

Jan smiles at the Dutch perception that Austrians are just Germans with marketing genes. His first review of the proposal is that it will work. Volumes will be a concern until a substantial inventory of treated firewood is distributed to coastal residents. He hopes the team meeting produces some computations of cords required to meet and survive at least the initial assault by these masses. Oh, Lord. Has anyone thought of covering the wood to keep it reasonably dry in monsoon season?

Firewood ferry boats, lighters in the vernacular, would be necessary adjuncts to any horizontal cable systems. They can serve as backup for cable shut downs for maintenance or part failure, which will inevitably occur, or if there are Bangla Bhai strikes. Every major project has some severe parameters.

"Well, they will address this tomorrow." He e-mails Maartje with his thoughts. This meeting must be free from any perception that the leaders are defensive. Such indications can permeate team psychology. So far, this team is on board and operating at a high level. During the Delta Project the RWS was so focused that it created a confident belief that once the underlying data had been analyzed, and all on the team were confident in the conclusions drawn, they couldn't lose.

On the highway from Delft to Rotterdam

Krystian had the two Smit freight specialists, Henrik and Julianne, and a concrete engineer in his Volvo station wagon for the 45-minute ride to Zierikzee. The ride is congenial. Because the team is a bit stressed out, everyone is unwinding. The concrete fellow volunteers to be the DD for the return drive to Delft.

Krystian says, "Good. I need some port to escape my analysis of the Austrian cable system proposal. They are very thorough and I was very tangled up until I ran my own computations. They were correct and, actually have a better margin than we normally work with. I am impressed. However, the cable speeds seem about 20 percent low. Assuming regular operation of several of these (at any given time assuming some are down for maintenance or safety reasons), later phase recommendations may be better served by another fifteen, twenty of these—no small cost item at 2-3m Euros each."

Passing through Rotterdam

The Rhine, Maas and Meuse rivers deliver Swiss and German mountain and ground waters into the massive RO-DAM sea port. One year it is the world's largest. The next it is second to Hong Kong or Seattle-Tacoma. The land peninsula fingers of the vast harbor are dwarfed by estuary waters whose speed here diminishes from 7 to 9 mph to about 1 to 2 in the spongy delta up river a few kilometers. Massive supertankers and giant container ships maneuver as if we are witnessing a slow motion ballet. On and off loading lighters, harbor service vessels scurrying everywhere. The lighters set Krystian to thinking out loud, "Would it make sense for us to beef up the lighter fleet in our wood off-loading program. How do we increase capacity, over there, of the lighters in case terrorists whack the cable systems?" One of the Smit people says, "I think each lighter could be goosed up to push or tow three to four canal barges. Fully laden barges cannot move upstream except when the tide is coming high. But when they are off-loaded or at low tide, empty barges move very well."

As they leave Rotterdam, they notice in the rear view mirror, a new ultra large super tanker (a ULCC), fully laden, which has left the English Channel and is being nosed to an outlying tanker pump-out float by 8 large harbor tugs. The tugs are working mightily, the super tanker is hardly moving, but they are very close to the pump-out float. God, they are massive, thinks Krystian.

Zierikzee

It is 14:45 and they pull up on an old cobblestone street in front of the Oosteschelde Inn. There are three other RWS vehicles there. Krystian is pleased. "Twelve minutes early and already we have a quorum." Maartje pulls up and pops out alone. "I came from Lisse and had a 15-minute head start."

They are seated at four tables in a large well-lit, dark oak room with a medieval flavor.

Maartje begins.

All are pleased to see her. It is clear she is feeling better. She puts a colorful transparency up on the meeting room screen. It's Pog's Burma-Shave sign sequence which makes everyone smile.

Stop the water
(Image: Tiger facing wave)

Save the tigers
(Image: Bernice)

Help our country
(Image: Flag)

Bangladesh
(Image: written in English and Bangla)

They are simple and communicative. Maartje, "These come from Pog Marenjar's studio—the artist hired by Dr. Rajiv and funded by Senator Mukherjee's assistant."

Henrik from Smit Transport asks, "Is it okay to ask questions? We appear to be the non-scientists here."

"Of course," booms Krystian. "Please."

"Bangladesh has so many people you might hire young adults by the thousands to create human unloading chains as a way to empty containers, then load and off-load lighters? I doubt Bangladesh could afford more than 6-8 cable systems until these first systems prove themselves."

One of the team says, "Why not pay these workers in firewood to ease the pressures on the Bengali budgets?"

"Might just be a stellar idea," says Maartje. "If the rest of you agree, I will run the concept by Khalil." The group agrees. They are well aware of the impoverished status of Bangladesh. "Let us shift subjects, to one of our greatest concerns—silt reduction. Our Director, Jan Greilingen has undertaken to design an embankment mattress for those areas most obliged to reduce erosion. We have several scientists assisting us—as some of you know. A plant genetics fellow in Arnhem is working on a deep and multiple root variety of embankment grass. He is optimistic this can be done. Krystian has someone in the States looking at pressure molded anchors to affix mattresses to the banks. We already know that we need anchors that will not shatter from the hydraulic or pneumatic impact."

Krystian, who is sitting in back, explains, "And when they are applied to anchor mattress in the embankments, the tips must be capable of having both a seed and time capsule fertilizer inserted before application. Also we need a method to allow water to flow into the seed chamber from bankside water. And the cost per Anchor should not exceed 22 cents ($.22) in American money. My math says if we make 1 to 2 million anchors this could be profitable enough to recover the mold costs, material and machine time. One resource says the mold must produce 25 to 35 anchors at a crack. The polymer chosen must possess impressive attributes. We are not there yet."

A team member says, "I am not yet convinced firewood procurement and distribution can work. Speak to us about this."

Krystian responds. "I believe we are solving—as we speak—the insecticide/fungicide process on board ship. Our Smit guests, Henrik and Julianne, have done some very significant conceptual work. Basically, we envision an on-board system moving four to five containers into a large autoclaving chamber at a time. The design of the container will allow both application and evacuation of the solutions required. Smit folks, would you care to comment?" Both amplify these remarks.

The questioning is spirited and drives itself. Clearly, opinion is divided among the teams: one faction assumes firewood and shipping will fall into place. The other is decidedly skeptical that any external firewood program will get off the ground, let alone succeed. After forty minutes, Maartje decides to steer the discussion toward another topic. She gets the whole group to quiet down and asks the skeptics to table their concerns until more pieces are in place—particularly money and shipping. She does this by saying, "Look, your doubts may be very well founded. Our perception of the necessity of this approach does not guarantee it will work. What I will promise you is that we will gather again, here, if you like, in two-three months to bring you up-to-date on developments. We know this is a lot to grasp. But I ask you, is this really all that much different from the now-legendary design of the massive drilling platforms in the 70s, which were designed and built as 'ships'; then towed from construction dry docks to the site, and their legs hydraulically lowered from towing depth to ocean floor? Or think about the Apple vision of a personal computer which had computing power, could connect to land lines, wireless and satellite to databases and people at their laptops, and link homes to PCs all over the world? Those were huge, multidisciplinary, visionary concepts. They are almost ordinary to us now, but once they seemed impossible. One day our project may be viewed in the same spirit."

In silence, the entire group ponders the significance, and, maybe just maybe, their being on a cutting edge. The lead dissident declares both acquiescence and appetite for a return to Zierikzee. Dissent in the Netherlands does not break up teams. It makes them more productive. Maartje, seizing the moment, summons the wait staff.

The entire group cheers. Krystian agrees with Maartje's perception that a new paradigm being tendered is worthy of a little grace. He is becoming a believer. But he is not ready to embrace and publicly declare his endorsement. Better, far better, to have the momentum build slowly. He wants the team to embrace this as a workable concept.

Moving as cautiously as that supertanker in Rotterdam, the group begins to respond to the insecticide-fungicide chamber. Most engineering and shipping types are of the opinion that a sealed, positive pressure for application and negative pressure afterward to evacuate residual fluid, is vital. But most want two chambers. And it is Julianne Hedin who presciently suggests autoclaving be done only in early and middle stages of transport so the holds can be subjected to massive circulation to pull as much fumigant as possible out.

Krystian is very pleased. His hunch to invite Henrik and Julianne may have paid off nicely.

"CLEVVV-RRRR," says a seasoned team member.

"We believe," says Henrik, "a Bangla business group with some established shipping contacts in Hong Kong has put out feelers to charter four super tanker VLCC's and one ULCC with options on three more for two years with two two-year extensions. Somebody is out there working this. We believe the first two are set to commence 18-24 months out. The next two at 30 and 40 months respectively. I dare say this involves a lot of money. And, interestingly, the requirements are for Malaysian and Vietnamese officers and crew. Both countries produce remarkably capable crews."

"Not the usual scum of the Earth," says another. "Have you ever been on a ship where the officer and crew are Malaysian or Vietnamese? They are very, very good. Nowhere near as costly as Norwegians, Danes or Germans. They sail for six months, are off for two and come back reliably. They are clean, tidy and abhor alcohol. They bank 85 percent of their earnings. They should mingle very well with locals, during off loading." The team nods.

Krystian states, "In this Phase One budget, there is funding projected to fill and transport three super tankers, at fifteen to twenty months out. And two more at 22 to 29 months. The Senator and Khalil are working with a Bangla PR agency on a 'prepare the coastal villagers' campaign, to head off riots and panic as much as possible. We project a six to eight month campaign. Mobile riot squad training has been assigned to the Bangla army and navy. The campaign cannot begin until just before the first wood vessels off load. The time lag must be a narrow window—just enough to create hope and not too long so the Bangla Bhai militant war lords create major difficulty due to delayed distribution. The Noakhali region has been targeted as the first area to benefit. The village leaders have a solid reputation for cleaning out gangs of dacoits and protection schemers. And they are among the most weather vulnerable peoples in the coastal areas."

"For crying out loud," says another, "without an army of trained riot police, the risk of the masses panicking and creating chaos is 100 percent. You'll need a NATO army not those UN troops who sat on their thumbs, the 'smile and stay holstered' peacekeepers in Rwanda. Remember how our Dutch UN troops were humiliated during their service in Bosnia? This must be a battle-hardened force. The PR must make clear in all the local dialects that no theft, rioting or piracy will be tolerated. Clearly, the first free wood deliveries must not occur until after monsoon."

"Maartje, I do not have an answer yet," Krystian says.

"Neither do I, but I'm guessing these trays of port, Amstel and some cheese might facilitate some creative ideas."

"Hip! Hip! Hooray" shouts everyone.

For the next half hour, liters of wine, massive chunks of cheese—kominekaas, Gouda, Saenkanter, French Roquefort—are consumed. Badly needed lubrication. Everyone is famished. The noise level and laughter suggest that fifty are present, not fifteen. The cheeses and elegant European breads vanish in 30 minutes. Dinner menus come out. For now, they take a few minutes to review the menu.

Krystian says, "I know the specials here are generally exceptional and the house table wines are excellent. And please make certain each returning car has a non-drinking designated driver." The wait staff takes dinner orders from a menu of fish, chicken, pork, soups, rabbit and spaetzle. Krystian clinks a glass until the group settles down. With 15 happy people, is there such a thing as quiet? They struggle back to a working mode.

Krystian laughs. Maartje smiles from ear to ear. "Anyone have a solution to the 'guard the firewood' issue? We had best plan against multiple assaults, until the people discover they can trust their government to keep delivering the firewood. A vital bridge to cross."

Maartje says, "I think we need a political statesman to help prepare for this. Who could do this? Krystian, any ideas?"

"Yes," says Krystian. "I have a couple of ideas. Let me take responsibility for this."

The host and wait staff arrive with more liters of wine, Amstel lights and, much to everyone's delight, Caffrey's ale. Krystian has ordered a separate salad bowl for each table. Balsamic vinegar, French bleu cheese and creamy, red Italian. Platters of wine-marinated and creamy-garlic herring are served at each table.

Liters of Evian find their way to the table. Large family-style dishes of spaetzle steaming, oozing with the best Dutch butter and nutmeg are served along with toasted egg breads garnished with paprika, garlic and melted cheese. Rabbit is as popular as mutton chops. The baby sole (tung) are sautéed to a grand finish.

One team member walks over to Maartje and sits down next to her. He says, "In World War Two, early on after the Nazis occupied the Netherlands and leveled Rotterdam, American and British intelligence agents were put ashore by British submarines. They helped form and train resistance units. After two years, the Germans had sustained such losses, they retaliated and executed hundreds of innocent Dutch. The resistance dug in and kept striking hard and fast. Major enemy officials were assassinated regularly. Only when resistance leaders eliminated the bodies, was retaliation reduced. By then, the resistance focus changed to military fuel and supply trains from Bremen and Frankfurt which were regularly picked off by American and British strafing fighters. The Dutch were able to tip them off as the trains crossed the border at Venlo-Kaldenkirchen. My point is this. I think we might quietly arrange to move some trained Bangla people as soon as possible into coastal villages and give them radios to monitor activities which may be a source of concern. Today we call these Special Force units. If we have a one-year head start on this, we may be able to head off trouble from extremist gangs and other nasty groups." Maartje reflects on the utility of this insight and quickly perceives wisdom. She calls Krystian over and explains the idea to him. She thanks the thoughtful fellow.

Then she responds, "Recruiting and training takes time and careful selection. And they must be able to slip into the culture and become invisible."

Maartje continues, "There is such a lack of medical, health care, hospital and dental work. What if there were a way to create teams of medical workers consisting of some special forces people who could be the eyes and ears of the Bangla intelligence services?" She thinks immediately of Rajiv and how he might benefit. "The Bangla special forces troops who went to Afghanistan as NATO-support earned a reputation as ferocious fighters. I would welcome their presence. But where would funding come from?"

Krystian says to the creative team members, "Your ideas may have real merit. We need a high level Dutch statesman, a NATO intelligence resource, to open the dialogue. Funding will require a major effort. Your medical personnel idea may have promise."

Then Maartje cautions the group. "We must limit dissemination of these ideas drastically lest security be compromised. From here on, no e-mails to anyone but Krystian or me but only if he is not available."

Krystian adds, "This must stay under wraps."

Everyone is now in good "spirits." A good team, eclectic and multi-disciplinary, muses Krystian to himself, basking in the good feelings of such a cohesive unit. Who, he wonders, might he talk to about this special forces concept? There is someone but he is unable to extract this from memory.

After dessert, cigars, cigarettes, genever and a winddown, Maartje stands up and says, "We should close up shop pretty soon. We have an hour drive. I am very pleased and so proud of all of you."

Krystian tells the group, "During the tense days of Delta Project national funding debates, we had several conservative politicians and their press attacking us daily, it seemed. Even after the Prince intervened, altering the mood of our legislature became a formidable challenge. Convincing recalcitrant legislative leaders was the beginning of a new era. There are solutions out there. The hard part, here, is that we operate in another culture."

Maartje thinks to herself that a meeting with Rajiv may be necessary. He has to be in this loop. Although he operates alone so much, he has such a wide angle lens approach so he could be very helpful. Besides, she enjoys being around him.

The team applauds Krystian for making this meeting and dinner happen. And they applaud the host and wait staff for the wonderful food, drinks, and service. Krystian winces—internally—at the 1300 Euros bill, but he feels good about having done it. Sixteen people. Wow. The price of leadership and an overdue "let your hair down" session is almost double what he'd expected, but it has been worth it.

Maartje collapses when she arrives at her apartment. She is still too weak and tonight too tired to e-mail Jiv and is wondering how Theophane is doing. As she drops off, she wonders how far it is from Denver to the Saratoga Valley in Wyoming where Theophane lives. Maybe if she and Jiv do the presentation with Senator Mukherjee and Royce Brenden at the GWF in Boulder, she could rent a car and drive up? Or over? She's not sure of the distance or time involved. Mapquest will come to her rescue tomorrow.

In the morning, there are questions from Jiv regarding the GWF application. These deal with application of funds, quantifying results and audit procedures. He has already sought help from a Matlah colleague regarding the health, safety and care for any GWF staff or volunteers traveling to Bangladesh. Since Krystian is an old pro at grant nomenclature, he and Rajiv address those matters first.

Then, Maartje and Jiv get their heads together—via modem—on species enhancement quantification. It turns out Smeeta, besides loving monda, is concentrating on this piece. She has spoken with the San Diego Zoo, the Beijing Zoological Gardens, the Swiss Tier Park in Lausanne and a well-staffed facility in Rio (which has almost the same equatorial latitude and weather as Bangladesh). They each indicate interest and are initially willing to take tigers short or long-term. Tigers are such popular residents. Some are willing to conduct fund raising to enhance habitat and, as Smeeta suggests, "…to support economically the foundational steps to secure habitat…" She dares not breathe a word about Nafis and Junaid's desire for a new high impact rifle.

Dr. Jiv is truly burned out. Last evening while working late on the GWF grant application, he fell asleep. After medical school and these first "riverboat medicine years," he was becoming very tired. What is going on? Tonight, he caves in and goes right to bed, but he takes two sleeping tablets. That is something he never does. After half an hour, he is out for the duration.

In the morning, it is clear he is overtired and badly in need of a break. This hasn't happened for years. Perhaps it is time for a trip, the same trip he, his father and brother, Assam, have taken many times. They go to the mountains. They pack food, drink, bed rolls, rain, sleet, and snow protection and hike up to a 14,000 foot high plateau along India's corridor border with Bhutan. They go for the peace, the intimacy and rare air. Father is such a pillar of strength. Being with him is like having your own personal mountain of calm. Rajiv does not know how to explain this quality. A homeopathic seminar he attended as a second year med student touched upon it. It was called Chi, the Chinese concept of personal energy, and how it affects others. And he thinks of the wonderful high altitude foods such as nut cocoa bars his mother always prepares. There is still a good month or six weeks to do this. Very few others venture into these high plateaus except for goat herds and their flocks. Even the plunk, plunk, plunk, plunk of their bells means tranquility. Maybe this is what I need, Rajiv says to himself—a little plunking.

What he also thinks, and does not need to say out loud, is how much his father has provided the entire family with a spiritual common sense philosophy. Clearly, the clanking, clunking bells of the goats and father's "keep steady" attitude speak to him. He places the call. Just dialing brings some peace.

Talking with both parents for a few minutes is very pleasant and comforting. The trip onto the high plateau appeals to Father. And he volunteers to clear the dates with Assam. As he drifts off to sleep, Rajiv muses about what he might be like as a father. He pictures having a family but, perish the thought, not on coastal Bangladesh.

Next day, during one four-hour period, he receives helpful, detailed e-mails from Smeeta, Nafis, Khalil, Maartje and Krystian (jointly) responding to his grant application cries for help. Maartje has also sent a warm, friendly note in a second, private e-mail. Smeeta and the Maartje-Krystian team provide help right down to specific wording of some responses. He analyzes each, then folds them into his numbers spreadsheet and narrative. Their help puts him over the hump. When he hears back from Khalil, he will circulate an editing draft for everyone. He decides to request an uninterrupted two hours to present the persona and merits of this proposal and a one-hour response time for GWF questions. He envisions a presentation team of four. Maybe he is to lead off, Maartje to follow, then Krystian then closing with, yes, Mukherjee. He wants to hold Brenden, Nafis, Smeeta and Khalil in the wings for their technical expertise. On second thought, it may be better to roll the Senator in, to bat third. Maartje or Krystian should be the book ends as they could refer questions to the best resource. He should open with coastal and Sundarbans reality pictures, then put maps and climate change data before the panel. He is concerned about Nafis, who is one of the brighter team members, but the one who seems to possess the most narrow focus and a seeming insensitivity to context. Maybe Nafis should sit on the sidelines during the first part of the presentation so he might better observe the bigger picture and acquire a feel for the GWF. Then, if the GWF panel concentrates on grass and roots, he will bring Nafis forward. The last thing he wants is a prima donna who irritates the GWF.

He will work with Khalil to bring the Senator to readiness, attitude and cultural sensitizing. No looking down his massive nose at any women on the panel or GWF staff. This is America, not Bangladesh. Clearly, he fears both Nafis and the Senator could be problematic. He will rely on Maartje and Krystian to speak to quadruple match grant money in Bangla government funds. They have been through this before.

It will be Rajiv's job to inject the tigers, Bertram and Bernice, in a low key fashion to lighten the air and create a pair of appealing creatures. Already Junaid and Jagdish have been coaching him on material to keep the panel focused on goal #1, tripling, at least, the population within 10-12 years. The Senator will cover the container port and shipping economics. Maartje will handle the ski lift wood transport system and off loading by lighters. Rajiv senses there is an important conceptual piece missing but is unable to put his finger on it. It has been nagging him for some time now.

His parents call back. The trip is set, two weeks from now. He will leave the coast Wednesday evening. Change trains in Dhaka. Home by 7:00 a.m. Thursday. Nap—visit—pack and head out and up by 1300. They will take the train for one hour, hike about two miles to a first camp site at 11,000 feet. From there, only weather and stamina determine how much farther they go. He can hardly wait. He asks Father what hiking gear he might like from Dhaka.

Father tells mother, who relays it, that he has heard of hiking sox which breathe. The first layer absorbs no moisture. Instead, the moisture is wicked out by the second layer where it dissipates in ambient air. Rajiv thinks it is a probably polypropylene for layer one and wool or silk for layer two. He will purchase three pairs of each for father. He's happy to be able to do this. It is good to see his parents enjoy things that were not possible while he and his siblings were growing up. The mill injuries and the lack of company or government workers' compensation system put inordinate strain on family economics. He and his siblings went to work and donated 80 percent of their earnings to mother and father. That helped a great deal. They all made it.

While father was recovering—during those difficult two years—he had often talked about and helped Rajiv understand how the people, scavenging for firewood, were eliminating trees, shrubs and roots throughout the low areas. Father even predicted a day when wildlife would disappear and he predicted that this would be the beginning of the end. This year Rajiv was comprehending the moment of this concern.

Rajiv then concentrates on something else. Nafis wants a tiger gun to protect forestry people and animal habitat workers in the Sundarbans. Maybe after the presentation in Boulder, he or Nafis could shop for one. Probably Denver. There are plenty of elk, bear and mountain goats just hours from Denver. There should be gun shops galore. He and Nafis could delay his return for a day to get this done. He wonders about exporting guns after 9/11. But this rifle would be leaving the States. Hunters do this all the time. He'll ask how guns are imported into India or Bangladesh. Ammunition, too. They should buy probably six or seven 25-cartridge boxes at a minimum. Maybe his friend, Nartan, a Bangla military internist, could help. Yes, he would know. Then he remembered Professor Goggan, a vascular surgeon who taught vessel repair using lasers. Dr. Goggan was a hunter. Rajiv remembers all the pictures on his office walls; water buffalo, African tigers and leopards, elk, caribou, moose, Kodiak bear. He would obtain Dr. Goggan's e-mail address from Dana and ask him directly. However, he would speak carefully about his coastal protection efforts lest he be misunderstood as dabbling inappropriately outside the realm of medicine. Others might not understand how a gun related to the health of his coastal patients. He would not have made the connection himself just a very few months ago.

The grant application will be transmitted electronically before he heads home to hike with father and brother. Actually, it is ready to go except for Khalil's commentary on the Senator's remarks.

What a team! muses Rajiv. These people come together very well. The synergy is productive. But they must not get shot down by the GWF. That would be devastating. Have they anticipated the concerns of the GWF? With all the battling, historically, between eco-environmental groups and slash and burn forestry concerns from Japan, this proposal sets up huge returns potentially for forestry firms, especially those seeking markets for second tier (pulp and firewood) lumber and also for ocean shippers. He figures the Finns were on to this well before his team was. Both Brenden and Maartje have made him aware that GWF struck it big on a massive charitable gift from an American timber family. How would this proposal sit with such people who probably already had a seat or two on the GWF board? This all seemed as far beyond his control as his limited ability to mitigate health care issues that plagued coastal villagers. It wasn't insignificance. But sometimes he felt helplessness. Maybe, he thought, I am just growing up. He dashed off a quick e-mail to Dana seeking Professor Goggan's e-mail. Then he asked a governmental service colleague to cover for him during the four days he would be unavailable. His colleague asked politely whether he cared to tell why he would be off. Jiv responded, "Just a short escape to the high plateau with my father and brother." To which the colleague quietly commented, "Is it the trip there or the high plateau itself which is the relaxing joy?" Jiv quickly said, "Both." Knowing he would owe his associate the same time at a future date, he simply said, "And Taj, let me know as far in advance as possible when I may repay you for this accommodation."

"Not a problem Jiv, as long as my health holds up. In the last cyclone, I developed a very bad case of stomach turbulence. Took me almost three weeks to recover. And I needed two IV's of electrolytes to replenish lost fluids. Say, did you know that Matlah has put out a worldwide call next year for cyclone season, for several hundred visiting physicians who would each bring with them a maximum of meds we cannot get enough of here?"

"Wow," said Jiv, "a wonderful development." Jiv wonders to himself whether he might interest his medical school to donate a half dozen doctors to do boat clinics with him. After he hears from Professor Goggan, he will ask. For now, he can wait and inquire of Matlah about their effort. Just imagine what an army of doctors, nurses and supplies could do alongside firewood project. Health care boats combing the waterways and lowlands while the firewood lighters and cable transport systems distribute their packages of firewood. Compound visible, tangible statements of delivered hope. Maybe, just maybe, a new beginning.

Senator Mukherjee's adjutant, Khalil, is busy pulling together useful tidbits from the Senator's sea port investment cronies dealing with shipboard fumigation and insecticide "po-neg (for positive-negative) pressure applications." Those people, seem too greedy for their own good. However, there are some diamonds among the sands of their avarice. He extracts them carefully, has the Senator approve and fires off his comments to Dr. Rajiv, Maartje, and Krystian. Then he sends off a note to his brother, Ermadi, an electrical engineer for a motor builder in Tajikistan, telling him what he is working on and who he is working with. Ermadi is intrigued and asks Khalil to keep him informed. Khalil is only too happy to accommodate. It gets a bit lonely in Bangladesh for a Tajik. And Khalil would not be in such a significant political position had not Senator Mukherjee worked several years earlier with a Tajik regional governor who commended Khalil, the brilliant son of a loyal tribal elder, to the Senator. The governor was right and both the Senator and Khalil were better for the nod and Khalil's willingness to leave Tajikistan for a more advanced political system. Thank Allah for cell phones and the Internet. Connectors they are. Anywhere. Khalil's work as a senate staffer to a powerful senator is a very important career step in Khalil's future political aspirations back home if he decides to return. The climate here is much warmer than the three seasons of wind, cold and dry snow that comprise most of Tajikistan's year.

His sister, Elizabeth, works for a biology company in San Diego. They do cat, dog and horse strain enhancement research. Khalil remembers how she loved animals, especially small ones, from the time she was two. She ministered to every stray dog and cat in the village besides the two family pets. It was clear she would, one day, be a veterinarian or zoologist. She married a Hispanic zoo worker she met. He was as much an animal lover as she was, but his loves were Kiwi birds and Koala bears. In fact, he was now the lead assistant to a post doctoral fellow on a funded Kiwi project.

How far his parents had flung their children! They had had modest but respectable careers as school administrators in Tajikistan, but dreamed of different lives for their children. Khalil wanted to return to run for mayor in Ghorm, but the weather here and his job as a part of this now stimulating political environment had become addictive. Whether it was the power, status or both, he wasn't sure. But he was settling in and had noticed that daughters of important constituents were noticing him even though or perhaps because he was a foreigner. Some were siren-like, dark skinned, jet black hair, beauties. It was hard not to enjoy the opportunities this provided. And now he had the privacy of his own apartment. And how he loved rum and coke when entertaining. He must remember to hide the rum—and his DVDs—when his parents visited. His mother would be horrified. How Western and cosmopolitan he was becoming. Khalil loved both worlds and, was equally at home in each. Sometimes he forgot one of the cardinal rules the Senator often emphasized: keep secret what you don't want any member of the public to know.

Back home, Ermadi, his brother, proudly explains Khalil's current work to his pals at a café near the motor company R&D facility in Dushanbe. He describes Khalil's work on coastal protection and the involvement of the Dutch. One person listens intently as Ermadi describes the merger of interests of the Bangladesh government and Western technology. Later that evening, this fellow sends an e-mail to a compatriot in the Tajik Army: "A project on coastal Bangladesh being done with Western (Dutch) water scientists should be assayed as a potential 'item of interest' for our organization. The project will take perhaps many years and will involve some structures which could be easily isolated as 'focus pieces.'"

An immediate reply, "Noted. Keep us informed. Allah is great. Ahmed."

Bildstein, Austria

Kleinhold Dalmer is finalizing the Kloppleser proposal for cable lifts to transport firewood into the coastal villages. He feels good about the tower footing design and the market that might open up for similar jobs over the next ten years. The boring data is satisfactory except for one spongy area. He includes an additional 15,000 Euros in the proposal for completing a deeper test boring there to ensure respectable footings for piers. The gondola conversion processes are being simplified. That will mean a significant cost-of-manufacture reduction. The Bangladesh government has just agreed to the exclusive-dealing covenant and non-disclosure of cable systems technology. This has Dalmer in a secure place. Ski area capital equipment expenditures are influenced by the climate extremes, and this has compelled ski equipment manufacturers to both consolidate and diversify. On this project, Kleinhold has been comforted by the presence of the RWS as a principal. These are technical folks. Working alongside them will give Kloppleser credibility on future projects elsewhere. Dalmer knows he will want several swings through Bangladesh as the first cable systems are being installed and tested. Any design variations must be carefully monitored during field start-up and thoroughly tested. Thoroughly tested.

Fort Collins, Colorado

Manny Kowalski is hard at work with his millright, Alois Dotzen-roth, on die design for the anchors.

Alois asks, "What do you think if—looking at these rotational CAD-CAM screens—we thicken the anchor shaft by 250 thou-sandths and then machine several more seed injection cavities? As long as the installer can put a fertilizer pellet and one seed in a hole and we use the fertilizer pellet with a proper diameter as a plug, the seeds won't fall out during injection into the embankments. As the fertilizer plug dissolves, the seed should germinate."

"It might work as long as we rotate the anchor each time we bore by at least 36 degrees. This way, we probably do not set up axial stresses which could produce anchor failure. And it certainly in-creases germination odds. At a nominal cost."

"Let's run this by Kpoczek and Jan Greilingen, the Dutch mat-tress guy," says Kowalski. "And I'll let Royce know what we are doing so he is not blind-sided if Jan or Krystian calls him out of the blue. Vital communicative diplomacy, Sherlock."

"Thank you, Watson," quips Manny.

Delft, Netherlands

In the morning, Jan and Krystian find Kowalski's e-mail waiting for them as each boots up. Jan is elated at the cleverness. Krystian takes this in stride. He is very used to creativity that percolates during these more effective processes. Here, it makes a great deal of sense. It won't add a huge cost. Krystian, in his way, suggests to Jan that if anchors and mattress are applied to the embankments at low tide, and because slack tide period is limited, a fixture might be designed that could do three anchors, at a time. Jan likes the idea and forwards it verbatim to Kowalski, who promptly turns it over to Alois.

Manny responds, "A productive idea. Right now, I do not see a solution. Let me play with it and we'll see. It would be a lot easier for a hydraulic unit rather than pneumatic—too much cyclic impact pressure with pneumatic." Manny is working on a different tangent. He doesn't tell Alois this yet. Manny is thinking about vessel design and Jan may have just opened up a concept for development. Manny calls Royce with the idea. Brenden says, "Manny, let me think about it. Vessel redesign is not my bag, but I wonder whether we should make it part of our job. Who do we know who is good with vessel design? I suspect we will have time to work up a proposal."

"Without legal protection, the idea can be picked off by any lazy opportunist. I will call my lawyer. He will show me the way. I think our best time to present this could be after the GWF presentation—assuming the Bangladesh-Netherlands proposal is favorably received and I am able to make a contribution during the presentation."

In fact, thinks Brenden as he hangs up, the proposal should be ready to e-mail the day we learn the outcome of the grant application. No better time to make such suggestions. And for our protection, I'll copy Krystian and Maartje. They may have enough clout to protect our interests.

"Angie, would you get Allen on the phone ASAP? If he is tied up, have him call back later today or tonight. Thank you."

Boulder, Colorado, GWF

Three weeks after Dr. Rajiv submits the application, a GWF e-mail goes out to Dr. Rajiv Gaol, Senator R. Modondas Mukherjee, Krystian Kpoczek, Maartje deBouter: "We have done a preliminary review of the Sundarbans tiger habitat enhancement proposal. We find it appropriate to invite you to make a presentation not to exceed three hours, divided into one and one-half to two hours for presentation and one hour for questions. We will select a panel of three to five staff members to hear this matter. Based on our experience, the question period may be spirited. We will hear this presentation beginning at

10:00 a.m. RMT on Tuesday, May 18th, 2006. This gives everyone 60 days to arrange travel. We caution you that your entire presentation team should be in the Denver area by 2:00 p.m. (1400) on Sunday, May 16th. We advise you to arrive on Saturday. The air up here is comparatively rare. Minimum physiologic adaptation time is 24 to 48 hours. Consumption of an additional 1½ liters of bottled water for three days before and during travel and 3 liters a day after arrival is strongly recommended. In extreme cases, bottled oxygen is desirable. If you would like the name of on-call physicians in downtown Denver or Boulder, we will provide them. Low country people are more susceptible to oxygen deprivation issues. Therefore, it is best to allow two 24-hour periods to adapt. Headaches, drowsiness, aching joints, and feeling faint are the usual symptoms. Please be advised accordingly. Kind regards, Conrad Josephson—Executive Director."

Dhaka, Bangladesh

Khalil is excited and reports immediately to the Senator. Rajiv is ecstatic. Maartje, Krystian and Jan are on the edge of astounded. Many, many e-mails dance among and between the concerned units. Rajiv asks the Senator to notify Smeeta, Nafis, and Khalil that their airfare, meals and lodging will be provided on the presentation trip. No excuses will be tolerated and their passports, finger prints, iris scans and exit visa applications must be in hand by April 1st without fail. Airline reservations for the Bangladesh delegation (of course the Senator flies first class) in coach will be booked by next Friday. A clothing and health at high altitude memo will follow. A hotel and food allowance will be provided so nobody should be out of pocket.

Delft, Netherlands

Jan is quite pleased. Maartje is somewhere between cloud 9 and 10. This project is moving. She calls her parents and siblings and plans a long weekend at home. It is North Sea herring time. The eels are plentiful and baby sole will be around for two more weeks.

Her technical message to Jiv has added warmth, "I am very much looking forward to being with you and, of course, will bring the lovely sweater. Please rest up and take very good care of yourself. Krystian thinks we should all arrive in Denver on Saturday, May 15, to altitude adapt and sharpen our presentation and concise answering skills. We will schedule a 3-hour work session Sunday a.m. and two 2-hour sessions Monday. Right now, I suggest you, Jiv, be our lead off presenter, followed by Krystian, then me, then Senator Mukherjee. I favor holding Mr. Brenden, Smeeta, Nafis and Khalil as experts in reserve. I suspect this panel will be tough. Krystian has asked you and me to prepare a detailed—and annotated—presentation outline for everyone within two weeks. We want focus as we head into the presentation. Everyone has one week (no more) to edit and comment. Then we will prepare a list of hypothetical questions panel members are likely to ask. We must not appear amateur. One poor presentation on the Delta project, Jan told me, cost two years of miscommunication, distrust and millions of guilders. We cannot be anything less than prepared AND professional."

Separately, Maartje is sending a letter to Theophane. Before or after the May presentation, she wants to visit him. Goodness, she wonders, why not include him as a resource? With a little preparation, he might provide the "caregiver army" perspective. She looks in her trip notes and there it is—his e-mail address. She sends him an e-mail telling it just like it is: 1) She wants to spend some time with him at the monastery; 2) informing him about project developments since they met, and 3) the grant application presentation in Boulder on May 18th. Would he consider being there? And she explains why his presence might be very beneficial to the panel. She would like him to discuss the children of Bangladesh and how loyal and hard working they and their parents are.

After sending off the "Theo-mail" she lays out her game lineup much as a soccer coach would do:

Presenters

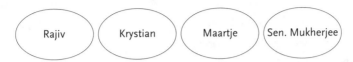

Resources

Next, she builds an Excel spreadsheet. On this, she, Krystian and Rajiv will list the topics for each presentation team member. At the end of the presentation, she will hand out this spreadsheet to the GWF panel. She wants them to remember who was who. No secrets here. This is showtime in a $50 million way. Maybe billions, if future phases are ultimately implemented. This team must be ready on all fronts. As an added thought, she includes at the base of each person's section, a bio and title/function.

As she lays this out, a, "You've got mail" icon pops up. She cannot believe her eyes. The UNICEF World Food Program has sent an inquiry. "We learned about you through a World Bank contact and have been following the project(s) you are proposing for The Interior Ministry of Bangladesh. Would you object if we contact the GWF to inquire whether one or two of our staff might attend your presentation, when it occurs? We followed up on the preliminary study you did for the Ministry. One of our staff was asked to review your proposal. She found it interesting enough to forward it to our attention. Mind you, we would only listen and would otherwise stay out of the way. Kindest regards, Rachel Odallah, Asian Specialist."

Maartje takes a flyer. She replies immediately, "We would, of course, have no objection whatsoever and you may inform GWF of this. (Attn. Carolyn Mack). E-mail *CMACK@GWF.com*." What a break, muses Maartje. As a matter of protocol, she forwards both to Carolyn Mack.

She copies Krystian, Jan and Rajiv. On the (blind) note, she types out, "What do you think of this? I remember Dr. Rajiv's telling me, on my first trip, that there were 35-50 agencies from all over the world who came regularly to assist the coastal Bangla villagers. But there was never sustained coordination between them despite extensive, duplicated effort and funding."

She wonders, might this effort evolve into an improved road map?

Rajiv is pleased. Jan has no reaction. Krystian sees something. He is beginning to formulate a master plan, but some pieces are still missing.

Krystian wondered how many times he had looked into the heavens at night and had never seen what Van Gogh saw or could understand how he could express these images as art. Is this what made him an engineer? How fortunate that the way he saw things was appropriate for an engineering project manager!

First, you made an assessment of feasibility. His experiences had markedly expanded his universe of the high water–lowland relationship. Then focus on the stages of project efforts. Then run preliminary estimates on a preparation phase, i.e., who must do what before the next teams begin? Which interest groups might be attracted to and also be opposed to the effort?

Then you do a preliminary costing of the stages. After this, he did some "where will funding come from?" analysis. Because he thought in 30-40 year processing spans, he had developed the ability to sprinkle funding along the time line. He had learned that stages could be flip-flopped if required by funding limits. In the vernacular, his critical path dependencies allowed many sequence changes and the dependencies thereby became less dependent. His Excel program had a list of 170 "project influencing" factors, only 25 of which were the usual architecture-engineering factors. He had a unique way of isolating momentum creating synergistically productive factors. He understood the interfaces between technology and culture. And he had become an architect of processes which transcend technical, cultural and geographic boundaries.

He was where he belonged. And how proud his mother was of

what he had become. Would he ever be able to do enough for her to say "thank you" for the love, values, brain power? He loved his father, too, but had only recently come to understand how Soviet communism destroyed generations of Czech males. The family and societal role of males was utterly blotted out by party apparatchiks. The consequence was that men lost self-esteem and pride, turned to alcohol, strong cigarettes and slovenliness to compensate. His father gradually acquiesced in this role displacement. Father probably died thirty years too soon because he had no motivation to get better from bad health. Any man who fought the system became visible. Under communism, being visible was a kiss of death. Behind Krystian's squinting malemute blue eyes lay a detachment easily confused for nonchalance. It was not. He held a deep, near violent, rage at the Stalinist system. This anger was deeply held in a remote sector of his brain. Only Arrianne, his wife, and a thoughtful Danish psychologist in the Hague, were aware of this, and of the care and support treatment that helped him cope. He was a classic case of negative emotional wounds driving positive outcomes.

In contrast, women, mothers, grandmothers all over Russia, Hungary, Poland, Czechoslovakia and Yugoslavia (as he still calls it), Romania and Bulgaria worked, dressed with pride, held children's hands at bus stops, stood in endless lines for food. The tragedy of the systemic effects on men could last another 100 years. Male youth, always inclined to emulate father figures in their lives, not coincidentally, manifested severe alcohol and drug issues. It was an endless cycle, a perpetuated tragedy. Until recently, Krystian had not appreciated the courage of his father who angrily pushed him to escape west and seek political asylum; preferably the Netherlands or Sweden. His father as Krystian finally saw, cared very deeply.

Even now, when he went to visit his mother, he always went to a local restaurant to have a beer and three vodkas (at least) with his father's cronies—those still living. Under the veneer of communism, these were fine, decent, caring men. They welcomed him with great affection. Just now, Krystian realized he had become an embodiment of all they longed for and could not be. Holy Mother of Christ! Why had he not taken the time to bring them something or more importantly, to recognize and thank them for their helping keep his father alive as long as possible and for being such important caretaking friends for himself? Guilt came crashing in.

He must go back soon and try to show his appreciation for those who embraced this "gone western" fellow and to show that he did not reject them for what they had not become.

My goodness. How unusual when I spent time thinking about things like pride, feelings, dignity, faith, spirit! If I were to make these ponderings productive, maybe I could take work crews of Dutch and Belgian youth home to the Czech Republic to interface with local youth (maybe a week long program) to renovate houses, shingle roofs, and apply weather proof siding, insulation, wiring. At least now supplies could be brought in without bribing border agents with half the cargo. My son and I could work on this, he thought. Shades of Theophane casting his own Grace-filled Penumbra on the Bengali children. What would Arrianne think? His minister and youth group could be a "hiring hall." And parents could lead work crews. We would need stand-by power, fuel, safe water, medicines, for sure. This may be a way to demonstrate to those youth something about pride and dignity. Our youth could be the ambassadors for re-introduction of these values. And he had a cultural welcome home ticket because everyone knew he was one of theirs.

Sundarbans, evening

It is an extremely humid, zero breeze evening. Jiv notes this stillness often precedes a storm.

Jiv writes Dana an e-mail: "During the dry season, I wonder whether you and several others in our class might consider coming here for two or so weeks each to assist with clinics. Were this possible and were you each to bring or advance ship some medicines and equipment, I believe we could persuade the government to support the expanded medical care to demonstrate good faith to our coastal villagers and to give them hope while other parts of some extensive projects are being brought about. Positive PR is really in need by our politicos.

"If you think there are possibilities, I will send you a pre-travel immunization schedule, anti-malarial work-up and a list of the medicines we most need and are unable to afford. Also suggested travel routings. I am almost a pro at this travel stuff. Calcutta is the closest international airport. Do you think Dr. Thomas Kristopher (an infectious diseases professor) would consider joining or publicly supporting this initiative? His name would be a formidable ally to accompany any requests to pharmaceutical companies for donations. For lack of a better title for this project, how about MMAB (Mobile Medical Assist for Bangladesh)? And Dana, please patch this to any classmates you can think of. Give my very best to your husband, Brent.

Jiv.

P.S. I'll be happy with any medical discipline, but pediatrics, cardiology, endocrinology and family practice are the greatest needs. We might 'tolerate' a radiologist."

Another evening—Matlah

He is thrilled at Maartje's latest e-mail about UNICEF and the alignment of talent for the presentation. But, he thinks, she should follow me. She wants to open and close with nationals from Bangladesh. How do I keep from letting my team down? I am only a physician. He shares this post haste with Maartje. Her response is caring and helpful. "Jiv, take your doctor's jacket off. You are a caring visionary. You have a ferocious national pride and an abundance of communication skills. These are gifts. If you are stumped or have a concentration lapse, defer to me, or Krystian for help. Fear not, we will all be ready for this presentation. This is why we must all arrive in Denver on Saturday. I arrive Thursday and will visit Theophane Friday. He is a two-hour plus drive from Denver. This additional time will also facilitate my own altitude adjustment." She does not share her thought yet to use Theophane as a resource to maximize the necessary contribution of the army of volunteer and philanthropic groups. Her assessment is that no current team member has the skill sets or background for this perspective. Theophane does. This could be important. This void has been amplified by UNICEF's indication of interest.

CHAPTER 20

Tenebrae

In the southern part of the country, Senator Mukherjee's parents are on a train returning to Dhaka from a visit to one of their many textile mills and sewing centers. On trips, they routinely demand the devotion of personal service from all those who they encounter. They are protocol-oriented, elegantly-clad—too much so—and abusive to a young waiter. He is working very hard to serve them professionally but lacks training, and confidence. The senior Mukherjee chastises the young man while Mrs. Mukherjee looks down her nose at him. He shoulders this abuse and leaves the table to head back to the dining car kitchen to correct the order—an error which was not his fault. Mrs. Mukherjee had ramblingly confused her order and insensitively failed to clarify what she told him. As he leaves their table, she patronizingly mutters, "How rural and backward these servants are. It's as if they just came from a fishing boat on the Bay." Her husband declares, "Is it any wonder these lesser souls never get ahead? What would they do without the benefits we provide them in mills and sewing centers?"

It is night time as their train wends its way inland from the Bay toward Dhaka. The wind is shrieking in the electrical wires above the train and the spring tidal waters under the viaducts have risen ominously. About a mile ahead, a tidal surge has ruptured a dike holding the rails. The weather is so frightening and the darkness so black that personnel operating the train do not notice one rail moving ever so slightly as the concrete ties under the rails begin to shift. Even at slower bad weather train speed (10 mph vs. the normal 33 mph) the rail cars begin to wobble and sway beyond margins of safety. As the engine reaches these rail sections, the mass of the engine pushes the rails just too far apart. The last wheels of the engine drop onto the dike under the rails. A tragedy which began fifteen hours earlier, but had no witness, strikes in agonizingly slow motion as first the coal car, then five passenger cars slide forward and descend down into the dark angry water. Parts of the roof section of each passenger car are above the water, held there by the tether to the engine. The front of the engine lies on the rail while the back is in the water.

The abused waiter, who moments earlier was tending the Mukherjees, is frantically trying to locate them by diving into the black water, through a mass of suitcases, clothing, dishes, linens. Coming back up for air, his head and right shoulder are a mass of cuts and torn tissue. He dives until he feels the car shifting dangerously down. He reluctantly abandons his search, sensing grave danger to his own life and his now exhausted body.

Hours pass. There are very few survivors in the submerged passenger cars. The waiter, Edmond, lies on the rails ahead of the engine. The surge recedes as the tide begins its outflow. Rescue teams arrive by rail, boat, helicopter. Large crane barges are maneuvered into place. These massive, buoyant vessels enable a sturdy deck crane to lift and drag whole rail cars up out of the murk as the water drains out. The grim job of identifying and tagging bodies is well underway. First estimates are that as many as 500 died. In Bangladesh, train cars are always packed. More bodies are brought out of the sludge-filled cars.

A government helicopter arrives and hovers some distance inland on a substantial dike, holding the storm-immune rails which lay a league too far for the engine to reach. This impressive aircraft set-

tles on the safe zone. Senator Ram Mukherjee and Khalil emerge—
the first of six exiting people. A railroad safety manager had noticed
the names of the Senator's parents on the passenger manifest and
contacted him immediately fearing greater consequences were there
a delay.

Over the next hour, the bodies from the passenger car are extracted from the distorted interior. Broken glass is everywhere. Body
removal is difficult and unpleasant. Recovery personnel stiffen as
word spreads that the powerful politician's parents were on the train.
One by one, body bags are lined up and unzipped for family members
and others to make the grim identifications. The recovery personnel
are a mix of Muslim, Hindu, and Christian. The process melds them
into a fabric of solemn presence. It is as if each appreciates that death
takes them all in. They wear their roles in a quiet, deliberate, professional cloak. They carefully watch as these apprehensive, anguished
people are folded into these moments.

The Senator's magnificent stature and poise vanish as he is led by
a recovery supervisor to a flatbed train car where several body bags
are opened up. It is clear from the Senator's face that two bags hold
his mother and father. How vulnerable he is in this moment! Fear
dictated the way he walked to this area. Apprehension is now over
and grief commences. He returns to the helicopter, now stooped and
appearing thirty years older. The life extracted from his parents by
these powerful processes of nature slowly passes to his shoulders.
Any soul who has buried a parent or child has experienced this heavy
initiation.

A quiet conversation occurs between the helicopter pilot and a
railroad track specialist:

Pilot, in wonder, "These massive dikes seem to shout at nature,
'How dare you assault us.' Nature shouts back. 'Get out of my way,
little berm. Do not resist. You have not a chance. If we cannot rip
your top off, we will rip the bottom out from under you.'"

Railroad official, with resignation, "Yes, some of our politicians believe they can legislate a successful storm protection system. It's much
like the American Corps of Engineers who duped legislators, farmers,

and millions of innocent others into believing they could fence in the mighty Mississippi. They were so wrong. In 1993, those dikes failed in many places as flood waters reclaimed the spongy wetlands created millions of years ago. When will our politicians wake up and hire real storm and flood experts to create some truly effective systems?"

The pilot replies, "I think they may have. I hear that there is a small study now that seeks help from a reputable Dutch team. This, however small, is very positive. I understand the Senator has provided some support for it. Amazing that he loses his parents in an accident on a dike approved 15 years ago by his senate and assembly cronies. That will compound his tragedy."

The railroad man comments, "It's one thing to participate in legislative processes. But it is quite another to blame others for the consequences of legislation which just happens to place huge dike construction contracts in the hands of companies owned by family members of certain legislative leaders. There will be a reckoning over this. We are a smarter people than this. Why do we remain trapped in such unproductive processes?"

Sadly, Rajiv reads the e-mail from Khalil with the news. He wonders whether the track was on top of one of those dikes hurriedly pushed up for political reasons and shoved into nature's way. He fears about the impact of this loss on the Senator's support of the grant application and his promise to quadruple any award. As he copies Maartje and Krystian, he fears this trauma may just provide opposition forces the opportunity to gain legislative control and drive the country back into the isolationist extremism from which the Awami party had taken Bangladesh these past few years. His anxiety level goes way up. He can feel his blood pressure taking off. He includes his concerns in his note to Maartje. At the same time he sends a sympathy e-note to the Senator via Khalil.

Maartje and Krystian are huddling. They wonder whether one of them, probably Maartje, ought to make the long trip to the funeral or to separately pay respects in a planned visit. They also e-mail Dr. Rajiv about his new ideas for using the symbolism of tigers and firewood; they like the tack he and Pog have been on for a couple of months.

Rajiv is also beginning to wonder whether Theophane may have a role here. The UNICEF interest infers this. He takes no credit. Maartje and Krystian are clearly the impetus. They, like some giant magnet, seem to know how to weld diverse parts together and bring focus and energies to the concepts.

From a personal perspective, he takes comfort that it all started with his grief at losing Sabjada. Losing her provided a cause. She had been his secret hope for the future Hatayia health care team. Someday, a clinic standing securely above tidal surges, named for her, might be a fitting tribute. And how proud her mother, Manja, and father, Shukendu, would be. He will stop again to see them next month. He will bring some special medicines for the beginnings of a household emergency kit, knowing Manja would also use it to serve others no matter what instructions he left with her.

Now he and Maartje, with significant input from Krystian, are finalizing the team's presentation to the GWF panel. Interestingly, their presentation converges with the notes compiled by Conrad and the GWF team. Their format is very different. The conceptual inferences are similar:

1. The overriding theme for our 5-18 presentation in Boulder is that tigers and firewood are inextricably connected.

2. The impact of climate change on Bangladesh; changing the culture of using shrubs and trees for cooking and heat; and the fact that tiger habitat can be vastly improved.

3. There are six steps to habitat enhancement: education; funding for firewood; political and religious inclusion; silt and embankment mattresses; health care, replanting and restocking.

4. Transporting and distributing massive volumes of firewood can be accomplished through deep water seaports, ship charters, and horizontal cable distribution systems and a fleet of lighters.

5. We must also be mindful of the political realities in Bangladesh.

Maartje sends Rajiv a sympathetic response, suggesting he advise them on burial customs and grieving and suggesting that Maartje visit in two-three weeks. It will be a push but there is time. The GWF presentation is 4½ weeks away. The opportunity to be in Maartje's company and sharpen the presentation outline seems too good to hope for. He knows which he desires more. After clearing the date with Khalil, Rajiv pencils in three days, two weeks hence. That's when Maartje should arrive in Calcutta. That evening she and Rajiv will meet with Pog to finalize the presentation screens. The next day, they will meet with the Senator in the morning and then Smeeta, Jagdish, Junaid and Nafis. This will help Smeeta and Nafis prepare for Boulder.

How bewildering, Rajiv reflects, that a tragedy should befall this influential politician, one whose mantle of resources seems limitless. In the middle of all this, Rajiv realizes how limited his knowledge is of the Senator's upbringing, career path and political links. Perhaps in such information lies the justification for Rajiv's uneasiness about vesting hope in the Senator. He thinks the Senator represents child labor, cheap adult labor, no unions, and vast profits from Western clothing buyers. Somehow, it doesn't feel right. Should he share this with Maartje and Krystian? He concludes he must and does so in a concise, careful e-mail to both. Maartje asks Krystian for his reading. Krystian, as expected, looks at the totality and says to Maartje, "What positive things do these projects hold for him? Is he a stake-holder in the charters, the seaport, autoclave manufacturer, on board firewood ships? Who owns the land where the deep water port will be located? How did he get to Yale, as Rajiv learned some time ago?"

Maartje suggests to Dr. Jiv that he call Pog Marenjar to see if he can learn more about the Senator's background. Pog's response is a thunder clap, "Allah is great, Jiv. You want me to end up dead in a rotten, sewage canal? This is way out of my league. But of course, I will get it done for you. I trust you. I know you would not put me up to this unless the information were vital. But please understand the personal risk I take. This will surely cost $1000-2000 USD extra. I cannot be visible on this. My in-laws could suffer grievously. As you know, they are partners with the Senator's in-laws, the Kapoors, in a massive new sewing and distribution center."

"I understand, Pog, honestly," replies Jiv. "But I need to know. And I wouldn't ask unless it was very important."

"Of course, Jiv. I just don't like being an exposed goalie with no defenders in front of me."

"And Pog, thirteen days from now, Maartje will be here and we (you, she and I) are having a working dinner to finalize our presentation screens; 6:00 p.m., April 27. So be sure to bring your laptop and all the files with you and two duplicate disks. Maartje has a larger screen but I want you to have a complete set here. She will bring the updated presentation outline so we can work from it. I may have it before she takes off from Amsterdam. If so, you'll have it five minutes later. You'll finally get a chance to meet her. And I welcome your impression. I am very excited over her coming."

"Jiv, you're falling, man. Allah, help you. What will your parents say?"

"They will meet her this time. We'll see. But I am certain my mother does not envision her to be anything but a professional acquaintance. By the way, I'll be absent for the next three days on a 'high plateau' trip with father and my brother Assam."

The train ride home for Rajiv is a good wind down from the demands of the past months. He needs this trip, like so many he has taken in the past with his father and brother. If the weather holds, they will have respectable trekking and little rain to keep them from enjoying high plateau air and scenery. Rajiv has obtained two added trekking tools—a titanium alloy walking stick for each and a fine pair of Canon binoculars with image stabilizing technology. These binoculars are 12 power magnification with a panorama setting and configuration for viewing the mountains at all times of day. The low light fluorite lenses are really helpful. He borrowed these from a military doctor friend, pledging his life to do so. He sleeps most of the way.

His mother, Trishana, and sister Gerga meet him at the train. It is 6:00 a.m. After close hugs, they have tea nearby to catch up before father, Sanjay, and Assam take over. He decides to tell them about the lady for whom mother knit the sweater. They listen intently as he explains how their relationship has developed. After a few minutes, mother influenced by her British education says, "I had an inkling the sweater was more than a welcome-to-Bangladesh present."

They take two rickshaw taxis home. Each is beautifully and colorfully painted. Father Dal is there smiling and, though older, appears physically strong. Assam arrives and then, two hours later, Sanjay. They all talk non-stop as mother and Gerga fix a fine meal of chicken and pork tandoori, rices, curries, naan (three kinds). The aroma of peppers, cumin, ginger and garlic are delectable access points to the past. It smells, tastes and feels so good to Rajiv.

By noon, Rajiv is fading fast. Sanjay has to head back to Dhaka regretting he is unable to come along. He hands out the trekking sticks and father's socks. Both are well received.

With the upland train leaving at 3:00 p.m., Rajiv wakes at noon. It is time for packing. Mother's prepared foods fill one back pack. Storm gear and spare clothing are in the second pack. Stove fuel, water and first aid items are in the third. Sleeping pads and bags are rolled on top of each pack. Dal's strength and balance are manifest as they get ready. A very good sign. Assam has no problem. He is agile, strong and in very good condition. Rajiv is the question mark. He will make the trek on pride.

The bags go by rickshaw to the train while Dal, Assam and Rajiv hike and chatter, chatter and hike. The one hour ride on what looks like a 1920s train sails by even at forty miles per hour. Everyone is too busy reclaiming the relationships to pay much attention. Assam, now 26, admires his older brother for his academic and professional achievements. Everyone in Sherpur knows and reveres Rajiv for those same abilities. Assam is known as a good musician; a string instrumentalist who happens to love Smoky Mountain bluegrass. He plays mandolin as well as several Indian stringed instruments. He and Rajiv have always loved climbing steep rock outcrops and cliffs. Assam still climbs to 20,000 feet regularly. He does so still with ease but has lost the desire to climb glaciers or ice fields. Rajiv and Assam used to read the many stories of climbers who traveled to Nepal, Tibet, and Pakistan's Karakoram Range to conquer the waiting giants.

Dal is camp maker and designated cook. In the years preceding Rajiv's departure for medical school, Trishana was the co-captain of the campsites and Gerga was the tomboy sister who did everything her brothers did.

During the mill injury recovery years, while healing, Sanjay and Assam took Dal's cooking place alongside Trishana at camp. Dal would lie in the sun, covered with robes, soaking in the warm rays as the robes heated up his frail body. To this day, Dal claims that Trishana's cooking and the tightly wrapped robes were key to his healing.

Now Dal delights in his grown sons and how much they each nurture him and Trishana. And they regularly send respectable monthly stipends which he and Trishana put aside for "hoped for" grandchildren. What little they spend is for home improvements.

Exiting the train at a border town where the sliver thin India corridor lies, they hike about 2½ miles up onto a high plateau. Setting camp takes the rest of the day. The 50°F weather is clear, with light breezes. Rajiv and Sanjay gather firewood, which is far more plentiful here than on coastal Bangladesh. Dal is a tea master. He loves Darjeeling tea. He adds spices which help everyone adjust to the altitude. They are now at 11,000 feet and tomorrow will hike to a new campsite at 13,500. Evening falls as they eat the first full meal Trishana lovingly prepared for "her boys." The night sky is stunning. Even though the temperature drops to 35°F, they all watch the night sky, playfully awarding prizes to the one who spots the most shooting stars. Dal wins with thirteen. Sleep comes quickly in their warm goose down sleeping bags which Rajiv had sent last year.

Dal rises early to get the stove started for coffee and warms oat cereal with nuts and dried fruits. Rajiv is last up. Clearly, he needed this diversion and rest. The air at this altitude is therapeutic. But his adaptation, of course, takes the longest. He is now a lowlands boy. Constant consumption of water facilitates his adjustment. By 9:00 a.m., they head east, then north, all the time going up. Ridges and outcrops swallow them. They stop twice for water and rest.

It is two p.m. before they find a suitable campsite. This one has a fine wind break for the now freshening north winds coming down off the massive slopes above. With his borrowed binoculars, Rajiv has spotted flocks of Himalayan snow geese sitting on the snow and ice about 1500 feet above them. Assam and Dal are intrigued with the lens' sharpness and image stability. Dal spots a pair of mountain sheep 1000 feet above them. But then clouds come rolling down and they vanish. They quickly set camp should the weather degenerate, which it does. Because the weather is only intermittently bad, they are able to maintain a pleasant campfire. Kindling is abundant and the boys bring back enough for evening and until they break camp in the morning. Dal works so hard that his sons worry and finally insist that he take a nap and they will prepare dinner.

He does. They do. An hour and a half later, he emerges from the tent to a supper call. The boys serve a rich grain-filled chicken soup and some pan-fried bread they have made on the portable stove. With the wind coming up and the weather unsettled, they eat quickly. They clean up and head into the small tent which is barely big enough for them. The crisp, high altitude air quickly lulls them into deep sleep.

Dal wakes up at about 1:00 a.m. responding to a call from nature. The sky is clear, the mountains in the light of a slivered moon and stars are so bright. Hiking now with two of his three sons makes it hard to remember the injury years when he could hardly walk or bend. His new sock combination renders his feet so comfortable, too. He crawls back into his sleeping bag until 6:00 a.m. when the eastern light creates a visual reveille.

Today they will head down. Because each pack is now fifteen food and fuel pounds lighter, the descent is easier. So far, the day is pleasant. The weather, if it is changing, will tell them so over the nearest mountain top. When the wind shears cloud tops above them, they can expect a marked weather shift in about an hour. They break camp as they have done many times over the past twenty-some years. Rajiv, the least physically active of the three, is actually in good shape, certainly due to hauling his baggage on and off the river boat. He feels his emotional batteries being recharged. It has been wonderful.

He muses that, someday, Maartje might enjoy a modified form of this trek. "Can she cook?" he wonders for the first time, gently comparing mother, her intelligence and many roles with Maartje and her life. He decides she probably could do it. Maybe his mother should show her the spice cabinet so necessary to Bangla cooking.

The trek down is markedly easier, less load, gravity as a partner and by now, they are altitude-acclimated. Given the tolerant weather, they decide to hurry for the train so they can spend this last night at home. They catch the 7:00 p.m. train and are home having tea by 10:00 p.m. Trishana is thrilled. All the food is gone. As a proud cook, she would have been sorely disappointed if they had brought any home.

The next week flies by. As usual, Jiv's clinic schedule is on overload. Maartje is swamped but Krystian and the rest of the team rise to the occasion to cover for the week that will be consumed by her 'pay respects' trip. Above all, Krystian understands doing what is politically correct. He approves the €9,000 voucher for the trip in a nanosecond. The RWS may be on the edge of billions here. Some empathy capital is much in order.

Delft, Netherlands

The next morning, Krystian receives a serious e-mail from Oron, his Special Forces friend. "Krystian, contact has been made at very high levels with Bangla Special Forces headquarters. I am deliberately not furnishing names to minimize 'broadcast leakage.' Please understand. These folks are very adept and, using their extensive NATO training, have begun an operation consistent with your concerns. They favor the medical team approach we discussed. Do not be surprised if your Dr. Rajiv acquires some 'assistance' in the coming months. In fact, a special medical supply boat is being fitted out to mask the accoutrements of this vessel. Already Bangla SF (BSF) Intelligence is reporting markedly increased cellular and wireless traffic between some folks in Chittagong and suspected undesirables in Tajikistan. Something is going on.

"Do not, under any circumstances, share this with anyone except Jan Greilingen. My superior has been in dialog with him."

Krystian, both gratified and apprehensive, sends a confirming note. This subject mirrors a concern he's harbored for years that the Delta Project has been wide open to a terrorist strike. The Netherlands security folks finally acknowledged a need to respond to these long overdue concerns. 9-11, Madrid '04 and London '05 were the catalysts.

CHAPTER 21

Epiphany

Schiphol

Maartje is waiting for the flight to Calcutta. She is finally healthy, but still tires easily. The presentation outline is in acceptable form and has been transmitted to Jan, the Senator, Khalil, Dr. Jiv, Krystian, and Royce Brenden. The major bases are covered, even tiger reproduction/propagation thanks to Smeeta. Maartje chose not to copy UNICEF fearing pre-presentation politicking. In fact, she was obliged to tell them a small untruth: the presentation would not be finalized until the day of the presentation—technically true but clearly a shading. With her, she brings a copy for Theophane.

As the flight is called, she downs two Extra Strength Tylenol and some lemon grass tablets. She boards, welcoming the almost horizontal sleeper seats in business class. KLM has long understood how hard and long a sixteen-seventeen-hour flight can be without sleep. Wine and dinner are welcome. She is fast asleep after only three hours. Five hours later she wakes to the welcome aroma of Dutch coffee. Three cups and 35 minutes later she is her usual warp-speed-coherent. After her morning toilet, she looks fine, feels wonderful and enjoys fresh fruit and a Leerdamer, sausage and chive omelet, takes in the BBC news and reads droves of technical material from the team.

Arriving in Calcutta a half-hour early (11:00 a.m.), she cannot wait to see Jiv. As she clears customs, there he is, smiling broadly. He is wearing gray silk slacks, a short sleeve silk, white dress shirt and a warm, red tie. They embrace—more than politely—with a long kiss as each looks into the other's eyes. No longer just the eyes of an engineer and doctor. Rather of two humans growing toward each other.

Their ride to Dhaka in yet another colorful Bengali rickshaw is filled with the pleasure of exchange. They hold hands and touch. It is mid-afternoon when they arrive at the Regiment Hotel, a clean, comfortably lit place whose stately pillars suggest the British Colonial era. Jiv insists Maartje rest for two to three hours before he picks her up for dinner with Pog. He shares some preliminary information Pog and his ferrets have developed.

Maartje collapses in a post-travel-heap and wakes up barely fifteen minutes before Jiv calls. When he shows up, she is transformed for the climate. She wears a fluffy mandarin orange, long sleeve blouse and cool pressed cotton, kitten grey slacks with open toe thin strap sandals. The thin straps are perfect for her well proportioned feet. Jiv smiles to himself thinking it would be hard to believe she is an engineer. She looks more like a Michigan Avenue public relations executive. This time she paid a great deal more attention to the clothing she brought. It shows.

Jiv smiles broadly as she steps out of the hotel. Now he is wishing they could be alone for dinner. But Pog e-mailed him saying some items of significant "archaeological" value had been unearthed. It is not far to dinner but traffic is at its absolute worst (normal for Dhaka) and it takes 20 minutes to go just seven blocks. As the valet takes the car, there is a smiling Pog, trying to not stare at Maartje. Jiv makes introductions and the three settle in to a softly-lit corner table. Pog and Maartje crank up their laptops.

Pog looks around and almost whispering, "Jiv, here are the newest developments on our subject. His Yale admission and all college and travel expenses were sponsored and paid by a Jewish clothing company in Atlanta, Georgia. Rajiv shudders. If Bangla Bhai knew this, all hell could break loose. Atlanta purchases about 50% of the production from the Senator's in-laws, the Kapoors. Part of the deal involved the Kapoor #3 sewing center being owned by Mukherjee's parents. At least 40% of that production is purchased by these same Atlanta people."

"My God," mutters Maartje. "These connections mean he might torpedo our entire project just to maintain the revenue flow from Atlanta. We may be dead."

"I don't like it," sputters Jiv. "No wonder he's been so smooth with us."

"Hold on," says Pog. "This may be more important."

He explains, "The Senator is an equal partner among eight who have taken options on the land slated for a new deep water seaport."

Pog thinks the Senator has put himself between a rock and a hard spot. His parents are gone. He and his two siblings are inheriting the properties. The Kapoor mills currently enjoy some of the lowest production costs in the world for blouses, shorts, and jeans. Pog had been in one of their mills and found it incredible. Well-lit, well-run, and efficient. The child labor was very well-fed and cared for. They hold sewing and ESL classes each afternoon after work. Children under fourteen must attend.

"He cannot be trusted," says Maartje, angrily. "He will do whatever fills his pockets, not what is good for the ordinary people of Bangladesh. I am angry at myself for having been so gullible."

Jiv says, "Wait, Maartje. This seaport piece creates some new possibilities. Let's cool down and get more information. Pog, who are his option partners and are they different from the Kapoor family and their usual cast of lawyers, bankers and accountants? This is very important."

"Jiv, sorry I have those names but I did not bring them with me. And, of course, I cannot call my wife and ask her because she is part of the Khan clothing family. She doesn't miss a trick. I will call you later this evening. I do know that two of them are Hong Kong Chinese who reside there. The other names didn't make any impression on me."

"Pog, we'll come back to this later. Let's talk screens and logos so

Maartje can add and edit. We are getting close to crunch time."

Pog turns his laptop so Maartje can see. Jiv has his own screen. One has no words, only well-finished caricatures of Bernice and Bertram. They are smiling. Mischief seems part of Bertram, perhaps a little Dennis the Menace. Bernice has earrings on each ear. Girls all over the world will love her. Screen two is one paragraph:

> As of 1-1-06, there are 297 tigers in the Sundarbans region of Bangladesh down from a population of 32,000 in 1901. This presentation addresses two programs:
> 1) restoring habitat and actively strengthening the tiger population to complement
> 2) a major coastal protection program to enhance the safety and security of millions of coastal villagers, agriculture, and ecology.

They flip through the next fifteen screens, editing as they proceed. All are conversant with the presentation, each from a different perspective. Pog's visual presentation skills are evident. He loathes words. Three hours later, after dining and cool beverages, Maartje says, "I feel fifty screens are 15-20 too many. We have only two hours max to present the essence. I believe, not more than thirty will be effective. We can incorporate the rest in our written/CD Rom submission. Let's hold them ready just in case we get a question that can be answered by one we have not shown."

"She's right, Jiv," says Pog, "but I think twenty-five is the max. We could combine maybe ten. This might create word overload. And, I would find it necessary to ask for additional funds. I am way over the $1,000 as you know, Jiv,"

"How much?" says Maartje.

"Probably $2,800 beyond," says Pog.

"Pog," says Maartje, "I will cover that for you and request those funds while I am here. Do not combine these. Each contains one or two thoughts max. This is better. At the conclusion of our presentation, why not give them the whole set? It would be best on a CD-ROM. Actually, better than writing so much. Remember, we have interest from UNICEF. There may be others we do not know about, like Senator Mukherjee's seaport partners."

Maartje yawns, deeply. Jiv notices and says, "Sleep time, Madame Traveler. We have a big day tomorrow."

As the dinner meeting ends, Pog says, "I'll clean up the ones we've talked about and only combine if two thoughts are presented. Better yet, Maartje, would you do this first and let me work with your edits? Let's try to close with P 30. That's a light but effective set of "Burma Shave" waterway signs."

Jiv advises not taking the humor too far. "We must be careful to not lighten up this presentation so we offend the panel." All agree.

Maartje apologizes for being too tired to have late tea with Jiv. It is clear that he is as tired as she is. Nonetheless a second deep kiss is still in order; a kiss that lingers a long time.

The next day it rains hard in the Sundarbans. Fortunately, Jiv and Maartje are in a covered, chartered boat working their way to the forestry regional offices where Smeeta and Nafis are waiting. In such a downpour visibility is bad and they proceed with care. The charter captain only knows how to go full throttle, so he misses two turns and they arrive half an hour late.

Despite this, the reunion is joyful. Once they finish talking about monda, they begin their prep session for the presentation. Jiv hands them the completed grant application while Maartje discusses health and altitude adaptation before shifting to protocol and process issues in Boulder. Then Maartje and Rajiv work through the screens and presentation outline. Smeeta gets it all. Nafis struggles and keeps introducing technical facets of grass and root biology. Maartje patiently and deftly teaches Nafis not to provide Ph.D. answers to basic panel questions. Answers must be brief, thorough and pertinent. Jiv emphasizes the "connection" necessity. Their presentation must clarify the links between:

- tigers and firewood

- silt and coastal protection

- shipping economics and attracting international funding

"Always connect what you are answering to tiger habitat and species propagation. This group is ONLY interested in tiger preservation and prey habitat. Anything else is irrelevant until GWF makes it otherwise," Maartje advises.

"Never lose sight of this," she adds. Slowly, Nafis is coming around. It's like turning a fully laden super-tanker in a very small harbor.

When Jiv and Maartje are satisfied that Smeeta and Nafis understand the most important items, they ask to be brought up to date on continuing efforts with grasses, shrubs and trees. Smeeta is very pleased that both have been invited to be part of the presentation team. Maartje appreciates how significant this is in their careers. She will use some special words to introduce them to the panel. More than ever she likes the evolving line-up.

Rajiv provides travel itineraries Khalil prepared and informs them when to pick up tickets, travel funds and passports so all will be in hand at least a week before they leave. Smeeta and Nafis are radiant and excited. They will be ready. Maartje does not tell them about an added treat: she has planned a Sunday tour to Estes Park where they may see elk and mountain goats. An opening pizza party is planned for the working suite on Saturday evening. Nafis asks what pizza is. Rajiv tells him it's tomato covered dough with onions, sausage, garlic and cheese. They leave each other with an American, "So long. Until we meet again." Excitement is building.

On the boat ride back, the weather improves and again the beauty of the Sundarbans is compelling. They hear and see so many birds. Maartje thinks of Krystian. He would be in Swarovski-heaven, reflects Maartje.

Now Maartje wants her own binoculars. Getting €800 into her budget might take some doing. Bonuses at the RWS are few and far between. She is certain Krystian justified his through some "far-sighted" reasoning process. Oh well. Another time.

In the meantime, Nafis has carefully garnered the cash for his "elephant gun." He has €1900 for the acquisition. This includes €500 of his €1,000 travel money.

Over tea back at the Regiment Hotel, Maartje and Jiv hold hands and chat like chickadees. Any observer would conclude they were love birds. But both are sagging and the evening ends at ten with a smile and a kiss. Maartje asks for one more. They part with both engines running in overdrive.

By the time Jiv picks her up at noon for the meeting at the Senator's office, he is bubbling with excitement. Never having seen the doctor "bubbling," Maartje asks, "What is going on?"

"Maartje, can you believe this? I just learned I am to have a new clinic supply boat and two, believe this, two medical assistants."

Maartje, having been tipped off by Krystian, already knows what is going on, but she plays along and shares Jiv's excitement. For Jiv, this will almost triple his effectiveness and significantly improve recovery rates for dysenteric and choleric children. The joy on his face warms Maartje, just in case she required warming. She is taken by the emotion radiating from his excitement.

As they arrive at the Senator's office, Khalil greets them softly and warmly. He explains the Senator's vast mood swings since the tragedy and counsels both to tolerate wide margins of error in their conversation. After a few moments, they are welcomed by a subdued but ever charismatic statesman.

He begs them to be seated and asks an attractive female attendant to provide tea. Once again, they are elegantly served. Maartje's first remarks are personal ones. She tells the Senator how sorry both she and Krystian are over the loss of his parents and the even more horrible way it happened. Clearly, the Senator is touched deeply that she traveled all the distance to show her sympathy. "In my grief, Miss deBouter and Dr. Gaol, I have become witness to the power of the presence of those who come, care and often say nothing. It is very powerful, this being present. Until this loss, I always found it necessary to move into someone else's grief, make appropriate noises, lighten the mood. You know. Be a politician. How very mistaken I have been. Given the work you must do for the presentation in two weeks, that you would devote a week to come here says much. I found myself becoming, for the first time excited about seeing both of you.

This is out of character for me. More tea, Miss deBouter? Dr. Gaol?

"Now, if you will indulge me, I have some ah, delicate things to share with you. So please, sit back and listen while I lift some weight from my chest."

He explains that marital and family clothing interests have always dominated his political actions. Thus, while he has been specifically very supportive of their efforts, always running in the back of his mind was another message. It was that, because he had calculated their odds at less than one in 200, it was very easy to proffer first double, then a quadruple match of funds if they received a grant from GWF. However, their resourcefulness, diligence and brilliant sense of connecting seemingly unrelated pieces now gave them, in his opinion, better than a 50-50 chance. Khalil thought the odds were even better. He takes a long, deep, breath. It is clear to Rajiv and Maartje that this is heavy going for the Senator.

Several months ago, he tells them, he formed a partnership with some non-family shipping interests based in Kowloon, Hong Kong. Because he foresaw a glimmer of economic return in a new deep water port, this partnership took options on all the parcels which might comprise a sea port. His involvement in this deal provided a way to decrease his dependence on both families. He found himself in an emotional vise. The clothing interests were keeping him and frankly, his country, from attaining a better life for millions of its citizens. In doing so, he had neglected wisdom imparted by the Chaplain of the Yale Divinity School when he had been a student there. He had actually immersed himself in a Western theology course on personal faith, spirituality, and choice. He became enthralled with this Chaplain and what he stood for. The man spoke from his deepest deep to the Senator's previously unvisited deepest deep. It mattered not that he was Muslim and the chaplain, Christian. The chaplain's values resided at the top of a mountain. Mukherjee wanted a mountain top for his own spiritual life. But twenty-five years of kow-towing to the pecuniary avariciousness of the clothing industry kept him, he had felt, in the choleric gutters of Bangla society. He'd had great success, but at a price. As long as he obeyed family rules he benefited.

What he lacked was self-esteem. He had become disloyal to the tenets the Yale Chaplain had ascribed. And it was tearing what soul he had into shreds. "Sadly, I feel I betrayed this noble man and all he stood for. Then you, Dr. Gaol, then you, Miss deBouter, and your Krystian Kpoczek, came 'galloping along'. You allowed me to see parts of myself I did not like. Your compelling presence in these hours and days of darkness following my parents' death is supportive.

"There is one fact I am certain you do not realize. You see, I am somewhat at fault for the loss of my parents. The dike system, which failed, was one of the many expedient political fixes we politicians made to keep clothing workers from gaining access to higher wage construction and shipping jobs. The faster the fix, here in our culture, the less likely it is that construction labor costs will rise to levels seen in Malaysia, Taiwan, or Thailand. Those regions are now economically far ahead of Bangladesh. Our clothing mill wages and prices continue to please our clothing customers in the West. I was a point man orchestrating this system.

"Now I feel I must atone for this. To this end, I wish to pledge my allegiance to support the grant."

Maartje and Jiv are amazed. Maartje speaks first. "Senator Mukherjee, we are obliged to earn any successes we have. As a stranger to your culture, I am helpless, except technically. Both Dr. Gaol and I feel you are key to obtaining the grant, and every related project in the short-term future. We are not troubled by your economic partnership interest in a new port. In the western world, this is quite commonplace.

"We would like you to close our presentation in Boulder in two weeks. The rest of us will serve as technical resources, but the grant has no chance if the panel concludes that Bangladesh lacks a genuine presence in the outcome or that Bangladesh is a shill. They have to understand that Bangladesh is this project. We plan to have five Bangla nationals on the presentation team."

Dr. Rajiv is uncharacteristically silent. However, he does pick up on one major point. "Senator Mukherjee, it will be vital that all of us stay on plan and stick to the presentation outline. Panel questioning may take us far away from the focus of our outline. The GWF takes a fairly significant risk should they award us a grant. We must provide reliable evidence of solid returns to them. Namely, that this work will help tigers. They care about tiger population. Everything else is our stuff. If they come to doubt our credibility or feel we are insincere in our pushing tiger success to obtain money for other purposes, all our efforts are dead."

Maartje concludes, "Sir, we have taken too much of your time. We are deeply sorry for the grief which has visited you. You have inspired us today out of great personal searching. We thank you. Until we meet in Denver on Saturday the fifteenth."

Back at the Regiment Hotel, Rajiv says, "What just happened back there?"

Maartje said, "First, all your concerns and discomfort were justified. Your perceptions were right. We were in trouble. It seems his personal loss has stimulated what Christians call an 'epiphany.' We witnessed a confession, the beginning of a powerful healing process."

Jiv takes the chance to change the subject, "What about us, Maartje? Might we realize our own epiphany? Aren't we moving way beyond project partners? You are always on my mind. Our last couple of 'good nights' were difficult. At least, this is what I feel."

"Jiv, I am as ready and willing as you are. I want you. And there is no one back in The Netherlands. Please know this. I am not an experienced bed partner, believe me. So I may be clumsy."

Jiv says, "I'll be back in three minutes."

And it happens. Clumsy it is. Desire, caring and biology, the order of which is uncertain, carry the day in the morning. As Maartje is hurriedly packing, Jiv is the happiest and most contented she's ever seen him. Both sets of eyes sparkle. Jiv's schedule leaves him no time to take her to Calcutta. She must go by rickshaw taxi. They part as new lovers. The next two weeks will seem like six months.

Maartje's flight back is long and uneventful. She sleeps in huge blocks and muses on their first intimate night. It now feels difficult to ramp back up as the massive 747-400 approaches the cloudy, windy, rainy Netherlands.

However, she composes a detailed report for Krystian about their meeting with the Senator. She believes the developments are quite favorable. When she and Krystian meet the next morning, she mentions that her relationships with Jiv is no longer purely professional. His only response is, "I like the vibes about this fellow. He has talent and a soul. I could not help but see how at ease the two of you were together. Just manage it carefully in Denver and Boulder so others do not panic and skew the presentation. Cross culture relationships could offend the Senator or panel members. Be very careful."

Maartje's work now seems to come in soft pastels. Love casts the glow. The sun shines even when it doesn't. Even her walk seems more fluid. Her e-mails to Rajiv are candlelight soft. His are the same. She is less intense, more facile and inclusive. She calls Solongo to share her romantic news. They chatter like magpies and advance their dinner date to a few days before she leaves for Denver. She wonders whether to share this with Theophane. She hesitates then realizes he, of all people, deserves to know it. How could she obscure truth in the presence of God, of all people? Candor first, not last. The Senator is teaching her something.

In the few days before she leaves and Krystian follows, the team meets each day to go over the engineering and technical data and the now tighter presentation outline. They discuss money, shipping, and pesticides. Maartje connects with Khalil, Anna Godsen and Dr. La-Vie in some final preparation. She maps out work session topics. She has a long phone conversation with Royce Brenden on silt and the subjects she wants him to cover. The day before she leaves, she sends a "We are coming" e-mail to Carolyn at the GWF, a diagram explaining the order of the presentation and the supporting resources.

Still basking in the glow of gentle loving, Maartje is technically and emotionally ready. And she is physically stronger. Krystian notices her glow and takes it in stride. He prepares very thoroughly, then cuts himself loose to become an observer, monitor of mood and sensor of momentum in the presentation room. He confers with Jan Greilingen for an update on the BSF insertion. He decides not to share Maartje's relationship with Dr. Rajiv, calculating that for now, the downside exceeds the upside. He sees Maartje off at Delft head-quarters as she taxis to the Schiphol train. He feels the excitement and the tension. Show time again.

This time, Maartje's flight takes a great circle over southern Greenland where she sees icebergs calving, then across Hudson Bay and Upper Lake Michigan, cuts across Wisconsin from northeast to southwest, next southern Minnesota, South Dakota, northwestern Nebraska colored by the celery greens of spring plantings. The Front Range Rockies appear during a long flat approach to DIA which seems to take an eternity. The snow-capped mountains—above 9000 feet—are breathtaking to Maartje. Even traditionally dry eastern Colorado is green. There must have been plenty of spring rain and mountain runoff this year.

Maartje fetches her bags and heads for the car rental office. Alamo-Emerald provides a new Subaru station wagon for her drive to Fort Collins. She plans to spend the night there before heading up the Cache Le Poudre canyon, and the drive to the seminary.

Before heading to dinner, she asked Royce Brenden to arrange a visit and plant tour with Manny Kowalski and Alois Dotzemoth at their molding company in Fort Collins. They are gracious and helpful in explaining the die design and anchor manufacturing process. She sees several anchors being molded and observes the machining center operator at his computer-numerically-controlled (CNC) equipment. It sequentially bores, drills, faces and finishes the rough cast anchors for seed and fertilizer pellet insertion. The first end of the anchor to be inserted is milled for the later addition of the flare out (opening like a parachute) flukes as the anchor is slightly retracted—about one inch—just before the hydraulic bank inserting machine lets go the anchors, three at a time.

She asks Manny and Alois for a half dozen anchors for the presentation. They of course are thrilled to send out their product. It even has their Internet address molded along the length. And an 800 phone number. A hamburger, French fries and malt at the Silver Grill near the C.S.U. campus bring early closure to the long travel day. Too tired to jog or even walk, she is asleep in minutes.

The wake up call at seven scares her. The bright light pouring into her window shocks her out of bed. With morning sun at her back, she begins a colorful and exciting climb. The spring runoff on the Poudre River is a kayaker's magnet. Kayakers in droves are risking the heavily flowing spring waters. She stops several times to watch. How carefully they study downstream rocks, eddies and depth. They make her sailboarding seem tame. At the top, she gazes south toward Estes Park and Long's Peak, heads down into the valley to Walden, east of the next mountain range. A colorful, alive time of year. But this one is special.

Walden is a flat, sleepy town with one wide street, three restaurants, four taverns. A rancher's town. She stops briefly for breakfast and gas and then heads north on Colorado 25, then Wyoming 230, to Riverside and Saratoga. Armed with two Diet Cokes and peanuts, she heads toward a point 50 miles north of the birthplace of the Platte River. Following the Platte brings her into another verdant, wide valley. An abundance of mountain water sustains this valley. A private jet-strewn airport crowded with small jets is evidence of the millionaire's club to the East. Then she spots several understated, low profile, single story cabin-like buildings: the Saratoga monastery. Whether it is the delightful aroma of the cookie bake shop, or the clear, mountain air gently whispering, the place feels charmed, like a suddenly reappearing Brigadoon.

She is glad she decided to come here. A brother fetches Theophane. Theophane walks up to her calmly. He is gently smiling and takes both her hands and says, "My, look at you. You look wonderful. Already, you bless us by just being here. I have missed you. How is Dr. Gaol?"

Maartje, emotionally caught up, refuses to let go of Theophane's hands, saying softly, "Theophane, not only has he become a valued professional colleague. We have developed a personal relationship. He has become very special to me. I believe I am in love."

"Ah," whispers Theophane. "No wonder you have such a lovely glow about you. Come, let's walk up and I will introduce you to some of my brothers. We'll dine, then talk privately." She is disarmed by his graciousness. He has the same energy here that she witnessed when she first met him. The grief in his Bangladesh eyes is not evident today.

Such gentle people, Maartje observes, as Theophane introduces several brothers over the next twenty minutes. They all seem intense but a quality of tranquility hovers. The austerity of monastery life is eclipsed by a compelling easiness about faith and life in this place. The ageless mountain ranges framing the valley help her appreciate how the agonizing daily traumas in the lives of the less fortunate Bangla coastal peoples can be managed by a man of God so deeply steeped in tranquility.

Maartje finds herself relaxing among the gentleness. She is reminded how intense her Western European life is, with its schedules, deadlines, peer and other pressures, demanding travel, and project-filled calendar.

After lunch, they move to a small alcove just inside the main building entrance. Maartje takes out her computer and as it boots up, she hands Theophane the new twelve-page presentation outline. He studies it slowly and carefully. She waits. And she waits. And waits some more.

Finally, he looks up and says, "This is a well thought out presentation. I would never have connected tigers or firewood with the safety and health of the coastal peoples. It makes eminent sense, as I reflect upon it. However, you barely touch on concepts that could make or break such a significant effort."

Maartje, "What are you referring to, Theophane?"

He explains that if he reduces this whole thing to a blur, he envisions an invasion force headed for Bangladesh, perhaps like that which arrived off Omaha beach in France in June, 1944: silt mattresses for embankment stability, shipping to implement the firewood piece, construction to do the horizontal cable delivery systems, coastal storm surge barriers, health care platoons, security, communications, public relations, political forces within Bangladesh, financial interests from all over the world, seaport construction efforts, the entomology and fungus army, agronomists, foliage specialists and others, of course. "The missing piece is what I call the support army of nurture and caring." But he observes, "You are coming close with the appeal to schools, children, museums and zoos. Bertram and Bernice are clearly magnets for children of all ages.

"Funny," quips Theophane, "talking about really caring, when the Christmas tsunami of '04 struck at Banda Aceh and over the Indian Ocean, I do not recall seeing any Bangla Bhai terrorists volunteering to help victims. What does this tell us about any underlying commitment of these people?"

"May I respond?"

"Please do," says Theophane.

"In an unsolicited contact three weeks ago, UNICEF requested the opportunity to audit our Boulder presentation. This may be a beginning 'support army.' Of course, it may not amount to anything. However, UNICEF and the World Food Program are formidable. GWF is aware of this interest and consented to their presence."

Theophane responds, "Maartje, yes, this is very positive, but only a small part. I am talking about those who communicate with grade, middle and high schools, zoos, wildlife organizations, parents and grandparents of children who donate money for wood or buy these Bertram and Bernice stuffed animals. How about churches and Sunday schools? Who will write and e-mail them regularly with news of developments and hopefully, successes? Who will write books, make videos, do in-school presentations, take tigers on tour? Who will tell the stories which develop? I think you are talking about twenty years here—maybe thirty or forty. The children of today will become productive adults while all these efforts take place. All these nurturing resources must be kept informed, kept interested, brought close to the project. I see nothing here about this."

"Theophane, I have two reasons to be here. First, I continue to find your presence in my life very comforting. I want to understand more of the spirit in your life. Maybe then I might develop more spirituality in mine. A significant part of my coming to you is, selfishly, to benefit from your spirit."

"I am but a honey bee," says Theophane. "The pollen I carry from flower to flower is an utterly simple faith and an imperfect sense of spiritual being. The pollen is the pixie dust of Christ. I just pick it up and move it along. As a young monk, I used to think I would go out to the world to deliver grand wisdoms. It did not take long to discover that nobody out there was listening. However, when I pass out polio vaccine and candy to the children in Bangladesh, it is a health care delivery system in action, however modest. So the candy and chocolate chip cookies are a sort of nectar to prepare children to receive a vitally important immunization dose, painlessly and joyfully. And also to receive the message that someone really cares about each one of them. So you see, I deliver the wisdom I dreamt about. However, it is not mine. I am just a courier. Patiently, the Lord waited for me to 'get the message.' Previously, I had succumbed to my intellectual arrogance."

Maartje senses how seemingly narrow her technical focus is. This fellow scratches her soul. She recalls that once the RWS sent many of its newer managers to a program on servant leadership. At the time, she had not really understood it. Now, she did. Theophane was servant leadership in the flesh.

Theophane tells a story. Once there was a playful young puppy that was taken to a humane society and was then purchased for the price of anti-rabies and other immunizations. The family who bought him had three young children. They all loved him. He relished in this and began to grow nicely. Somewhat abruptly, the little dog stopping eating, stopped growing, didn't look well and was losing his fur.

Concerned, the family took him to a veterinarian. After drawing blood for chemistry, the vet did a thorough physical with his hands. As he ran his fingers over the dog's neck, he felt something. A closer examination of the neck revealed a fine wire collar. It had been a small puppy's collar which, because of the way it was bent, could not expand as the puppy grew. With a wire cutter, he carefully snipped this wire. Over the next few weeks, the puppy improved in all health categories and went on to live a full life.

"And so it is for the lives of many. Until we identify and loosen those wires which constrict us, restrain us, we are unable to grow psychologically, spiritually, or even in productivity. Perhaps, Miss

Maartje, you are in a process of removing some wire from your life. If so, rejoice," Theophane concluded.

Maartje swallows, breathes heavily and her eyes well up. The moment of the minute is overpowering.

After a few moments, she pauses, then says softly, "And Theophane, just in case I required a second reason, it was to ask you again, invite you, to Boulder on Tuesday for our presentation to the GWF.

"I want you there. You have just said why. You are the piece we have not yet thoughtfully developed. Look, we are concrete, steel, and mattress people. We're not purveyors of human software. I would like you to comment and answer questions as you see fit. There will be nine of us. Four will make our initial presentation. The remaining four are resources to answer panel questions and amplify or clarify that which we may not have effectively put across."

"I will consider it, Maartje. I sense the gravity of this matter for all of Bangladesh and I admire your commitment and tenacity. What you are doing—and Dr. Rajiv too—is noble. It is spiritual. Regarding UNICEF, I suspect it is searching for wisdom. I find it hard to believe UNICEF wants to continue in the business of supplying food and aid today to victims who survived a tragedy yesterday and who will die tomorrow in a repeating tragedy.

"Come, let us walk in this valley before we have an early supper. Also, I wish you to see our mountain sky at night after supper. We market this grand scenery to our new students and fraters—I mean priests in training. Take a half hour to freshen up. Dress warmly. The afternoon winds assault us regularly."

In a dormitory-like guest room, Maartje, very much looking forward to dinner, cleans up, puts on the sweater Rajiv gave her, buttons up and meets Theophane at the front entrance. They walk for 45 minutes and Maartje can feel how hard her lungs are working. She is glad she has three more days to acclimate. Her joints ache and she has the beginnings of a headache. Dinner helps.

What really helps is a grace offered by Brother Samuel. "Heavenly Father. A faith in God adds life to our life, adds life to people who seem only to know suffering, pain and degradation, adds life to all that has come before and adds life to death. Help us, we beseech you, to lead lives of caring and devotion to all those we serve and to thoughtfully inspire them to see and feel your light."

The brothers are hospitable and listen intently to her whistling Dutch tones. The food is plain but very tasty and nutritious. Pot roast, potatoes, carrots, a rich, succulent beef gravy—not lumpy like the gravy she's tried to make, and freshly baked (of course) dinner rolls from the monastery bakery.

After supper, with shadows reaching across the valley toward the Snowy range on the East, Theophane beckons Maartje to join him for a star gazing session. Stars pop out every other minute, low in the eastern sky first, then overhead and everywhere over the next half hour. It is the breadth of the sky which strikes Maartje. Theophane's understated style masks his own awe. As they gaze up sitting at a picnic table, she says, "Theophane, how did you choose the name?"

"As you know, it means "the presence of God." I chose it because my counseling brother, twenty-five years ago, told me he felt the presence of God when I walked into a room. I thought this very special. It has significantly shaped my life. In coastal Bangladesh, what little I bring to the children lies in the delivery to them of an invisible spiritual sense from hands-on touching these remarkable children. Frankly, I receive far more from them than I give. It is as if they are the presence of God touching this candy vendor."

Maartje feels warm, safe and cared about here beneath the magnificent evening sky. All her presentation anxieties now seem more manageable. Until now, she has not felt this. She knew she needed to come here. She needed to be in the presence of a person who really understands. This is sanctuary. It is very enabling.

Then, a huge yawn visits her. "If I do not get to bed I'll be a zombie. Is it okay if we sign off for the night?"

"Of course," he says.

"I should leave by 9:00 a.m. to get back to Denver to greet the team as they arrive."

"We'll have juice, tea or coffee and rolls at 7:30," says Theophane. "I am so grateful you have seen me and will seek permission to come to

Denver Monday for dinner and the presentation Tuesday in Boulder."

"Theophane, we are at the Best Western Hotel between the new DIA airport and downtown Denver. This makes our run to Boulder easier. And I offer you funds for your travel. Of course, we pay for your room, parking, and meals."

"Not at all necessary, Miss Maartje. We have a generous donor who created an endowment that generates investment returns annually for travel. This fund gets me to and from Calcutta, Dhaka, Hatiya and the Sundarbans. Thank you for offering. I am well covered for this."

"See you at 7:30 a.m."

Her room is austere with modest plywood paneling and simple pine trim. The blankets are maroon wool, heavy and warm. Theophane has provided an extra pillow and a down feather comforter. It is wonderful. She can see some night sky from bed. She goes to sleep watching the stars above the Saratoga Valley. Morning comes slowly but she is up at 6:00, showered, packed and in the dining room by 7:15 for two mugs of coffee. She still has a headache but her joints are better and caffeine is her headache elixir.

Theophane comes from morning mass. They share breakfast. He walks her to the parking lot.

"Miss Maartje, your visit was a gift to me. Your invitation to Denver has me thinking. I am not at all sure that any meaningful contribution will be forthcoming. However, having re-studied your presentation papers, I will be happy to comment on the Army of Support concept. It has been absent in so many other efforts. That is, should you call on me to do so. I will limit my comments to not more than three to five minutes. Early this morning, I recalled a conversation with an Islamic mullah who tends his faithful in the Sundarbans. It will be vital that he and many other imams and mullahs become part of this process. There is so much they can do to support your causes. Now have a safe trip. I will be there Monday by 5:00 p.m. and will call your cell phone if I am late." She writes the names of the hotel meeting and dinner rooms and her room number on a note card.

"Tot Ziens," whistles Maartje.

CHAPTER 22

Going Home

Maartje drives away from the monastery on a cloud. What a mistake it would have been if she hadn't come here.

While it's too late to roll these new perspectives into the written presentation, there can be comments to the panel. And she would call Theophane just before closing with Senator Mukherjee.

She feels good. And very excited to see Rajiv.

Coming back down the Cache Le Poudre Canyon into Fort Collins is no less exciting than going up. The mountain water run off mesmerizes the weekenders and passers through. She arrives at the hotel a half hour before Krystian does. Then an hour and a half later Rajiv, Smeeta, Nafis, Khalil and the Senator wander in. All are tired. She schedules a half hour warm up in a conference room, complete with bottles of water, plain and carbonated. The chatter is endless. She lays out the Sunday morning work, the Estes Park tour in the afternoon and another session over dinner. She explains that Theophane and Royce Brenden will be with them Monday morning.

The troops are beginning to sag so they close up shop early. Maartje shares her altitude aches, pains and breathing shortness with them so they will greater care to drink fluids and walk. She,

287

Rajiv and Krystian go back to her room to talk presentation. Krystian, being nobody's fool, exits early, blaming fatigue. The old pro.

Rajiv and Maartje quickly re-nourish their relationship. But he falls asleep in her bed. She doesn't dare, nor does she want to, move him.

Sunday begins slowly and becomes a gallop. They begin with a two and a half hour session mostly to inform and prepare Senator Mukherjee. He is in the throes of high altitude and travel fatigue. He listens carefully, especially to Krystian. Khalil is coaching him with the presentation materials. Attention is paid to Smeeta and Nafis because their apparent lack of presentation experience remains a concern. Avoiding errors from too much excitement and straying from the big picture are Rajiv and Maartje's concerns. Maartje announces that Theophane will be part of the presentation team and will join them for Monday dinner. She does this as a fait accompli and then initiates discussion on the support Army concept. The team's response is all over the map. The Senator is skeptical; Krystian is thinking; Rajiv is quiet. Smeeta and Nafis are curious. Khalil gets it.

They table the discussion until cocktails and dinner that evening. Adjourning to get ready for the van trip to Estes Park, Krystian sidles up to Maartje. "You are right about Theophane. Maybe when you do the introduction take a few extra minutes to describe his work and experience in Bangladesh. This sets him up for panel receptiveness. See if they nibble."

Maartje said, "Because we have not developed this in our formal materials, we dare not risk elevating him to a prominent role. The panel might conclude we feel our position is so shaky that we reached for him in a last minute panic. Having him present—even if he says nothing—is useful enough especially if Dr. Rajiv's references his hands-on polio vaccine work."

Rajiv chimes in, "I couldn't agree more. He speaks to an inner dimension in all of us. He is appropriate. You are right to include him. My concern down the road is how we build a bridge to Islam. Not necessarily for this presentation but as we proceed, the wholehearted support of Islamic religious leaders throughout Bangladesh is a must. Might Theophane help us with this?"

"When he gets here Monday. Touch on this with him, Jiv."

"Yes," Jiv says, "better me since I was such an antagonist a year ago."

Estes Park in May is spectacular. The Rocky Mountain goats come down below 8000 feet to eat grasses, because the lichens higher up are still under deep snow and not accessible until June. The goats wander along the roads and sometimes drift on to the highway. Elk also come down to graze. There is plenty of snow above 9,000 feet. Rain and snow in April has blessed most of Colorado this spring and markedly ameliorated a three-year drought. Long's Peak is the dominant sentinel in this area. Everyone enjoys looking through Krystian's Swarovskis at the animals and the panorama. Rapidly advancing clouds, wind and rain shorten their round trip. Most are asleep in the van before they leave the park. Ah, altitude. Even Rajiv is whipped. Maartje is two days better. She is spunky and ache free. It helps that she is drinking more water than a camel.

Everyone crashes from four to seven when they reconvene for wine, hors d'oeuvres and a salad, main courses, vegetables, served on a buffet in their private meeting room. Talk among and between the team is comfortable and pleasant. Even the Senator is engaged with Smeeta and Krystian. It is clear he wants to and needs to be here. During dinner, he asks for the floor from Maartje.

"I would like to share some political and economic developments back home with you: all the land for a new deep water port is subject to options, which expire in nine months. An assembly committee has been established to move the quadruple funding bill forward expeditiously. Conditional three year ship charter options have been negotiated with super tanker owners. Given the escalating oil pricing and a dearth of newer vessels, these options are obscenely expensive but better having the ships locked in. We do not have to exercise these until 12-18 months from now. Some of you are aware that recently signed timber land leases with the Finnish paper companies have provided Bangladesh with funds to cover this first phase of our relationship with the RWS." Rajiv smiles.

"And there may be funds left over to apply to some of the other efforts. I am pleased to state that a Bengali steel fabricating company has just agreed to travel to Helsinki, Finland, to design and install the wood treating chambers on each ship. Finland and Sweden are very forestry-oriented. They make everything from chain saws, pulp wood defibrators, crane saws that grasp a whole tree, fell it, and cut it into 100-inch standard pulp log length, then stack it. Companies from both countries have approached our embassies for information about our efforts and to indicate their interest in selling firewood. Apparently the movement of pulp mills to warmer climates has depressed many local markets. This is very good for us. And they are talking with schools and zoos about this project. This is unexpected. It could be major. A three-year supply of firewood for Bangladesh is a massive volume."

Everyone applauds the Senator's words.

"Thank you. I caution everyone that if Muslim imams and mullahs are not invited and included in this entire process, our best hopes will surely be doomed. The tragedies of 9-11, Madrid ('04) and London ('05) are never far away. In this world, people are either included or they are excluded. There are millions of Muslims out there who feel passed over by opportunity, security, health care, dignity, disposable income. They have been subordinate for generations. Along come some brilliant manipulators who promise a land of honey, dates, and palms if they destroy Western cultures and peoples, especially those who support and do business with Israel or western nations. And they are given guns and clothing. Our greatest fear is that Bangladesh will become a haven for terrorists like Afghanistan."

A hotel clerk comes into the room and asks for the Senator. He leaves to take a call. He returns five minutes later. His face is grief-stricken. "I've just been informed that Muslim extremists have bombed the Assembly chambers in Dhaka. The Prime Minister narrowly escaped. We've lost perhaps 25 legislators and many more are wounded. A broadcast has just stated that a cell of Al Qaeda claims responsibility. Khalil and I must leave immediately. I am so sorry. I will give you, Miss Maartje, the text of my remarks. Actually, you have just heard part of them. Under the circumstances, I suggest Mr.

Krystian deliver my remarks. Please carry on. Khalil will e-mail you with more presentation tidbits while we are en route. This is a national crisis and I need to be there as soon as possible."

The team is shaken and agitated. Krystian leaves with the Senator. Maartje ends the meeting saying, "Tomorrow will be a busier day than we envisioned. The GWF panel must sense our unwavering commitment in spite of this development."

About 15 minutes later, Krystian joins Rajiv and Maartje in Maartje's room. A long silence occurs. Krystian opens, "As if he has not endured enough grief. Now this. He gave me a few comments on Bangladesh culture and politics. With some effort, I will weave it into a coherent package. His thoughts will take at least ten minutes besides my own twenty. Should I do them together?"

Rajiv answers, "No. First do yours, then close later with his. The contrast may be helpful. I believe the presentation should move crisply lest we become bogged down by questions. Would it help to have Smeeta do some of his presentation?"

"Yes, I like that," says Krystian.

Maartje, haltingly, murmurs, "I cannot think clearly right now. We're down two on our team. I must process this."

Rajiv, "Maartje, let's call it a night. I have some thoughts to share privately with both of you over breakfast. Let's queue up early, say 7:00."

"Done," says Krystian who diplomatically takes his leave.

Maartje is in tears. Rajiv senses this, holds her closely, says nothing until she settles down. He says softly, "It is vital you sleep well tonight. I'm going to my room to get some lemon grass pills. Now that we have a situation, rest is required to cope and make a decent presentation."

Maartje takes two. Jiv stays until he is sure she is settling down. He leaves her a bottle of carbonated water to settle her intestines. She fights sleep for about half an hour, finally realizing that she is not resisting sleep, she is battling fear. It is 11:30 p.m. Sleep finally arrives and at 6:45 a.m., her wake up call happens. A shower helps. She is five minutes late joining Krystian and Rajiv.

Krystian greets them by saying, "In 1978 when we had a crucial legislative presentation for funding the final phases of the Delta Project pieces, our lead presentation engineer suffered a stroke three days before the hearing. Everybody wanted to postpone it. That is but for one economic fellow. He suggested we simply divide up our fallen warrior's presentation. Which we did. There were some laughable imperfections and lapses. In fact, everybody laughed. When the legislators saw that we were able to laugh at ourselves and our own lapses, they became very sympathetic. The proceeding went from hostile to positive. They allowed us to supplement our presentation with an unprecedented 'list of corrections.' What really happened was that we stepped outside our fears and performed quite well." Even Maartje smiles.

"I like that," said Rajiv. "May I share a thought with you?"

"Of course," say both.

"We, actually mostly me, have done a very bad job of dealing with the 'soft' stuff, which lurks all around this complicated thing. Why not elevate Theophane to spend, say ten minutes on this, in the third or fourth position? I feel he would add a quality none of us has. We are so busy in our respective fields of knowledge, especially me, we may be running right by synergies that make or break projects of this magnitude. As you know, I was not sure about Theophane for a long time. In retrospect, this may have been because he was holding a mirror to my face and I did not like what I saw. It had nothing to do with his being Christian and my having been raised Muslim. It had to do with allowing my faith and spirituality to go dormant. Dormant is too nice a word. I liquidated it to simplify my life. Theophane has inspired me to reactivate it. I do not believe Theophane will hurt us and, with a little coaching by you two, he may deliver something vital that we cannot."

Krystian quietly says, "Look, we also have Royce Brenden in the wings. I now think we would be foolish not to bring him front and center. His Three Gorges Dam work is recognized all over the engineering world as careful and reliable. I think we should divide the Senator's talk into two pieces and, Maartje, you must zealously guard the time. I will help you prepare both. You know, we could have planned ourselves right past these resources."

Maartje asks, "How do we rectify the written presentation materials?"

"We do not. We supplement. At the outset of the hearing, we ask for five days to supplement based on the unavailability of the Senator, our last minute adjustments and probable imperfections. Let's not kid ourselves, mistakes will be made. And we need to be open about this. I fear the Senator and Khalil's departure may render the panel uptight. We must loosen them up."

Maartje says, "When I introduce Theophane, I will tell the panel we are very early into the support system curve and will happily keep them apprised of all these developments as part of grant reporting. I do intend, unless you override me, to describe my first encounter with him while I was with Rajiv for my first survey. I believe it is telling."

"Well, I remember," interjects Rajiv.

The rest of the team begins shuffling into the hotel dining room. Some appear refreshed, others seem still in the grip of too much altitude, too little oxygen. Royce Brenden is at the maître d's station. Maartje jumps up just as he spots her. They greet each other and she introduces him to Krystian and Rajiv. Right off the bat, he and Krystian hit it off. A pair of technical birds.

Maartje explains to Brenden about the Dhaka bombing and the Senator and Khalil's departure. "We think we would like to move you to a presentation position to fill what we fear is now a considerable hole."

"What in the world might I say that would be of consequence?" queries Brenden.

Rajiv says, "If you create a verbal bridge between the Yangtze and our project commenting on our silt approach, your local persona may actually help us as much as the Senator's presence would have defined Bangladesh. Even though I am pure Bangla, I have no presence or political power. Smeeta and Nafis, over there at the round table of five, give us 'real local color.'"

Brenden remarks, "Wow, I must do some serious thinking so I can be effective. How much time will I have?"

"Five to ten minutes," responds Maartje. "This means a really tight, crisp set of remarks," Maartje hands him the written presentation. "After we get started this morning, take an hour to digest this. Then when we break, we'll talk more specifically about some things you might say that we could not say effectively. A good night's sleep (and musing to herself, Rajiv to tuck me in) and I have become an opportunist. You and Theophane are the persons who provide the American perspective. The GWF is a U.S.-based group whose donors are 89% U.S. citizens.

"I must go to begin our teamwork session. Rajiv will bring you along shortly. Actually, if you want to stay here to digest the presentation, I'll introduce you when you come in. We are in the Curecanti room. Try not to be later than 9:45. Dialog and interplay among the team is important today. I do not want them to see you as some "expert" from far away and that you are here to rescue us. Allow them to see such human frailties as you have, if any. This renders their own acceptable."

Off she goes. Krystian and Rajiv are already in the Curecanti room.

"Let's begin today the way we envision proceeding tomorrow," Maartje says. "Royce Brenden is here, but he is in the lobby studying the presentation. Actually, it will be fine to interrupt each of us with reasonable questions. This could happen tomorrow and each of us must remember where we were when a question is put to us. Use a blank index card or a pen to mark this spot on your materials.

"I will open with an introduction and overview, then Dr. Rajiv, then Krystian. Back to me to cover the seaport facets, which the Senator was to present. Then we have decided to elevate each of you from a resource spot to a presenter. Smeeta, Nafis, Royce Brenden, Theophane. Rajiv or Krystian will close. We will decide this later.

"Some of you already know that UNICEF has picked up on this matter and is sending one or two representatives from New York. Their presence is probably more significant to GWF than to us. However, it touches on what Theophane refers to as the Army of Support in Bangladesh and back home for all project stages. Note that we are acquiring new perspectives as we go. You must be prepared for questions anytime, from anyone. By the way, Theophane will be here shortly. I expect each of you to introduce yourself, talk to him, make him feel welcome and treat him as a partner. He is. Treat him as Minister of the Army of Support."

After Maartje's dry run introduction, Dr. Rajiv picks up. He traces the topography of Bangladesh and geographical matters, the specialness of the Sundarbans, tigers, the denuding of the forests and loss of habitat. Then he begins his transparency show. Everyone in the room has laptops. He hands each a disc and shows them the roadmap to presentation screen 1. Everyone smiles at Bernice and Bertram, giggles at Pog's Burma Shave signs and the accompanying Bangla text. Brenden quietly enters. Everyone knows who he is but Maartje introduces him anyway, "Royce is a silt consultant who has worked with the World Bank on a Yangtze River project and has helped us a great deal. Krystian's and my director at the RWS asked us to utilize him as we put together our silt containment proposal. In an hour and a half, we will take a 15-minute break for WC's, tea, coffee and the marvelous morning buns they serve here."

Rajiv finishes his screens, turns to Krystian who, ever prepared, steps up. Before he opens, three hands go up. "Questions, OK?" Krystian says. "Sure. For Dr. Rajiv."

Smeeta, Nafis and then Maartje all fire away. The questions are helpful and Rajiv answers them fairly well. On one, he defers to Maartje and Krystian and another, about embankment mattresses and anchors, he asks Royce if he would help. Brenden contexts first, then homes in with a useful answer. Everyone there sees the fellow is a natural. He talks about the anchors as if he were the designer. He has stage presence in a golf shirt and cowboy boots. Maartje reins him in a little when he describes the specific polymer being used in the injection molding process. "I suggest you defer on the specific polymer. We never know who desperately wants this specific info to compete head on against the Fort Collins shop."

Brenden. "Of course, quite correct. Even an innocent slip by a GWF panel member at a cocktail party could be harmful."

Rajiv says, "I suggest we pass an anchor or two to the panel—but only after Krystian or Royce discusses their use. The one who first discusses them should hand them out. Hands-on items help connect with a panel. My cardiac surgery professor always brought samples of arteries when he was explaining vessel bypass techniques. I have never forgotten those methods."

Maartje takes 30 minutes to introduce screens 12-23, the RWS and the Delta project.

Krystian summarizes the construction and effectiveness of the Dutch design. He takes another 15 minutes to show a climate change snapshot and hands out a Dutch book, "The Effect of Sea Level Rise on Society" saying, "I have two more copies for the panel."

Krystian playfully teases Maartje. "If you will shoe horn my 31-minute presentation into twenty, we'll be fine."

"I will work on this. I have some ideas," Maartje says.

Rajiv responds, "Better for me to give up five minutes. It is very important for this material—the stuff of hope—to be carefully presented."

"But Jiv, yours is vital."

"I can do it," says Jiv. "I just have to think about it. Perhaps I'll omit explanations for several presentation screens."

The group differs sharply on this, but it's time for lunch. They head for the buffet room and a one-hour (actually one hour, twenty) break. It has been a busy and productive morning. Everyone needs protein and a breather. Smeeta, Nafis and Royce sit together. They are discussing grasses. Maartje is very pleased.

The afternoon finds Maartje adding content to the concepts laid out by Rajiv and Krystian. She is less poised and more technical but no one doubts her competence. Rajiv picks up on her edginess and suggests that he add some comments to his presentation on several subjects to ease her burden.

Theophane drifts into the meeting room. Maartje pauses to introduce him to the team. He and Rajiv nod affectionately to each other.

Royce responds to several direct questions by Maartje and Krystian. His material needs tightening but he takes part in an enthusiastic dialog with Smeeta and Nafis as they excitedly discuss the porcupine quill retention attributes of the anchors—the ones Maartje handled in Fort Collins last Thursday afternoon. Manny Kowalski developed this concept to keep anchors from pulling out of the embankment due to tidal currents and resulting pressure. "We're beta testing now," says Royce. "It should work. Making it cost effective, well, this is another matter."

Krystian is confident the GWF panel will show some hands-on interest in the anchors.

Maartje beckons Theophane forward. He's been chatting quietly with Rajiv. Maartje asks, "Has Rajiv filled you in on the developments?"

Theophane says, "I was so looking forward to seeing the Senator again. He is such an effective statesman. I met him on my first work trip. And I am deeply saddened by the bombing in Dhaka. It is clear Bangladesh, despite its Islamic population, is not immune to terrorism."

Maartje turns to Theophane and takes a chance. "Theophane, I would like you and Royce Brenden to fill the Senator's time slot, with a somewhat different focus. We will use Smeeta and Nafis to amplify tiger habitat and how to grow the tiger population. Mr. Brenden is our silt containment consultant."

"The muck man," says Royce.

Theophane picks up an anchor from Smeeta and says, "I heard, as I entered, some remarks about Mr. Kowalski's anchors. These are fascinating. I happen to 'sell,' if you will, a different kind of anchor. It is the anchor of our Creator's love if you are Christian, Allah's if you are Muslim." The entire group smiles at the metaphor. How quickly this quiet soul is becoming part of the team—a team that right now needs a boost.

Maartje, now operating on full alert, says, "Theophane, please use this metaphor in your presentation."

CHAPTER 23

A Foreign Affair
Turns Domestic

Sundarbans, Bangladesh

Dr. Rajiv's two new medical assistants—the BSF plants—are in the new clinic boat anchored deep in the Sundarbans. Even though there are only 250 tigers in the whole of this vast water-soaked area, the men still have the infrared sensors on. These sensors detect mammalian body heat within 150 yards. Safety first. Right now, there's nothing on the scope to worry about. However, they are busy using some very sophisticated "medical" instrumentation to listen to something else—they are tuned to cell phone conversations coming from outside Bangladesh to a GPS-located spot in a Cox's Bazaar café. They have directed local contacts there to observe and listen. They are transmitting this conversation to team leaders and an on-site-fellow. Actually, the "fellow" is an attractive young woman who appears to be waiting for friends. What they overhear is a planning session for a "project." Someone wants to use Semtex—the Eastern European equivalent of C-4—for a target. While not imminent, several couriers are to bring fuses and plastic explosives to Dhaka over the next few weeks. The target will be the cranes at the newly constructed deep-water port side. The discussion is about the movement of fuses and plastic explosives via several couriers in the next two to four weeks.

The on-site agent does her work. Vehicle licenses are noted. The locus of the reception site is carefully staked out. It is the back room of a tea shop. Every entrance/exit is covered. Backup teams are in place. This is not a bust operation, only "who is who" so the ultimate event can be squelched after the players are identified and located. The source of the call is in Tajikistan. A fellow named Ahmed is calling from a remote village up about 9000 feet. The "Project" will involve divers and stealth. It will be in the evening at high tide.

In Denver at the Monday evening dinner, Maartje asks Theophane to offer grace as the group prepares for dinner. For Smeeta and Nafis' benefit, he offers an Islamic prayer—which he delivers in Bangla and then translates to English. The prayer is softly delivered and leaves an impact for its breadth. It is very inclusive:

> "With all due regard to the religious faith of each person here, we pray to our highest spiritual power. We seek the comfort of your grace as we struggle to live lives which respond and caringly so to your hopes for each of us and for this unified team. We ask your loving arms to find and wrap themselves around Senator Ram Mukherjee, Khalil and those who suffered so grievously in the Dhaka explosions. Gather with us now as we commune in your spirit and with each other."

The meal is very good, a fusion of Asian and Southwest American foods. The tension is mounting. After dinner, Maartje and Rajiv do a brief summary for all. The closing remarks from Krystian deal with expected and unexpected questions. "Remember, mark your spot. Deal with the unexpected. Always return to where you were. Take your cues from Maartje and Rajiv. Do not venture into uncharted territory."

The team is advised to be in the lobby at 8:30 dressed as discussed with no strong perfumes, deodorants or colognes. "Remember," they are advised, "this is a fresh air—no smoking—climb mountains culture."

As the group trickles out, Krystian approaches Royce Brenden, Rajiv and Maartje to suggest a half hour to share thoughts. They welcome the opportunity.

Krystian, mindful of everyone's need for a good night's sleep, starts right in. "I have always found it helpful to make a list of the tilt points. Tilt points would be the concerns of the GWF. What can hurt their reputation? What will help them accomplish their mission in this project and others? What developments external to the project can kill it and harm the GWF? We must cover all these and emphasize them appropriately. And, in the panel's questioning, interrogation may be the better word, they will be signaling topics they consider vital which perhaps are not developed to their satisfaction. We must respond right then and there. If you say, 'I will cover this later,' that will not work.

"I feel we are most vulnerable on firewood. They will certainly focus on the funding, the supply, shipping, distribution and security to assure fair distribution and keep terrorists and dacoits at bay. They may conclude this is a too high risk approach, the odds of success are against us (and them) and there may be nothing their money can do to turn this into a winner."

Rajiv suggests, "It may help to use the satellite photos showing the denuding over 30 years to help them understand just how vital a piece this is. Without firewood, nothing of consequence will occur. This is a story being repeated throughout the rain forest areas of the world, whether mining, oil, strip logging or just firewood for cooking and warmth."

"Excellent," says Krystian.

Maartje says, "I have the text of the Senator's remarks regarding the Deep Water Port and the shipping charters. Perhaps I should read those three to four pages.

"Absolutely, but tighten it down to one page," chimes in Rajiv, "and then, after you have read *only* the key parts, pass out copies to each panel member. Who will close our presentation?"

Maartje says, "It should be one or the other of you or both. I would like to make this decision on the fly after we have seen how the panel responds to each of us."

"Fine," says Krystian. "I will do an outline for Rajiv and me and will hold it until we see how the presentation is going. I may have time to make copies."

Maartje comments, "I will ask for a five minute time out to tighten up our closing. I will ask this at the outset so we know their position."

Rajiv says, "Krystian, I think you should close. I do not have the presentation expertise you do. My ego will not be wounded. Trust me."

Royce adds, "If the panel demonstrates some leniency, each of you might take three to four minutes. Let's wait and see."

"Dr. Rajiv, you are from Bangladesh. I am just Krystian, the engineer. It is far more important for you to make our closing impression."

"Now, men, let us wait. Off to bed with both of you. And Royce, thank you for investing this long day in us," Maartje says as she heads for her room.

The next day arrives like most mountain mornings. There is the light over the Eastern skyline, the always large, open sky. Bright, bright air. Maartje is up at 5:30 a.m. having coffee in her room. She is doing a concentrated last review of presentation materials. She finishes by 6:40 a.m., takes a long hot shower, does her hair, and puts on a black pant suit with her mandarin orange silk blouse and scarf in both colors. She heads down to the coffee shop at 7:45. Everyone, in varying degrees, is ready. Rajiv smiles warmly and appreciatively as Maartje strolls in. She is classy. He is wondering why he did not spend the night with her. Smeeta is wearing a lovely celery green silk blouse (made by her mother) and a long, darker pastel green skirt with midnight black medium heels. Maartje tells her she looks very professional. Everyone claps. Smeeta blushes and shyly looks down. Theophane slips in. He has taken measures to iron his sedate monk's garb—no robe this time, just a clean brown suit with a creamy beige shirt and dark brown collar.

Maartje hands out the final lineup. They each check it out. No one gasps or groans. Each realizes that his or her part, small or large, is important and that effective delivery is at least 50 percent of the total.

Royce shows up at 8:20 with two bottles of 20 ounce water for each and passes them out. They are becoming accustomed to this Colorado gesture.

Brenden has four anchors tethered to his briefcase by nylon connectors. He pulls Maartje and Krystian politely aside, "I understand that GWF board member Alex Gardner will chair the panel. He is a no bullshit, retired, construction executive. Gardner turns stuffy presenters inside out and often re-sequences meetings out of the blue. So be advised." Krystian is thrilled. To have a seasoned construction executive couldn't be better for the Dutch team members and Royce Brenden. Maartje thinks she likes this, though right now she is hardly sure of her name.

They pile into two vans for the 40 minute trip to Boulder. Some are quiet. Some chatter. The University of Colorado campus lies along the front range of the Rockies. It is about six to eight blocks wide and about a mile and a half long. Their destination is a small multi-media room at the Buffalo Alumni Center which holds a maximum of 50 people. All chairs are on the same level. The meeting room faces north. Five 24" x 30" computer presentation screens are set so wherever a person sits, at least two screens are visible, just like the layout in a sports bar. In front of the GWF panel is a U-shaped arrangement of tables. Maartje arrays her team around the U.

At 9:45, six people enter the GWF panel has arrived. Conrad Josephson, the Executive Director GWF, does the honors. "This is my assistant, Carolyn Mack. Maartje and Rajiv already know this, but new to them are the panelists. Our panel chairman, Alex Gardner, Maria Nunez; Nancy Johnson, and a GWF director; Orville Roser, panel member." To Maartje and Rajiv, their faces are hard to read. Maartje realizes suddenly that they know little about these people who will pass judgment on their application. Are they scientists, humanists, or engineers? Too late now to find out.

Rajiv is already tinkering with the hookup from his laptop to the presentation monitors. His presentation begins with a title screen which reads, "A presentation to support and explain the Grant Application of Bangladesh to the Global Wildlife Federation May 18,

2006." Thanks to Pog and his graphics, the colors are crisp and sharp. Maartje is doing her table diagram with names for both her teams and for the panel. She uses full names and puts a major subject of emphasis or two by each. Nafis and Smeeta beam as they see their names. To each, it is as though they were star performers, names blinking in neon lights in front of a famous hotel.

At 10:00 sharp, Alex Gardner clinks on a glass, "Let's get to work." Everyone promptly sits down. Gardner opens by explaining, "This is a presentation by Bangladesh and several interested supporters to the Global Wildlife Federation seeking a grant of ten million dollars to support its proposal to strengthen habitat and Bengal tiger population in Bangladesh. In a moment, Miss deBouter, I will recognize you. First some basics." He covers rest rooms, beverages, lunch (all on the team wonder why—as they thought the meeting would be over by noon) and asks each presenter, while presenting to speak up, to stand either in place or at the podium as each chooses. He introduces the panel carefully, saying, "While I may chair this panel today, I assure you each panelist has skills and interests that are being focused on this matter. And, please, when one of us asks a question, do not ramble. Answer it, continue or finish, and sit down. Our format as scheduled is one hour and thirty minutes for formal presentations, one hour for questions, then 38 minutes for you, Miss deBouter, or whoever you designate to finish up. It may be more than one of you. Either during your presentation or during the question and answer period, in our grant process we are always interested in the activity of militant terrorist groups in any country or territory to which we allocate grant money.

"However, and because of the complexity of this matter, not the least of which is the worldwide nature of resources you propose involving and which you have already brought to bear, after 1¾ hours, we will all break for lunch. The panel, plus Conrad and Carolyn, will use this room. You will have your catered box lunch delivered here, then you'll go upstairs to room 404A. I want the GWF panel to have at least an hour to discuss what we have heard. Then we will reconvene and I am sure we will have more questions or will ask some of you to amplify certain items. We are not trying to trip you up, but let's face it, if we are to view your application favorably, we don't just call our controller to wire ten million dollars to the Senator's office and wait for your project to make us look brilliant."

For Krystian and Rajiv this is good news. The GWF would never consider extending this presentation had they already turned it down. Maartje is thinking ahead. She says, "Chairman Gardner, would it be possible for us to do our closing at the very end of the second session rather than before we break?"

Gardner says, "Excuse us," while he polls the panel as well as Conrad and Carolyn, who clearly are considered valued resources. After five minutes, Gardner says, "That will be fine, Miss deBouter. Let's get to work. Carolyn will pass out a lunch choice check sheet."

At that moment, in walk three "suits"; people dressed in typical East Coast fashion. Carolyn whispers to Gardner who says, "You must be the UNICEF representatives." Only one is a "zipper."

"Yes, sir, we are," says the obvious leader of the trio. "I am Rachel Thomas. This is Dr. Farouk Zeir and Claudia Abendstern."

Gardner, "Welcome, and please be seated where you are able to see at least one monitor."

"Miss deBouter, proceed."

Maartje rises carefully and walks to the laptop on the center table. She carefully arranges her materials, sips a glass of water, and smiles. "I am Maartje deBouter, a hydrology engineer, a graduate of the University of Utrecht with emphasis on culturally integrated major construction projects. I also have an M.B.A. in Technical Communication from M.I.T. I have been with the Royal Water Service (RWS) of the Netherlands for three years. I report to Krystian Kpoczek, a senior hydrology engineer for the RWS. I live in Lisse, very near Keukenhof Gardens. My supervisor, Mr. Kpoczek, (Maartje gestures to Krystian) has a bachelor's degree in civil engineering from the Czech Engineering Institute in Prague and a master's degree in hydrology from the Munich Institute for Advanced Construction Technology. Mr. Kpoczek was a project manager of the pier and gates group for the storm surge barrier of the Oosteschelde (Maartje always seems to whistle when she says this) coastal protection project. We call it the Delta Project. It was begun in 1970 and was completed in the fall of 1986. This project was our national response to the huge storm—a high tide, North Sea, force 9 Beaufort Scale storm in spring 1953. It manifested itself as a major surge. As you may remember, that storm ruptured dikes and then allowed a nine-foot surge wall of sea water to flood 500,000 hectares (one hectare is 1.6 acres). 1853 people drowned, millions of animals died, soil was salt poisoned and it took 8-10 years to purge excessive saline content from soils in the region.

"Dr. Rajiv Gaol, a native of Bangladesh, is a practicing pediatrician and infectious disease specialist. He attended Northwestern University Medical School in Chicago, graduated from there, did a residency at Northwestern Hospital and returned to Bangladesh to perform government service, the six years of service he owed in return for the medical education he received under a Bangladeshi program to strengthen its health care system. He has served three of the six years. We call him our 'river boat doctor.' He serves villagers in the Sundarbans and coastal islands, mostly visiting by boat. There are few roads and only one railroad which, of course, travels only where there are large dikes to hold track bed.

"As some of you may know, a tragic bombing occurred in the assembly hall in Dhaka this past Saturday, one day after Senator Ram Mukherjee and his staff assistant, Khalil, arrived in Denver. Hundreds were injured and 50 people died. The Senator who is a leading political figure in Bangladesh, and Khalil were obliged to return immediately. Several of us will present the essence of their remarks.

"Smeeta Pal is a habitat specialist with the Interior Department of Bangladesh. She is our expert on Bengal tigers. She earned bachelor's and master's degrees from Srinigar College in species enhancement and ecology. Nafis Ahmad is a grass, shrub and tree forestry department chief in the Madpur district of Bangladesh. He has a biology degree from the University of Calcutta." Nafis smiles politely.

(Smiling inwardly to himself, Rajiv silently thinks, And after tomorrow, Nafis will be a dead shot with his new .375 Magnum rifle.)

"Brother Theophane is a monk from a monastery in Saratoga,

Wyoming. Every year since 1991, he has visited coastal Bangladesh to assist with polio vaccine distribution for children. His monastery makes and sells chocolate chip cookies with the brand name of Holy Smackers! We have invited him here as our resource on the levels of support, caring and nurture which must be developed for any project, or series of projects, to have a decent chance of success.

"Royce Brenden is COO of IEC Denver, a widely known engineering consulting firm. Mr. Brenden is our silt containment consultant. He was a World Bank consultant for the massive Yangtze River Three Gorges Dam project." She sits down.

Rajiv rises, bows politely, moves to the station, switches on his lap top, looks carefully at the panel and smiles. He nods courteously to the UNICEF people, saying, "I wish we had 20,000 of you in Bangladesh." They glow.

"I will take ten minutes to explain the geography and topography of our country, five minutes to describe the consequences of the absence of effective storm surge protection systems. In my last ten minutes I will explain what in the world the first two have to do with the Bengal tiger population. Miss deBouter, Mr. Ahmad, Miss Pal, Mr. Brenden and Mr. Kpoczek will explain our proposal and planning to markedly improve the tiger population in coastal Bangladesh. Our project is multi-national and multi-disciplinary involving the considerable skills, experience and resources of the Netherlands Royal Water Service.

"Our country, first created in 1971, lies at the north end of the Bay of Bengal (P-1). In many ways, we are an Asian geographical equivalent of the low countries—Belgium, Luxembourg and The Netherlands—in Western Europe. Our coastal islands are so low we hardly refer to them as barrier islands. They are but moderately foliaged sandbars. During the three to six cyclones we have every year, these islands often disappear under tidal surges which rise 5-10 feet above normal high tides. We lose thousands of people to lesser force storms and hundreds of thousands to more intense storms."

"Dr. Gaol," pipes up Maria Nunez, "if these savage storms occur so regularly and, seemingly, so predictably, why are there so many annual, shall we say, tragedies? Do not even the least of your people know the consequences of location there?"

Rajiv responds. "In varying degrees, they all know the consequences. We have a very large, rapidly expanding population of illiterate, impoverished, near starving people—millions of them. Because they lack funds to acquire food, they will, and do, risk everything to live there or in the Sundarbans (P-2). This is a large delta-like estuary where edible foods, fish, shrimp, clams, oysters all thrive in those waters. In these dangerous areas, despite the risks, they are able to feed their families. We are not a wealthy country. For us, risk is taken by necessity. Inland, in the cities, the open dumping of sewage is a fertile source for cholera, dysentery and a host of parasites. People there live in shanties (P-3) which they do not—and never will—own. Gangs of vicious thugs—we refer to them as 'dacoits'—extract protection money from people who have little. To escape this violence, people flee to the vulnerable coastal islands for survival. They know the dacoits will not risk following them. One group of dacoits who did was annihilated by villagers who rose up against them."

"Thank you," says Ms. Nunez soberly.

Rajiv continues, "Storm surge flooding coming from the Bay of Bengal is compounded by the mountain waters of three significant rivers—at spring melt—the Brahmaputra from East India which becomes our Jumuna, the Megna and the Ganges. So our country gets its water, good and bad, both ways. Now the Sundarbans and many other areas just happen to be (P-4 and P-5) remarkable wetlands. They are similar to your wetlands, the Mississippi River delta south of New Orleans; that is the way it was before offshore oil rigs came in the 70s. Also, the Everglades, until the Corps of Engineers dammed off the water supply there in the late '40s. Our wetlands serve to absorb seasonal flood waters, even storm surges, and runoff from high snowfall winters in the Himalayas.

"Because the Sundarbans are so lush, tropical, and fast growing, animals like deer, wild pigs and tigers select them as habitat. Around 1860, our Bengal tiger population was estimated to be between 40,000 and 85,000." P-6 is a remarkably clear photograph of a large male Bengal tiger that had no idea he was being photographed as he washed his nine-inch paws in the silty water off a Sundarbans embankment. Carolyn and Conrad are mesmerized, as is Ms. Nunez. It's hard to read the reaction of the other panelist. Nancy Johnson shows no visible affect. Mr. Roser seems detached. Alex Gardner is neutral.

Rajiv then introduces the current situation. "For almost 100 years, as you know, tigers became an important trophy for hunters from abroad. Others hunted tigers for their parts. Psychological and perceived male sexual prowess is said to increase after consuming certain tiger parts. (Everybody smiles.) This has contributed to near extinction of the Bengal tiger. The population today is perilously perched at 265-275.

"Everyone in Bangladesh requires wood to burn for cooking and, during monsoons, to keep warm. P-7 is a satellite photo taken in 1975. The darkest greens are trees and shrubs. Already we see vast deforestation and defoliating along all coastal areas, not only in the Sundarbans. By 2002, looking at P-8 (his audience stares and gasps), you are able to observe a major color shift. Note the browns and reds in all coastal areas. Approximately half of this land is worthless, not even swamp subsistence level. The other half is top soil from up river embankments. As you may see, this silt (the suspended top soil) has moved out into the Bay of Bengal basin from what was one mile off-shore between 1890 and 1905 (Bhatchayara coastal survey) to 7-10 miles in 1990 and today in some sectors (P-9) as much as 35 miles."

Chairman Gardner stares at this. He is troubled.

"Dr. Gaol, would you bring back P-7 and 8 again, please?"

"Certainly, Chairman Gardner." And he does so. A thirty-second silent study period ensues.

"In our proposal, the tiger is a key player in any process to reduce erosion and improve the shrub, grass and tree cover. As you see, this tiger is alert, in no apparent distress, appears mature, well developed and nourished. This is a healthy tiger, at home and at ease in his environment as we'd like all tigers (and people, I might add) to be.

"Before I stop, allow me to state, so there may be no doubt, the

aim of our proposal is not just to strengthen the Bengal tiger population. This is one prong of a major convergence. The other is the
compelling necessity (P-10) to reduce the tragic loss of life, severe
disease, and starvation which endlessly impair the dignity and well
being of the peoples of Bangladesh. In my medical practice, I see
these problems every day. We never seem to get ahead of this. Our
health care, even the care I provide with the best possible treatment
and medications will, without major structural engineering and social improvement, fall further and further behind. This is part of why
I, a medical person, have become part of this proposal team."

He sits down, leaving P-10 on the screen deliberately. The panel
stares at a horrible scene of sewage and filth, children floating boats, tin
cans, cardboard, whatever, in the toxic effluent of canals and swales.

After a long pause, Maartje comes back up to the podium computer. She knows now she must push off from the necessary sadness
and pain of P-10 to a fix—at least a debatable solution—to the monumental issues presented out by Dr. Rajiv.

She shows P-11. It is the Delta Project in a wide angle helicopter
shot early one rare April morning when the sun was shining on the
Haringvliet piers, gates and super-highway over the top. Maartje remembered how Rajiv gasped as they drove over the rise, out of the
farmlands south of Rotterdam, almost fifteen months ago. Smeeta,
Nafis and Theophane are as impressed as the panel. Chairman Gardner is in his element. This is big stuff. World class, 200 year life. He
knows how good the undersea foundation had to be for these structures. No silt there. All take in the stunning North Sea background
of ominous gray blue brightening to a white tipped sky blue just beyond the structures, then to a gray green brown of the estuary waters
between land and the gating structures. The serene colors change
the mood in the room. Here they can see a very serious problem has
been confronted and solved.

"This is the Dutch response to our 1953 tragedy." Then she shows
P-12, P-13, P-14, P-15, and P-16. "These are other major pieces of the
current era of Dutch coastal erosion, protection, and… wetlands
preservation, projects." Each slide shows a fish, oyster, starfish, lim-

pet clam or crab caricature on it—a Pog Marenjar idea to link the Bengal tigers, Bertram and Bernice, with some Dutch counterparts. P-17 introduces Bernice and Bertram. Everyone smiles, especially Carolyn and even the skeptical Mr. Roser.

Conrad understands quickly. "Miss deBouter, are you suggesting, or inferring, that oysters, clams, and crabs in the Netherlands are vanishing species?"

"No, Mr. Josephson." Maartje turns to Krystian.

"If I may," he says softly but precisely, with barely a hint of Eastern Europe in his voice. "During the design period of the Delta Project, in 1963-1974, a major negative consequence of the design, as it was then, would have extinguished these marine populations in project areas. The engineering conclusion was that it was absolutely necessary to create closed barriers, permanently closed, in the entire Delta except for shipping locks and dams.

"A massive outburst came from commercial fishing, shellfish and crab interests, who saw centuries of North Sea livelihoods and culture vanishing, being sacrificed on an engineering altar. We experienced violent protests for almost two years. Of course, the government proposed buying them out. Then consumers, buying cooperatives and food stores joined the protests.

"One, and I mean just one person, a free spirited engineer spoke up at one of our planning sessions in 1980 at the RWS. I was present and the discussions were teetering on futility. The government was about to reach a 'cram down' decision on project approval.

"This fellow said, 'Might it be possible to design piers with some sort of hydraulic gating that could allow sea water, nutrients, food and all to arrive and depart with the tides? These gates could then be lowered only when storm surges threatened this area of the coast'?

"The room—there were 26 of us present—became so quiet for a very long time. (Very much like the 1980s TV ads by E. F. Mutton, was it?)"

The panel laughs. Krystian is purple with embarrassment, yet he doesn't know why. Chairman Gardner says, "Mr. Kpoczek, forgive our terrible manners. We knew the brokerage house as E. F. Hutton."

Krystian blushes and laughs at himself. Everybody shares the rejoinder. As he recovers, Mr. Roser observes, dryly, "In fact, E. F. Hutton ultimately went to the financial slaughterhouse just like mutton. So you were more correct than you realized. It is we who did not get it."

Recovering, Krystian continues. "In this deadly silent room everybody responded positively and negatively. We began a vigorous discussion of how to incorporate the major objections of the political greens, the commercial fisherman, the consumers and seafood sellers.

"Two weeks later, our Prince met with opposition leaders to outline the engineering shift and put things in perspective. This session at the palace defused much of the dissent. Ecologists, biologists, and fishing interests were, for the first time, added to several design and implementation committees. In undertaking the redesign, we lost more than three years. But we gained national harmony and political support which, of course, was tantamount to funding.

"The rest is history. And Chairman Gardner, I apologize for providing such a wandering response to your question.

"The coastal flood population systems we propose for Bangladesh are in phases or stages. We speak here only of Phase 1 and perhaps 2. To rebuild tiger population we must restore habitat. To restore habitat we must inspire the local population to stop foraging for firewood. Mind you, at present, they do not have a choice. Survival comes first. Therefore, a system must be created—and initially funded—in part by you and in part by a quadruple matching grant of the government of Bangladesh.

"The project requires a two-to-three-year supply of firewood; a massive amount. This can only come from outside Bangladesh. The acquisition and transportation of this wood, delivery in a vermin free, disease free, condition and a reliable distribution system to keep the coastal populations from panic have been the subject of our efforts for many months. Miss Pal, Mr. Ahmad, Dr. Gaol and Miss deBouter, Brother Theophane, Senator Mukherjee and his assistant Khalil Khan have been vital parts of this process. Our executive director at the RWS suggested (Maartje chuckles to herself, "he demanded") we retain an experienced silt containment consultant. An expert with worldwide credibility is here in Colorado, Mr. Royce Brenden. He was retained to evaluate our proposal.

"Halting the foraging and denuding (seen on slides P-7, 8, and 9) is a must. Then replanting embankment grasses, shrubs and trees for the growing areas are the beginning steps toward habitat enhancement."

The panel is listening intently. Each senses that Krystian knows what he is talking about. His experience and confidence are clear from his tone, concise statements, and body language.

"Mr. Junaid Caterlee and Mr. Jagdish Rao worked on embankment grasses, the seeds for which will be imbedded in the mattresses and embankment anchors for a two or three-meter wide three-inch thick, slowly biodegradable, polymer woven mattress. Our RWS Executive Director, Jan Greilingen, is a well-reputed mattress designer. For the Delta Project, he designed the .72 meter thick (almost 2') mattresses (not degradable) on which the piers (P-11) rest out in the North Sea."

Gardner breaks in, "Mr. Kpoczek, perhaps I am ahead of myself, but how in the world do you propose anchoring these mattresses throughout Bangladesh and how in hell could embankment grass, especially baby grass, not be flushed into the Bay of Bengal on tides or floods?"

Krystian replies, "I would gladly answer that. However," and he pauses looking at Maartje. She stands and says, "Mr. Ahmad and Miss Pal will speak shortly to the grass matters. I will discuss the genetic engineering we are having done to develop an optimum deep root embankment grass. However, both Mr. Kpoczek and Mr. Brenden may wish to respond now" and she looks directly at both so neither misses the signal.

"Mr. Brenden, would you briefly discuss the anchors? I will comment later on the application process."

Royce Brenden rises, reaches into his briefcase, thinking to himself, God bless Manny and Alois, pulls out four anchors and hands two to Gardner who gives each a lengthy visual examination, a touch and pound on the floor "kick" test.

"Mr. Chairman, Ladies and Gentlemen of the GWF panel, I am Royce Brenden, a native of Colorado. I worked as a State Highway designer for the CDOT for eight years, rose to project manager, then left to set up IEC with four other engineers, biologists and scientists. I was an I-70 consultant on the Keystone-Vail stretch and the 20 miles east of Glenwood Springs. I suspect most panel members remember how difficult the design of this segment was. Environmental and ecological parameters were at least as demanding as the structural parameters. We also had to make sure that traffic continued to flow. My resume is in the presentation submission on page 197 which Miss deBouter will present at the conclusion.

"This 18-inch gray thing is an embankment anchor co-designed by Mr. Greilingen in Delft, Holland, and Messrs. Kowalski and Dotzenroth of IMKC in Fort Collins. These are injection molded from very high impact resistant biodegradable polymers. You will note several angled back holes" (he shows diagram P-18) "and a harpoon-like device at the tip or small end. These were designed to be hydraulically injected into canal and river beds from a special barge; three anchors at a time—over eight feet—the mattress width.

"The harpoon tip, like a porcupine quill or parachute, spreads out upon penetration and slight retraction to optimize mattress retention. Within each anchor are ten radially drilled holes (see P-18, 19). Into each hole is first inserted an embankment grass seed followed by a plug of slowly decomposing fertilizer for germinated roots. The Bengali researchers and Mr. Greilingen have determined that the water, quite brackish in the canals, sloughs, rivers, and streams will, by a slight pressure differential, and some osmosis, penetrate through the fertilizer to nourish germinated seeds so the grass may find—actually grow—its way out of the anchor into the embankment."

"Very helpful," says Mr. Roser. "Why can't you inject them pneumatically using compressed air rather than the added expense of hydraulic pumps, hoses and controls?"

"Because," answers Krystian, reclaiming the floor, "we found they shatter with the staccato impact from pneumatics—a jackhammer sort of effect. Hole machining itself sets up stress points which are not insignificant even under steadily increasing hydraulic pressure."

"I see. Thank you," says Mr. Roser with an accepting smile. He thinks to himself, Jesus Christ, these folks not only think about problematic stuff, they field test it. This may not be the dreamy stuff I was afraid we were being asked to fund.

Brendan sits down.

Maartje continues, "Please assume, for the moment, that the Netherlands Delta coastal protection system, has worked without major incident since 1986. However, also recognize that we have not yet had another 1000-year storm, but we have experienced 37 major storms.

"Our on-site research in Bangladesh revealed that even the very best coastal protection systems stand no chance of reducing the population's craving for firewood. Observing this early on during our preliminary survey almost a year ago challenged all of us to find a method to alleviate the consequences of the desperate daily scavenging. It became clear that importing massive tonnages of firewood while the silt containment project was in process held promise. It passed all our feasibility tests.

"Senator Ram Mukherjee is, perhaps, the most effective political statesman in Bangladesh. Not only was he willing to sign on politically but he has become a participant in a partnership to acquire land and build the new deep water cargo seaport capable of receiving ULCC's and VLCC's, Ultra Large and Very Large former oil tankers which would bring the firewood.

"As we speak, a marketing campaign is being developed, using the tigers, Bernice and Bertram and their offspring Banjo (P-17) to appeal to schoolchildren, teachers, zoos and other ecology organizations in America, Scandinavia, Europe and South America to pay for containers filled with firewood for shipment to Bangladesh. We expect this will require two to three years of wood being shipped in. We expect our silt containment efforts to take from year two to year ten to be fully implemented.

"In a recent breakthrough, Senator Mukherjee and his assistant, Khalil, prevailed in efforts to convince the Bengali legislature to allow the export of 25 Bengal tigers for reproduction at leading zoos and species enhancement facilities throughout Europe, the U.S., South America and Australia. The major component of this effort was the government's agreement that all offspring may be kept by their birthplace zoo or transferred to another approved facility. The original 25, or healthy replacement offspring for those who die while overseas, must be returned within ten years. An endangered species firm in Sausalito, California, is volunteering to drastically reduce its cloning costs for these tigers assuming appropriate DNA extraction and preservation are provided. Our program marketing consultant explained that schoolchildren and teachers all over the world would not be very supportive if they had no chance to obtain and see a tiger cub where they live. We envision posters, stuffed Bertram, Bernice and Banjo toys, species enhancement data on an Internet site and many other pieces to evolve.

"The transport of unwanted foreign insects or fungi into Bangladesh by means of this firewood importing system has been a major concern for Jagdish Rao, Junaid Caterlee, and me. We concluded early on that we could not be partners in creating an invasive species problem.

"About six months ago, we retained a widely respected expert in Great Britain, Dr. Anna Godsen, to help us. From all perspectives save cost, a shipboard treatment system is necessary. It is similar to autoclaving used to treat construction timber which will be used outdoors, underground, or underwater. This was a process developed in America. In Oregon, we believe. Mrs. Johnson, the timber lady, knows all about this and is very familiar with injecting saline born preservative under pressure. This requires a pressure vessel, called an autoclave, to drive the fungicide and insect inhibiting agent to the very core (center) of each piece of firewood. This process, on board ship, requires a container movement system to shuttle firewood containers around inside the hull during transit. This has been accomplished and is being beta tested in Finland now, where several dormant oil tankers are moored. For political reasons, it must be a company majority owned by Bengali nationals."

Roser and Maria Nunez are scribbling notes furiously. The UNI-

CEF personnel are clearly waking up and showing far more interest than at first and so is Nancy Johnson. Maybe she is a bug person, thinks Krystian. Maartje notices the same thing but thinks she is a shipping person.

In fact, Nancy Johnson is part of the container freighter fleet-owning subsidiary of a timber family. She is vice president of her family's foundation. She also oversees investments for the $300 million endowment donor. What the first three generations made in timber is now significantly invested in shipping. Ms. Johnson has a more than casual interest in this aspect of the project. A resourceful donor who, right now, looks like a canary eating cat.

Maartje concludes and Krystian steps back up, "The use of funds, should GWF look favorably on our application, is detailed in section 17 of our presentation paper. In fact, I am handing each of you a disk and a paper copy access outline to our documentation and the presentation statement Miss deBouter will provide at the conclusion of our presentation later today. Actually, Maartje, why don't you hand it out now? Then, when we separate for lunch, the panel will have all the materials at least to peruse as they prepare their questions."

Maartje does so promptly taking the hard copy. "You will find this is topical. In our presentation, for example, you will find the major categories on P-18 and 19. There are 33 access phrases from funding sources to application of funds; firewood obtaining, treating, packing, shipping, distribution, storing, combustion safety, donating for, cost to obtain, cost to ship, tracking, required containers, and so on.

"I would like to turn to a feature we call 'Cable Distribution of Firewood.' I assume most all of you are snow skiers." Everyone smiles or laughs.

"Our Austrian vendor, Kloppleser, has modified its vertical ski-lift system design to accommodate firewood rather than people. And to operate horizontally, rather than vertically up and down mountains. When there is no need to move firewood, the cable systems will move people, six per gondola. The wood bearing gondolas must drop off the drive cable just as skiers' gondolas do at the wheel house.

This is for unloading and reattachment to the cable powered by the bullwheel motor. The greatest difference lies in the fact that firewood gondolas take longer to unload than people. This modification is not yet perfected. However, as of yesterday, it became ready for field beta testing so we are pleased to have this up-to-date status for you. Now images P-20, 21 and 22 demonstrate, in sequence, the cable system proposed installation sites. As you will quickly note in 22, the initial cable systems do not cover even a fraction of the coastal areas, i.e., those within ten miles of the Bay of Bengal. As Bangladesh has an over-abundance of water, we will also require lighters, fully loaded shallow draft vessels which can proceed up river or canal on a moderate high tide and return on a 'coming low.' They look like miniature World War II LST's. In fact, they are. However, they use jet thrusting for power and bow and stern thrusters to supplement the shallow draft rudders.

"In addition to these systems, we need people power. Bangladesh has a very large labor pool of enthusiastic hard working people from age 12-50. Our proposal suggests a work-for-firewood pay system for many thousands of these. We hope to add free health care for all these workers, just in case Dr. Gaol does not have enough to do." He smiles at Rajiv. Rajiv smiles back, and at the panel, too. "When the system has served its purpose, these laborers will be offered work in the new coastal lightering system. Vast loads of shrubs, small trees, mulch and biologic fertilizer will be required over the next 2-50 years. And we propose holding 'agronomy and selective harvesting' mini-courses on board as these lighters, initially 200, are proceeding to their destination. Ah yes, I almost forgot. Senator Mukherjee has introduced legislation to provide seasoned military troops to accompany these lighters right through unloading and stacking to deter dacoits and water pirates. The Bengali Army and Navy are thrilled to have such a training opportunity. We are informed that both services intend to market military careers using the visibility of this program."

Conrad is in awe of the extent of this effort and the brainpower applied, far beyond theoretical. Yes, tigers are only part of this but they have the potential to be a catalyst for synergism. He wonders whether they might be looking at a blueprint for other such projects all over the world in reclaiming denuded rain forest of Brazil, Sarawak, Indonesia, Malaysia, Africa?

Gardner speaks up. "Mr. Kpoczek, it is almost time for lunch. I do not, however, wish to cut you off."

Krystian, sagging significantly from the high energy of the past days and today, shrugs and says, "A perfect break point." He only has one or two minutes left but breathes nary a word lest he forget some vital piece later. He halts immediately.

Maartje interjects, "We still have Smeeta, Nafis and Theophane. May we finish their presentations after lunch, 20 minutes max?"

"Yes," says Gardner, "we've peppered you with questions already. Take the first 30 minutes when we reconvene."

"Oh, the lunches are here. It is 12:05 p.m. We will reconvene at 1:30. You grant application people will go up two floors to your room. UNICEF, we have booked a smaller room in the 320 Building next door (Room 203). After you eat, I might suggest taking a 15-20 minute walk around this campus. It is typical Colorado landscape with red rock, orange rock and stone everywhere."

At the back of the room, everyone finds a lunch box with his or her name on it, accompanying beverage, utensils and heads out to nourish, rest, recover and prepare to finish.

Maartje says to Theophane, "I would like you to speak for five minutes on the Support Army and the importance of Hope and Faith in this process. Would you do this?"

"Yes, I will try. I am so pleased you asked me to come in yesterday. Now I have a much greater understanding of this entire matter. I might mention that I have met Mr. Roser and Mr. Conrad before. They are regulars at our 'Faith Journeys' workshops and also annual purchasers of Holy Smackers at Christmas. It is a very small world within a very large world, isn't it?"

"Wow," says a tired Maartje.

Upstairs she tells everyone to rest their brains for 15 minutes. "Then we will focus for 15-20 minutes and, I implore all of you take a quiet walk. Do NOT be late back to the presentation room. In fact, be there at 1:25 sharp. It is 12:18 now." Everyone except Theophane is sagging. He looks like a marathoner at mile 18.

Krystian says to Maartje and Brenden, "Thank you for your foresight on the anchors. Did you notice how all panelists and the GWF lady assistant studied them? They are cleverly designed and seem well made." They eat in silence. Maartje dozes for ten minutes. Krystian nudges her.

She convenes the group. "So far, we seem to be doing fairly well. I expect the questions will continue to be thorough. Be very careful. Repeat all questions out loud. And I mean out loud. Nafis, Smeeta, and Theophane, each of you speaks far too softly for this room. And trust me, I will prompt you on this. Smeeta, after Krystian finishes, I want you to speak for five minutes on critical facets of tiger habitat, prey and how our proposal will facilitate this. Speak confidently of your approach to population enhancement when habitat is developed and poaching contained. Theophane, you will speak about support and coordination. Has anyone been observing the UNICEF team?"

Theophane says, "They are extremely attentive and two are taking copious notes. When we recessed, their leader asked Mr. Josephson whether they could obtain a copy of our presentation. He deferred to the panel."

Krystian responds, "By all means. We have nothing to hide. All our materials are copyrighted and declared as confidential and proprietary. If we are successful, they will surely ask us to waive, which we will. But only if we are successful. We do not and will not waive copyright protection."

"I want you, Nafis, to explain in not more than six minutes, your long root grass successes, transmission of the samples to Dr. LaVie and his genetic efforts. And Nafis, both you and Smeeta must help them understand Bangladesh. They must conclude that you will succeed in this project before they commit any significant dollars. In other words, a significant return to the GWF. Do not forget: a grant is their investment in you. They expect results. It will be measured in the strengthening of the tiger population. Deliver the character of Bangladesh. You are Bangladesh. Because we've lost the Senator and

Khalil for this presentation, the panel must see Bangladesh in you. If you ramble, I will tell you to stop. Do so immediately, without fail."

"Dr. Rajiv," she smiles at him in her newly emerging spunky demeanor, "Do not fail to discuss Matlah. They are known worldwide for their databases."

Rajiv says, "The only other thing we're known for all over the world is storm surges and floods."

Nafis says, "I have been in three Matlah studies over twelve years. On the strength of their gathered data. I was given a series of tests for a stomach disorder. They told me of a medication. It stands a 97 percent chance of totally inhibiting further development of my condition and they provide it to me free of charge."

Rajiv says, "Nafis, when I call on you, tell the panel this story exactly. No more. No less." Theophane smiles. He just remembered something.

Maartje, "Dr. Rajiv, do not forget to go over P-23 through 26. Again, maybe close with those?"

"Thank you for the reminder. Yes, I will do this. And I will take about 45 seconds to do so."

"I have you on my stop watch," says Krystian.

"When we are done, team, take time to introduce yourself to the UNICEF people and thank as many panelists, Director Josephson and Mrs. Mack, as you are able. If they have questions, answer them. Make positive eye contact. I am very proud of all of you. We will unwind in our hotel meeting room. Dinner this evening will be at 6:00 p.m. Our cars will leave the hotel for the restaurant at 5:40 p.m. Sharp."

They separate, most walk in the clear, bright, mountain air of Boulder. The campus is lovely, full of flowers, and with mountain snow runoff there is plenty of enveloping nature noise especially near the surging mountain streams.

At 1:30 p.m. Panel Chair Gardner calls the session to order. Krystian finishes. Nafis rises and walks to the podium. Maartje is worried. He looks down at his notes, then looks up at the panel, Conrad and Carolyn. He smiles beautifully, using his warm eyes and great set of white teeth. "Member of the Panel, GWF staff, Mr. Josephson and Ms. Mack, UNICEF representatives, and my fellow team members."

Maartje, Dr. Rajiv and Krystian are astounded. This tightly focused, head down, research-oriented, grass collector has a stage presence. His black skin contrasts well with his yellow-green silk shirt.

"I am a botanist with a bachelor's degree from the Agricultural College in Kolkata, formerly Calcutta. I am a 5th generation member of a family which has lived within 180 km of The Sundarbans since the early 1800s. My great-grandfather and grandfather were bush beaters for Indian and British high officials who hunted, actually slaughtered, tigers by the hundreds, just for the sport of it.

"Our family culture has evolved from tiger and elephant killing to re-establishment of habitat and food for these elegant animals. There is now a compelling need to nurture them and to enhance the well being of Bangla peoples, who, as you understand all too well, are sadly impoverished, health care deprived, endlessly battered by weather and harassed by 'pay protection' gangs. The merger of these human interests with the needs of the tiger population and habitat is well thought out. To the credit of my fellow teammates, processes have been developed that promise—with your support—to create a quite meaningful beginning. I am honored to be a part of this multicultural, multidisciplinary effort and I will stay with it as long as I am welcome." He is mesmerizing the room.

"Re-establishment of grasses in canals, embankment walls and on top of the islands and peninsulas that make up coastal Bangladesh, including the Sundarbans, are a crucial first step. Manufactured mattresses and anchors are far beyond me. But the grasses we embed in them are not. In our research, we have located several long root—and by long, I mean twelve inches or more—embankment species. With Junaid—and Jagdish Rao's help, these were obtained, preserved in their native waters, and dispatched to Dr. Henry LaVie in Belgium. He is the bio-genetics plant specialist whom Miss deBouter has retained on behalf of the RWS. He is, as we speak, genetically engineering grasses whose root ends already demonstrate an ability to grow shoots from the root tip upwards to the surface. This will tie an embankment grass germinating in an anchor tip to an offspring grass on an island. This may seem logical and easy. It is not. Should we perfect this, the silt containment effort holds more promise. This should significantly accelerate the rate at which we decrease silt. However, we do not yet know whether the vertical shoot will get to the surface from the lowest anchor in an embankment mattress. It may take two years to determine this so please understand, we have some way to go.

"Hard work and hope define the Bengali peoples. The sickening conditions in which millions of my fellow countrymen, women and children live their entire, often abbreviated, lives has actually militated against our living better. Both India and Pakistan (formerly West Pakistan) cast us loose because they thought we were utterly bereft of hope. I believe we have much to hope for. This project, this team, your willingness to take risk, great risk I might add, offers our people, our tigers, our country, a hope that has not yet arrived. I thank you, on behalf of all Bengal tigers and my people, for your courtesy here today and for your willingness to assist should you find it in your best interests to do so." Nafis tells his Mathlah experience, then sits down. The long silence is telling. Smeeta softly rises. Her eyes dance.

"I am Smeeta Pal. I hold a master's degree in Tropical Animal Biology from the Kashmiri Community College in Srinigar, Kashmir, generally known infamously as a disputed territory of endless violence. It is true. Going to school was being in a war zone; except we never knew which street or building the war would be in next. I lost several classmates to bombings and shootings." She pauses.

"Nafis has spoken about grasses, silt, and foliage. I have a few brief remarks on the subject of animals and man, especially tigers. Assume for the moment we are successful at increasing the numbers from 275 to 1,250 within ten years. Contrast this with a despicable animal pit in Colton, California, where, very recently, some sadly misguided people collected, bred and sold hundreds of tigers, and starved hundreds more. More than 50 dead kits were found in a freezer and the bodies of some 35 large cats were strewn around the property. It will become your role and that of other concerned organizations to prevent such tragic abuse of animals. When people can buy, over the internet, a tiger for $500, we have a deadly system. No matter how much money you spend or how intelligent we are, these people impede our efforts. We will achieve tiger population enhancement and coastal protection. Please expect bumps on the highway. We know the road; with your help, we will travel it and you will have a noble hand in the process and certainly be able to take credit in the outcome. Thank you."

As Smeeta sits down, Theophane arises. He is so tall that all of him does not get up at the same time. It is as though the upper trunk operates on one hydraulic pump, the middle on a second with a two-second delay, and the lower legs and ankles on yet a third. He moves to the speaker's table.

"Ladies and gentlemen of the Global Wildlife Federation and grant panel, I am Theophane, a brother from the Saratoga, Wyoming Monastery, a Roman Catholic order which dates to the 13th century in southern France. I was born in Hyde Park, Illinois. Because I was perceived to be a decent student in grade and middle schools, my parents sent me, sacrificed to send me, to a seminary preparation high school in Maywood, Illinois. I have been attached to this order for 37 years.

"Each brother has a calling to community service outside the monastery for six weeks each year. Serving children, their siblings and parents in coastal Bangladesh has great appeal for me. The work has significant rewards, largely in the faces and warm, touching hands of these youngsters, who possess so little and yet provide so much. It is also an exercise in managing grief to return every year and learn how much loss has occurred during my absence from the storms and surges we've learned about today and the grim toxic and infectious conditions which permeate so much of this overpopulated, under-served, country. I mean utterly no offense to Dr. Rajiv Gaol and his Herculean efforts. He makes, and has made, thousands of children well. The children and their parents love and respect him. He makes do with grossly inadequate medicines and supplies. Before he came, there was very little health care in and among the coastal islands.

He makes a difference with each family. He stays among them and becomes one of them. He is a role model for children who dream of becoming nurses, technicians and doctors. I sense he is now being summoned to a higher calling. He is the rare person who can lead such efforts as being considered here. He would never tell you this nor would he seek out the position. He is truly gifted. As with Smeeta, Nafis, Jagdish and Junaid, he is Bangladesh. But he is also a part of you and me after his seven years in Chicago.

"Now I would like to speak to what I refer to as the invisible armies of support for such an extensive series of projects and subprojects as is being proposed. All five technical facets—engineering, botany, biology, ships and firewood—will fail of their essential purpose unless extraordinary effort is allocated to those who serve invisibly on the periphery of each tangible, funded piece of this effort. It will be the Mullahs, the ministers, the volunteers, the teachers of schoolchildren worldwide who will utilize Bernice, Bertram, and Banjo as stuffed animals and posters in acts of concert and responses to it. It will be the parents of the schoolchildren in Parten Kirchen, Germany, Bolzano, Italy, Mexico City; Memphis, Tennessee; Chicago, Illinois; Manitowoc, Wisconsin; Ypsilanti, Michigan; Spokane, Washington; Burlington, Vermont; and Moose Jaw, Saskatchewan, who will also acquire a deep empathy for the tigers and people, especially children, of Bangladesh. And docents and tour guides at zoos and museums. Somehow, somewhere, a methodical delivery of a caring attitude must be established, nurtured and reaffirmed for the entire duration of this project. Your money alone will not do it, nor will the skills of these fine presentation brethren. UNICEF has a solid reputation for providing a component of this support. I seek not to condemn when I say one of the drawbacks to its vast growth and funding strengths is a politically compelled and perhaps institutional constraining. Of course, UNICEF has a role, maybe a large one. The interpersonal connectionalism, to use a Methodist Church concept, emphasizes the power of a person's presence. The sense, yes, the sense felt by an eight-year Bengali child that someone far, far away cares enough to send letters and an occasional package, is an example of connectedness and of presence. Enclosing pictures, paper, envelopes and postage stamps so the Bengali child can write back and have the postage prepaid—to do this—is going one better.

"In one sense, it is not your responsibility to compel this dimension. Nor is it the role of all these gifted technical people to do so. However, unless each and all of them feel and act upon a personal sense of responsibility to be this, support this, and facilitate it, we will be in this room 30 years from now starting all over. I, of course, do not have any magical software. Nor am I certain I have properly diagnosed the need. But I have felt it. I hope some of this has been transmitted to each of you. In this day and age, we simply do not wait for Bangladesh to share the Christmas 2004 Indonesian earthquake and tsunamis resulting in the death of more than 170,000 people. These wonderful adults and children as hard working, colorful, sunny and loving as they are, deserve some of the grace the rest of us enjoy. It is only by a fluke of nature that they live in Bangladesh, and that we live here. We are spiritually connected. I am willing, as long as I am able, to commit myself to this."

And with particular regard to the UNICEF representatives in the room, he turns to them, "I do not believe UNICEF wants to continue to supply food TODAY for people who survived a tragedy YESTERDAY and who will die in a repeating tragedy TOMORROW.

"In response to chairman Gardner's concerns earlier about militant Muslim terrorists, I was in Bangladesh and coastal India after the 2004 Christmas tsunami. Not once, anywhere, have we ever seen any terrorist organization deliver any care to a single person.

"To close, I brought with me an afternoon snack of Holy Smackers," and he reaches over to his briefcase and pulls out four bags each containing a dozen cookies. "With your permission, Mr. Chair."

"Of course," booms Gardner. "Just do not overlook the panel with one of those bags—at least." Everyone relaxes as Gardner says, "Let's all take five minutes before you close with Mr. Brenden and Miss deBouter and after that, we begin with our questions."

Folks head for the restrooms. There are soda and bottled water on a white table clothed table. A University of Colorado food service employee is assisting. Royce Brenden moves carefully to the podium, puts on his black and pewter half-lens reading glasses, looks at his materials, then at the panel, making eye contact with each:

"Members of the Global Wildlife Federation panel, each of us grieves at distant tragedies which involve loss of life, permanent emotional and physical injury and despair. Despair is an inward manifestation of loss of hope, a letting go of an underlying faith which generates hope. Whether it is massive flooding, AIDS, Ebola, there are two major responses. First the crisis response teams—those who respond promptly to a disaster. Then later come the "design better for the future" professionals. They look at the causes and study the issues of necessary collection of forces, people, money, and knowledge which might prevent or contain the consequences of future repetitious tragedy. Unfortunately, most of these efforts go nowhere, particularly in underdeveloped nations.

"Then there is another approach.

"This panel and every single person in this room are vitally concerned. Each of us operates from a markedly different discipline or perspective. Some are concerned about Bengal tigers, other about food and medical care to poverty-stricken masses in Bangladesh, firewood for cooking and warmth, personal safety in the endless cyclones in the Bay of Bengal. Others are concerned about economic enhancement and creation of opportunity for less educated, less trained, poorly geographically situated people, exploitation of women, men, children, and tigers by those who care only for the rock bottom sewing cost of a t-shirt or the profit from selling medicines containing ground up tiger parts.

"The capacity and power in this room properly directed, funded and focused, has an opportunity to do something about this. Something formidable.

"I know something about silt. I am satisfied that the joint proposal of Bangladesh and the Dutch RWS contains a most well developed effort to restore habitat, restrain creation of silt, and markedly expand the Bengal tiger population, to provide firewood for essential cooking and warming and to markedly strengthen flood protection for the millions of coastal, river and canal people of Bangladesh. Better than anything we've yet seen.

"The embankment mattresses, the seed and fertilizer containing anchors" (he picks one up and deftly rotates it) "are a vital first engineering and bio-genetic step. Nothing of a major construction nature can happen until silt is first contained, then reduced.

"Even were the GWF to pass on this application and instead award vast grant sums to support, say, the cloning of endangered tiger species, habitat must, of necessity, be provided for these elegant creatures.

"This application is an opportunity to place your funds, not on a roulette table, but rather on a team in which you will become a vital participant, not a distant investor. The forces present in this room are at a confluence of opportunity.

"Favorable action by the GWF means you embrace processes by which a myriad of fixes for animal and human suffering will be addressed, created and applied. I believe these processes may then be revised, amplified and applied to other instances of animal and human endangerment around the world."

He sits down.

Maartje is in awe of Brenden's comments. He has said it all in six minutes. She realizes the very best she can do is to be very brief and sit down.

"Panel members of the GWF, Director Josephson and Mrs. Mack," and turning deferentially, "visiting UNICEF team, our planet is very large and very small. It is large when we become insular within our historic culture and discipline boundaries; we live out, work out and then fade out of our life times. However, when during our lives, we are inspired and compelled to break out, reach out, and venture out, we find we are not more than a plane ride or a nanosecond by e-mail from anyone.

"There is often talk about the human cost of projects like this. I suggest we might rather think in accounting terms of the expense incurred to achieve a human and ecologically sound life for creatures and people who enjoy much less than any of us in this room.

"I believe we can work together. We would like this opportunity." She sits down.

"Thank you, Miss deBouter. Now we have questions. Miss de-Bouter, we assume you will refer questions to a responder of your choosing. However, some of us wish to ask particular members of your team questions directed specifically to them. I trust this will be satisfactory."

"Of course," says Maartje deferentially. "If you want someone to supplement the response, feel free to do so."

"Maria Nunez, you have a question."

"Were Senator Mukherjee here, I would ask this of him. In his absence, anyone from Bangladesh may answer. In this country, we hear endless reports of child labor, children 7-8-9-10 years old being forced to work 40-50 hour weeks in sewing mills or rice fields, being paid a pittance, all to feather the nest of wealthy clothing families and land owners. Were the GWF to become part of a funding process for your proposal, how might we reconcile our apprehension that all we are doing is padding the nest of a few wealthy Bengali families while the masses continue to suffer as before without any benefit from your or our efforts?"

Maartje is tired and the question causes her to hesitate. She turns to look at Rajiv, Nafis and Smeeta. Rajiv stands immediately, "Miss Nunez, when I was 14, that is 18 years ago, my father was badly injured in a mill by a large rug loom. His injuries required two years of medicine and healing. There is no workers' compensation system in Bangladesh such as workers in Illinois or Colorado have. The USA system, at a significant cost to employers, provides remarkable health care and quite extensive income replacement. My brother, sister, and I became the workers' compensation system for our family. All three of us were taken on as employees by my father's mill. Yes, we worked 50 hours a week for almost two years. Our earnings, however meager, provided food, clothing and health care for all of us. The mill, actually owned by Senator Mukherjee's in-laws, the Kapoors, fed us while at work and required us to attend English classes three days a week for two hours. It was those classes that allowed me to take the medical school tests—all in English—and qualify for the very significant scholarship I was awarded. I offer this not in defense of child labor. Yes, the Kapoors made a lot of money off us. But there was, for us, a compensation system and it worked."

"Dr. Gaol, my point is slightly different. The GWF could not tolerate the bad publicity of funding an effort in a country that fails to distribute its wealth more proportionate to the laborers who have such fine hard skills and work so hard."

"I feel we must begin somewhere," responds Rajiv. "I wish the Senator were here. He struggles with this inequity."

Krystian arises, "I would like to supplement Dr. Gaol's response to your question. In the middle of the 16th century in The Netherlands, during the lives of Rembrandt Van Rijn and Franz Hals, Holland had a significant textile industry. I believe 20,000 people were so employed in Leiden and neighboring areas. Four or five thousand of these were children taken from the orphanages of Germany and Belgium. By fiat, a rule was embraced by the community that children could not be forced to work more than 14 hours a day. I suggest your question and public relations concern, in the context of such European practices then and slavery in the USA in the 17th, 18th and 19th centuries, infers we are all sadly bonded to some historically undesirable social practices.

"Until Bangladesh climbs out of the filth and poverty that shackles millions to despair more than hope, major efforts such as this grant application are one of the few processes which will deliver a hope fulfilled. You may find it appropriate to condition any grant award on putting in place machinery to develop those processes which will lead to the ultimate elimination of these practices." (long pause) "I believe the World Bank has only recently begun to condition its participation, on the presence and effectiveness of these processes."

Royce Brenden pops up, "He is absolutely correct."

Krystian sits down. Brenden does the same.

Maartje rises, "I wish to thank the entire GWF and this panel for the gracious treatment you have accorded us, without regard to whether you act favorably on our application. I wish to close with one of Bangladesh's approaches to preparing the population for things to come. It is a waterway equivalent to Burma Shave signs on country roads in the USA. Should you act favorably on this application, we intend to place these along the mangroves in coastal Bangladesh and the Sundarbans."

She puts up P-27 A-B-C-D. They are four-color photographs taken late in the day along a Sundarbans waterway. The signs read: "Hope is Grand." "Some Relief is Near." "Free Firewood next year." "Keep watching here." Bertram and Bernice appear on the first and fourth.

Gardner says, "Miss deBouter, we thank you all for your testimony and visual materials. I must confess, had we undertaken to prepare a similar analysis and presentation, we probably would not have developed anything at this level. Our compliments to all of you."

Maartje rises. As she does, Roser says, "Mr. Kpoczek, you used the phrase referring to the LST lighters, 'when the system has proved itself…' When will this be?"

Krystian stands up, "Mr. Roser, I believe this will occur between 17 and 24 months from now. I am satisfied the design is sound and we expect testing in the Netherlands and Bangladesh to require about eleven to twelve months. Final lock-down on manufacturing software will follow almost immediately. The first order for six has been submitted for delivery four months after implementation of this software."

"And," continues Roser, "if the first 40-50 million USD achieves the initial goals aptly summarized on P-24 and 25, what do you project the cost for future phases and please include in your response, where this work will go and who will receive the funds."

"Our preliminary—and these are only preliminary estimates— are that over a 30 years period, the costs will exceed in today's dollars between $14 and $29 billion USD," answers Krystian.

Maartje continues, "Our goal initially was only to create a coastal protection system to reduce the severe cost, in human terms, of storm surges and other flooding. Only as we began our survey analysis did it became apparent that the recovery of the tiger population was on a precise parallel to the well being of the coastal peoples. In the USA, the post DDT recovery of the Bald Eagle and in Europe and Scandinavia, the restoration of wood stork habitat and population, have had as much to do with the well being of the peoples there as the Bengal tiger will have to the people of Bangladesh, especially of the Sundarbans.

"We all echo Dr. Gaol's closing remarks. None of us would be here today had it not been for his ability to see way beyond present day Bangladesh."

Rajiv was sitting back and for the first time in many months, relaxing.

History was rolling across his mind's eye, Gandhi's dream and ultimate triumph: independence from Great Britain, had rapidly dissolved into the same day tragedy of Partition—West Pakistan, East Pakistan, and India. Rajiv was just now beginning to see that his beloved Bangladesh had not only survived a violent struggle from August 1947 to 2006 but was, for the first time, poised on a launch pad toward fulfillment of long standing hope.

CHAPTER 24

A Well-Oiled Security System

Nafis is preparing for a day of research way back in the northern sector of the Sundarbans. In his lab, he is petting the stock of his new tiger rifle. It is of the highest quality rosewood. He checks the clips to find eight .375 Magnum cartridges in each. He savors the blued steel barrel, shorter than most. Before he gathers Smeeta and Junaid for the boat ride, he basks in the formidable elegance of his new insurance policy. When he first sighted it in six months ago, he could not believe how the KA-BOOM vacated the foliage for an hour. And thanks be to Allah for the heavily shoulder-padded short sleeve jungle shirt and rain jacket the Denver gun store owner suggested he buy—having noticed his slight physique.

A Lovely Day's Beginning

One year later, Mullah Bassam and Theophane are on their way by boat to a village on Hatiya Island. It is a lovely tropical morning on the water. The sun is barely above the horizon. The tranquility is interrupted only by the occasional jumping mullet.

The Mullah says, "Well, Brother Theophane, we are now to be

visited by an invasion. I am told we will be invaded by wave after wave of ships containing foreign firewood, people and equipment. Is it true this could last for twenty years?"

"Ah yes, Praise Allah and Jesus Christ, Mullah Bassam." Theophane says, "When the 10 million dollar grant was awarded by the GWF last year, your government matched it times four. Since then, things have happened rapidly. And yes, this invasion could outlast us both."

"I must share with you the atmosphere in Boulder last May. The Global Wildlife Federation personnel, the Bengali-Netherlands team, the visiting UNICEF people. It was as if the award of grant money became superfluous. Right in front of our eyes, a process emerged. The GWF board required a four-year, full-time commitment from both Miss deBouter and Dr. Gaol. That made good sense. They are so in love with each other anyway. GWF has assigned Carolyn Mack to be on site monitor four to six months a year. Director Conrad will make four trips a year.

"As we left the presentation room, I heard Mr. Krystian say, 'You know I've been wanting a new pair of gyro-stabilized Swarovski binoculars.' This told me what he thought would happen."

Mullah Bassam says, thoughtfully, "Brother Theophane, we have much to do, do we not? If this invasion and these armies are to outlast us, we must be about training our replacements."

They come around a bend. There a six-vessel array is positioned, three on each bank: a towing vessel and two shallow draft barges. One barge in each group has solar and diesel-powered hydraulic pumps and lines over the shoreside gunwales. Cheerful Bengali workers are carefully "injecting," three at a time, dark gray anchors, some 18 inches, some longer, with funny harpoon-like tips, through brown polymer mattresses into the embankments.

Throughout coastal Bangladesh, careful listeners could hear a bird sing.

Epilogue

Successfully using human, political, religious, technical and financial momentum to carry out the many phases of the flood and storm surge management system becomes the working theme of this project. Maartje and Rajiv remain devoted to each other but the subject of marriage has an uncertain "do not discuss" flag hovering overhead. The complexities in their relationship at 12,000 miles, often on a computer screen, orbit all they do with each other.

Rajiv has taken an 80 percent leave of absence from Comilla as he teams with Khalil and Maartje to drive the project. He is both overextended and uplifted by the demands of the role. Help arrives in strange baskets. Trouble shows up in every conceivable form. Khalil's suggested division of accountability strengthens the team and facilitates enhanced prompt, competent, decision implementation.

The GWF assigns Conrad and Carolyn to monitor the application of its funds. For one week every six months, they are in Bangladesh together.

Several terrorist efforts are disruptive but the earlier intelligence network leads to a major and bloody rupture in their seaport attack plans before any harm is done.

Shipboard application of Anna Godsen's pesticide-fungicide becomes a comedy of errors on the first three supertankers. However, all three arrive in Bangladesh with their firewood cargoes having been appropriately treated—after Krystian, Royce, Alois and Anna G. come on board by helicopter in the middle of Charter Number One.

Pog's picture signs are a huge success and their use spreads rapidly—after villagers figure out that they don't burn. The villagers respond more confidently with each firewood pick-up.

Jagdish and Smeeta coordinate with two armies: the local workers who load and unload and the Bengali Army units assigned to secure the wood from theft. Delivery lightering and transport to the designated areas is clumsy at first. The dacoits are an endless harassment. However, a Special Forces unit is now tracking two gang leaders. And, in several villages, local villagers adopt a vigilante "we've had enough" mindset and eliminate a number of dacoit leaders.

Theophane and Mullah Bassam are very effective servant leaders of the Army of Support. They cooperate fluidly despite the diverse theological routes they travel. Grace and Acceptance are their raison d'être. They are so successful they become targets of a major terrorist assassination plot.

The Senator and his cronies begin to roll in profit from the shipping partnership. Pog Marenjar and the Senator team up in a nationwide postage stamp-poster effort. Fifty percent of the net funds received from sales are allocated to tiger population strengthening. The posters are sold all over the world in museums, zoos, animal parks, schools and Disneyworld. GWF gives them to donors of more than $100. GWF buys them from the government of Bangladesh at a deep discount.

Financing the larger phases takes hold, due unexpectedly to word spreading from firewood shipping-delivery successes. The data on these shipments convinces even the most conservative economists that the project has merit and, more importantly, contains significant financial benefit to those who participate. Silt reduction is measurably significant about 18 months after the first 500 miles of river, canal and Sundarbans banks are mattressed. Jan is ecstatic. Dr. LaVie's genetically engineered bank grass from Smeeta and Junaid's discoveries, his "snorkel grass", are attracting interest from many watery parts of the world.

Krystian and Royce Brenden meet with Kleinhold Dalmer to explore a better design of a horizontal transport lift system. The design is performing solidly in beta testing. Each gains "company" approval to create a new business entity. It is an LLC (Limited Liability Company) created under Wyoming law. The law was developed from earlier Panamanian and German laws. Of course, each employer extracts warrants for future participation in member shares.

Theophane is stricken with a virulent and terminal cancer. Maartje and Rajiv visit him in Saratoga and arrange with the Senator and Khalil to personally transport him to Bangladesh where he wishes to spend his last months with "his" children. The village children adopt him and now lovingly minister to the minister who, for so many years, ministered to them.

Amplified health care throughout the Barrier Islands, the Sundarbans and other coastal areas is happening. This is due in large part to Rajiv's med-school classmates and several professors. Other Big Ten schools sign on. They come in regular teams (clad in school colors and bearing hats and pennants for kids) for two-week roving river boat clinics. Currently four floating clinic vessels are operating. Six more are in the works. The schools are bidding for naming (Christening) rights. Rajiv serves on the newly commissioned *Sabjada Singh* Children's Clinic. The in-flow of medicines is facilitating a significant spike in the Matlah database amplifying local quality of health care. This is a huge politically marketable item for Bangladesh. Khalil and the Senator capitalize on this to gain support for major construction phase funding. Sabjada's mother, Manja, is the lead nurse on the *Sabjada Singh*. (Pradeep is chief engineer.) Sabjada's brother is in training to be a medical technician. Rajiv is his mentor and this becomes an unexpected bond to his now joyful memories of Sabjada.

Shrub and tree planting in the mattressed areas are generally well secured and successful. The Finns are really good at timber management. Their meticulous research, before making commitments, pays off. And they were dead-on in their perception that a nine-year growth cycle works in Bangladesh. It also appears that many of their Bangla contacts are developing a taste for flavored Finnish vodkas, especially pomegranate. The Army Reserve, the forestry police and the generally invisible Special Forces work together to preserve this new growth. In the fourth year, a selective harvesting plan is presented for discussion. The first harvest will occur in year six (smaller kindling and medium size firewood only). It is now projected that Bangladesh will not require firewood imports after years six or seven.

Theophane's death occurs at a floating clinic in the Sundarbans. He is honored and respects are paid in a five-day river, canal and coastal islands shipboard caravan. Maartje, Rajiv, Khalil, Pog and even the Senator (for one day) are part of this river train. Like a kite with a very long tail, the following of devoted, grateful villagers inspires everyone and, of course, the tail gets longer, much longer. Their way of saying goodbye and thank you is well beyond trumpets and bouquets.

In year four, Rajiv appropriately resigns his lead role as does Maartje. They nominate Khalil to be new chair and Smeeta as Executive Assistant. The Senator's power makes this a rubber stamp.

After serious negotiation sprinkled with more than a little love making, Maartje and Rajiv decide they must visit both sets of parents to obtain parental blessing to a union. Because each recognizes the importance of parents and siblings to their emerging unit, the frightening realization is that any one of the four parents can veto a marriage. Happiness abounds as blessings are given by all four parents. The outcome of family input is that there will be two weddings, each attended by both sets of parents and some siblings; one in the Netherlands and the second two weeks later in Sherpur, Bangladesh. Planning by the mothers is underway. They communicate with each other by e-mail.

On a visit to Sherpur, Maartje and Rajiv just happen to digress to Muktagacha for, you know what. They act like adolescent lovers at their favorite monda shop.

Afterword

It is the 15th anniversary of Rajiv's first meeting with the Minister. Six major phases are completed and have been storm tested many times. Coastal Bangladesh is 42 percent under flood management systems. Tiger population in the Sundarbans has quadrupled not counting the export of 56 Bengal tiger cubs and young adults to far corners of Europe, South and North America, and Russia, Africa and Australia.

Maartje and Rajiv live in Fort Collins, Colorado, where they are under contract to GWF as an evaluation team of health care and human support systems for complex grant proposals. They have a son Theo, 7, and a daughter Sabi, 4, who see their grandparents, aunts and uncles at least twice a year. Annually, Rajiv teaches a pediatric tropical illness seminar at his alma mater in downtown Chicago.

Mullah Bassam is escorted to New York by Rajiv, Maartje, Khalil, Krystian and Conrad to receive, on Theophane's and his behalf, the UNICEF "Over the Horizon" prize. His acceptance speech contains sensitive echoes to the cross culture efforts and commitments which were the underpinnings of this effort.

In Krystian's office, a pair of Canon image stabilizing binoculars hang alongside his Swarovskis. On the wall of his office hangs a lovely *kantha* depicting a multi-colored butterfly newly emerging from its cocoon. The butterfly is a beauty from the Madhupur Forest. At the bottom is written the Bangla phrase which translates: "You can fly but... that cocoon has to go."